THE WILDWOODS

Family Secret

CATHY WILSON

This is a work of fiction. All names, characters, places, and incidents either are the product of the author's imagination or are used fictitiously. Any resemblance to actual persons, living or dead, events, or locales is entirely coincidental.

Library of Congress Registration Number TXu002203039/2020-06-10
Library of Congress Registration Number TXu002203241/2020-06-11
Library of Congress Registration Number TXu002235101/2020-12-21
Library of Congress Registration Number TXu002237035/2020-12-31

ISBN:978-0-578-83412-2
Ebook ISBN: 978-0-578-83413-9

Author bio and back cover photos by Chelsea Schmitz

John – My love, courage, and perseverance
Sis – My Opey; may we always keep laughing.
Mom – My passion and imagination
Dad – My ambition and practicality

ACKNOWLEDGEMENTS

To my editor, Cassandra A. Dunn, thank you for your help. Your thoughtful suggestions and advice were invaluable.

I wish to recognize the following people for lending their support and encouragement. I am grateful for their friendship, kindness, and sincerity. Whether or not they were aware, their respected reviews and feedback kept this writer moving forward; pushing to accomplish a long sought-after goal. Thank you,

Bill and Colleen Reid, Paul and Cindy Allsing, Joe and MaryKay Malone, Donna Wilson, Guy Ott, Tony and Carolyn Andrade and Leslie Lehr.

THE
WILDWOODS
Family Secret

CHAPTER 1

G ina Teducci glanced behind her. Every row of benches in the stifling courtroom was occupied now. She wondered what was keeping her supervisor Roger Mattison and coworker Claire Chu.

Her eyes probed the gallery. Her father Carmine hadn't arrived yet, either. He would be late, like every other day for the past two weeks, wanting to enter the courthouse from one of the side entrances to avoid the media hounds.

Gina was in her third year working as a forensic science technician at the Central Regional Crime Lab for the New Jersey State Police Department. She had tested and reported on DNA and trace evidence samples in this case, connecting to crime boss Joe D'Amato and several of his associates. She was confident the crime lab had supplied plenty of ammunition for the prosecutor.

Across the aisle, nearly all the seating was occupied with the D'Amato family and affiliates in support of the defendant. Most of them Gina recognized. She'd known the D'Amato family since childhood.

"All rise," the bailiff called out. "The honorable Judge William Bailey presiding once again. Hudson County Superior Court."

Gina stood along with everyone attending. The judge entered through a side door to the left of his bench. The long folds of his black robe billowed against his tall slender frame. The grey of his hair matched the wire rim of his glasses. He was reputed as being intolerable of corruption and organized crime, which boosted Gina's optimism for the outcome of this trial.

Judge Bailey took his seat. "Please be seated."

A faint whooshing sound filled the courtroom as everyone sat down.

"Bailiff, will you bring the jurors in please?" Judge Bailey asked.

The bailiff opened a door to the right of the judge and the jury filed in. Six men and six women. The morning sun poured in on them through the red velvet draped windows behind the panel. They took their seats and settled in for another day of trial. The bailiff moved to adjust the blinds in the windows to deflect the sun.

Roger pushed through the rear courtroom door followed by Claire. They made their way to the front row where Gina sat. Roger wore his one and only tweed blazer jacket that was too small for his bulky frame, leather loafers and no tie. He preferred a lab coat to a dress coat.

"We had to park three blocks away." He huffed out of breath. "What'd I miss?" He settled in next to Gina, combing a hand though his thick brown wavy hair. His flushed cheeks popped above plenty of facial hair.

"Nothing," Gina whispered in response.

Claire acknowledged Gina as she shed her cumbersome nylon ski jacket. She rolled it into a ball and pressed it down on the bench beside her. Her face was void of make-up and her jet-black hair was pulled back in a ponytail. As an avid marathon runner, she appeared to handle the three-block trek much better than Roger.

"How the city thought parking restrictions during this trial was a good idea is beyond me," Roger muttered.

Gina looked to the defense table where Joe D'Amato sat with his attorney, Mark Delano.

"Attendance control was expected," she whispered.

"Let the record reflect today's date." The judge spoke to the stenographer sitting at a small desk to his right. "Friday, May seventeenth, two thousand nineteen. It's…" He consulted the wall clock. "9:06 a.m." He surveyed the courtroom. "Is counsel ready to proceed?"

District Attorney Benjamin Forrester stood at the prosecutor's table in front of Gina.

"Yes, your honor," Benjamin responded.

It was shaping up to be a landmark case for the D.A.'s office. Two weeks in and he still had the floor. Benjamin's prosecution rate was in the high ninety percentile. That made Gina hopeful.

His co-counsel, Cynthia Holden, sat next to him and Chris Schuler sat next to her. Their table was ladened with three-ring binders, folders and note pads. Leather attaches and briefcases were stowed at their feet.

"Yes, your honor," Mark, Joe's attorney, responded.

Mark headed up the successful Delano and Associates firm. A firm well-acquainted with defending organized crime cases. Both he and Joe appeared composed and reassured even though there had been plenty of damaging evidence and testimony brought against Joe during his trial.

Second-degree murder, aggravated assault, bribery, extortion, money laundering, false contract payments, and leader of organized crime had been the charges presented against Joe in the grand jury's indictment.

Associates of Joe's that had been implicated would be indicted separately. The state did not want to take any chances with a mistrial by proceeding against multiple defendants. They were only interested in this one...for now.

"The prosecution has only one more witness to question before the defense begins presenting, is that correct?" Judge Bailey asked, looking to Benjamin.

"That's correct, your honor," Benjamin replied.

"Very well, counsel," the judge said. "Call your last witness."

"The prosecution calls Detective Nick Casey to the stand," Benjamin responded.

Detective Nick Casey was highly regarded and well-respected by his peers and the department. He'd been reserved as the winning drive for the prosecutor's case to convict the infamous crime boss. He also held a special interest for Gina, which brought an elevated level of anticipation to today's proceedings for her.

The bailiff stepped out to retrieve the witness, then returned with Nick Casey. A few people in the gallery shifted in their seats to watch them enter. Gina was one of them.

It had been a while since she'd seen Nick. He looked better than she remembered. A lot better. His tall, athletic frame seemed to tower over the slighter bailiff. His light brown hair was cut much shorter now. He was clean shaven, outfitted in a sharp blue suit and tie, and he walked with an assertive air.

Working in the crime lab had given Gina insight on his career over the years. His arrest record was impressive for a thirty-two-year-old detective. He kept his focus straight ahead as he was led to the witness stand. He was sworn in and he took his seat as instructed.

A flutter of intimidation stirred in Gina, knowing how it felt to be sworn in and having to testify against a man like Joe D'Amato. But Nick appeared unfazed, fearless. It was how she remembered him being when they were kids.

The rear door opened once more followed by a small wave of commotion. Gina turned to see her father, Carmine Teducci, arrive. He looked handsome and confident as always, rousing the interest of the media that was lining the back wall of the courtroom. Her uncle Anthony, Carmine's younger brother, followed close behind. They both acknowledged Gina as they took a seat three rows back.

Roger leaned into her. "Your father grabs as much media attention as Joe does."

Gina had stopped reading the online fodder after the first day of proceedings. It was unsettling because she had mixed emotions about the outcome of this trial. In the corner of her mind was a troubling reality; her father Carmine could easily be in the position Joe was in right now.

"Yes, he does," was all she said, bringing her focus back to Nick.

Benjamin crossed the courtroom to stand near Nick in the witness box. "Mr. Casey, can you please state for the court your full name and occupation?"

Nick leaned forward to speak into the microphone. "Nicholas Daniel Casey, Detective One with the Hoboken City Police Department Detective Bureau."

"In what division?"

"Homicide."

"And how long have you been a detective?"

"Eight years."

"And of those eight years, how many of them have been served in an undercover capacity?"

"Six."

"And you're comfortable with today's proceedings?" Benjamin asked. "With testifying here today in this courtroom?" Benjamin looked over to the D'Amato clan of attendees. The jury followed Benjamin's gaze.

Nick cleared his throat. "Yes."

"Good," Benjamin chirped. He moved back to the prosecutor's table, collected his yellow notepad, then strode back to the witness stand. "I'm going to begin with the deposition you gave three months ago and work forward from there, OK?"

"No," Nick replied.

"I'm sorry?" Benjamin asked.

"No, it's not OK to begin with the deposition I gave to you three months ago."

A soft murmur floated throughout the courtroom.

The judge chimed in. "I will ask that the courtroom please refrain from any outbursts. Thank you." He looked to Benjamin and Nick. "Is there a problem, counsel?"

"I don't believe so, your honor," Benjamin said, then returned to Nick. "Detective, I want to bring the jury up to speed from the beginning from your point of view, just as I've done with every other witness up to this point. Through the course of your investigation with Detective Jerry Pulia, there has been a multitude of evidence from several individuals including yourself. With your testimony today, it is my intent for you to corroborate not only your own, but other witness statements and accounts. Statements and accounts that have not only been heard in this courtroom over the past two weeks, but also in written and interviewed depositions over the past three months. Again, yours included. I want to be sure that the jury has a clear and concise understanding of each of those accounts."

Nick looked to the defendant's table, then back to Benjamin. "At this time, I wish to recant my deposition."

Collective whispers drifted up from the gallery.

"Excuse me detective?" Benjamin blurted out.

Nick leaned forward, speaking close to the microphone. "At this time, I wish to recant…"

"I heard you the first time, detective." Benjamin cut him off.

"Counsel…," Judge Bailey cut in. "Please do not interrupt the witness."

Benjamin held up a hand. "My apologies, your honor." He looked to Nick. "Detective, I'll need to clarify for the jury. What part of your deposition do you wish to recant?"

"All of it," Nick replied.

Gina gasped. She swore the ground shifted under the bench she sat on. Nick's statement caused an uproar in the courtroom. Judge Bailey pounded his gavel several times to bring order to the courtroom. Gina's heart began pounding just as hard.

"I'm not going to ask this courtroom again," the judge reprimanded. "If you cannot contain the outbursts, I will clear all of you from the courtroom." He waved his gavel to the gallery.

The judge regarded Benjamin. "Would counsel like a recess to consult with your witness?"

"No, your honor." Benjamin spun back to Nick, baffled. "What the hell are you doing, detective?"

"Counsel…," Judge Bailey interrupted. "I don't advise…"

"Regarding this case, detective…" Benjamin ignored the judge. "Did someone speak to you before court today?"

"No," Nick replied.

"Counsel," Judge Bailey called out.

Benjamin ignored the judge again and nearly shouted at Nick, "Detective, I'll remind you again that you're under oath. And the deposition you gave to me outside of court was also under oath. Now, regarding this case, detective, did *anyone*, besides myself or my staff, contact you at any time prior to today's proceedings?"

"No," Nick replied.

"I don't understand, detective. Why would you want to recant your deposition?" Benjamin asked.

"Because none of it is true," Nick stated, looking directly at the jury.

Gina was finding it difficult to breathe. She gripped the bench tightly with both hands. This was supposed to be the day that Joe D'Amato's fate would be sealed. Nick's testimony to corroborate prior witness testimony, the investigation, and her office's DNA and trace evidence findings, would have created no doubt for the jury. There would have been enough evidence to convict Joe and put him away for a good long time. Nick was destroying that.

Gina couldn't believe what was happening. *How could the witness accountings and evidence over the past three months not be true? Why would he testify to that? What was he doing?* She wanted to stand up and shout across the courtroom along with Benjamin. She looked over to Joe. His focus on Nick was unwavering. Gina guessed that he had everything to do with what was happening now. She felt sick.

She had her hopes pinned on closure with this trial. Closure for her and her family. Closure for her sister's murder sixteen years ago. Gina and her family had been robbed of that closure. There hadn't been a trial for her sister Sirrina's murder because the killer, Joe's nephew Guiseppe, had been killed as well. And even though Sirrina's murder didn't pertain to this trial, it was a murder that was connected to Joe D'Amato. Nick had just stuck a needle in that balloon of hope.

The gavel was hammering down again. The courtroom quieted down. It was obvious the judge was just as stunned with the turn of events.

"Will counsel please approach?" the judge ordered.

Both Benjamin and Mark approached the judge's bench. Judge Bailey covered his microphone and spoke to the attorneys. He nodded furiously, but the courtroom couldn't hear what he was saying.

Nick's focus was set to the rear of the courtroom. Gina pivoted to see what had his attention. In the last row sat her cousin Jimmy Teducci. He must have entered quietly after her father and uncle had arrived. He and Nick had their eyes locked on one another. There was plenty of tension between the two that Gina wasn't understanding.

She glanced to her father and Uncle Anthony sitting two rows in front of Jimmy. Both sat stone-faced. Gina assumed this was upsetting her father just as much, if not more. *Why wasn't Jimmy sitting with them?* she wondered. Her focus shifted to the media, furiously texting the current event. An Alice in Wonderland moment. Nothing was making sense.

7

"Counsel may proceed," Judge Bailey said curtly.

Gina turned back to face the front of the courtroom. Mark returned to his seat. He leaned into Joe, speaking in his ear. Joe gave a quick nod, keeping his focus on the judge.

"He sits at that table like he's attending one of his corporate meetings," Roger said, jarring Gina from her thoughts. "Calculating...wise...self-assured," Roger continued. He shook his head turning to her. "...and responsible for decades of corruption."

Gina didn't respond. She knew the D'Amato connections cast a wide net. Senators, congressmen, county supervisors, and mayors of both New Jersey and New York had some involvement at some point. And some had been imprisoned for their actions.

Benjamin retrieved a three-ring notebook from the prosecutors' table, then walked back to Nick.

Gina leaned over to Roger. "Why didn't they call a recess? What's Benjamin doing?"

"I'm not sure," Roger replied. "I'm hoping the D.A. has something up his sleeve. Otherwise, this trial is over."

Gina deflated. "Please don't say that."

Roger only shook his head, looking dismayed. He'd completed two days of testimony three days ago on the lab's behalf. Claire was busy texting on her phone.

Benjamin flipped through the notebook. "Detective, just to be clear, your deposition that I'm holding in my hand...a deposition given to me and my staff over the past three months, you're now claiming is all untrue? Again, you were under oath when you gave this."

"If that is my deposition that you're holding there, then yes," Nick replied.

"Detective, your deposition corroborates sworn witness testimony this court has heard over the course of the past two weeks from several witnesses, some of which include detective Jerry Pulia and forensic scientist Roger Mattison from the crime lab, as well as Sergeant Marco Rotello and police officer Danny Nunzio, both from your precinct. Is it your sworn testimony now that everything that has been revealed to this court throughout the course of this trial is untrue? All previous testimony and evidence that has been brought to this trial to date not only from those that I just mentioned, but others as well, is incorrect? Is that what you're saying?" Benjamin's voice cracked.

"Counsel…," the judge cut in again. "I'm not going to remind you again. One question at a time. The jury needs to hear the witness answer each of your questions."

Benjamin waved a hand to the judge in acknowledgment. He turned to Nick. "Detective Casey, there's been quite a bit of evidence to support this case and reports to corroborate that evidence. You're saying the entire lot of that is untrue?"

Gina sat rigid, holding her breath. Part of what he was referencing was her crime lab's work. *Her* work.

"As it pertains to this case," Nick said. "The evidence, yes, and the testimony corroborating that evidence, yes."

Benjamin slouched his shoulders, caving to the pressure he suddenly found himself under. Something Gina had never seen him do before. His usual charismatic positive force was now diminished. He looked down to his shoes, gave a small laugh, and shook his head in disbelief.

"Oh boy," he said.

Then he looked back to Nick and blurted out, "Detective, how do I know that what you're telling me right now isn't untrue? How does this court know that you haven't been contacted or threatened or manipulated by the defendant in some way?"

"Objection," Mark called out. "Inflammatory."

"Your honor," Benjamin pleaded. "This goes to the credibility of this witness."

"Sustained," the judge responded. "He's your witness, counsel. Establishing credibility is on you. Re-direct your line of questioning. And this is your last warning. One question at a time."

Gina was grateful that Judge Bailey was exercising incredible tolerance of Benjamin this morning.

"Detective…" Benjamin turned back to Nick. "I want to be absolutely clear on this, so I'm going to ask you once more. Have you been contacted by anyone other than myself and my staff regarding this case?"

Nick glanced to the judge before answering. "No."

Benjamin addressed the judge. "Your honor, I have no further questions for this witness." Benjamin walked back to his seat and plopped down, appearing defeated.

That's it? Gina thought. *What are you doing? Call a recess. Consult with your witness. You can't be done yet.* Dread washed over her. She was astonished at what was happening. She didn't believe that Nick hadn't been contacted by someone from the D'Amato side. Something made him change his mind and change his testimony.

Nick's nature and expertise in his work were solid. Gina knew this from personal experience, and from trusted co-workers. His evidence was irrefutable. He was a highly regarded detective. *Why was he blowing up the prosecutor's case?*

There had been no reaction from Joe. He sat calmly with his hands folded together, looking polished and regal in his tailored attire.

The six men and six women of the jury sat without expression. *Were they surprised at what they heard? Or had they expected something like this to materialize considering the defendant?* Gina's thoughts were spinning.

Judge Bailey gave Nick a long considerate look. He turned his attention to the defense table. "Does counsel wish to cross-examine this witness?"

"I do, your honor."

"Very well. Your witness, counsel."

Mark stood and strode across the courtroom to Nick with an air about him that things would soon go his way.

"Detective, please explain to the court how it is you arrived at the conclusion that the accountings of your deposition and the evidence in this case are untrue?" Mark asked.

"Through my own investigation," Nick said.

"A separate investigation?" Mark questioned.

"Correct," Nick answered.

"An investigation not associated with the district attorney's case?" Mark extended a hand to the prosecutor's table.

"Correct," Nick answered.

Benjamin and his co-counsel looked to one another as if baffled by what they were hearing. Benjamin scribbled notes on his legal pad.

"Interesting." Mark looked to Joe then back to Nick. "Who authorized you to perform this investigation?"

"No one."

"No one?" Mark asked. "You just took it upon yourself to conduct a parallel investigation?"

"Yes," Nick answered.

"Is that protocol for your department, detective?"

"No."

"Is this representative of you in all of your cases, detective?"

"No."

"Just this particular case?"

"Correct."

Mark rested an elbow on the witness stand, as if engaging Nick in friendly conversation. "What prompted you to run this second investigation, detective?"

Nick hesitated before responding, "Intuition."

Anger rose inside Gina as she listened. Every word Nick said felt like a stab to her gut. Nick was coming off more as a defense witness than a witness for the prosecution. *Why? Where was this coming from?* she fumed.

"Can you elaborate, detective, based on this case?" Mark asked.

"I believed this case had the potential for certain people to go to extreme measures and do anything to convict the defendant," Nick replied. "Turns out I was right."

"How so, detective?"

"The evidence supplied in this case was falsified," Nick concluded.

There was commotion in the courtroom once again. Gina was floored. She looked to Roger and Claire in desperation. "How can that be?" she whispered to Roger. "What's he talking about?"

"I don't know. Stop talking or we'll get thrown out," Roger whispered back.

"Order," the judge called out once more.

Gina frowned, but didn't pursue her remaining questions. She wouldn't risk being removed from the courtroom.

Mark continued with his cross-examination. "Your testimony now, detective, is that the evidence and testimony corroborating that evidence was falsified, correct?"

"Yes."

"Do you have proof of your findings, detective?"

"I do," Nick answered.

"Can you confirm that the evidence was, in fact, planted to use against my client?"

"It was," Nick replied.

Gina realized she was holding her breath and exhaled.

"Detective," Mark folded his hands behind his back. "Did you yourself falsify evidence to use against my client?"

Nick's focus landed on the defense table. On Joe. "I did not," he answered.

Gina's high hopes for a conviction fizzled. Mark walked in front of the jury and asked his next question, keeping his focus on the jury.

"Why did you not inform the D.A. about the falsified evidence?" He spun to Nick. "Why wait until today to inform this court of that fact? Why did you allow this case to come to trial, detective?"

"Counsel," Judge Bailey spoke out. "I've already reiterated this to the prosecution. The same applies to the defense. Please direct only one question at a time to the witness and allow him to answer before asking your next question."

Mark gave a slight bow to the judge. "Of course, your honor, my apologies." He looked at Nick. "Detective, why did you wait until today to inform the D.A. and this court that the evidence was falsified?"

"I was curious," Nick said.

"Curious?" Mark chuckled. "About what?"

"About how far the corruption reached," Nick replied.

Another small wave of commotion bristled through the courtroom.

"Objection, your honor," Benjamin called out. "Counsel is grossly misleading the jury."

Mark whirled around to face Benjamin. "Counsel, might I remind you that this is your witness up here." He then looked to the judge. "Your honor, I believe this witnesses testimony is pertinent to my client's defense."

The judge gave Mark's request long and serious consideration before giving his ruling. Losing a conviction in this case would not bode well for his reputation.

"Overruled." The judge finally spoke. "Counsel, you will redirect your line of questioning."

"I will not, your honor." Mark stood his ground. "My line of questioning is clearly within the bounds of cross-examination. This witness can prove beyond a reasonable doubt that corruption has infected this case, stemming from the police department, the crime lab, or possibly even the district attorney's office." Mark strode to the middle of the courtroom and faced the judge. "Your honor, pardon my boldness, but the fact you want me to redirect my line of questioning begs the question whether you yourself have been corrupted."

"That's far enough, counsel. You're speeding towards a contempt charge." The judge looked to the jury. "The jury will disregard counsel's last statement." He looked at Mark. "Redirect your question, counsel."

Mark held out his hands, pleading. "I'm sorry, your honor. With that request, I move for a mistrial." He extended his arm toward the jury panel. "This jury has been influenced by what has taken place here today." Mark was in his element.

Another uproar swept through the courtroom. Judge Baily hammered his gavel, calling out "Order," but no one would listen.

Gina was completely stunned.

"Holy shit," Roger muttered. "I can't believe this. We've gotta go."

Roger and Claire collected their things and moved to leave.

"Where are you going?" Gina grabbed at Roger's arm. "It's not over yet."

"I've got work to do," he said. "Stay till the end if you want to but get back to the lab as soon as you can." He scooted from the bench, following behind Claire. Gina watched them leave the courtroom in a rush.

Her cousin Jimmy walked out behind them. Her father and Uncle Anthony whispered to one another without expression. Gina gathered her coat and purse and moved to sit with them. The judge continued calling order to the courtroom. He pounded his gavel again and the courtroom eventually quieted down.

Mark stood in the middle of the courtroom with his hands clasped behind his back. He displayed a knowing expression with his chin held high. He was rounding third and heading for home.

"Your honor, clearly this witness has perjured himself, or at the very least is guilty of obstruction of justice. I'm gonna go out on a limb here and express that it's apparent to me and it should be to the court that this witness has in fact had some sort of communication with the defense prior to today's proceedings. Without my knowledge, of course."

Gina's stomach churned. *Could that be true? Had Nick communicated with Joe D'Amato's side prior to testifying?* She gripped her coat and purse. She glanced down. Her father's fists were clenched tight in his lap.

The judge rubbed his temples. Dread developed in his expression. He was obviously not happy with the way the trial was proceeding.

Judge Bailey raised his eyes to Nick. "Is that true, detective?"

Nick looked straight at the judge. "Yes."

Gina heard herself gasp. More commotion erupted. The judge sat back in his chair as if trying to understand what was happening in his own courtroom. He didn't call "order" this time. Nick had flat-out lied. Perjured himself.

Judge Bailey seemed to need a few moments to collect his thoughts. He waited for the gallery to quiet down. When it did, he directed his attention to Nick.

"Detective, I must express my deepest disappointment in your absurd conduct in my courtroom this morning. You have displayed disregard for the law and disrespected my courtroom. I'm charging you with one count of perjury under New Jersey State Statute 2C:28-1. You are to be taken into custody to await arraignment." Judge Bailey turned to the bailiff. "Bailiff, please remove detective Nick Casey to a holding cell."

The bailiff made his way to the witness stand. Nick stepped down from his seat. He seemed relaxed, maybe even relieved. The bailiff took his arm and led him across the courtroom. Nick kept his focus straight ahead, avoiding looking to the gallery as he was led out.

Gina grabbed her father's arm. "Jesus, Dad. What's going on here today?"

Carmine shook his head. "I have no fucking idea."

"Would you tell me if you knew?" Gina asked.

Carmine shot her a look of anger but didn't answer. Gina had struck a nerve with that question. She settled back in her seat to wait for the trial to end.

The judge scanned the jury panel. His complexion paled and his composure was weakened. Nick's testimony had been a blow to his self-esteem. Benjamin appeared just as shattered.

"Ladies and gentlemen of the jury, after today's proceedings, I must rule this case a mistrial."

Again, the court burst out in commotion and the judge banged the gavel several times.

"Order," he shouted to the gallery.

When the courtroom settled down, he turned back to the jury. "This court appreciates your time and service. Thank you. You may be excused."

The jury panel stood and filed out of the courtroom.

Judge Bailey looked to the defense table. "Mr. D'Amato, your posted bail will remain with the court, pending an investigation of today's proceedings. You're free to leave my courtroom, but not the state. This court is adjourned," he said curtly. He banged his gavel one last time, then stood and abruptly exited.

Gina's mouth was dry as cotton. She wanted to jump up and shout, but no words would form. And what could she say? The judge had made his ruling. Court was adjourned. Joe was a free man. She was numb.

Benjamin and his co-counsel packed up their case load and exited the courtroom with heads hung low. The press followed on their heels. It was going to be a media frenzy outside the courthouse today. She watched the hugs and handshakes taking place on the defendant's side.

Carmine tapped her arm. "Come on. Let's get out of here."

CHAPTER 2

Gina rode the elevator down to the first floor of the courthouse with her father Carmine and Uncle Anthony. There were four other occupants along for the ride, so they remained quiet. When the elevator doors opened, a small mass of reporters converged on them. Camera lights flashed and microphones were shoved in their faces as they continued to walk. The four other occupants scurried in the opposite direction.

Reporters were all shouting at once. "Carmine Teducci, tell us your thoughts on the proceedings today." "How do you feel about Joe D'Amato not being convicted?" "Some feel this is the Teducci and D'Amato stronghold on government. Any comment?" "Business as usual for organized crime?" "D'Amato murdered your daughter sixteen years ago. How does that make you feel about today's mistrial?"

Gina stopped in her tracks and spun to face the reporters. Cameras flashed. She felt her father's grip on her arm. "Let it go," he whispered in her ear.

Carmine looked to the reporters and calmly replied, "No comment." He spun around and pulled Gina with him.

Gina and Anthony fell in step with Carmine and headed out the side door. Gina couldn't resist looking back, fearing they were being followed by media hounds. Thankfully, they had moved on to other prey. That last comment had been so galling. Anything to spur a reaction.

Once outside the courtroom, chilled May morning air prickled Gina's cheeks and nose. Spring seemed unwilling to pass the baton onto summer, and it felt refreshing and calming. She inhaled a few deep breaths, then asked her father, "What happened in there today? Why would Nick do that? Perjure himself. It makes no sense. Something happened. Something big happened."

"I don't know, sweetheart," Carmine said. "And if I knew something, I would have told you."

"I'm sorry I said that to you," Gina said. "I was just surprised by everything that was happening."

"We all were," Anthony chimed in.

He was a shorter, leaner version of her father, with chiseled facial features. Her father's features were softer and more rounded, but still handsome just the same. The Teducci family had been blessed with excellent genes for many generations.

When Gina's grandmother was alive, she had boasted their Italian lineage, saying Teducci women were strong, passionate, and mysterious. Beautiful inside and out. And Teducci men were gallant, competitive opportunists. Confident and amorous.

Gina missed her grandmother. She had died the year before Gina's sister Sirrina died. Seventeen years ago. She would have stood up and spoken her mind in court this morning.

"I'll go get the car," Anthony said. "Gina?" He gave her a peck on her cheek. "I'll see you soon, sweetheart." He trotted down the stairs to the parking lot. He and his wife Loretta were Gina's godparents.

"Dad, I'm scared." Gina said. "There's going to be an investigation into this, into the office I work at. An investigation into my work as well. What if they find something? What if what Nick said today is true?"

Carmine took hold of her shoulders. "Gina, don't get worked up over this. You did your job. You did as you were asked. Nothing about this can come back at you."

"How do you know that?" Her voice sounded shrill.

"Because you wouldn't have done something illegal," he said. "If you had known you were reporting falsified documents and evidence, you wouldn't have done it, right? And you would have reported it to your director. I know you. You're a good girl." He squeezed her arms, then let go. "I'll deal with this. Don't worry, hunh?"

But Gina did worry. *What could her father do? Was he somehow involved?* She didn't even want to know that right now. Gina nodded, accepting his suggestion for the time being.

Carmine scanned the parking lot, "Where are you parked?"

Gina pointed to the furthest part of the lot. "Out there. How's Mom?"

"You want us to give you a ride to your car?" he asked.

"No, I'm good. How's Mom?" Gina asked again.

"Your Mom is fine. You know it would be too hard for her to be here."

Gina agreed. Her mother and Joe hadn't spoken for sixteen years. Gina knew her father's position with Joe D'Amato put a strain on their marriage. She sometimes thought of her father as selfish in his commitments to Joe. But she also knew his walking away from those commitments was not an option. He'd become too ingrained in the life to ever turn his back on it.

Her mother knew it, too. She was strong. Supportive. Devoted. Gina wasn't sure she could be as devoted as her mother. She certainly couldn't be as forgiving as her parents.

"After today, I'm glad she wasn't here," Gina said, stuffing her hands in her coat pockets warding off the chill. "How are you after all of this?"

"I'm not sure," he said, watching cars exiting the parking lot. He turned back to her. "Pissed. Concerned. I think some people have some explaining to do."

His words lacked conviction. There was a long history between the Teduccis and D'Amatos. Not all of it was bad. Gina wondered how he truly felt. She wouldn't ask because she doubted that she would get a straight answer.

"I'll come by the house either tonight or tomorrow to see Mom," was all she said.

They walked down the steps as Anthony pulled up in his Cadillac. Carmine pulled her close for a hug and kissed her cheek. "I'll see you soon, honey, and don't worry about this."

"O.K. Bye," Gina replied. She wished he would stop saying that because she *was* worried.

Carmine opened the door and climbed into the passenger seat.

"You need a lift to your car?" Anthony called out.

"No, I'm good," Gina said. "Take care."

She waved to them as they drove away. Gina didn't walk to her car. Instead, she went back inside the courthouse to find the bailiff. It took thirty minutes to find out that they would be taking Nick Casey to the Hudson County Department of Corrections after his arraignment.

When she asked if she could see him before his arraignment, they told her no. She expected that answer but asked anyway. When the bailiff couldn't give her any more information, she went to the division manager's office on the third floor. She needed answers, and she wanted them from the source. She wasn't sure what her father could do to help with this situation, and she didn't want to wait to find out.

The third floor of the courthouse held none of the opulence and carved wood finishes as the first, second, and fourth floors. White granite covered the floors, and the walls were beige with bulletin boards in place of artwork. There was a series of corridors with small offices and minimal furnishings. A bullpen area held five desks, with storefront glass offices on three sides. Gina smelled coffee and heated pastries in the vicinity.

She had never had a reason to visit the division manager's office. Her job as a crime lab technician only required her to testify on certain cases. She never met with defendants during a trial. This was a first for her.

She passed a uniformed police officer escorting a handcuffed prisoner down the hall. She tried not to imagine that they had done the same with Nick. He would be in the basement of the building now. The holding cell section. She passed attorneys carrying attaché cases and government employees going about their business. The third floor was apparently the hub of the courthouse's operations.

Gina made her way to the division manager's administration desk at the far end of one of the corridors. A heavyset woman sat at her desk, engrossed with her computer screen. She had short cropped black hair with maroon tinted tips. Her "L" shaped desk was littered with framed photos, silk flowers in clay pots, and ceramic Rottweiler figurines. Her workspace resembled an art class more than it did official government business. A stacking tray crammed with paperwork shielded her from the front counter.

"Excuse me," Gina said.

"Be right there," the woman said without looking over.

A long minute passed before she swung her ergonomic chair to face Gina. "How can I help you?" Her tone lacked any possible interest in Gina's needs.

"I'm here to see Detective Nick Casey," Gina said.

"Does he work out of our precinct?" she asked.

"No. He would be in a holding cell."

"Come again?" the woman asked.

"This is pertaining to Judge Bailey's trial this morning," Gina said, trying to be patient.

"He was arrested?" she asked louder than necessary.

"Yes."

"Hmm. That's a first for me." The woman spun back to her computer. Her long white fingernails typed in some information. It looked like they had been painted with liquid whiteout. She waited for her computer to tell her something. "What for?" she asked.

"Perjury," Gina replied.

The woman shook her head in disappointment. She reviewed her computer screen.

Gina turned to watch the workings of the courthouse continue around her. A phone was ringing somewhere down the corridor that apparently no one cared to answer.

"He's still being processed," the woman said.

Gina turned back to look at the woman. "What does that mean? Will I be able to see him?"

"That's all my computer is telling me," the woman replied.

Gina forced patience. "Can I bother you to please go ask someone if I'll be able to see him anytime soon? It's important."

Gina didn't think she should have had to add "it's important," but apparently that's what finally got the woman to move off her ass. She hefted her girth from her chair using one hand. The other hand she had wrapped in a neoprene wrist brace.

She shuffled away, getting easily distracted by co-workers. She disappeared through a door, then returned a few minutes later. She told Gina to come back later in the day. She seemed bored and uninterested in Gina's urgency. Gina wondered how much effort she had put into trying to locate him. She took notice of her name badge. "Thanks for your help, Wanda."

"Of course," Wanda said.

Annoyed, Gina left Wanda and the courthouse and headed back to the crime lab. She needed to talk with Roger and Claire. Their abrupt departure from the courtroom concerned her. It wasn't like Roger not to stay for the entire proceeding.

She made her way south on to Interstate ninety-five, heading to the lab in Hamilton Township. If she had blown through a red light, she would have been oblivious to it. She feared plenty right now. Her job was possibly in jeopardy.

There would be investigations, plenty of investigations, from many different agencies. *Would an investigation find fault in her work? In Roger and Claire's work? Had they been careful in their lab screenings and reporting?*

She tried not to over-analyze the situation while driving in traffic. She would get back to the crime lab and go over details of the case with Roger and Claire. They had made a good team in this investigation.

Nick's testimony had implied that the corruption had affected not only the crime lab, but the police department and the district attorney's office as well. It had been a bold statement, but their director, Detective Jerry Pulia, oversaw every aspect of their work on this case. It's why they worked as a team, so no mistakes, or in this case, corruption, could take place.

She feared for Nick. She couldn't understand why he'd done what he did. He perjured himself. A Class Three felony on his record. He threw his career away today. Why? He was going to prison. She was angry, sad, and scared all at once. He would be incarcerated with felons he helped put away. He would be stripped of his medals and achievements. His undercover status was blown. He would be in danger.

Gina's chest tightened, and tears welled up in her eyes. *What happened to him? What made him change his testimony?* She wiped a tear that ran down her cheek. She rolled down her window and inhaled deep breaths of the cool air to calm her nerves. She would stop by the courthouse this afternoon on her way home. They would have finished processing Nick by then. He would be in a holding cell awaiting arraignment.

Gina arrived at the crime lab less than an hour later. She had been speeding and wasn't even aware of it. It wasn't like her not to pay attention. The drive had been a blur.

The Hamilton County forensic science lab occupied one hundred thousand square feet of space within the New Jersey State Police Technical Building. Ten thousand of it was for the DNA lab alone: an advanced high-tech facility. The rest of the building contained the New Jersey police headquarters technology campus and the Office of Homeland Security.

She parked and walked to the single level brick and glass building that housed the crime lab. There were four white panel vans backed into parking spaces near the entrance, and two black suburban SUVs parked next to the vans that she didn't recognize.

Gina swiped her lab ID attached to a lanyard around her neck through the card reader. She pushed through the double glass doors and made her way to the corridor of private offices. The interior of the crime lab had undergone a major remodel the year before.

Wood plank floors, soft white walls, stainless steel, and pine furniture had replaced the dark industrial look originally constructed. Their equipment was state of the art, which was something the state of New Jersey always made sure was in the budget. Backing their law enforcement was a priority.

There was a buzz of unusual activity throughout the crime lab. Men and women whom Gina didn't recognize were swarming the lab, cubicles, and private offices. Some were carrying boxes, while others supervised with clip boards.

Where were her colleagues? Gina went to her cubicle. Her laptop had been removed. The Janet Sardello car bombing case file had also been removed. It was the next case she was going to start on today. She went to go find Roger.

He was in his office, packing files into an evidence box. A young man in khakis and a white dress shirt with the sleeves rolled up stood close by with a clip board in hand. He appeared to be taking inventory of what Roger was packing into the box.

"What are you doing?" Gina asked.

Roger looked up. "Packing up the D'Amato case files. Bring me what you have at your desk, so I have everything put together. The D.A. wants our case files sealed and placed in the evidence storage as soon as possible." He glanced at the young man in the corner quietly observing. "Can you give us a minute, please?"

"Sure. I'll need you to stop working on that until I return." The young man referred to the box Roger was packing.

Roger lifted both hands in the air as if in surrender.

The young man scooted past Gina and left them alone.

Gina stepped further into Roger's office. Boxes, files, and report folders were neatly stacked, some occupying floor space, some were on pine bookshelves. Everything was labeled and in its proper space.

There were no signs of a personal life. No photos, no awards, no magnets with clever sayings stuck on the file cabinets, no magazines to show any areas of interest. There was nothing to identify who Roger Mattison was. He immersed himself in his work.

"There's nothing for me to bring you," Gina said. "They've already raided my cubicle."

Roger nodded. "I'll get the files from them. I want to keep everything together so there's no questions or mishaps. I don't trust these bozos."

"They took the Sardello case from me, too."

"Actually, I took that after I got back here," he said. "It was requested by Detective Pulia. When I delivered it to him, he said it was being re-assigned."

"Re-assigned?" Gina asked not happy to hear this bit of news. "To who?"

"Whom," Roger corrected her. "Another tech. I don't know. He's the director. He didn't specify and I didn't ask. It's kind of crazy in here today." He paused on her reaction. "Look, don't get worked up about it."

"It doesn't look good for me to have a case re-assigned, Roger. Especially right now."

"I'm just doing what I'm told."

"Do you want to talk about what happened today?" Gina asked.

Roger straightened, huffing a few breaths. The bending and stretching of packing had overworked his dormant muscles. "Not right now." He plopped his weight down in his chair.

"Aren't you concerned about this investigation?" Gina asked.

No answer.

"What do I say if someone questions me?" she asked.

Roger sat up straight. He hesitated before answering. "The truth, Gina."

"I wasn't implying I was going to lie about anything. I just meant…I don't know what to expect."

"Expect the unexpected."

"That doesn't help."

"Expect to answer questions about your past."

"My past? What about my past?"

Roger hesitated, seeming uneasy. "Expect them to ask about your affiliation with the D'Amato family."

Gina detected bitterness in his words. She didn't appreciate him making the association. "I don't have an *affiliation* with the family."

"I mean about your sister," Roger concluded.

A man cleared his throat close behind Gina. She startled and turned to face him.

Roger said, "Gina, this is FBI agent Chris Collins and his partner, agent Danielle Stevens."

The agents held up their badges. Gina was taken by surprise. *How long had they been standing behind her? Why hadn't Roger given her some sort of warning? How much of their conversation had they heard?*

Both agents tucked their credentials back in their jacket pockets. Chris had a military presence to his stance: tight buzz-cut red hair topped his pudgy face that expressed a happy-go-lucky smirk, like he was your best friend. She wasn't sure she trusted him. Either of them. She wasn't sure who she should trust. Everything was in a delicate balance now.

The fallout from the trial left her with a sinking feeling. She'd keep her guard up. So many questions needed answers and she didn't know who could answer them for her. She would be cooperative but cautious with the information she gave to the two agents.

Danielle was every bit a tomboy. Her faded blonde ponytail was pulled tight to the nape of her neck and she wore no makeup. Her navy suit and black rubber shoes said she had something to prove, most likely to herself.

"Are you Miss Gina Teducci?" Chris asked.

"Yes, I am." Gina looked to Roger. He busied himself labeling the box with a Sharpie.

"Will you come with us, please?" Danielle asked.

Gina nodded. This was happening much faster than she anticipated. The FBI investigation had been underway within an hour of the trial results.

CHAPTER 3

Gina and both agents were seated in one of the crime lab's three interview rooms. Rooms normally utilized for interviewing witnesses in a case, or interrogating criminals. Gina had been in these rooms more times than she remembered. But this time had an entirely different feel.

She was on the opposing side of the table being interviewed. It was a first for her and she wasn't liking it. The glass partitions allowed her to see into the lab area where the FBI carried on their activities.

She wondered where her co-workers were. Gone for the day? Gina felt uninformed, like she was hanging from a limb about to snap and drop her fifty feet into an abyss. She leaned back in her wire mesh chair with her hands tightly clasped together in her lap.

Collins and Stevens settled into their chairs and opened their case files to begin the interview. They each had a notepad with pen in hand, ready to take her report.

"Should I have my lawyer present?" Gina asked.

The agents looked to one another, then to her.

"Do you think you need your lawyer?" Danielle asked.

I don't trust either of you. "I'm not sure," Gina replied. Her palms were damp.

Collins set his pen down and folded his hands over his notepad. "This is an inquiry into the D'Amato case that you worked on. If you think your work somehow requires you to have your lawyer present, we can stop and continue once he or she is present. Or we can begin, and if at any time you wish to stop, we can certainly do so and have you contact your lawyer."

He had a way of making it sound like she was over-reacting by wanting her lawyer present. "Fine," Gina said. "Let's start and see where this goes."

Danielle removed a tape recorder from her black canvas bag and placed it on the table between them. "We'll be recording this interview, ok?" she said.

Do I have a choice? "I suppose," Gina replied.

Danielle switched on the recorder.

Chris leaned forward and scribbled something on his notepad. He spoke to no one in particular giving a verbal introduction for the recording, then began the interview. "Miss Teducci, first I'm going to ask some questions for clarification, and then we'll move on to the case." He looked up at her. "Just some general housekeeping." He gave her a squinty smile.

Gina nodded.

"I'll need for you to speak your answers as we move forward," he said.

Note to self, head nodding isn't accepted, Gina thought.

Chris looked at her expectantly.

"Oh. Yes...ok," Gina replied. Her nerves were shot, and they hadn't even begun.

"I'll read off the information I have here in my notes. Please correct me if I have anything wrong."

He looked at her with his little smirk.

"OK," Gina replied. She decided she didn't like him.

Chris began his housekeeping. "Gina Marie Teducci, single, age twenty-eight, born February fourth, nineteen ninety-one in Englewood, New Jersey. Parents are Carmine and Jacqueline Teducci." He looked up to her. "You want to know something? My uncle...top notch FBI agent. New York. He knew your grandfather Stefano Teducci."

"My grandfather's still alive," Gina replied.

"I know. My uncle isn't. Murdered. An unsolved murder, in fact."

Maybe he was taken out for manipulating interview information, Gina thought.

She responded with silence. He continued. "OK then…," He went back to his notes. "You reside at seven-o-two Jefferson Avenue, apartment B-3, Cliffside Park, New Jersey, a…one-bedroom apartment. Let's see…owner and landlord are Paul and Betty Schaffer." Chris looked up at her. "Good so far?"

"Yes," Gina answered.

"Good," he replied and continued. "You graduated University of Albany – SUNY – New York, a bachelor's degree in Natural Science-Biology specializing in DNA studies. You also had classes in business and finance. You're employed as a Forensic Science Technician here at the New Jersey State Police Department Crime Lab in Hamilton County. Your supervisor is Mr. Roger Mattison and your director is Detective Jerry Pulia, correct?"

"Yes."

"For the case in reference, the Joe D'Amato case, who did you report to?"

"Are we moving on from housekeeping?" Gina asked.

Chris smiled. "Yes, I suppose so."

"Roger," Gina replied.

"No one else?"

"No."

"Did anyone assist you in your work besides Mr. Mattison?"

"Claire Chu," Gina replied. "Actually, I assisted her."

"Anyone else?"

"No."

"Did you conduct any reports to Claire directly or just to Roger?"

"To both." Gina decided it was best to keep her answers short and to the point.

"Were you part of this case from the beginning?"

"Yes."

"Claire as well?"

"Yes."

"Did you have any reservations when asked to work on this case?"

"No. Why would I?"

Danielle chimed in. "Please only answer the questions your asked."

"No." Gina answered again. She decided she didn't like Danielle, either.

Chris continued, "Did Roger or Detective Pulia ever ask you if you had any reservations working on this case prior to your involvement?"

Gina hesitated on this one. She was getting a feel for where Chris was going with his line of questioning. The last thing she wanted was to inadvertently place blame or cause on Roger or her director. But she also had to keep herself in the clear.

"Gina?" Chris presented his happy-go-lucky grin.

"No."

Chris made some notes on his pad. "Can you explain your history with Mr. Joe D'Amato?"

This is what you really want to know, isn't it? Gina thought. *To somehow tie me to the mistrial this morning.* Gina would be overly cautious in her answers. "I don't think it's any secret that our families have known each other for over sixty years. It might even be longer than that. What does the media say these days?"

Chris smiled again. "We'll leave the media out of this."

"That's a long time," Danielle said. "One big happy family?"

"Aren't all families?" Gina shot back to her.

Danielle sat back in her chair, stepping out of the ring, and allowing Chris to finish the interview.

Chris spoke up again. "I only want to hear about what happened with your sister, Sirrina."

"Only?" Gina scoffed. "It was a very significant and painful experience."

"Yes." Chris recoiled. "My apologies, Gina, for making that sound anything other than what it was."

"I don't know what I can tell you that you don't already know. Between the investigations and the media, you should have a clear understanding of the events that led to my sister's death."

"I'd like to hear your recollection," he said.

Gina would give him the media's version. It was already public knowledge. There would be no harm in recounting the events as they had been reported, since she didn't have an attorney present to protect her rights. "It was sixteen years ago," Gina began. "I was twelve and Sirrina was eight. We went down the shore to the Wildwoods."

"That's a theme park?" Chris asked. "In Wildwood, New Jersey, correct?"

"It's the boardwalk. There's an amusement and water park there," Gina replied.

"Had you been there before?" Chris asked.

"Yes," Gina replied. "My parents and aunts and uncles would rent summer houses there and we would go usually three or four times throughout the summer."

"And do you and your family still go there for the summers?"

"No."

"When did the vacations stop?"

Gina was quiet.

Chris looked up from his note taking. "Since Sirrina's death?" he asked.

Gina nodded.

Danielle spoke up. "Can you please answer for the recording?"

"Yes," Gina replied.

"And where exactly was the house your family rented the time you went when Sirrina was abducted and eventually killed?" Chris asked scanning a report in his file.

Gina got quiet again. She hadn't expected to have to share this story with the FBI. She had tried her best to put the pain of this experience behind her, and now this jackass was asking her to recollect a very painful time in her life while he scribbled on his notepad. Expect the unexpected. Isn't that what Roger had told her just before these two appeared in his office earlier? This was unexpected.

"Gina?" Chris was prodding her again.

"I...um...no. My parents hadn't rented a house." Gina collected her thoughts. "That trip was just a group of us kids going to the Wildwoods for the day."

"Go on," he said.

Gina recalled the Suburban and minivan carting the kids and teenagers. Innocent joy cruising down the highway. Heading to the Jersey shore for a day of fun in the sun at the amusement park and water slides. "My cousin Jimmy drove his parents' Suburban." She remembered them all laughing and singing their favorite songs for the two-hour drive. "It was Sirrina, my friend Chloe, Nick and myself. My brother Christopher rode with my other cousins Steven, Jeanine, and Joey in Steven's parents' minivan."

Chris interrupted, "You mentioned Nick. Is that Detective Nick Casey?"

See? You already know this. That wasn't just a lucky assumption, you ass. "Yes," Gina answered.

"You grew up with him as well?"

"Yes." *And I had a crush on him that summer too, but I'm leaving that detail out.*

"Continue," he said.

"We got there around eleven in the morning."

Gina remembered their group having so much fun on the rides, playing games and playing at the beach. They ran around all day in bathing suits and flip flops, riding the giant water slides and baking in the summer sun. Nick and Christopher won stuffed animals at one of the games. A pink teddy bear for her and a black and white tiger for Chloe.

"We did what kids do at the Wildwoods," Gina said. "Conquered the water slides, played games, ran down the beach and played in the surf. Rode the park rides."

Gina recalled how she couldn't keep Sirrina off the Ferris wheel. She loved being up high in the sky at the water's edge. Each time they rode it, Sirrina pretended she was a seagull soaring above the ocean. Gina laughed and joined her little sister, spreading their arms wide while the giant wheel carried them to the top.

The sweet innocence of Sirrina giggling and squealing. Both girls flapped their arms right as the big wheel rounded the top and began to descend. The vast ocean was splayed out in front of them as far as they could see. That moment of weightlessness had them screaming with delight. Catching their breath, they held hands, waiting for the next revolution.

Gina felt tears well up in her eyes. She quickly wiped at them, not wanting to embarrass herself in this interview.

"Do we need to take a break?" Chris asked.

Gina shook her head no. "The sun was setting, so we all decided to go grab a slice of pizza before driving home. Sirrina needed to use the bathroom, so I went with her and my cousin Jimmy came with us. He didn't want the two of us going off alone."

"He was the oldest one in your group?" Chris asked.

"Yes. Eighteen."

Chris wrote this down. He looked up at her. "Continue."

"The rest of the group went over to the pizza place to get a table. There was a line at the bathrooms. Jimmy waited outside. I let Sirrina go ahead of me. When she came out, I told her to go wait with Jimmy. Two girls pushed ahead of me while I was talking to her, so I had to wait my turn."

Gina was trembling now. No matter how many times she had to recite the events of that night, it never got any easier. If anything, it was harder each time. She drew in a breath. Her voice was ragged and shaky.

"When I came out of the bathroom, there was all this commotion. My cousin Jimmy was freaking out about something. He came up to me and said Sirrina was missing. I didn't understand it. At first, I thought he and Sirrina were playing a joke. Like she went off to hide around the building and Jimmy would try to scare me, for fun."

Gina paused again remembering how that hadn't been the case. She remembered the surge of emotions as those moments drew on; when she came to realize that Jimmy wasn't kidding. This wasn't a joke. Sirrina had disappeared for real.

"Did Jimmy play games like that on a regular basis?" Chris asked.

"No. Well, no more so than any other kids would do. It was harmless fun."

"Except this time," Danielle chimed in.

Fuck you, Gina thought.

"What happened next?" Chris asked.

Gina recalled Jimmy pacing and flailing his arms, shouting out Sirrina's name. His eyes wide with fear, his nostrils flared. He looked crazed and scared all at once. He had been hysterical.

"People started gathering around us," Gina continued. "Jimmy asked one of the adults that had come over to go find the rest of our group at the pizza place. By then two security officers arrived and began to question Jimmy."

Gina recalled clinging to Jimmy's side. When she began to cry, he held her hand. She remembered his palm was sweaty and his hand shook with fear. The sun had set by then. The night sky was black against the neon lights of the amusement park. She remembered feeling like she'd been cast into a twisted dream at that point. Fun and entertainment continued around them. Gina held tight to Jimmy and their group huddled close with the police and security. They were like the axes holding the world in place as it continued to revolve around them.

Rides spun, twirled, and twinkled high above. The boardwalk thudded underfoot as strangers passed by. Some pushing baby strollers rushed past the scene, avoiding possible danger. Other folks gathered around to see what the police excitement was all about.

Bells, buzzers, and tinny music rang out from the game booths. Screams from kids enjoying the rides echoed around them. The smell of popcorn, hot dogs, candied apples, and cigarette smoke filled the air. Gina felt dizzy and sick to her stomach. The twisted dream had turned into a nightmare.

She remembered Nick had been there, holding her tight. She had let go of Jimmy at some point and clung to Nick instead. Her brother Christopher was holding Chloe. Everyone was crying. The police arrived. The fire department arrived. Their parents arrived. And Sirrina was gone.

"What happened next?" Chris interrupted her thoughts.

Gina sifted through her recollections. After the chaotic scene died down, the crowd dispersed. There had only been Gina, her family, and friends left standing on the boardwalk. The two-hour drive home had been a quiet one. Gina kept looking out the back window of her parents' car, thinking they left her sister behind. If they turned around and went back for her, she would be there waiting for them.

"We went home," Gina answered.

"But that wasn't the end of it."

"No," Gina barely whispered.

Her hesitation caused Chris to lead the accounting. "Your cousin Jimmy took it the hardest. He had turned his back on Sirrina for just a moment to take a phone call, and she was gone. He later tried to commit suicide, isn't that right?"

Gina nodded yes. She pulled a Kleenex from her purse and wiped her eyes and nose since both were running now. "How does all of this have anything to do with the trial this morning?"

"I'll get to that," he said, referring to his notepad and file. "Your cousin Jimmy was committed to a private mental facility and during that time he was contacted by Sirrina's kidnappers, correct?" Chris asked. "What was the name of the hospital he was committed to?"

The Pines. "I don't remember," Gina answered. "It's in his report. All of this is in the police reports. And apparently, in your notes there." Gina pointed to his notepad and file. "Obviously, you already know all of this, so why are you making me relive these painful memories? You already know what happened."

"I have a statement from a twelve-year-old girl," Chris said. "A scared and traumatized twelve-year-old girl. I'd like to hear your recollection of the incident now. I'd like to hear your thoughts on the D'Amato family as it pertains to your sister's death."

Why? So, you can pin the blame on me for what happened this morning? Wouldn't that be a neat and tidy solution for you. "I think I would like for this interview to be over with now."

"I'm sorry, Gina," Chris apologized. "That was an insensitive thing for me to say. I would appreciate your continuing with your recollection. This way we can be done and gone."

Gina liked the sound of that. She wanted to be done and gone right now. She would give them what they needed so she could get the hell out of there. *Control your anger, Gina,* she thought.

"I can only relay what's in the police reports from this point on. Like you said, I was a twelve-year-old kid at the time. I wasn't privy to most of the conversations and interviews. I'm not sure what I can tell you that's any different than what's in those reports."

"You'd be surprised, Gina." Danielle spoke up again. "Body language tells us a lot. When victims or criminals recount their stories, a lot is revealed through their body language."

Chris shot Danielle a hard look, not appreciating her interjection.

Gina caught the silent communication between them. "I'm aware of body language," Gina said. *See? Keep your cool. They're watching your every move. Keep your posture relaxed, hands loose in your lap and your eyes steady on Chris or his notepad.* She wouldn't give them any reason to raise their suspicions about her.

Chris looked back to Gina. "Please continue. What happened after Jimmy went to the private hospital?"

"He was contacted by the kidnappers," Gina said.

"And how was this possible?" Chris asked. "It's my understanding that there is no outside communication allowed for patients being treated at those types of facilities."

"He had his cell phone. I remember that because it was stolen."

"Really?" Chris asked, sounding surprised.

"It's in the report," Gina said.

"And never recovered?"

"No. Not that I know of."

"Hmm. That's convenient," Chris said, half to himself.

Gina had to admit that it sounded a little suspicious as she reiterated the events. Or maybe sitting here being interrogated by these two agents had her thoughts spinning out.

"So once Jimmy was contacted, what happened?" Chris asked.

"Apparently, a meeting was set up on a yacht in Lincoln Harbor in New Jersey. Jimmy was supposed to bring ransom money: one hundred thousand dollars to trade for Sirrina."

"But that never happened, correct?"

Gina was quiet.

"Gina?" Chris prodded her again.

Gina looked down to her hands folded in her lap. "No." Her voice strained to say the word. Tears filled her eyes again.

"There was an explosion on board the yacht before Jimmy arrived," Chris said.

Gina kept her head hung down and only nodded yes.

"Let the record show that Gina has responded yes to my question," Chris said. "Do you want to stop here and take some time to regain your composure, Gina?"

35

You're a lousy prick, she thought. "No." She raised her head and wiped at her tears with her wadded-up Kleenex. Danielle pushed a box of Kleenex closer to her. Gina plucked two from the box this time. Danielle settled back in her seat like she was bored and had heard this sob story a hundred times. Her disposition seemed heartless and unemotional. Gina assumed she would go far in her career as an FBI agent.

"What was the outcome from the investigation of the explosion?" Chris asked.

Gina looked past Chris to the happenings outside the room. Agents continued going about their business of boxing up files and computers and removing them from the crime lab. She wondered if Roger and Claire had been put through the same scrutiny she was being put through.

"Gina?" Chris called out.

"Yes, um…" She didn't want to answer any more questions. She wanted to leave the interrogation, leave the building, leave this tragedy behind.

Chris interjected, "The investigation found four people on board the yacht. Joe's nephew Guiseppe D'Amato, his two college friends Greg Plumber and Josh Dietrich, and of course…your sister Sirrina."

He might have seemed sympathetic at that moment if Gina hadn't already thought him a heartless prick. She wasn't sure if it was genuine or not.

He continued, "Most of the evidence was destroyed in the explosion, but the evidence they were able to recover led to identifying these four individuals, correct?"

"Yes." Gina strained to answer his question.

"What was the reason for the kidnapping and ransom in the first place?"

"I don't know."

"Business? Personal? Random?"

Gina shrugged. "I don't know."

"How did your family respond when they were told Guiseppe D'Amato had been your sister's abductor and murderer?"

"I'm sorry?" Gina asked. *So much for sympathetic,* she thought. *He's here to pick at the scab until it bleeds. Until I bleed with any information, he can use against me.*

"Did they lash out? Was there retaliation? Anger? Hatred?"

All the above, you idiot, Gina thought. "I'm sure they were upset," Gina replied. "Just as upset as any parent would be under the same circumstances."

"Yes, but the fact this was someone known to you and your family. A personal connection. Joe D'Amato's nephew. You yourself said your families have known each other for sixty plus years. That's a lot of history. A lot of history that's contained plenty of criminal behavior between the two families. And maybe some unsettled grievances, too. There had to be another level of anger altogether. A vengefulness maybe?"

Gina wasn't liking his accusations one bit. He was forcing that retaliation scenario again. She remained quiet.

Chris added, "Couple that with the fact there was never a trial in your sister's murder case, no one to blame, no one to convict…no closure. I would imagine that to be upsetting. Devastating, for sure."

Gina practiced restraint. A current of anger coursed through her, but she remained quiet. She wouldn't give him the satisfaction of seeing her coming unglued.

Chris didn't stop. "Tell me, Gina, did you become a crime scene technician because of your sister?"

Yes. "No," Gina replied.

"No?" Chris asked.

"Did you become an FBI agent because of your uncle?" Gina shot back at him.

"Yes, I did."

At least he answered her honestly. She wouldn't do the same for him. She had, in fact, become a CSI because of her sister's death. She wanted to understand why they couldn't find Sirrina after the boat exploded.

As a kid watching television, she had seen explosions blow people up and away. She had hoped Sirrina was blown far from the boat. She'd hoped that Sirrina was floating out in the Hudson, that they would find her that day. Alive.

But her work as a forensic tech taught her plenty about what explosions could do to a person at close range and on the water. The blast would certainly kill. And any remnants would either have been eaten by marine life or currents would have swept her away.

It was unimaginable to think of her sister's life ending so horrifically. A year of therapy had helped Gina overcome most of it. Immersing herself in her work has helped, too. She knew Nick had become a cop because of Sirrina's death.

Gina never wanted another family to go through what she and her family went through. In her sister's case, evidence had been destroyed and poor samples were turned into the lab. The crime scene had been compromised by onlookers and inexperienced port police. She knew every case couldn't be contained, but it made her extra careful and vigilant in every piece of evidence she collected and analyzed.

"What are you asking, agent Collins?" Gina questioned. "If I was looking for revenge with this case?"

"I was thinking closure. Funny you should say revenge."

"There's nothing funny about any of this," Gina shot back. "You're the one who implied revenge in your earlier question. I was just clarifying whether that's what you were in fact asking me. If I was out for revenge in my analysis of this case."

"Were you?"

"No."

Both he and Gina shared a good long stare before he finally spoke. "Then I guess we're done here." Chris capped his pen and set it on his notepad.

Danielle moved to switch off the tape recorder.

"That's it?" Gina asked.

"For now," Chris said. He stood up and Danielle did the same. They collected their things. "We'll be in contact if we have any more questions."

Gina watched the agents leave the room. She sat in silence for a long moment. She realized she had been trembling. She wondered if her body language made her appear guilty of something. The whole ordeal left her feeling wiped out.

CHAPTER 4

It's difficult to define the ethical and moral standards of the lobbyist. Jimmy Teducci had been referred to as a crafty hustler, a low-level con man and everything in between. Truth be told, there wasn't much difference between any of those and a lobbyist.

Jimmy worked in the private sector, persuading and influencing government officials to better serve the interests of his clients. It was his job, and that of his office, to sway legislators and regulatory agencies in their policies and often-times have new legislation or policies created.

Savvy was how Jimmy saw himself. He could successfully have laws changed. Whether it was for the good of the public or not didn't concern him. His only concern was the needs of his clients. They paid for results, and Jimmy delivered.

Jimmy tossed aside the financial magazine that he was reading. It was another article centered around him and the lobbying profession that he'd read four times already. Something to keep his mind occupied while he waited, but it wasn't helping.

Four text messages and three phone calls to Detective Jerry Pulia went unanswered. Jimmy needed answers. Joe D'Amato's trial vaporized after Detective Nick Casey's testimony. Nick and Jerry were partners on the case. A solid case. A slam dunk case. Joe D'Amato should have been going to jail and instead he walked, free of any charges.

The outcome of the trial had Jimmy reeling. All that work, flushed down the toilet. He propped his elbows on his glass desktop and rubbed his temples. A blinding migraine had hit an hour earlier and hadn't subsided with the three Excedrin pills he took. The burning sensation in the pit of his stomach made him gulp down the last of his coffee. It didn't help. And it didn't matter.

What mattered right now was talking to Detective Pulia. Why the hell wasn't Jerry returning his calls or text messages? He needed to make sure the players were honoring the deal and following the plan. Obviously, one player had already strayed. Jimmy's stomach churned thinking about the consequences Nick's actions would have.

Jimmy's plan had too many moving parts. Too many avenues that could go south. He realized that now. He felt like walls were closing in and the roof was about to crush him, thanks to Nick pulling the foundation right out from under his feet. It just went to prove he couldn't trust people even when they had been paid a shitload of money. A mistake he wouldn't make again.

Nick had double-crossed him and left a lot of people in precarious situations. Jimmy would see to it that Nick didn't make it out of prison alive. He wondered who else would turn. This was going to cost him. A lot.

Thinking of how many deals he would have to broker in the coming weeks made his head spin. His lobbying efforts would be put to the test. It was going to take a miracle to keep all the players in check. Yes, this was going to cost him plenty.

He stood and walked over to the wall of windows of his fourth-floor corner office. He pressed his palm against the cold glass. An orange Staten Island ferry made its crossing through the murky waters of the Hudson, bringing passengers from Manhattan to Staten Island.

Looking down to the water's edge on the Jersey side, his thoughts swirled like the river's current. He was confident he could rise above this situation and still carry out his plans for New York. Nick Casey wouldn't stop him. No one would. Nick may have the power of law enforcement on his side, but Jimmy had political power backing him. His foothold in the city and state government would make him a wealthy man someday. He had learned to wield his power behind the scenes.

His Uncle Carmine wanted him in a permanent position within the building department. A commissioner would have been fine for Carmine. A position that could control from the inside. But Jimmy preferred the freedom of being a lobbyist. And the many perks that went with it.

Jimmy's sights were set for across the Hudson. The New York side. The D'Amato side. That should have started with Joe going to prison. Jimmy should have been planning his next move. Instead, he needed to focus on damage control.

He heard a commotion outside his office. A moment later his door swung open and district attorney Benjamin Forrester strode in. Jimmy's assistant Jeanette followed on his heels.

"I'm sorry, Jimmy," she said. "He didn't give me…"

Benjamin held up his hand to stop her, but his focus was set on Jimmy. "We need to talk. I need some reassurances, Jimmy."

"Benjamin. What a surprise," Jimmy replied with sarcastic pleasure.

"Cut the crap, Jimmy," Benjamin retorted.

Jimmy looked to his assistant. "Thank you, Jeanette. Will you please excuse us?"

"Can I bring either of you anything?" she asked.

Jimmy looked at Benjamin.

"No," Benjamin snapped.

"We're fine, Jeanette. Can you please close the door on your way out?"

Jeanette excused herself, closing the door behind her.

Jimmy gestured to one of the client chairs at his desk. "Take a seat Benjamin."

Benjamin walked to the leather chairs and plopped down in one of them. "Please tell me that you have some idea as to what the hell happened this morning?"

Benjamin's career was crashing down around him. Jimmy could see it in his expression. He sounded desperate. His shoulders bent forward from the weight of the mistrial. It had been a crushing loss for him.

"First of all, Benjamin, I'll ask that you refrain from barging in my office, shouting and making a scene in front of my employees."

Benjamin pivoted with a look of surprise as he glanced at Jimmy's office door, then back to Jimmy. "Who? Jeanette? I didn't think I had to sensor my conversations in front of her."

"You do. Because you don't know who else is listening in the office," Jimmy said.

Eavesdropping wasn't a real concern, but he wanted Benjamin to respect keeping his big mouth shut.

"No one's ever here except you and Jeanette," Benjamin said. "I didn't think…"

"Right. You didn't think," Jimmy cut him off. "And you need to start thinking. Thinking about how you're going to handle your end."

"Handle my end?" Benjamin scoffed. "Why the hell do you think I'm here, Jimmy? I was blindsided this morning. Tell me what you think I should do with my situation, hunh? I'm going to have the Attorney General crawling up my ass, not to mention the FBI and who knows who else." He sat rigid on the edge of his chair, expecting answers.

Jimmy remained standing. He walked in front of Benjamin and leaned his weight back against his desk. He wanted the power position of standing above Benjamin. He wasn't appreciating Benjamin panicking the way he was. Panic caused mistakes, and no one could afford mistakes right now.

A little calming reassurance would control Benjamin. He had proved to be a ball of playdough that Jimmy could easily manipulate. If Benjamin possessed half the boldness he projected while trying his court cases, Jimmy could have considered him a man. But the sad truth was that Benjamin was a weak man who lacked confidence. He hid behind his cases and Jimmy to feign power. It worked well for Jimmy.

Jimmy relaxed his arms and clasped his hands together. "You didn't do anything wrong, Benny. The truth about what happened today is that you and Judge Bailey didn't win your landmark case against Joe D'Amato. And Detective Nick Casey perjured himself on the witness stand, obviously in a deal made with Joe D'Amato. Nick will be going to prison and Joe will be a free man. Nothing else."

"Nothing else?" Benjamin scoffed. "What about all of the fabricated testimony and evidence that Nick revealed?"

"Think about it, Benny. Technically, Nick didn't reveal fabricated testimony or evidence. He only testified to that fact. That's Nick's word against everyone else who testified."

"But he said that he completed a separate investigation. Why would he have done that?" Benjamin asked.

Good question, Jimmy thought. He walked around his desk to take a seat in his high back leather chair.

"Benjamin, you heard Joe D'Amato's attorney this morning. He was making exaggerated statements simply to win his case. I can't believe I'm having to explain this to you. It's what defense attorneys do. Anything to sway the jury or influence the case to secure a win. The fact that Nick was your witness and not the defense's witness...well...that put a tailspin on things." Jimmy paused for thought. "Whether Nick has evidence or testimony from a second investigation is irrelevant at this point. The judge made his final ruling. I would put money on it that Nick Casey flat out lied up on that witness stand this morning."

"We know he did, Jimmy. He perjured himself. That's why he was arrested."

"I meant he lied about the second investigation."

"Oh. I don't know," Benjamin said. "Why would Detective Casey do that? Why would he perjure himself and go to prison? He's a decorated detective with a flawless arrest record. I've worked on a lot of trials that relied on his work and I've never had anything like this happen to any of my cases. It makes no sense. He just threw his career in the shitter this morning and for what?" Benjamin stated.

Benjamin was starting to spiral out of control. Jimmy needed to get him back in line.

"Why do any witnesses change their stories or their testimony, hunh?" Jimmy asked.

"A lot of reasons," Benjamin said.

Jimmy leaned forward on his elbows. "Right. But most times it's either because they're rewarded with something very appealing or because they're scared. They've been threatened in some way, which is where my money is at. It was obvious this morning that Joe D'Amato or one of his associates got to Detective Casey." Jimmy sat back in his chair. "Hell, it's what I would have done if I were in Joe's shoes. That's why he fabricated that nonsense this morning. Joe D'Amato can be a very persuasive man. He must have something pretty big hanging over Nick's head for him to have lied on the stand this morning."

"How can you sit there so sure of yourself?" Benjamin asked.

"Why else would Nick perjure himself?" Jimmy asked. "It could be bribery, but I doubt it. I'd put money on it that Joe D'Amato had something on Nick."

"I don't know. Maybe," Benjamin said, looking past Jimmy, out the windows to the Hudson. He brought his attention back to Jimmy. "What about us? Our deal?"

Jimmy folded his hands together and rested his chin on the tips of his knuckles with a slight grin. He knew this was the real reason for Benjamin's visit. "What about it?"

"What if the investigations find something. Connects me and you to...you know." Benjamin was cowering, almost groveling.

"What we do, Benjamin, has nothing to do with what they'll be investigating. It's a separate matter entirely. Rest assured your re-election campaign account will continue to flourish." Jimmy fanned his hands to mimic flowers blossoming.

Benjamin slouched down in his chair, looking defeated. Jimmy stood up and came around to stand in front of him once again. Jimmy bent forward to talk close to Benjamin. "You need to snap out of your slump here, Benny. You're looking pitiful and guilty. Face the investigations head on. Like I said, you didn't do anything wrong. You need to show force and commitment by standing by your case. Let them find fault in what Nick said today. That's not on you."

"What about Joe's attorney implying my office corrupted the case? That I was corrupt."

"You are corrupt," Jimmy replied. "It's just not pertaining to this case."

Benjamin's attention floated away again, looking out the windows. He apparently didn't like hearing the truth. Jimmy grew impatient. He bent down, getting in Benjamin's face, and placed a hand on Benjamin's shoulder. He gave a slight squeeze. "Do I need to be concerned here?"

Benjamin pressed himself back into the chair. "No. No Jimmy. I'll handle it."

Jimmy patted his shoulder and straightened. "Good." Jimmy walked back to his chair. "Ask Jeanette to come in when you leave."

Benjamin remained seated.

Jimmy looked over to Benjamin, annoyed. "We're done here."

Benjamin stood and walked to the door, then turned back to Jimmy. "I'll let you know how the investigations go."

Jimmy opened his laptop without looking at Benjamin. "The less communication between us, Benny, the better." He typed on his laptop until he heard his office door close. He looked up and Benjamin was gone. Benjamin was going to be a problem. Just like Nick had turned out to be a problem. Jimmy would put a tentative plan in place to deal with both.

Jeanette knocked as she walked into his office, looking sexy as always. She could make him forget his woes even if only for a moment. She carried file folders and mail in one arm and a white sack in the other. She reminded him of his cousin Gina in every way, only four years younger. And if Gina weren't his cousin…

"I ran downstairs to grab us a couple of sandwiches. Are you hungry?" Jeanette asked.

High heels carried her stunning twenty-four-year-old body across his office. The skin-hugging knit dress brought indecent thoughts. It was dark blue with a plunging neckline. He imagined black lace undergarments to match her black stilettos. She had every color of the rainbow in undergarments. He'd seen her in most of them. Half of them he'd purchased for her.

She came around to his side of the desk and set the folders and mail on the corner of the desk. She plopped the sack lunch in front of him. The aroma of pastrami wafted up out of the bag.

"I'm hungry all right." He pulled her onto his lap.

"Of course, you are." She smiled and kissed his cheek. "But not here. Not at the office." She moved to stand, but he held her tight. "Jimmy…" She looked at him, less than pleased.

"All right, all right." He released his hold on her. "Let's have dinner tonight."

She rummaged through the sack lunch and pulled out two sandwiches. "Mmm, I have plans tonight. Maybe tomorrow night." She took one of the sandwiches and went around to the other side of the desk, taking a seat in the chair Benjamin sat in earlier. She unwrapped her sandwich in her lap.

Jimmy was fantasizing about taking her to a hotel for the afternoon and then dinner. Instead, she brushed him off like she had something else more pressing than spending time with him. It bothered him more than he wanted to admit when she did that. But he also respected her for it. She wasn't one to be tied down. Jeanette liked her freedom. She was smart, sophisticated, and independent. Jimmy was helping fund her college education. She wanted to be a photojournalist.

He unwrapped his sandwich and took a bite. He liked spending time with her. They shared lengthy conversations about his lobbying efforts, politics, travel destinations, food, wine whatever. The list of subjects was broad. She was a great conversationalist. Very articulate for her twenty-four years. And sex with her was phenomenal.

The time he spent with his fiancé,' Chloe Morgan, was different. Their sex was great, too, but infrequent. Chloe was more focused on her career with Morgan Publishing than on Jimmy's career. But that didn't matter. He wasn't marrying her for her attention. He got that from Jeanette. He was marrying Chloe for her parents' money and use of their publishing firm.

The Morgans owned Morgan Publishing House, a third-generation marketing and publishing organization with offices in New York, Chicago, Los Angeles, San Francisco, Seattle, Dallas, and Miami. Yes, Jimmy would be well cared for.

"Where are you at?" Jeanette asked.

Jimmy looked up to her, not realizing his thoughts had trailed off. He took another bite of the sandwich.

Jeanette stood and walked to his mini refrigerator, grabbed two bottles of water, then returned to his desk and set one down in front of him. Jimmy was turned on by the simple task.

"I was thinking about the future," he replied.

"That's unpredictable," Jeanette said. "Let's talk about something else."

He didn't agree with her, but he didn't tell her that. He wasn't in the mood for a lengthy debate. "Tell me what plans you've made for your trip to Paris next month."

He was jealous he wasn't going with her. She'd decided to go with a girlfriend, which made him a little more than furious, but he wouldn't tell her that, either. And he couldn't blame her. She'd planned to go the week of his wedding.

"Oh, yes." she said, and launched into her travel itinerary while they ate their sandwiches.

Jimmy tuned her out. He had work to do after this morning's debacle in court, but he wouldn't share his thoughts on that with Jeanette. Instead, he quietly finished his sandwich, allowing her to carry on about her travel plans.

CHAPTER 5

After regaining her composure from the FBI interrogation, Gina went back to her cubicle. Any article belonging to the lab had been removed. Her file drawers had been emptied out and left half open. Only her personal belongings remained: framed pictures of her and her sister Sirrina and some of her friends. They'd been kind enough to leave her bamboo plant behind, unscathed.

She considered packing up her things, but she wanted to keep a positive outlook. She wanted to believe she still had a job to come back to on Monday. Gina closed her desk and file cabinet drawers, straightened up the disarray the agents left behind, then went to find Roger.

Most of the agent activity had filtered out. The crime lab was practically empty, with only a few agents still packing up and hauling boxes to the exit.

Gina found Roger alone in his office, texting on his phone. He had a notepad on his desk with some sort of list written out. Gina knocked on his door. Roger looked up.

"Is it safe to enter?"

Roger took a deep breath. "Yeah. Have a seat."

Gina set her purse on the corner of his nearly empty desk and took a seat across from him.

"How did it go?" he asked with concern.

"How do you think?"

"I couldn't say anything, you know," Roger offered with some discomfort. "I have to protect the lab."

"I know." And she did know. It was all such a big fucking mess, starting with what happened in court.

"What about you?" Gina asked. "How did your interrogation go?"

"Mine? Hunh." He scoffed. "Mine hasn't even begun. What they did here today is just the tip of the iceberg. I'll be dealing with this for quite some time."

"What about Claire and me?"

"You're good, Gina. They got what they wanted from you."

"And what was that exactly?"

"The truth."

"Did they say something to you?"

"Oh, yeah," Roger replied. "Agent Chris stopped by my office on his way out. Said you responded with clarity, whatever the hell that's supposed to mean. But he said he's done with your piece of his investigation."

Gina felt a wave of relief wash over her, but she couldn't help noticing the bitterness in Roger's tone. "So where does this leave you and Claire?"

"Claire? I'm not sure. She left as soon as we got back here this morning. Claimed she had a migraine or cramps or something. I didn't ask for details. I gave Collins her information. They can catch up with her at home."

"And for you?" Gina asked.

"I'll be questioned on my conduct as supervising CSI in the D'Amato case."

"Why?"

"Honestly, I don't know what I was thinking, including you on this case in the first place."

His words surprised her.

"The conflict of interest," he responded off her look. "I never considered it. It's so clear to me now. It wasn't when I included you on the forensic team for this case."

Gina remembered Chris's question about whether Roger or Jerry had asked if she had any reservations about working the D'Amato case. They hadn't been interested in her reservations, they were inquiring as to whether Roger or Jerry had considered the conflict of interest. "Shit!" Gina said aloud.

"What?"

"Chris questioned me about having any reservations working on the case. I didn't realize he was using that information for a different matter altogether. I'm sorry, Roger. I hope I didn't…"

Roger held up his hand, stopping her mid-sentence. "Don't, Gina. If you spoke the truth and didn't leave anything out or mislead them with anything, that's all I'm concerned with."

"I did…didn't. You know what I mean. I was honest with my answers."

"You're in the clear then."

"But what about you and Claire? And Jerry?" Gina asked.

"I don't know."

"They shouldn't be able to call my family's history into question with regards to this case," Gina said. "I did my job as a professional. I worked this case just as I would have worked any case. You and Jerry oversaw every aspect of my work, and Claire's, too. If something were questionable, I have no doubt you would have caught it."

"Well, thank you for your vote of confidence."

"I'm being serious, Roger. Nothing in our work warrants any red flags. I've thought about the evidence we analyzed. We had clear positive results on blood and fingerprint analysis on three key pieces of evidence."

"I agree with you, Gina. But they're going to want someone to pay for this mistrial fiasco."

"Well, it shouldn't be you or this lab."

"Again, I agree with you."

There was a moment of silence between them before Gina asked, "Why do you think Nick changed his testimony?"

"I don't know, Gina. But in doing so, he threw a lot of people under the bus, including this lab. I hope he was well compensated for his actions."

Gina startled at his accusation. "That's not fair, Roger. We've known Nick a long time. Known him to be a standup detective. That's not who he is. He wouldn't have gone against his partner, the department, and the D.A. to accept a payout."

"You sure about that?"

Gina hesitated on this one.

"You've known him a long time," Roger continued. "Grew up together, right?"

Gina nodded, not appreciating his accusation of Nick. But she and Nick had also grown apart starting with attending separate colleges. Then he joined the Army. It wasn't until later in their careers that she interacted sporadically with him. But even then, his undercover work kept him away. She'd known him, yes. But how well?

"Don't let that cloud your judgment," Roger added.

"I can't be sure about anything right now," Gina replied. "But deep down I don't believe Nick would do that. I don't doubt there was serious cause for what he did today, but what you're suggesting…I think is way off the mark."

"I wish I could share your opinion, Gina, but right now…"

He didn't finish his thought. Both sat quiet for a long moment. She wasn't ready to agree with Roger's assumptions of Nick.

"What happens now?" Gina asked. "They cleared out all of our cases."

"My guess is some of the techs and investigators will be reassigned to other labs, and some of us will be on suspension pending the investigation."

A sinking feeling hit Gina. "Suspension? Really? For how long?"

"As long as it takes," he said. He leaned forward to place his elbows on the desk. "Look, it's Friday. Take the weekend to recoup from all of this. Come back here on Monday and we'll see what's what. Ok?"

"You've been doing this a long time," Gina said.

"Eighteen years."

"Has anything like this ever happened that you know of?"

"No. Which is why I can only guess with my answers to you."

Gina accepted his response.

"Go home. Leave. Vamoose," he said, waving his hands for her to scoot.

"What time is it?" Gina pulled her cell phone from her purse. She still needed to get to the courthouse to see Nick. "Four o'clock!" She bolted up from her chair. "Geez, I'm going to be late."

"Hot date or what?"

"Not funny," she replied. "I…um." She couldn't tell him where she was going. "I just need to be somewhere." She slipped her purse strap over her shoulder.

"We'll talk on Monday," he said. "Enjoy your weekend."

"Thanks. Try and do the same." She left his office thinking he would be doing anything but enjoying his weekend. She stopped by her cubicle for her coat on her way out. Hopefully, she would make it in time to the courthouse. She hadn't realized how fast the afternoon had slipped by. She needed to see Nick before they carted him off to prison.

CHAPTER 6

Gina sped north on highway ninety-five back to the courthouse. She would be cutting it close. She hoped Nick had been processed by now and was in a holding cell awaiting arraignment. They would most likely have him scheduled on the evening court docket. She thought about Wanda and her lack of interest earlier today and realized that she left without asking what the visiting hours were for the inmates.

Inmate. She hated to use that term in reference to Nick. It was so inappropriate. She didn't want to accept the trial's outcome. He wasn't an inmate. He wasn't a criminal. He wasn't a liar.

So why did he perjure himself? He had certainly caused problems for the prosecution. For a lot of people in fact, including himself. That much she was sure of.

Which made her question his being an inmate, a criminal…a liar. They had spoken briefly over the years, but it only pertained to work. A case they might have had in common. But what did she really know of him? Personally? Nothing. Shortly after Sirrina's death, she had lost touch with Nick. He had moved on. It broke her heart at the time. She'd had such a crush on him.

And the handful of times they worked together on cases it had been all business. Something had changed in him. And something had changed in her. She had always had a fondness for him and found him attractive, but she never acted on it. *Why?* she wondered.

In some ways, Sirrina's tragedy had driven them apart. She didn't even know if Nick had liked her back then. They were just kids. And he was three years older than her, which was like a lifetime between them.

He would have been interested in high school girls. Gina was only twelve. Just a kid as far as he would have been concerned.

Gina thought about his career. He was a decorated detective with a sterling reputation in the eyes of his fellow officers, and the public. The crime lab and district attorney's office had nothing but praise for him. She knew from reports, media, and her own office that he had earned medals for honor, valor, honorable mention, commendation integrity, and meritorious police duty.

But the fact she didn't know anything about his personal life made her uneasy. It brought Roger's question to the forefront now. *You sure about that?*

She didn't want to think about that now. She wanted to wait and talk with Nick. To get more information about why he did what he did this morning. His explanation would clear any questions she had about his involvement with Joe D'Amato.

She dodged recklessly in and out of traffic, trying to get to the courthouse before five o'clock. She was cursing herself for having lost track of time. If she missed Nick now, she would have to wait until he was transferred to the Hudson County Department of Corrections. That could take another day or two. She didn't want to wait that long to talk to him.

Gina pulled into the parking lot at ten minutes to five. She had made it in record time. She rushed from her car and into the courthouse. She whizzed through security and rode the elevator to the third floor. She practically ran down the corridor to Wanda's desk, but she wasn't there.

Gina caught her breath from her sprint. A fluorescent orange sign clipped to an easel on the counter caught her eye. Visiting hours were from eight o'clock a.m. until seven o'clock p.m. She'd made it. She would have time to see Nick.

Wanda appeared, carrying a large soda in a pink plastic tumbler. It matched the one she used as a pencil holder on her desk. She set the drink on her cluttered desk and walked over to Gina at the counter. "You're back."

"Yes," Gina replied. "Is Detective Nick Casey available for visitors yet?" Gina wasn't sure why, but it seemed important to refer to him as detective.

"Sign in on the computer there." Wanda pointed to a tablet anchored on the opposite end of the counter. "This is your copy of the rules and regulations." She handed Gina two pages stapled together. Her claw-like liquid whiteout nails were a distraction. *How did she do anything with nails that long?*

Gina walked over to the tablet, pressed a key to start and then followed onscreen instructions for the first and last name. The next question: business or personal visit. Gina selected business. It asked for a business name. She put in the crime lab's information. Reason for visit? Gina paused on this one. She typed one word. Clarification. The last question asked if she'd received a copy of the visitor's rules and regulations. She typed yes, then signed out and went back to Wanda.

"I'm finished signing in," Gina said.

"I need a photo ID," Wanda said, sounding bored.

Gina handed her driver's license to Wanda.

"I need to make a copy."

Wanda walked to a copy machine. There were no pleasantries when it came to Wanda. No "please" or "thank you" or "excuse me a moment." It was just a series of tasks she performed to the least of her abilities. Gina watched her move with the pace of molasses as she made a copy, then returned to Gina and handed back her license.

"Have a seat in the lounge. Someone will come and get you." She pointed in the direction of a small waiting area with six black plastic chairs and two glass end tables.

"Thank you," Gina said, and took a seat as instructed. Her breathing had returned to normal, but her nerves were flaring. She couldn't help but feel skeptical and anxious to see Nick. What if she didn't like hearing what he had to say? She tried not to think about that. It was a bad idea to start second-guessing this visit.

She plucked a wrinkled copy of *People* magazine from the side table. It was well worn and sticky. Gina returned it to the table and wiped her hands on her pant leg.

The corridors were quieter now. Most of the activity had ended by five o'clock. The waiting was testing her patience. It seemed silly that she felt nervous to see him. It was Nick, after all. She'd known him since childhood. She took a few deep breaths. She smelled fresh brewed coffee somewhere in the vicinity, but caffeine was the last thing she needed right now.

A uniformed officer walked with purpose towards her. His shoes echoed on the granite floors. He approached in a serious manner. "Gina Teducci?" he asked.

"Yes." Gina stood up.

"Sergeant Jim Slater," he said, sounding stern and impatient. He held out his hand.

They shook hands. "Nice to meet you," she said.

She realized too late that her palms were sweaty, but the Sergeant didn't let that bother him. His firm handshake, and quick release, was all business. He was stocky with a round face and squinty brown eyes.

"Follow me, please," Sergeant Jim said. He turned abruptly and walked back in the direction he'd come from. Gina followed close on his heels.

They entered a small office off the corridor and walked through another door leading into another corridor. Gina knew she would get lost trying to navigate these halls.

They entered a blue carpeted room with plain white walls. A Formica wood desk and four blue plastic chairs were in the middle of the room. There were cameras in two corners and a framed one-way glass window on one wall.

"Please take a seat, Miss Teducci. Can I bring you anything?" the sergeant asked.

A double shot of whiskey? she thought. "No, I'm fine. Thank you," Gina replied. She was one step closer to seeing Nick and feeling shaky now. The sergeant left the room, closing the door behind him. Gina was surrounded by unbearable silence.

The anticipation was taking its toll. She looked to the one-way glass window and wondered who, if anyone, was standing behind it, watching her every move. She felt like an ant under one of her microscopes.

The doorknob clanked, jarring her. The door swung open. Nick stood in the doorway. Gina's breath caught. He was dressed in orange prison scrubs and white slip-on canvas shoes. His face was expressionless. Gina slowly stood up, pressing her hands on the table for support.

Sergeant Jim gave Nick a nudge in his back. Nick stepped into the room. At least they didn't have him handcuffed. That probably would have sent Gina over the edge.

"Take a seat, both of you," Sergeant Jim said.

Nick walked to the table and stood across from Gina. She didn't know what to say. Apparently, neither did he. They both just stared at one another.

"I'll only ask once more," Sergeant Jim remarked.

Gina flinched, realizing she hadn't followed his orders. "My apologies, sergeant." She quickly took her seat.

Nick eased into his seat. His movements were slow and careful. Gina sensed he was on edge. Serious. Cautious. Maybe even insecure? Uncertain? Those last two weren't words she would have ever used to describe Nick. He seemed more like a stranger suddenly. His eyes bore right through her, causing her to shrink back in the plastic chair.

"I'll be right outside the door," Sergeant Jim said. "No physical contact is allowed. The detainee leaves first." He looked at Nick. "Knock when you're finished."

Sergeant Jim looked back to Gina. She nodded.

"And be aware that everything in this room is being monitored and recorded." The sergeant pointed to the cameras, each bearing a little red light indicating they were active.

"Yes," was all that Gina managed to say. Her mouth was sandpaper dry. She felt hot and uncomfortable. This wasn't how she'd imagined this going.

Sergeant Jim left, closing the door behind him. There was a long silence between her and Nick. She wasn't sure where she should start.

"What are you doing here, Gina?" Nick asked.

His tone caught her off guard. His posture was erect and closed off. His jaw clenched and his pale steely blue eyes were narrowed. She had never seen him like this before. Cold. Calculating. Did she know him? Had Roger been right? Had her judgment been clouded? She wasn't sure what she expected, but this wasn't it.

"I should ask you the same question, Nick," she shot back. Her tone came across harsher than she meant it to.

"I can't answer any questions, Gina."

"Is that what your lawyer advised?"

Nick didn't respond.

Gina took a deep breath and softened her defense mode. "I'm sorry. I…This is the last thing I wanted, Nick. I don't want this to be a hostile meeting between us. I think we both deserve more than that. I was hoping for clarification. Hoping to understand what happened in court today. Or at least an explanation of why I'm sitting across from a decorated detective on his way to prison."

"I don't have an answer for you," he replied.

"Can you tell me anything? How you're doing? How you're holding up?"

Nick spread his arms as if to gesture, 'look at me, I'm fine.'

Now you're being a prick, Gina thought. "Why did you agree to see me? You had to know I would want some answers. Want to know why you perjured yourself and destroyed the prosecutor's case. Why you threw your career away today and the crime lab under the bus."

"You're going to be fine, Gina."

"You don't know that. There's going to be investigations. What if…"

"You're going to be fine." He cut her off.

Something about the way he said that gave her pause. There was a quiet sincerity about him now. His body language and demeanor threw her off. She couldn't figure him out. There wasn't anger or hostility and certainly not fear. He was calm, like he had everything under control. Gina wished she felt like she was under control. She pressed her palms to her pant legs to absorb the sweat.

"I don't know how you can sit there so relaxed and reassured," she said. "Have you thought through what you did this morning? I mean really thought about it? The repercussions?" She hesitated for a moment. "It was a mistrial," she continued. "A mistrial. And…and your career? Why did you do that? Why didn't you let the D.A. know before the trial? Why even allow a trial?" She hated asking that last question. She wanted Joe D'Amato on trial. She wanted him in prison.

Nick sat quietly looking at her. Gina drew a deep breath. He wasn't going to say anything she wanted to hear.

"I'm babbling." She sat back, feeling defeated. "I don't know why I'm telling you this. You already know."

Still, nothing from him.

"I wish you would say something, Nick. I didn't expect this to be a one-sided conversation. I wouldn't have risked the speeding ticket getting here."

He grinned at her sarcasm.

"Well, a half-smile, it's something, I suppose," she added.

He leaned forward, placing his elbows and forearms on the table. "I agreed to see you, Gina, because I wanted to see you. It's been a long time."

She liked hearing him say her name. His smile tugged at her heart. His eyes looked clearer now and brilliant blue. The way she had remembered them from so long ago. Something passed between them in that moment. He seemed ok with his situation. Accepting of the consequences.

But Gina felt anguish deep inside. She wasn't ok with his situation. She wasn't accepting of the consequences. She felt defeat wash over her, realizing there was nothing she could do for him. She just needed to be here for him. Gina reached across the table and placed her hands on his forearms. His skin felt warm to her touch.

Nick pulled away just as Sergeant Jim's voice boomed over the intercom. "No contact."

Gina snatched her hands back, not expecting the intercom. "Sorry," she said to Nick. She forgot they were being monitored. She had to be careful. The last thing she wanted was to cause Nick further complications.

She sat back in her chair. "I wish you could help me understand this, Nick. I don't know what to do now."

"Now, you go back to work, and I go off to prison."

Tears welled up in her eyes. "I don't want to hear that, Nick. What happened? Why? Why can't you tell me? Who can explain this to me? *Please?*" She heard how desperate she sounded.

Nick closed his eyes and took a long deep breath. "You're going to be fine, Gina."

"You told me that already. Tell me something else."

"That's all I have."

"It can't be. Please don't do this. Don't shut me out. Please talk to me, Nick."

He only looked at her with that same half-grin, his eyes holding hers.

"That's it?" Gina said.

He sat back in his chair and folded his arms across his chest, "That's it."

Gina wasn't sure if she wanted to hold him or punch him. She wanted to reach out to him, but Sergeant Jim would most likely appear in the doorway this time. Nick was shutting down, withdrawing from her. It made her sad and angry.

"So, we're done here?" It tormented her, saying those words. She wanted to stay with him. Talk with him. Hold him. Kiss him. Curse at him.

"We're done here," he said. She thought she detected sadness in his tone as well.

Gina felt a knot form in her throat.

Nick stood up. "I have to leave first."

Gina shot up from her chair. "Where will you be incarcerated? For how long?" she cried out. She surprised herself saying those words.

"I don't know," he quietly replied.

"I'm sorry I asked that." Gina winced. "I'll get the information and I'll come to see you."

Nick shook his head no. "This is the last we see of each other. I don't want to see you in prison."

Gina wavered and placed her hands on the table again for support. Nick's hardened expression forced her to accept his request.

He turned from her and walked to the door. He knocked twice. Sergeant Jim opened the door and led Nick out of the room. The door closed and he was gone. Gina sat down and cried…for Nick, for Sirrina, and for herself.

CHAPTER 7

Jimmy sank into the oversized leather chair in Carmine's study, twirling ice cubes in his whiskey glass. The room resembled a rich man's smoking lounge. Carmine sat across from him in a matching chair with his own whiskey in hand. They were discussing the happenings from court while Jackie finished cooking ziti in the kitchen. Jimmy studied Carmine in his plush leather chair. Everything in Carmine's life was plush. It always had been.

A forty-five hundred square foot Spanish colonial in an upscale neighborhood. A vacation cabin in the mountains. Sport and luxury cars tucked into the six-car garage. A beautiful and intelligent wife with an unlimited credit card account. And four grown successful children.

"Earth to Jimmy." Carmine was waving a hand in the air.

Jimmy snapped from his reflecting. "Yeah. Sorry about that."

"Don't get too worked up over this thing, hunh?" Carmine said. "I told you, I made some calls this afternoon and I'm going to see D.A. Benjamin Forrester on Monday."

Jimmy tensed at this. "Let me handle Benjamin."

Carmine shot him a look of disapproval.

"Carm, you need to focus on Derek Brooks and LeAnn Sardello. The building department is still reeling from Janet's death. Her car bombing has everyone on edge. It's the perfect time to strike. It's time for the Teduccis to control New York."

"You think Janet Sardello's death changes things?" Carmine asked. "It changes nothing." Carmine took a drink of his whiskey. "Jesus, you're an ungrateful prick. Have I taught you nothing? It's precisely the wrong time to strike. Is it not clear to you what happened in court today? Joe still controls New York. And it's going to stay that way."

Jimmy didn't like the response, but he didn't want to piss off Carmine. He would think of a way around this. A way around Carmine. Just like he'd always done. He watched Carmine down what was left of his drink. He held up his glass. "Join me for another one?"

"Sure," Jimmy replied. He swigged what was left in his glass.

Carmine walked to the bar tucked in the corner of the room. He retrieved the whisky bottle and poured Jimmy a double shot.

"It's not that I don't appreciate your enthusiasm, Jimmy. I do. But there's plenty you still don't understand."

Carmine poured himself a shot then set the whiskey bottle down. He remained standing in front of Jimmy: a drink in one hand, the other tucked in his pants pocket. Jimmy thought of him as a mafia do-gooder.

"You're right, Uncle Carm. I forget sometimes just how much you and Aunt Jackie have done for me," Jimmy said.

Carmine stood with a blank stare. Apparently, he wanted the song and dance.

"You took me in when my old man kicked me out. I was only sixteen, still in school and not a pot to piss in."

"My brother had his reasons, right?" Carmine said.

Jimmy wasn't liking being made to feel like a chump. Carmine always did this to him.

"Maybe," Jimmy said.

"Maybe? You stole from them. And got caught. I would have done the same thing with my own kids."

But you never let my old man Frank know that, did you? You let him think he was wrong for having kicked me out. Shame on you, Uncle Carm. If you only knew what I was doing behind your back, Jimmy thought.

"I know," Jimmy said. "I've learned a lot from you and Uncle Anthony. I've overcome a lot of bad things, including my health. It's a big accomplishment that I'm proud of. I haven't needed a shrink for years now. You and Aunt Jackie helped me to overcome the worst experience of my life when Sirrina died."

Carmine flinched at his candid response. He took a drink of his whiskey and paced to the far side of the room.

Yes. Jimmy thought. *It's the same every time. All I need to do is mention poor little Sirrina and all is forgiven and forgotten.* "I'm fortunate that you and Aunt Jackie took me in," Jimmy said. "I think I'm a better person for it. You put me through college and gave me the support to get where I am."

Carmine turned to him and only nodded. Obviously, Jimmy's words had upset him. Too bad. If Carmine knew what Jimmy had been setting up behind his back for the past couple of years, his uncle would be kissing his feet right now. Unfortunately, things didn't go as planned this morning, but he would fix that, too.

Jimmy continued, "I sometimes imagine how different our lives would have been had Sirrina not died."

Carmine shot him a look of anger. "That's enough."

Jimmy held up a hand. "I'm sorry, Uncle Carm. I didn't mean that in a bad way. I just meant that I probably wouldn't have been given the opportunities I was given. And my parents, hell. They probably would have made better choices." *Choices like you made, Uncle Carm. Successful businesses. A beautiful intelligent wife. Four grown successful children. A vacation home in the mountains.*

Jimmy would have the same someday. Hopefully soon. He wouldn't wind up making the same bad choices his parents did. Bad investments and gambling left them with a mediocre house in Trenton and two dive bars to support them. Jimmy's oldest brother Paul was still in the Air Force. A career serviceman. He had enlisted right out of high school. Jimmy's second oldest sister Nicole was a checker at Costco with three kids and a pending divorce. Her second one. He wouldn't end up like either of them.

"My brother Frank wanted to do things his way," Carmine replied. "That's all I'm going to say."

Jimmy knew there had been plenty of arguments and fallout over the years. His old man detested the fact that his younger brother took Jimmy in. It defeated his purpose in teaching Jimmy a lesson. And the more successful Jimmy became under Carmine's wing, the angrier his father

Frank grew. His parents no longer spoke to Carmine and Jackie. And they rarely spoke with his Uncle Anthony and Aunt Loretta.

Carmine walked back to stand in front of Jimmy. "Look, we got off the subject here."

"I thought we were just talking, Uncle Carm. Sometimes these things need airing out."

"Well, I'm done airing out," Carmine snapped.

The doorbell rang.

"I'll get it," Jackie called out from the kitchen.

Carmine grabbed the bottle of whiskey and refreshed his drink. He offered another pour to Jimmy, but he declined. He needed to keep his head clear tonight. He wouldn't even finish the double shot still in his glass.

Jimmy had to make sure he convinced Carmine to leave Benjamin up to him. After talking with Benjamin earlier today, Jimmy needed to get him under control. If he talked with Carmine, he would say too much and that would provoke Carmine to start asking questions. Questions that Jimmy did not want to answer.

"Look who came to join us," Jackie said from the doorway.

Gina walked in behind her.

Great, Jimmy thought. *Does someone always have to fuck up my plan?*

"Oh ho, you made it." Carmine beamed when he saw his daughter. He set his drink down and met her halfway across the room, holding his arms out to her.

Gina wrapped him in a long embrace and kissed his cheek. "I did. How are you, Dad?"

"Good. Your cousin Jimmy and me were just shootin' the shit."

Gina walked to Jimmy and he gave her a hug. "Gina. Always a pleasure." *Except for tonight, but I'll work around it,* he thought.

"While all of you are standing, head to the dining room," Jackie said. "Dinner's ready."

They sat at the dining table and dug into Jackie's baked ziti, meatballs, salad, and French bread.

"Aunt Jackie, you outdid yourself again. You make the best ziti in this family. It was my favorite when I lived here…and it still is." Jimmy shoved a fork full of pasta in his mouth, chewing with pleasure.

"Thank you, Jimmy." Jackie smiled. "You're always welcome here." She cleared her throat and went back to eating her dinner.

Jimmy noticed she seemed on edge. She did that little annoying throat clearing thing again. She always did that after she addressed him. It made him wonder how sincere her comments were. He picked up the bottle of wine and refreshed her glass. She didn't acknowledge his effort.

"Gina?" Jimmy offered to pour her some wine.

She held up her hand. "No more for me. I'm driving."

Jackie placed a hand on her forearm. "Why don't you stay the night? Have some more wine and we can talk later."

Jimmy caught that Jackie was squeezing Gina's arm as he set the bottle down on the table.

"OK. Sure," Gina said. She looked to Jimmy and picked up her wine glass. "I guess I'll have a refill."

Jimmy poured her a glass. "Do I dare ask how bad it was when you got back to the lab this morning?"

Gina finished her sip of wine and set her glass down.

"Let's not ruin dinner with talk about this morning," Carmine suggested. He looked to Jimmy. "We can talk later over cigars."

"I don't mind," Gina said. She looked at Jimmy. "Why did you leave the courtroom early? You missed the final ruling."

Carmine looked up to him. His chewing stopped.

"I had to take a phone call," Jimmy replied, knowing Carmine's look had everything to do with the fact he hadn't been aware Jimmy was in the courtroom. "By the time I was finished, so was the trial. I got the recap from one of my media contacts." He looked back to Carmine. Carmine was slow to return to his ziti and meatballs.

"It wasn't what I had expected," Gina replied to his earlier question.

"No? What did you expect?" Jimmy scoffed.

"I don't know," Gina said. "Certainly not the rapid response from the FBI."

Everyone got quiet and looked at Gina like she'd announced she had murdered someone.

"The FBI?" Jimmy asked.

"What happened?" Carmine asked.

"I can't say much, you know," Gina replied. "It's an ongoing investigation."

"That was quick," Jimmy said.

"I know," Gina replied. "They shut down the lab. They boxed up the D'Amato case to have it sealed and delivered to the D.A.'s office."

"What about your other cases?" Jimmy asked.

Gina was about to put a fork full of pasta in her mouth, then stopped. "What about them?"

Jackie had stopped eating. She was sitting back in her chair holding her glass of wine and staring at her plate. Carmine continued to eat. Gina was waiting for Jimmy's answer.

"I was just curious is all."

"About any one in particular or all of them?" Gina asked. She followed through with her bite.

"The Janet Sardello case?" Jimmy asked.

Carmine snapped his head up, looking at Jimmy. His chewing continued but his eyes shot daggers at him.

"People in my office were talking," Jimmy said. "We're all lobbyists. She was a lobbyist. I think the car bombing freaked a lot of them out. It freaked me out."

Everyone sat quiet for the moment.

Jimmy added, "I just wondered if there had been any breaks in the case. Obviously, we'd all feel better if the bastard that did it was caught. I'm sorry I asked."

"No. It's fine, Jimmy," Gina said. "But I'm not supposed to discuss the cases. Any of them. I only spoke about Joe's because..."

"Because it hits home," Carmine said.

Gina nodded. "The Sardello case was given to another technician. I won't be doing the processing on it."

Jimmy nodded, seeming pleased with her answer. "That's good to hear."

"Why would you say that?" Gina asked.

"Oh. Um, because…"

"Can we please change the subject?" Jackie asked.

Everyone fell silent.

"Mom, you're not eating," Gina observed.

"That's my fault," Jimmy said. "I'm sorry Aunt Jackie. You cooked this wonderful meal and here I am ruining it."

"Not at all, Jimmy," Jackie replied and cleared her throat.

"I saw Nick today," Gina said.

Everyone stopped eating and looked at Gina once more.

"You're full of surprises tonight, aren't you?" Jimmy commented.

"When?" Carmine asked.

"Well, I tried to see him right after I left you and Uncle Anthony at the courthouse this morning," Gina answered. "But he hadn't been processed yet. So, I went back to work and then stopped back by just before coming here tonight."

"What did he say?" Jimmy asked.

"Not much, really," Gina replied. "His attorney advised him not to talk to anyone."

"Of course not, the guilty prick," Jimmy said.

"Hey," Carmine called out.

"What?" Jimmy said.

"That's not fair, Jimmy. You sound just like Roger at work. Nothing has been proven about what Nick said today in court," Gina responded.

"Are you seriously going to sit there and defend what he did today?" Jimmy scoffed at Gina. "That son of a bitch deserves to be behind bars. He turned his back on everyone that trusted and supported his investigation. Not to mention the family he kicked to the curb." Jimmy waved a hand around the table, referencing the Teduccis. "It seems that Joe D'Amato got what he paid for."

"All right. That's enough. Both of you." Carmine held up his hand to stop them. He turned to Gina. "I know it's not what you want to hear from me, but I'm with Jimmy on this one."

"See? You should listen to your old man, Gina," Jimmy called out.

Carmine snapped his head back to Jimmy, pointing a finger. "That's enough out of you. Are we clear?"

Fuck you, Uncle Carm. You don't control me, Jimmy thought. He held up his hands in mock defense. "Loud and clear."

Carmine turned back to Gina. "I understand your wanting to hear Nick's side of this, but you need to be careful here. What he did today…"

"What he did today was completely out of his character." Gina cut him off. "I can't believe you're both condemning his actions. This family has known Nick for a long time. We're all aware of his contributions to the police force. He's a damn good detective. The important question here is why?"

"I can't believe you're defending his actions, Gina," Jimmy shot back. "People change."

"I don't believe that," Gina said. "Something happened. Something made him do the unthinkable."

"You're right," Carmine added. "And until we know what that something is, he can't be trusted. You need to steer clear of him, you hear me?"

"Your father's right, Gina," Jimmy said. "For all we know Nick's had this planned from the beginning. He's probably been working with D'Amatos all along. Joe would have had to pay a pretty hefty price for Nick to…"

Jackie slammed her fist on the table. Silverware and glassware clanked. Everyone shut up and looked at her. She pushed her chair back and stood up. Tears welled in her eyes. She bolted from the table.

"Mom?" Gina went after her.

Carmine looked to Jimmy. "You just couldn't keep your fuckin' mouth shut, could you?"

"Me?" Jimmy sounded surprised. "I think it was the conversation as a whole that probably upset her."

"I think it's time for you to go," Carmine said as he stood up.

"But we didn't get to finish discussing…"

"We'll talk next week," Carmine replied.

"Are you still going to see the D.A. on Monday?" Jimmy asked.

Carmine turned from Jimmy. "I don't know." He started to walk towards the front door.

Jimmy threw his napkin on his plate, pushed his chair back, and stood. This night had not gone as planned. He would have to make some adjustments now. He walked towards Carmine and to the front door. "Say goodnight to Aunt Jackie and Gina for me."

"Do me a favor, hunh?" Carmine said. "Keep a lid on this thing until I have a better understanding as to what happened today. Keep your head down. Don't go asking questions or raising suspicions, alright?"

"Is there anything I need to know, Uncle Carm?" Jimmy asked.

"No. Just focus on the work you've been doing and if anyone asks, you know nothing," Carmine said.

What's the matter, Uncle Carm, afraid someone might connect you with the D'Amatos? Connect you with the crimes that were brought to Joe's trial? Maybe they would lock you up instead. Wouldn't that be a hoot. Then I would be out from under your thumb. I would be in control, Jimmy thought.

"Are we clear?" Carmine snapped at him.

"Yeah. Yeah. We're clear," Jimmy said. He held out his hand and Carmine shook it. "Thank you for dinner," Jimmy said, and walked out the front door. He heard the door slam harder than it needed to. Jimmy smiled. He climbed into his nine-eleven Porsche turbo and sped off.

CHAPTER 8

The wolves would come for him eventually, Carmine thought. It was inevitable. He reclined on a chaise lounge chair on the back patio, smoking a cigar after Jimmy left. It would be a mistake to assume he was insulated from prosecution.

Joe D'Amato had dodged a crippling bullet in court today. Carmine wondered what it had taken for Nick to change his testimony. Whatever it was, Carmine would have done the same. This trial had given Carmine great pause and reflection into his own life. That could have very easily been him sitting at the defense table instead of Joe.

Murder, bribery, extortion, contract fraud, bid rigging, false appraisals...the list went on and on. Charges that could easily be brought against him by the right person. *Who would do it?* Carmine wondered. *Who would have the most to gain?* Quite a few names crossed his mind. Carmine's life was a delicate balancing act between trust and betrayal.

Dinner tonight had left him unsettled. Jimmy just didn't get it. He wondered now if he ever would. Maybe he shouldn't have protected Jimmy the way he had over the years, keeping him in the dark about agreements made between the Teduccis and the D'Amatos. Gentlemen agreements. No contracts, no lawyers, no witnesses...just two men and their word. It was a process that had served the two families well for over ninety years.

Even when Sirrina died, and the families found out it had been Joe's nephew that caused her death, Carmine couldn't place the blame on Joe. His nephew had acted on his own. It hadn't been Joe calling the shots and lashing out. It had been his nephew Guiseppe D'Amato. Guiseppe had overstepped his bounds. He tried making a power move within the families that he had no business navigating. It cost him his life and Sirrina hers, not to mention two of Guiseppes' friends. And it had caused both families plenty of pain and grief.

Carmine could see Jimmy trying to step outside his boundaries now. His sights, set on controlling the building department in New York, would need to be shuttered. Jimmy had become greedy. And greed led to certain failure.

Carmine's foothold within the New Jersey building department was the Teducci's primary contracting focal point, and it was substantial. Hell, it was more than substantial. It was a product of endless supply. But it hadn't been easy. Too many years to count earning his place, his ranking, and respect from Joe. Theirs was an organization that honored its principles. He would need to make Jimmy realize this, and soon, apparently.

Carmine heard the sliding glass door open and close. Gina walked up, holding two brandies. She handed one to him.

"Thank you," he said, as he took his drink.

Gina reclined on the chaise chair next to his.

"How's your mom?" Carmine asked.

Gina unfolded a blanket that was at the foot of the chair. "OK. She went to take a bath." She covered up against the cool night air and looked up to the star-filled sky.

Carmine reflected on his daughter. She'd been through so much as a child, losing her younger sister. She'd weathered the storm. She'd grown into a beautiful, strong, successful woman. Her three older brothers had done the same.

Carmine toked his cigar. He held his glass of brandy out to Gina. "I'm proud of you, you know that?"

Gina looked over to him and smiled. "For what?" She clinked his glass and took a sip.

"A lot of things," he replied. "You've done good for yourself. You've got a strong mind and will about you. You don't let people tell you what to do. You don't accept what you don't agree with."

Gina sipped her brandy. "Just like you taught me to," she said.

"Your Mom had a lot of say in that, too," he replied.

"I'm sorry about dinner," she said. "I apologized to Mom, too."

"Your cousin Jimmy's an ungrateful prick sometimes."

"I'm sure he didn't mean..."

"He did." Carmine cut her off. "He's just like his old man, Frank. They don't look at the big picture. They think small. They always have." He toked his cigar. "I don't know, maybe I'm sounding like the ungrateful prick now."

"You have a lot to protect, Dad. This family has always looked to you for support and relied on you for that protection."

Gina got it, he thought. *Why didn't Jimmy?* "I was twenty-eight when we relocated to the states from Cortona. Same age you are now." He looked to her, reminiscing. "That hadn't been an easy decision. Your grandfather Stefano wasn't happy about it. He fought me on my decision."

"I know it made Mom happy." Gina said.

Carmine agreed. He and his two brothers were groomed at a young age to run illegal enterprises that his father Stefano had been born into. It was those mafia-run enterprises that brought the family's wealth.

Carmine also had the choice to stay in Cortona, Italy, managing the wine and olive oil production of their estate, but Carmine wanted more.

He thought about Jackie now. She had been born and raised in New Jersey. Carmine recalled how they met. She had been working for Joe at one of his restaurants.

He remembered having been taken with her almost immediately. She'd had an assertive almost pushy manner that had appealed to him. She had a mind of her own and wasn't afraid to speak it. Something she had instilled in their kids since they were barely able to walk.

When Carmine proposed to her, he'd been surprised at her willingness to leave her family in New Jersey and move with him to Italy. A choice he knew hadn't been an easy one for her to make. But it was Carmine that realized he didn't want to stay in Italy.

He and Jackie had moved to New Jersey just after their third son was born. Gina was born four years later in New Jersey, and her sister Sirrina, four years after Gina. It hadn't been easy raising five kids.

"I thought Grandpa was the one who helped you and Mom get established here." Gina looked at him. "With Joe, right?"

"More or less." Carmine replied. "The two of them had businesses established in the states together. Your grandfather would send me to meet with Joe on a regular basis because he didn't like flying. I was barely out of high school when he started doing that."

"That's right." Gina said. "I remember you mentioning that before. And that's how you met Mom, isn't it?"

Carmine smiled, "Eventually, yeah."

"Well, on the surface Grandpa may have responded to your decision to move to the states with anger. But deep down I think he probably knew you were the best choice to handle his business ventures in the states." Gina looked to him. "It's where his confidence laid. In you."

"Maybe." Carmine said reflecting on the memory. Stefano had arranged with Joe D'Amato for Carmine to oversee management of those established businesses. Carmine also began carving out his own future. "But in doing so, our move here created a lot of…turmoil within the family." Carmine studied his cigar lost in thought not wanting to elaborate on the memory with his daughter.

Not long after Carmine relocated to the states, to his father's dismay, Carmine's two brothers and one sister came calling. All with their families in tow. All of them wanting a piece of the action Carmine had been creating on his own. His youngest brother, Anthony, established himself right away, working under Carmine. The accountant.

Carmine's sister moved back to Italy almost immediately after arriving. She preferred Italy to the states. She and her husband would let Stefano support them, along with Carmine's youngest sister and her husband and family. Carmine knew that when his father joined his mother six feet under, he would have to return to Italy to take his father's place in overseeing the estate. Otherwise, that spigot would eventually run dry.

"Your grandfather's wish had always been to keep his family in Italy, but I wanted a better future for you kids," Carmine said. "For all of us."

"I'm sure Grandpa's proud of everything you've done. Grandma, too."

Carmine wondered if his father was proud of Frank. Jimmy's father. He'd been the worst. Frank had sucked the life out of Carmine until there was nothing left to give. The two of them came to blows on more than one occasion. Frank had nearly bankrupted Carmine when Carmine was still getting established, and then blamed Carmine for turning his back on him. Frank had been spending money that Carmine's company didn't have. It left Carmine no choice.

He'd shut Frank out of his construction company and told him he was on his own to raise and support his own family. Tough love, as Jackie referred to it. But it had to be done. Carmine and Frank didn't speak again until the night Jimmy pounded on Carmine's door.

Jimmy was sixteen at the time and sobbing like a little girl. Frank had kicked him out of the house. Carmine had never shared Frank's failings with Jimmy. He assumed Frank hadn't, either. Maybe that had been a mistake.

"What are you thinking about?" Gina asked.

"Family pride."

"Liar."

"Hey," Carmine shot back.

"Sorry."

They shared a quiet moment between them. Gina knew him better than he liked to admit. Jimmy's visit tonight was causing him indigestion. He didn't want to ruin his night with Gina by talking about his brother Frank.

"I like hearing you talk about Italy," Gina said. "It seems a shame that I only visit there once a year for Grandpa's birthday."

"Don't change the subject on my behalf."

Gina gave him a sideways glance. "I know how much you enjoy talking about Uncle Frank."

Carmine toked his cigar and blew three smoke rings. "Sometimes you're too smart for your own good."

Gina sipped her brandy.

"Your mother shouldn't have had to listen to all that talk tonight. I should have stopped Jimmy sooner. It upsets her. It's why she didn't go to the trial. I can't blame her."

"I don't, either," Gina said. "I should have kept my mouth shut about going to see Nick, too."

"How was he?" Carmine asked. He looked over to her. "Really."

Gina curled up into a ball under her blanket. "It was hard to tell. He was respecting his attorney's advice and not answering any questions I asked him. The room was being monitored, which made it that much more uncomfortable." She thought about the meeting. "He seemed ok with his decision."

"And that bothers you," Carmine said. It was a statement, not a question.

Gina nodded and took another sip of her brandy.

"Why do you think he did it?" Carmine asked.

Gina looked at him. "I don't know. I thought after seeing him today I would have a better understanding of his actions, but I don't." She looked up at the stars. "It's just so damn hard to believe he did this. Not only to himself, but to all the people involved in the case. It's hard to believe he turned his back on his peers and sided with Joe."

"Maybe it's hard for you to accept it because deep down you've always held something for him, in here." Gina looked over to him. He was patting a hand over his heart. "It's a betrayal and it hurts."

She turned back to the stars. "What do you believe?" Gina asked.

"He was always a good kid. Solid. He was a hell of a cop and a great detective. He caused me some heartburn now and then, but I respected what he did."

"Like what?" Gina asked looking over at him with a half-smile.

Carmine wouldn't go into any detail with her. "Some of my guys get out of line now and then. Joe's, too. He would set them straight." Carmine wouldn't tell her about the bid-rigging, contract bribes, gambling and extortion. He knew Gina understood his line of work. He also knew she wasn't accepting of it. But he was confident he had her loyalty and love.

"I'm sure he did," she replied.

"Nick was a rookie cop back then," Carmine said. "Coming up through the ranks. He was making a name for himself. And what better way to do that than to lock horns with me and Joe." Carmine chuckled.

Gina smiled at the thought.

Carmine added, "But like Jimmy said tonight, people change."

Gina looked over to him again. Her smile faded. Now, she seemed disappointed.

"I'm not saying he did or didn't change; I'm just saying keep your eyes and ears open. Don't be too optimistic and trusting," Carmine said.

"Do you trust Jimmy?" Gina asked.

"He's never given me a reason not to. Why do you ask?"

"Mom doesn't. She said she never has. She said he's conniving. An opportunist without a conscience. Her words, not mine."

"Jesus," Carmine said. "Well, she might be right on that last one." *Just like his old man,* Carmine thought.

"I never knew she felt that way about him," Gina said.

"Jimmy was heading down a rocky road when he came to stay with us way back when. He was sixteen with no guidance. Your Uncle Frank wasn't doing him any favors, either. I straightened Jimmy out quick. I think the real damage was done when Sirrina died. It hit Jimmy so hard that he tried to take his own life. We were all so concerned for him at the time. Even your mother. None of us noticed the pain she had bottled up inside her. The pain of losing her daughter. I didn't see it." He paused to reflect. "Your mother can put on a strong front when she needs to. I think Jimmy's issues robbed your mother of her needs at the time."

"Geez, Dad, I've never heard you talk like this before," Gina said.

"It was a tough time, for all of us," Carmine said. "But especially your mother. Sometimes I think she holds a little anger and hostility inside towards me. And I wouldn't blame her if she did. This life, what we do, how we go about doing things, it hasn't been easy for her. For any of us."

"Don't beat yourself up too much, Dad." Gina said. "Mom was aware of what she signed up for when she married you. She knew of Grandpa's connections to the D'Amatos. She knew leaving Italy wasn't going to change your commitment to the Teducci family. She knew that Joe was a powerful crime boss and that you would be working alongside him. Grandpa managed Italy and Joe managed New Jersey and New York. She was accepting of the fact that you would eventually take over managing New Jersey. She knew she was going to have to work just as hard in Italy as she did here in Jersey to keep all us kids from being involved in…that life." Gina made quotations with her fingers when she said that life. "But I do know she's happier to be here in Jersey than in Italy. Her roots are here."

"She told you all that tonight?" Carmine asked.

"No, Dad. It's been a culmination of conversations over the years. I just know how she feels about things. Because we talk." Gina looked right at him. "Communication is important."

Carmine tolerated her preaching.

Gina pulled the blanket up around her shoulders, warding off the chill of the night air. "I think she does hold anger and hostility inside, and maybe some regret, too." She looked at him. "But it's not towards you, Dad."

He considered her answer.

Gina continued. "Maybe you should share those thoughts with Mom sometime. I think she'd like to hear you say what you've said to me tonight."

Carmine crushed out his cigar in an ashtray on the ground next to his chair. "I'm glad you were here for her tonight. She misses you."

"And you don't?" Gina asked with a pouty face.

"Of course, I do, sweetheart," Carmine replied.

Gina swung her legs to the side of the chair, facing Carmine. "The blanket isn't working. Let's go inside."

"You go," Carmine said. "I'm going to stay out here a little bit longer. The cool air clears my head."

"OK," Gina said as she stood up." I'll leave this for you." She covered his legs with the blanket, then gave him a peck on his cheek. "Don't stay out here too long."

"I won't. Tell your mother I'll be up in a bit."

Gina squeezed his shoulder and left him sitting under the stars. Carmine heard the sliding glass door open and then close a moment later. The crickets took over. He sipped his brandy, thinking about what he and Gina had just talked about.

All this reflecting tonight made him realize how much he'd kept bottled up inside, just like Jackie had. Gina was right. He would talk with Jackie. Maybe he would plan something special for the two of them. He would wait for the dust to settle on the trial before doing so.

In the meantime, he would meet with D.A. Forrester. He would also set up a meeting to talk with Joe D'Amato.

CHAPTER 9

It was nearly eleven p.m. when Sergeant Jim Slater entered the private room Nick Casey had been ensconced in since being removed from the courtroom. Four white walls, one small desk with one chair, a black vinyl sofa, and a wall-mounted television furnished the ten-by-ten space. The television was tuned to a sports channel, recapping historical sports highlights.

It had been Nick's request that no one interact with him until his transfer. Gina had been the only exception. He hadn't expected her to come. It was a welcome surprise, but it pained him to treat her the way he did. She would know the truth soon enough.

"Let's go, detective," Sergeant Jim said. "Your ride is here."

Nick sat up on the couch. His unofficial investigation remained on track. Sergeant Jim stood with purpose and without expression. Nick knew him to be one of the good ones. The corruption that plagued Nick's division hadn't reached this man.

The selected individuals involved with Nick's parallel investigation had been carefully vetted. And they would continue to be until he had the answers he was looking for. Until the right people paid for the crimes they had committed. This case owed a lot of people the truth. People that meant a lot to Nick.

The sergeant led Nick down two long corridors. They took the elevator down to G2, an underground garage. The elevator door glided open. A black panel van was parked just outside the elevator. The side door of the van slid open.

"Good luck, detective," Sergeant Jim said.

"Thanks."

Nick climbed inside the van. Sergeant Jim remained in the elevator. The door slid shut and the van drove off. This garage level wasn't monitored the way G1's garage was. G1 was where they picked up and dropped off criminals. G2 was the garage for employees.

Nick acknowledged the four men inside the van as he positioned himself on the floor. He pressed his back up against the back side of the driver's seat. Nick had spent months planning with these men prior to and during the unofficial investigation that he'd been running alongside the D.A.'s investigation.

He looked to the four of them as the van surged through the city streets. He'd been adamant in recruiting them for his crew. All ex-military, like himself. They had made up a five-man SRT team in Iraq some twelve years earlier and had remained in contact.

SRT was Special Reaction Team. It was equivalent to S.W.A.T. They were trained to respond, react, and resolve high risk incidents. They were also special forces trained in close quarters combat. They were the initial team required to enter, clear, and secure whatever structure or situation was posing the threat. They also protected important dignitaries and high-ranking military officers.

Nick had been the only one of the five to continue in government law enforcement. The other four had forged separate careers in the private sector. But under special circumstances, the five of them came together as a team. Nick's unofficial investigation was one of those special circumstances.

Reuben Alvarez manned the driver's seat. At forty-two, he was six feet of brawn tucked under a Montecristi panama hat, earning himself the nickname Panama Al. He had been working undercover as an informant in Atlantic City, New Jersey on a trafficking case when Nick reached out to him.

Maurice Williams sat in the passenger seat, thirty-four with cornrows. During his college years he held his own in the fighting rink as an ultimate fighting champion. He and Nick were in criminal justice classes together at CUNY John Jay College in New York. Nick sparred in the ring with him during practice workouts before both enlisted.

Known as "Ice" in gangland Los Angeles, he supplied protection for a drug cartel.

Leonard Bradford sat on the van floor, his legs stretched out, with his back pressed against the back of the passenger seat. He was a personal bodyguard to a Wall Street giant. He also managed his money laundering operation from national and international accounts. His criminal affiliates referred to him as "the executive." Nick referred to him as Leo.

Chico Ruiz was perched on the van floor at Nick's feet, with his back to the driver's side panel. A twenty-nine-year-old master black belt, his flesh was covered in artful ink. He was a privately contracted agent, specializing in cyber terrorism and computer hacking, and working both sides of the law.

Joe D'Amato had left Nick to his own devices in selecting who would assist him with this operation. Unofficial meant just that. No other law enforcement agency had been or would be privy to Nick's second investigation. He still wasn't sure how far up the command chain the corruption within and outside his department rose.

Nick felt like a hypocrite going against his department. But what he hoped to uncover would be worth it. The knife of corruption sliced both ways.

Maurice tossed a duffle bag to Nick. "Orange ain't your color, detective."

"No?" Nick replied with a grin. He unzipped the bag and removed a change of clothes and shoes. He shed the prison scrubs and dressed in street clothes as Reuben kept the van in motion. Nick reached into the duffle bag and removed his badge. He wouldn't be needing that now. He tucked it into the pocket of his jeans.

Nick removed his gun and shoulder harness and tossed the duffle bag aside. He slipped the harness on, holstered his nine-millimeter, and covered up with a denim jacket. He looked to the rear of the van. He picked up an LED flashlight that was in a cup holder and switched it on. The light beam revealed a man's body lying face down, hands and feet bound with nylon zip ties and duct tape covering his mouth.

"Apparently not a willing participant," Nick said.

"They never are," Leo replied.

"Sorry for the delay, man," Reuben called out from the driver's seat. "Traffic coming up from Florida was a bitch."

"No worries," Nick said. He looked to Leo. "How'd it go?"

"Like you planned," Leo said. "His old lady wasn't there. And no one else was around, so no one saw us."

"Good," Nick replied.

Nick shined the beam of light on the man's face. It was beaten to a bloody pulp. Nick looked to Chico. "Your work?"

"Nope," Chico replied. "That was all Ice."

Nick switched off the light. He leaned his head back and listened to the rock music coming through the stereo. They hit up a drive through for a late dinner and continued to their destination. Twenty minutes later, they parked across the street from Manny's Tavern in Jersey City: a low one-story brick structure sandwiched between similar buildings lining the block.

The neighborhood was a mix of commercial and residential. Some buildings had been repurposed and some remained in a state of disrepair. It was a busy Friday night. Reuben parked the van so that the front windshield viewed the front door and side parking lot of the bar. Reuben lit a cigarette. He was the only one of the team that smoked.

"Now we wait," Nick said. "I thought you were quitting."

"I tried the patch. It didn't work," Reuben replied.

Chico plugged in his ear buds. He leaned his head back and closed his eyes. Leo busied himself with his cell phone. Ice kept watch out the front windshield with binoculars.

Nick rested his head against Reuben's seat. He looked to the bound and gagged man once again.

"Did Glen give up anything?" Nick asked to no one in particular.

"No," Ice said. He half-turned in the passenger seat to talk to Nick. "Because I didn't ask him for anything. This is your show, man. We're just delivering the goods."

"Why the beating?" Nick asked.

"La cucaracha," Reuben chimed in. "With a big mouth."

"Carrying on like a little bitch," Ice said. "Something about needing more time and some old folks' home or something like that. He wasn't making any sense. I think he thought we were there to collect on a debt."

"You were," Nick said. "Just not the one he thought." Nick kept his focus on the man's body.

Glen Langley. Fifty-two. Con man extraordinaire. His specialty was Ponzi schemes targeting college students and senior citizens. A bottom-feeder dressed to the nines.

Nick had done his homework on this guy before sending his crew to collect him. His Florida hacienda was a rich man's wet dream. Lavishly furnished, hi-end electronics, in-home shooting range, priceless artwork, collector sports cars, a yacht and powerboat and a helicopter to fly him and the honey to the Caribbean islands whenever. Nick was looking forward to his interrogation.

Nick's parallel investigation had led him to Steven's University of Tech Engineering in Hoboken. Guiseppe's college. Not far from where they sat tonight.

Joe had asked Nick to re-investigate Guiseppe's death. The explosion at Lincoln Marina. The explosion that also killed Sirrina and two of Guiseppe's college friends. A detective in Nick's position might have grappled with the request. But Nick's loyalty to Joe never gave him a moment's hesitation.

Guiseppe's college was the starting point for Nick's investigation. He had tracked down and interviewed college students that had gone to school with Guiseppe. Students that knew him and his two friends. Students that told him about Glen Langley's Ponzi schemes. Students that thought they were getting rich until they weren't.

For the most part, the next forty-five minutes passed with small talk about the case in between bouts of listening to the music. They were all up to speed on the plan, so it was just sit-and-wait time now.

"Show time," Reuben said.

Nick checked his cell phone. One a.m. He sat up and moved to look out the front windshield. The last of the lights in Manny's Tavern turned off. Closing time.

A man exited the front door, locked it, and began walking to the side parking lot. Ice watched him with the binoculars.

"Is that him?" Nick asked.

"Affirmative," Ice replied. "Manny Contreras."

Reuben extinguished his cigarette in the ashtray, started the van, and pulled up next to Manny. Chico slid the van's side door open. Ice and Leo pulled hoodies over their heads, jumped out, snatched up Manny, and threw him in the van. Reuben drove off without cause and without a trace.

Nick had climbed into the front passenger seat during the abduction. He listened to the scuffling and fist punches being delivered to Manny as he struggled to free himself.

"What the fuck, man?" Manny yelled out. "Let me go."

Another solid punch landed on him. It sounded like Manny threw up his guts.

Nick turned to them. Manny was a thirty-eight-year-old scrappy Latino with a shaved head and neck tattoos. "Relax, Manny. We just have some questions."

"Questions about what?" Manny's black and white Chuck Taylor's were pressed against the inside wall of the van. Ice and Chico had his upper body pinned to the floor. "Who the fuck are you guys? What do you want with me, man? I didn't do anything."

Leo slammed his fist into Manny's ribs. "Shut up."

Manny exhaled a growl from the hit. He whimpered. "Come on, man." He panted in pain, facing the rear of the van. Streetlights cast a strobe-like effect inside the van as Reuben drove through city streets. Manny caught a glimpse of Glen's body." Fuck!" He wriggled and struggled to get free. "Who the fuck is that? Is he dead?" More panting. "Aw, shit man. Is he dead?"

Leo braced both hands around Manny's neck, pinning him to the floor. "Shut the fuck up."

When Manny stopped squirming, Leo released him.

"We've got a long drive, Manny," Nick said. "Sit back and enjoy the ride. No talking. Is that clear?"

Leo, Ice, and Chico hoovered over him. "Yeah," Manny answered. "Got it."

For the next hour, rock music replaced conversation. And when the van rolled to a stop, Nick and Reuben climbed out. The gravel road crunched under foot as Nick did a once over of the area. It was just after two o'clock in the morning. The only sound came from the van's idling motor and a rusted "no trespassing'" sign that scraped against the chain link fence in the breeze. It hung upside down, anchored by one last screw.

Misty fog was settling in. The half-moon high above barely cast enough light for Nick to make out six abandoned metal buildings stretched out beyond the fence. Each one was the length of a football field. The four outer ones had long narrow windows near the roofline. The two middle ones were windowless. The place could have been any one of a hundred different businesses, but the stench that filled the night air made it easy to identify. Recent remnants of what used to be a thriving poultry farm. And on nights like tonight, when the air was damp, the stench was almost unbearable.

A thin ribbon of red and white lights marked the interstate miles away. Nothing else was around except empty marsh land. Reuben pushed the gate open. He'd previously cut the chain and lock. There was no graffiti on the buildings, which is why Nick chose this place. No one had been here. No one would be here after they left.

Nick and Reuben climbed back inside the van.

"We're good. Let's go in." Nick pointed to one of the middle buildings.

Reuben drove up to the building. Nick jumped out and walked to the warehouse door. He rolled it open, and Reuben drove the van inside. Nick closed the door and returned to the passenger seat.

The headlights cast a dusty haze. A layer of dirt covered the warehouse floor. Mice scurried across their path. A row of metal heat lamps ran the length of the building, high overhead. Used at one time to keep the hens in comfort. Exposed pipes ran down both sides of the building about a foot off the ground, that would have supplied water for the chickens.

Reuben drove to the center of the building and stopped near a large cardboard box. It was the only item in the massive warehouse. He killed the engine but left the headlights on. Nick climbed out and moved to open the side door of the van. His four partners joined him. The dirt and chicken manure underfoot reeked.

"Christ!" Reuben said to Nick. "You sure know how to pick a place."

"No one wants to come here," Nick responded.

"Yeah," Reuben replied. "I know why."

Nick flicked on the flashlight again. He set it on end behind the passenger seat to illuminate the cargo area of the van.

"Sit up," Nick said to Manny. "Back against the side of the van."

"What is this, man?" Manny whined.

"Do it," Nick ordered.

Manny complied. "Man, what's that smell?"

"Your fear," Ice responded. "It smells just like chicken shit."

Glen's body shifted. He moaned in pain. Leo removed a knife from his belt and climbed inside the van. He cut the ties from Glen's hands and feet and ripped the duct tape from his mouth. Glen quickly regained consciousness, yelling out.

"Sit up," Leo told him.

Glen winced in pain, struggling to move. Leo pulled him up by his collared shirt.

"Ohhh. Ow, ow, OW!" Glen cried out. "Son of a bitch."

"Move over here, next to Manny," Nick said.

Leo climbed out of the van and stood with Nick and the others. Glen looked through his good eye towards Manny. His other eye was swollen shut. "Who...who's he?" Glen asked as he scooted to sit next to Manny.

Nick reached inside his jacket and removed his nine-millimeter from his shoulder harness. He set one foot on the door jamb of the van and crossed his forearms over his knee. The gun hung loose in his hand, not pointed at either man.

"This is simple," Nick said. "I'm going to ask some questions. I expect honest answers. If I'm satisfied with what you tell me, we all go home. If not...I shoot you." He waved the gun.

"Jesus, I don't believe this," Glen muttered under his breath.

"I'll start with you, Glen," Nick said. "Since you seem eager to talk."

Manny looked to the beaten man. He studied him for a moment, then surprise registered on his face. He kept his mouth shut and faced Nick. This didn't go un-noticed by Nick. Manny recognized Glen.

"Your college Ponzi schemes," Nick said, looking at Glen. "I want to know about em'."

"Look, I don't know..."

"Don't waste my time, Glen." Nick waved his gun.

86

Glen deflated. "All right, all right." He looked down to his scraped hands and dirty clothes. "Hedge funds, mostly," Glen said as he lifted his head. His words were slurred from his beaten swollen lips. Blood oozed from his head, eye, and mouth. He looked grotesque in the flashlight's glow. "Phantom riches." He chuckled to himself. "No-risk investments with huge returns. These kids think they're going to be the next Warren Buffet." He shrugged his shoulders. "Who am I to bust their bubble?" He wiped at blood and drool with the back of his hand.

"But you do bust their bubble," Nick said. "Now I'm here to bust yours."

Glen shut up.

"I'm interested in sixteen years ago," Nick said. "The campus of Steven's University of Tech in Hoboken. Guiseppe D'Amato. Ring any bells?"

Glen thought for a long moment. He slurped his spittle, looking up to Nick with his good eye opened wide. "Hey, that's the guy who was just acquitted. A...a mistrial, right? D'Amato?"

"Wrong one. Try again," Nick said.

"Guiseppe you said?" Glen asked. "Sixteen years ago? That's a ways back. Let's see...that would be..."

"The summer of two thousand three." Nick finished his thought.

Glen did some serious thinking. "If it was summer, I was already gone."

"Gone where?"

"First Florida and then I...we, traveled for the next few months."

"We who?"

"Me and the misses," Glen answered. "Shirley. She's my gal."

"June twenty first two thousand three to be exact," Nick said.

Glen thought again. "No. I was gone. It wasn't us. Once summer came around and the students left campus, we quit the scheme. I waited until fall to start it up again. And I moved to a different campus. I never worked the same campus more than one semester. I stay on the move. Stayed on the move. I don't work colleges anymore."

No. Now you just prey on the elderly, you sorry prick, Nick thought. "Was Guiseppe invested in your Ponzi before you left for the summer?" he asked.

Glen pondered the question. "Geez man," he slurred. "There were a lot of kids. I didn't know them all by name, you know?"

"But you remembered D'Amato."

"Well, yeah. But that was because of the recent news, not because…" He paused as a thought came to him.

"Not because, what?" Nick asked.

A glimmer of recognition registered on Glen's swollen face. He looked up to Nick. "I do remember the name. I remember having his name in my client book. Two stars."

"Two stars?"

"Yeah," Glen replied. "I put a star next to the names of investors that were a sure thing. You know, an easy target. Easy to get money from."

"Why two stars for Guiseppe?"

"The kid was gullible." Glen half laughed, half coughed, obviously having a clearer memory of him now. "He had two buddies that were in with him. All three of them…naïve sheep. I could have sold the kid Fruit Loops if he thought he needed em'." Glen waved off the conversation.

Nick allowed the comment to pass. "Where's your client book?"

"That one?" Glen pondered. "Burned up. It got destroyed in the fire."

"What fire?"

"Someone bombed my office. At least that's what the police told me. They never caught whoever did it, either."

"Another satisfied customer," Reuben said.

"What did I care?" Glen added. "I collected from my insurance and moved on."

The bombing piqued Nick's interest. He filed that comment away. "Who's we?" Nick asked.

"Hunh?"

"Earlier you said once summer came around and the students left campus, we quit the scheme until the following semester came around. Who's we?"

Glen dropped his head back against the side of the van. "Why not?" he said, half to himself. "I feel that this isn't going to end well for me tonight."

"Shirley?" Nick asked.

Glen brought his good eye back to Nick. "Naw. Well, she was involved, sort of."

Nick couldn't believe this chump just gave up his girlfriend as an accomplice. *Keep talkin' loser,* Nick thought.

"But that's not who worked with me on campus. It was this kid. Jimmy Salazar."

Manny leaned forward to Nick. "Hey, just so you know, man, I don't know this dude. I don't know why I'm even here."

"Save it, Manny. I'll get to you in a minute," Nick said. "Your buddy Glen here already gave you up. Why do you think we have the two of you here tonight?"

"That's bullshit, man," Manny said. "I don't know this guy."

Ice climbed in the van and removed a pair of bolt cutters stashed behind the passenger seat. Leo jumped in behind him, grabbed Manny's left arm, and held up Manny's hand with his pinky finger exposed.

Manny struggled to free himself, screaming, "What are you doing? What are you…?"

Ice swiftly cut off Manny's little digit. Manny screamed out in pain. Leo released his grip. Manny pressed his hand to his stomach. He quickly wrapped his shirt around his hand to absorb the blood. He howled and cried in pain as Leo and Ice climbed out of the van and stood behind Nick once again. Glen sat quietly in shock.

Nick continued with Glen. "Jimmy Salazar. You were saying?"

"Yeah." Glen slowly brought his gaze back to Nick. "Jimmy Salazar."

"Manny kicked Glen in the leg. "What the fuck, man?" Manny was bawling. "Why you talkin'? Why are you telling him anything?"

Glen looked to Manny. "Take a look around, Manny. Things aren't lookin' good for either of us, kid."

"Fuck you, man," Manny shot back. "Speak for yourself."

Nick pointed his gun at Manny. "Shut up, Manny, or you're going to lose more than a finger."

"This is bullshit, man," Manny yelled back.

"For your sake, it better not be," Nick said.

Manny thought about saying more, but he reconsidered. He kept pressure on his wound, rocking back and forth in pain. Nick lowered his gun and came back to Glen. At least Glen had come to terms with tonight's events. He realized his luck had finally run out. He had nothing to lose. Nick hoped he would gain from that. Manny on the other hand...

"What else can you tell me about Salazar?" Nick asked Glen.

"Not much. I didn't care much for the kid. He was too pushy. Too aggressive. Drew too much attention to himself. That was going to draw attention to me."

"Jimmy Salazar." Nick repeated the name.

"Yeah," Glen said. "Only that was the name I set him up with. An alias, you know. To protect him. His real name was Jimmy Teducci."

Nick felt a shockwave shoot through him. He straightened his stance, holding the gun at his side. It was a connection he'd hoped to make in his investigation, but it still caught him off-guard.

"You know him," Glen said. "I can tell by your reaction." It looked as if Glen tried to smile but failed miserably. His battered face contorted unpleasantly.

"Aw, man," Manny moaned. "Why didn't you keep your mouth shut, Glen?"

"How do you know him?" Nick asked Manny.

"No way, man," Manny said, still rocking in pain.

"I can promise you, Manny, it's not going to get any better by holding out," Nick stated.

Manny dropped his head. "Aw, shit. Shit, shit, shit!"

"Give it up," Nick said.

"The guy borrowed money from me, ok?" Manny finally spoke. "A lot. Like a hundred Gs. Said this guy put him in contact with me." Manny pointed to Glen. "But he told me his name was Jimmy Salazar."

"And?" Nick prodded.

"I had people to pay, you know? Business associates."

Nick scoffed. "Manny the mogul."

"Hey, fuck you man," Manny shot back.

Nick was quiet.

"Anyway," Manny continued. "This guy Jimmy keeps giving me the runaround and not paying, so I kidnapped his little sister, you know, so he'd pay up."

Nick leaned forward on one foot, raising the gun to rest on his knee. He was getting somewhere now, and faster than he'd expected. "Keep going," he demanded.

"Only, well," Manny hung his head. "It got so fucked up, man."

"What did?" Nick asked.

"See, Jimmy told me he would have the money in a day or two and for me to hang tight," Manny continued, still wincing in pain. "Said he had to do some family stuff over the weekend and that he would get with me the following week. I didn't trust the dude anymore, you know? I figured the guy was skipping town or some shit like that. So, me and my guys, we followed him." Manny re-secured his blood-soaked t-shirt around his hand. "We ended up following him to the Wildwoods. It's a water park down…"

"I know of it." Nick cut him off. "Keep going."

"Well, at first I thought for sure the dude was skipping town, but he had a car full of kids. I assumed that was the family obligation he had to take care of. We followed him around all day. I was debating whether or not it was the right time to act."

Nick felt a cold stab of shock shoot through him now. He had been part of that group of kids being followed. He tried recalling if anything seemed suspicious that day. He'd only been fifteen years old then.

"Anyway," Manny continued. "I called Jimmy once I decided to go through with it. I gave him one more chance to pay up. He told me he was only going to pay half of what he owed me, or I could go fuck myself. So, we picked up his kid sister. Only…"

"Only what?"

"Only it wasn't Jimmy's sister." Manny rocked back and forth in agony. "Man-oh-man-oh-man." Manny exhaled, reliving the events. "Turned out she was the daughter of someone you don't want to fuck with."

"And who was that?" Nick baited him.

"She was Carmine Teducci's daughter, Sirrina."

A quiet moment fell over the group.

"Keep going," Nick said.

"Man, I wanted no part of that," Manny continued. "I didn't even know Jimmy was a Teducci until tonight. I knew him as Jimmy Salazar.

Shit." Manny tucked himself into a tight ball. "You working for the Teducci family? Is that what this is about, man?"

"No," Nick replied. "What happened after the kidnapping?"

"Shit, man," Manny said. "I didn't know this shit was going to come back to me, man."

"What happened!" Nick yelled.

Glen flinched and scooted a few inches away from Manny.

Something shifted in Manny. His expression changed. His posture changed. He stifled his whimpering. The reality of his position was beginning to dawn on him. He was ready to confess.

"It was a few nights later," Manny said. "Jimmy called to say he had the money. So, we set up a meeting. After hours at my bar." Manny looked down to his bloody hand and shirt. "He showed up with half the money he owed me." Manny looked back to Nick. "Told me that's all I was getting and for me to hand over Sirrina or the family would take care of me in their own way." Manny scoffed. "I knew what that meant. The fucker had the balls to short me and then threaten me."

"What did you do, Manny?" Nick demanded.

"I took the money and me and my guys beat the crap out of him. Told him if he ever came looking for me, I'd have him killed." Manny said, sounding proud of himself. "I turned the threat right back on him, you know?"

"What happened with Sirrina?" Nick asked, his stomach churned. He wanted to be done with these two assholes.

"Man," Manny said, some of his bravado slipping away. "What could I do?" He paused to reflect on the moment. "I sold her."

Nick flinched, not believing what he'd just heard. "You what?"

"You heard me, man." Manny smiled. A sick, twisted expression. "I had no choice. You would've done the same thing in my position, or maybe just killed her." He coughed out a half laugh, half sob. "I couldn't have that heat on me man. The Teducci family. No way. And I didn't want her blood on my hands. Selling her seemed an easier, cleaner way to get rid of her."

Nick took a few steps away to collect his thoughts. He wasn't sure what he had expected to find out from Glen and Manny, but it certainly wasn't this. His crew remained quiet, allowing him to process Manny's words.

They knew every detail of what Nick was investigating. No doubt they had been just as shocked to hear what Manny had said. *Sold to who?* Nick wondered. Had Guiseppe somehow been involved in this? Is that how she wound up on the yacht in Lincoln Marina? Nick was having trouble making that connection with Jimmy.

"Hey, I'm sorry man," Manny called out from inside the van. "For whatever that's worth."

Nick moved back to face him and Glen again. "Who was the buyer?" Nick asked. He felt bile rise in his throat having to ask that question.

"I...I don't know," Manny mumbled. "I don't remember, man. It was a long time ago, you know?"

Nick climbed inside the van and pressed his gun to Manny's forehead. "Think, mother-fucker, or it's lights out for you."

"No, no, no. Wait, man. Don't..." Manny panted. "It's, shit. I can't think with a gun shoved in my face."

Nick lowered the gun and pressed it to his gut. "Better?"

"Shit, no," Manny said. He took a deep breath, closing his eyes, trying to recollect that moment in time sixteen years ago. "Someone in my crew set it up. The guy's name is Horseshoe, Horshio, Horshey, shit. Something like that. He goes by one name."

"Horacio," Reuben said.

"That's it," Manny said.

Nick turned to Reuben. "You know him?"

Reuben nodded in agreement. "Not good."

Nick climbed out of the van. "You know where to find him?" he asked Reuben.

"Atlanta, Georgia," Reuben replied.

"Are we done with these two assholes?" Nick asked.

"We are," Reuben concluded.

Leo opened the passenger side door. He took his cell phone out of the center console. He ended the recording and held up the phone to Nick. "Got it." Then backed away from the van.

Nick turned back to Manny. "You were wrong, Manny. I would've never done what you did." He lifted his gun and pumped two bullets into him. He turned to Glen. Before Glen could get another word out of his mouth, Nick pumped two shots into him. Both of their bodies slumped in place. Nick turned back to his crew.

"Let's torch it and get out of here."

The five of them retrieved gasoline, rags, and glass jars from the large cardboard box. Supplies they had left when they scouted and selected this place as their interrogation site. They filled the jars with fuel, stuffed rags into the jars, and lit the rags with Reuben's cigarette lighter. They threw the flaming bottles into the van and watched it explode into flames. Ice retrieved the cardboard box, broke it down with his bare hands, and tossed it into the burning van.

Nick felt the heat of the flames on his face. It was nothing compared to the flame burning inside him. "Change in plans, boys." he said, focused on the flames. "Looks like we're heading south."

"What about Jimmy?" Reuben asked.

Nick thought about Glen's earlier comment about his office having been blown up. Nick would put money on it that Jimmy had been the one who did it. He turned to face his crew.

"Jimmy's not going anywhere," Nick replied. "Leo, I'll need you to sit on him while the rest of us go to Atlanta."

"You got it," Leo accepted.

"You think we can find Sirrina?" Reuben asked.

"You tell me," Nick replied. "You said you know of this guy Horacio. What are my chances of finding her?"

"A saint's chance in hell," Reuben said.

"At least you're giving us a chance," Nick said.

"Let's get out of here, man." Chico said. "I can't take this shit smell anymore."

Nick turned back to the flames. Satisfied with the extent of the fire, he moved to join the rest of them. Outside, they walked to a newer model extra cab pickup parked at the side of the building.

"Shoes in back," Reuben said. "I don't want that shit stinkin' up my truck."

They removed their shoes and threw them in the bed of the truck before driving off.

CHAPTER 10

Gina drove down second street in Hudson Heights at noon the next day. It was a narrow tree-lined street with cars parked on both sides. It barely left room for one-way traffic. She was looking forward to spending the afternoon with her two best friends. It would give her a chance to step off the emotional merry-go-round that she'd been on since yesterday.

Megan Fuller stood on the front steps of her four-story brick apartment building, busy with her cellphone. Gina stopped in the street. She honked twice, startling Megan.

"Come on, chica, I don't have all day," Gina called through the open passenger side window.

Megan made her way to the car. She had an easygoing southern California style about her. Nothing fussy. Straight blonde hair that hung like a veil down her back and short wispy bangs. Her bright green eyes were shielded with stylish shades.

She was thin. *Too thin,* Gina thought. She had the appetite of a lion and never gained an ounce. The two of them met their first year in college and had been best friends ever since.

Megan climbed into the passenger seat. She looked comfortably chic in jeans, a t-shirt and tan cropped leather jacket that matched her ankle high boots.

"Hi ya," Megan said. Her smile was bright and infectious. She smelled like freesia flowers.

Gina smiled back, "Hi ya, hon."

Megan pulled the door closed and Gina drove off.

"Where are we having lunch?" Megan asked. "I'm starving. I only had a yogurt for breakfast."

Gina navigated her way out of Megan's neighborhood. "A place called Lynette's Paris Café, not far from the Plaza Hotel and Central Park."

"It sounds French and expensive," Megan said.

"You know it will be," Gina replied. "Chloe suggested it. It's a friend of a friend who owns the place, or something like that." Gina waved a hand in gesture. "I guess Chloe is considering them for catering her wedding. She wants our opinion of their food before making her decision." Gina turned on Tonnelle Avenue and headed for the Lincoln Tunnel.

"You look pretty today," Megan said. "You look chic when you tie your hair up like that."

Gina instinctively ran a hand over her lap, smoothing her white knit dress. She wore knee-high black boots and a jean jacket.

"Thanks for that," Gina replied. "I was thinking the same about you." She glanced in the rearview mirror. "I tie my hair up like this when I don't have time to do anything with it."

"So, how are you doing?" Megan asked.

"I'm good," Gina said. "How about you?"

"I'm good. But really, Gina, how *are* you?"

Gina gave Megan a quick glance then returned her focus to the road without answering.

"I watch the news. I know what happened yesterday. You can't think I'm not going to ask you about it. Where are you at with all that?" Megan asked.

"Honestly, I'd rather not talk about it. This is Chloe's day and anything I have to share about yesterday would ruin the day today."

"No, it wouldn't. And besides, we've had enough wedding planning lunches with Chloe. In the end, it doesn't matter what you and I suggest, she's going to do everything her way. At least if we discuss the mistrial, we won't have to hear how wonderful Jimmy is, every five minutes."

Gina shot Megan a sideways look.

"Sorry. I know he's your cousin," Megan said. "But sometimes I think Chloe's trying to convince herself she's doing the right thing marrying him."

"You do?" Gina asked.

Gina knew Jimmy and Chloe fought occasionally, but several breakups and makeups over the past year hadn't stopped the two of them from wanting to tie the knot. Gina thought Chloe stood firm on her decision. That marrying Jimmy was what she wanted.

"I wish you hadn't said that, Megan. Now you've got me questioning their engagement."

"Chloe's just so independent," Megan said. "Did you ever see her settling down, getting married and having kids?"

"I did, but I always hoped it would be with my brother Christopher, not Jimmy. I always thought somewhere along the line her and Chris would hook-up again."

"Oh yeah." Megan smiled. "Chloe was Christopher's first love. How is Chris anyways?"

"He's good. Everyone's good."

How old were they?"

"That was a long time ago," Gina said. "Chloe was twelve and Chris was fifteen."

A long silence followed.

Megan squeezed Gina's shoulder. "You're thinking about Sirrina, aren't you?"

Megan knew Gina well. The two of them shared a sister-like bond. Even though Gina had grown up with Chloe and had been best friends with her since childhood, it was Megan that Gina confided in most.

Gina nodded, keeping her eyes on the road.

"Me, too. But I'm also thinking about that damn mistrial. That's gotta be eating you up inside, Gina. I wish you'd talk to me," Megan pleaded.

Gina forced a smile. "Let's enjoy today. Like I said, this is Chloe's day. She seems happy and I think we should support her decision. She's the first of us three to get married. It's a big deal."

"So is what is happening with you."

"We can talk about it later, you and me. After lunch. After Chloe leaves." Gina glanced to Megan. "Promise me you won't bring it up while we're with her. If she mentions it...different story."

"Oh, she'll mention it. I'll guarantee you that," Megan said.

They valet parked the car at the restaurant and entered Lynette's Paris Café. The place was packed.

It was a modest space on the ground floor of a multi-use ten-story building. The back of the restaurant shared a pretty garden courtyard with condominium residents on the floors above. The décor was charming rustic French countryside. On the way to their table, they passed a glass case crammed with French pastries and desserts. The aromas of grilled onions and fresh bread baking in ovens permeated the air. Gina wished she had an appetite.

The hostess sat Gina and Megan. Chloe hadn't arrived yet, but had apparently used her clout to reserve a window table overlooking the flourishing garden. You would never know traffic was keeping pace on Madison Avenue just outside the courtyard walls. Chloe appeared a moment later looking sophisticated in a pink and black Chanel suit and black heels.

Supported by her parents' successful publishing firm, Chloe was editor in chief for five of their magazines. Her striking appearance and style drew looks as she approached. She was New York through and through. Her sleek black hair was cut in a severe bob that curled right to her jutting jaw line. She removed her vogue sunglasses to reveal large brown eyes, detailed with heavy eyeliner and mascara.

Chloe gave Megan a hug, and then turned to Gina. "Come here, sweetie."

She pulled Gina into a tight embrace, holding her for a long moment before releasing her.

"Are you ok?" she asked with concern.

"Yes, and I'd rather not talk about it."

"We will at some point," Chloe insisted.

Gina shook her head as they took their seats.

A waiter approached. "Can I bring you ladies something to drink?"

"I was going to order our usual champagne," Chloe said. "But I don't think any of us feel like celebrating today."

"Yes, order the champagne," Gina replied.

"Gina," Megan said, placing a hand on Gina's arm.

The waiter was standing by, impatiently.

"You both want to make a big deal about yesterday. I don't," Gina concluded.

"Can you bring us a bottle of the two thousand sixteen Chateau Pichon Baron, please?" Chloe said to the waiter.

"Wait," Megan said. "If we're having wine instead of champagne, let's have a white instead. Is that ok?"

"Sure," Gina said.

"Of course," Chloe said and turned back to the waiter. "We'll have a bottle of the two thousand nineteen Chateau Sixtine, instead."

"Very well, madam," the waiter replied, then left.

"So, what happened yesterday in court, Gina?" Chloe asked. "Jimmy stayed at his apartment in New Jersey last night and we've been playing phone tag since yesterday, so I haven't had a chance to talk to him."

"Like I told Megan on the way here, I really can't say much about what happened. Not yet anyways. And in all honesty, I'd rather not talk about it. Let's enjoy lunch and discuss your wedding plans."

Chloe waved a hand. "Everything's planned already."

Megan shot Gina a knowing look.

"I want to know how you're holding up with the mistrial," Chloe continued. "What about your job? What's happening there?"

"I'll know more on Monday," Gina said. She wasn't about to share with her friends about the FBI interrogation she endured. She wouldn't do or say anything to jeopardize her position at work.

Their waiter returned with the wine. The girls ordered lunch, discussed Chloe's wedding, and enjoyed each other's company for over two hours. Chloe only mentioned how wonderful Jimmy was, twice. And both times Chloe said it, Gina thought she seemed anxious or tense. It was slight, an edginess Gina hadn't noticed before, but it was there. Gina wondered if there was some truth to what Megan had told her earlier.

More than once, Chloe and Megan raised the issue about the mistrial during lunch, but Gina skirted around the subject.

Outside the restaurant, Chloe hailed a cab back to her office. Weekends didn't exist with her career. Gina and Megan decided to take advantage of the sunny afternoon. They walked to Central Park, recapping Chloe's wedding plans. Chloe had made it sound like it would be a festive family gathering at the Plaza Hotel. Gina knew it would be anything but. Her parents would give their only daughter a million-dollar fairytale wedding. Gina wondered how her cousin Jimmy would handle it all. They settled on a bench in the warm sun overlooking the pond.

Megan's cell phone rang again. It had been going off non-stop during lunch.

"Do you need to get back to work?" Gina asked.

"No," Megan said, reviewing the text message. "I have three leases renewing this coming week, but the office can handle it."

Megan had received her real estate broker's license two years ago. Gina knew it wouldn't be long before Megan would have a shingle to hang on her own door.

"I went to see Nick yesterday after court," Gina said, focused on a flock of birds floating on the water.

Megan placed a hand on Gina's knee, squeezing, "Really? What happened?"

"He couldn't say much." Gina looked to Megan. "I wanted to be mad at him for what he'd pulled in court, but seeing him standing there in front of me, dressed in jailhouse scrubs…" She exhaled. "It took its toll. I felt like…it broke…" Gina choked up.

Megan pulled her close and embraced her.

"I'm worried about him, Megan." Gina wiped her tears.

"Nick can take care of himself," Megan said. "From everything you've told me about him over the years, he'll figure out a way to deal with his situation. And it *is* his situation. He brought this on himself. Remember that. You need to focus on you and take care of yourself and your job."

Gina sat up. "I know," she said. Without going into too much detail, she reiterated the events at her work with the FBI interrogation. It felt good to offload on her friend.

"I can see why you didn't want to talk about this in front of Chloe," Megan said.

"She was there the day Sirrina was abducted. I didn't want her to have to relive that nightmare all over again."

"You're a good friend, Gina."

"So are you, Megan."

They embraced each other for a good long moment, then pulled away, but stayed close to one another. Gina was grateful for the friendship she had with Megan.

"What will you do?" Megan asked.

"I don't know yet," Gina exhaled. "I'll show up for work on Monday and see what happens."

"Just keep a clear head. And if you need an attorney, I have one to recommend."

"Doesn't everyone?" Gina replied.

"Right." Megan bit her lip. "Your family probably has a team of them on retainer."

Gina looked to her friend, accepting that truth. "Hopefully, I won't need to call on them."

They left the park shortly afterwards. Gina dropped Megan off at her apartment then went home to prepare for Monday.

CHAPTER 11

"There's going to be a shitload of heat coming down the pike for this, Jimmy," Detective Jerry Pulia said. "I need to know how you want me to handle it. I'm not taking the rap. I need to know what to do. So, tell me what my options are."

Jimmy sat at his desk across from Jerry. It was Sunday afternoon. Jimmy had finally tracked the prick down. Jerry had been doing his best hiding out to avoid the FBI's inquiry. Jimmy had to threaten him with exposure to get him to show up.

And now that he was here, he was expecting Jimmy to clean up the mess. A mess that should have been in Pulia's control. A mess that Jimmy knew was going to cost him a small fortune to fix.

"Answering my calls, for starters," Jimmy said. "Sticking your head in the sand isn't going to make this go away."

On Sundays, Jimmy had the office to himself. It's when he was the most productive. And today, able to speak his mind freely. He had checked Pulia for a wiretap as soon as he had arrived. Jimmy couldn't be sure who Pulia was or wasn't talking to now.

"You guaranteed me that you had Nick under control," Jimmy continued. "I paid Nick half up front, as he requested. Just like I paid you half up front to guarantee results. Results that should have included a ruling in our favor, which you promised you could deliver."

Jimmy didn't expand on the fact that he'd offered Nick twenty thousand dollars, twice what he had offered Jerry.

"I have important clients and backers who were relying on those results," Jimmy said. "So, you can imagine the position I'm in now with this mistrial fiasco."

Jimmy's clients and backers would have gladly paid twice the amount Jimmy had offered to Jerry and Nick. They had plenty to gain in political and government roles. Roles that Jimmy needed to protect for his future in lobbying.

"None of us saw this coming, Jimmy," Pulia said. It was a feeble response.

Jimmy didn't answer.

Pulia squirmed in his seat. "If Nick hadn't been reassigned to me in the first place, none of this would have happened. I'd be sitting here collecting the second half of my payment from you instead of discussing options on how to clear my name."

"But the department did reassign him to you, and you assured me that it wasn't going to be a problem," Jimmy said. "And now it *is* a problem that's going to cost me. Cost you." Jimmy pointed to Jerry. "You convinced me that Nick's abilities were going to benefit our plan, that he would follow your lead and not cause us any setbacks." Jimmy scoffed. "You know, when you told me that, there was this nagging twinge I felt at the base of my neck." Jimmy's expression was pinched as he massaged his neck. "I hadn't been confident you'd be able to get Nick on board with our plan and keep him in line. I was right." Jimmy shook his head, disappointed. "I should have followed my gut instinct. That's a lesson I won't soon forget."

Pulia didn't respond.

"You didn't think through all of the 'what ifs' Jerry, did you?" Jimmy scolded.

Jimmy didn't feel the need to address him as detective. He was no longer deserving of the title. He was just another bottom feeder with mediocre capabilities.

Pulia rubbed his eyes in frustration. The dark circles under them indicated he hadn't slept much, if at all, since the mistrial. His forty-five years looked more like sixty. His hair was ruffed up like he'd just crawled out of bed. He wore a navy jog suit and sneakers instead of his usual sport coat and tie, and he smelled of perspiration.

"You're not instilling much confidence in me here, Jerry, and that concerns me."

Pulia's eyes snapped up to him. "Is that some sort of threat?"

In a word, yes, Jimmy thought. But he wouldn't go there, yet. He needed to coddle Jerry's fears for a little while longer.

"I don't appreciate the hostility, Jerry," Jimmy continued. "I have no doubt we can navigate through this, but I need to be careful how I go about doing that. Nick and I have a lot of history together. We grew up in the same neighborhood and hung out as kids together. It was…"

"That was a long time ago," Pulia cut in. "What's one got to do with the other?"

Plenty, Jimmy thought. "Karma."

"Hunh?"

"Never mind," Jimmy said, waving him off impatiently.

Jimmy had paid Pulia eighty thousand dollars over the past six months for falsifying documents and evidence on twelve other cases, paving the way for Jimmy to establish players for his lobbying practices.

Jimmy targeted Pulia because he knew he had debt, and he oversaw the crime lab. He was the perfect candidate: a puppet Jimmy could use to achieve his goal of sending Joe D'Amato to prison. Jimmy realized now that he had overestimated Jerry's abilities and commitment to his role. Jimmy's misplaced confidence in Jerry left a bitter taste in his mouth. It was a sobering reminder that reliability was liability in disguise.

"Well, I hope your navigating through this includes a guarantee that nothing from the D'Amato case will blow back on me," Jerry said. "And for my role in the Janet Sardello car bombing case, too."

Jimmy's eyes narrowed. *You can't just wash your hands of this, Jerry,* Jimmy thought. He was rapidly growing tired of Pulia.

"Do you have the files, Jerry?" Jimmy asked.

"What are my guarantees here, Jimmy?"

Guarantees. Jimmy soured at the plural form of the word.

"There are no guarantees in any of this," Jimmy said. "The sooner you understand that the better."

Jerry stared at him wide-eyed and dumbfounded.

"What do you want from me, hunh?" Jimmy asked.

"I want to know that when the D.A. and F.B.I. and whoever else comes pokin' around investigating this case, that I'm not going to be following my partner to prison," Pulia replied.

"Or what?" Jimmy asked.

Pulia didn't answer.

Jimmy propped his elbows on the desk and rubbed his palms together as if brokering a deal. He needed to appeal to Jerry's request and keep him sound.

"OK, I'll see what I can do," Jimmy said. "Let's have the files." Jimmy held out a hand, expecting Pulia to hand them over, but he didn't. He sat there stone-faced. Apparently expecting more than what Jimmy had offered.

Jimmy lowered his hand on his desk. "How do you expect me to make that sort of guarantee, Jerry?"

"You know people. You know you know people that can guarantee me that."

"So, you're going to pay *me* now to protect *you*?"

"No. I think you owe it to me."

"Jesus," Jimmy scoffed, leaning back in his chair, thinking how best to play his hand. *The chump actually thinks I can save him from this fuck up*, Jimmy thought. "Fine. I'll talk to D.A. Forrester. I'll see to it that the blame is focused on the others involved: the D.A.'s co-counsel, Chris Schuler, and the people from your department: Sergeant Rotello, Officer Nunzio, and Claire Chu from the lab," Jimmy said. "I can't guarantee that you're not going to feel some heat from this, but I can make sure all the others receive the brunt of it."

There was a long silence. Jimmy watched Pulia mull this over. Jimmy was doing the same. He had re-played his role in this over and over, making sure he would land in the clear of any investigations. He would. He had taken careful measures to make sure no one could connect any wrongdoing back to him. He had merely been a facilitator between the parties involved. One who held a common interest in politics and law enforcement through his lobbying efforts. He had been careful to document his activities with justifiable reasons.

"Look, Jerry," Jimmy continued. "You've gotta accept some responsibility on some level for what you did here."

"Yeah, maybe," Pulia responded, looking down to his hands clasped in his lap with a sulking expression. He was realizing the gravy train was coming to a screeching halt.

Jimmy assumed thoughts of regret were swimming through his head. The fear of facing indictments would eat him up inside. Jimmy needed to get him focused on something positive.

"What about you, Jimmy?" Pulia interrupted his thought.

"What about me?"

"What's your responsibility in all this?" Pulia asked with bitterness.

Go fuck yourself, Jerry, Jimmy thought. He moved forward once again, leaning on his elbows. "You know something, Jerry? We still don't know the extent of what Nick's supposed investigation is going to bring." Jimmy was deflecting.

Pulia studied him with squinty eyes.

"That's right," Jimmy continued. "All that Nick said is that he ran an investigation, and that evidence and testimony were falsified."

"Isn't that enough?" Pulia exclaimed. "Why am I asking you that? It *is* enough."

"Think about it, Jerry. The main players involved with the case were all part of the plan to convict Joe D'Amato. Nick is the only one who strayed from that group of people. It will be all of you against him. Your word against his. The result will be that D'Amato convinced Nick to take the rap. My guess would be in the form of a payment. We know Nick accepts bribes. He took a healthy one from me."

"But a prison rap?" Pulia asked. "I'm having a hard time believing that Nick would have gone as far as accepting prison time in exchange for a payout."

"You'd be surprised what people are willing to do," Jimmy said. "I can't believe I'm having to tell you that. Hell, in your line of work, you've probably come across some real douchebags. And besides, you don't know what the payout consisted of."

"It would have to be pretty fucking high," Pulia responded.

"D'Amato could afford to pay whatever Nick asked for. That much I know," Jimmy said.

Jimmy watched Pulia weigh his options. After a long moment, he bent over the side of his chair and picked up a thick brown file. He handed it over to Jimmy.

"This is everything on the Janet Sardello car bombing case," Pulia said.

"Who else had access to this?" Jimmy asked, containing his eagerness as he took the file.

"No one," Pulia said. "It had just been assigned to your cousin Gina, but I was able to retrieve it before she had a chance to review it. And before the FBI swarmed the lab."

"What will you say happened to this?" Jimmy gripped the file with both hands.

"That the F.B.I. mishandled the case file and it went missing."

"You can make that stick?" Jimmy asked.

"I can," Pulia replied.

Jimmy nodded, even though he lacked confidence in Jerry now, but he didn't have a choice. His options were limited, and he needed that file. He opened his top desk drawer, removed an envelope, and closed the drawer.

"I'll take care of you for the Sardello case files." Jimmy handed the envelope to Pulia.

Pulia took the envelope. He squeezed it, feeling its thickness, then he opened it to view the cash tucked inside.

"It's all there, Jerry," Jimmy said. "Four-grand, like we agreed on."

Pulia looked up to him, satisfied. "I thought you would have negotiated this down some, since I didn't have to do all the false reporting."

"I'm a man of my word, Jerry."

Pulia grunted.

"Take a walk, Jerry," Jimmy said. "You're certainly dressed for it. Clear your head. No amount of guilt can change the past, and no amount of worrying can change the future."

Pulia stood up. "You believe that?"

"I do."

"Lucky for you then," Jerry said. He turned and left Jimmy's office.

Jimmy sat back in his chair, breathing a sigh of relief. Having the Sardello car bombing case go missing was a far better conclusion than he had originally planned. With the D'Amato mistrial coming into question, the Sardello case would have certainly raised plenty of suspicion. He moved to his floor safe, crammed the file inside, then closed the safe.

He thought about destroying the file immediately but reconsidered. It seemed smart to hang on to it for a while. He walked over to the wall of windows facing the Hudson and watched traffic on the waterway silently glide past. Having gotten Jerry Pulia under control, he needed to consider what his next move would be. He glanced to his left. Just up the way, Lincoln Marina was in clear view from his office.

CHAPTER 12

On Monday morning, Gina arrived at the crime lab by seven forty-five. Fifteen minutes earlier than normal. One black Suburban and two Hamilton County police cruisers were backed into parking spaces outside the lab. No other vehicles were present. *Not a good sign,* Gina thought.

A uniformed officer sat behind the wheel of the Suburban as she drove past. This was feeling like Friday all over again. She had been hoping for something better this morning. She considered turning around and leaving but feared that would appear suspicious. The officer in the Suburban had watched her pull in, and most likely either photographed her car or recorded her license plate.

Gina parked her car. *Maybe you should wait in the car until others arrive,* she thought. But then that might appear suspicious, too. She grabbed her coat and purse and headed for the entrance. Another uniformed police officer stood just outside the door with an iPad in his hands.

"Good morning," Gina said, trying to sound positive.

"Morning, ma'am."

"Is it ok to go in?"

"I'll need to verify you're on the list of approved personnel." The officer readied himself with the iPad. "Your name please?"

"Gina Teducci." *This was different,* she thought. *New security measures already put in place.*

"Can you spell that for me please?"

"T.E.D.U.C.C.I."

The officer entered her name and waited. "You're clear," he said. "You're to go to interview room one and meet with chief of police, Stanford." He slid his security clearance card through the reader and opened the door for her.

Gina stiffened. *I'm meeting with the police chief?* A worrisome thought. *This can't be good.*

"Do you know if Roger Mattison is inside?" Gina asked. She knew he wasn't. His car wasn't in the parking lot. She was stalling, trembling with anxiety. Anticipating she would soon be unemployed.

"I'm just supposed to direct you to the chief, ma'am," the officer replied, still holding the door open for her.

"Thank you," Gina said as she walked through the door. This wasn't how she imagined the morning starting off.

Gina entered the reception area and stopped. The front door clicked shut. The lights hadn't been turned on. Only natural light from the entrance doors filtered in. It was unusual to be in the lab with no others around. It felt uncomfortable. Not one person was in sight. An eeriness crept over her. It was too quiet.

Gina moved farther into the lab. The absence of norm hit her with full force. The flurry of activity from techs working their cases and discussing results was non-existent. Equipment and machines sat dark and quiet. Their favorite music energizing the lab had been silenced, coffee aromas wafting through the air ceased to exist…nothing. This wasn't the crime lab she had come to know and enjoy working at. It felt more like a morgue.

After having the F.B.I. converge on the lab Friday, the atmosphere felt depressed. There was a sense of abandonment. At least in this part of the lab the corridor lights were on. They lit the only path leading to the interview rooms. *A path leading to doom*, she thought.

Her heels hitting the wood floor seemed louder than normal. Without the bustle of the lab, there was nothing to absorb the sound. She felt like a lamb inching towards slaughter as she continued to walk. She glanced in the private offices as she moved past. Since the lights were off within the offices, it was hard to see much. From what she could tell, all computers, laptops, and case files had been removed from everyone's workspace. Just like her cubicle had been cleared of.

Gina made her final approach to the interview room. Through the plate glass partition windows, she saw Chief Stanford sitting at the only table in the room. One uniformed officer sat across from him. Gina entered, pushing open the glass door.

"Good morning," she said. Again, forcing herself to sound positive.

The uniformed officer stood up and backed away from the desk. He nodded to acknowledge her.

"Good morning, Miss Teducci," the chief said. "Come in. Take a seat, please."

He already knew her name. The officer at the front entrance would have informed him of her arrival. And his tone was indifferent, not welcoming. Or maybe Gina was reading more into it than she should have. It was difficult to remain positive when she already knew the outcome of this meeting. She took a deep breath and moved to the table. She set her coat and purse on one chair and took a seat in the other facing the chief. The uniformed officer moved to stand by the door.

"I'm Police Chief Bruce Stanford," he said, extending his hand to her.

I know. Why are you here and not Roger? she thought. "Nice to meet you," Gina said, shaking his hand. Her palm was sweaty. Just like during her meeting with Sergeant Jim Slater when she went to see Nick. And like him, the chief didn't seem to notice the damp handshake. Gina knew who he was but had never met him in person. He was all business this morning. She noticed that he didn't bother introducing the uniformed officer.

Apparently, this meeting was going to be short and to the point. She was being let go of her position with the crime lab. They had sent the chief to dispense with the unpleasant task instead of someone from the human resources department. Or maybe he had requested to do it. Either way, the outcome for her wasn't good.

Gina wished Roger had at least been able to be present for this meeting. She would have liked the opportunity to thank him for everything he had done for her over the course of her short career at the lab. She would call him the minute she left the building.

Chief Stanford bent to the side of his chair where a box sat on the floor filled with different sized manila envelopes. He rifled through the envelopes. "This won't take long, Miss Teducci. We'll have you on your way shortly."

Gina deflated. So, they were letting her go. She would be unemployed. He seemed flip about the prospect of terminating her employment. She supposed he had to be. From the look of the box beside him, he had quite a few of these meetings to take care of today.

Gina felt a knot form in her throat. She tried imagining her future with this termination on her record. She wouldn't be rehired by another state agency. They would frown at her involvement in a case where documents and testimony had been falsified. Her career as she knew it was over. Just like Nick's. She swallowed once and cleared her throat, trying to dislodge the ache. She couldn't get emotional now.

"Here we go," he said.

The chief pulled a manila envelope from the box and placed it on the desk. It had her name spelled out in black block letters. Under her name, the word "CONFIDENTIAL" was stamped in red letters. The chief pushed the envelope to her.

"This is for you to take with you," he said. "Confidential means just that, Miss Teducci." He tapped his hand lightly on the envelope. "You are to share whatever contents are in this envelope with no one. Is that clear?"

Gina only nodded in acceptance. She suddenly felt small and insignificant. She wasn't sure she wanted to open the envelope or read the contents. *Contents,* she thought. He made it sound so official. Final was more like it. Why didn't he just come out and say what it was? It's not like it was a surprise or anything.

Maybe she would set it aside for a while. Bask in the light of the idea that she still had her job. One last fleeting…*No,* she thought. She would tear it open, read it, and accept it. Like ripping off a band aid. Better sooner than later to come to terms with this whole unpleasant mess.

Certainly, the state would want her taking care of the "contents" right away. It would contain instructions on where to go, who to see, and what to do once she was stripped of her credentials as a forensic lab technician.

Most likely she would have to report back with the F.B.I. after meeting with the detective's bureau. It was all coming to an end, and it had barely gotten started for her. She felt sad and hollow inside.

"That's all I have for you, Miss Teducci," the chief was saying. "Sergeant Donnelly here will escort you out of the building."

He wasn't even going to discuss what was in the envelope. Explain any circumstance with her or wish her well. Just an envelope to open on her own time. Time she wouldn't be compensated for, but that's not what mattered to her.

What mattered was that she was now an ex-employee of the state. A career she worked hard to attain. A career she enjoyed and would certainly miss. Chief Stanford didn't owe her any explanation. If anyone did, it was Nick. He was the reason she sat here today being handed her walking papers.

"I…um," she cleared her throat again. "I have some personal things that I left at my cubicle. Is it ok to collect those before I leave?"

"Sure," the chief said. "Sergeant Donnelly can escort you."

Gina nodded again. She stood, collected her coat, purse, and the confidential envelope. She was near tears but fought to keep her composure. "It's been a pleasure working here, sir. Thank you."

He gave her a quizzical look. "You're welcome, Miss Teducci."

Obviously, he wanted her to leave before she became emotional. Gina exited the room. Sergeant Donnelly followed close behind. They made their way to her cubicle on the opposite side of the lab. Gina gathered up the few photos that were on her desk and scooped up her bamboo plant. Sergeant Donnelly escorted her the entire way to the exit, holding the door for her as she left the building.

"Thanks," she said, barely containing tears as she rushed past him and out to her car.

She quickly unlocked the door and climbed inside, pushing her things over to the passenger seat before slamming the car door shut. She leaned her head back on the headrest and sobbed. She felt so empty now. Like she had no purpose suddenly. It was an awful feeling.

When her emotional outburst subsided, she wiped her tears and picked up the envelope. CONFIDENTIAL. Those bold red letters leaped off the envelope like a sentencing. She carefully tore the top open and removed the documents. The cover sheet had a bold-typed paragraph that instructed "READ THIS PAGE FIRST."

Gina read through the bold print. It was clear, concise instructions that indicated if the envelope had been opened prior to her receiving it, she was to report it to the authorities named within the document immediately. The remaining bold print instructed her to not discuss or share any part of the contents with anyone. Under no circumstance was she to leave any portion of the contents unattended at any time whatsoever.

Pretty explicit for termination papers, Gina thought. She flipped to the next page. The top of the page read "Temporary Transfer or Assignment of Duties." Gina read through the document, then had to reread it once more before it sank in. She wasn't being terminated. She still had a job with the lab. Only, it wasn't the Hamilton County lab.

"Atlanta, Georgia?" Gina said out loud. "What the…?"

She flipped through the remaining pages of the documents. She was to report to the Atlanta, Georgia Crime Lab Headquarters in Decatur as soon as possible. Her flight, hotel, and rental car had already been arranged. Per diem and expenses would be compensated. Her salary would remain the same. Her hours of operation had "flexible" entered. Gina wasn't sure what that meant. The next item got her attention. Dates of assignment read "Start: Immediately. End Date: Open."

What did that mean? Gina wondered. *Open? Will I be staying in Georgia forever?* The remaining pages held an employment application and all pertinent documents required for a new hire.

The questions came flooding. Why Georgia? How did this happen? Why me? What do I say to everyone I know? What about my friends? My parents and family? My co-workers? My landlord? If I can't talk to anyone about this, what do I tell them? And *why* can't I tell anyone about this? It's just a job reassignment. What's the big deal?

But then Gina thought about it some more. Maybe not everyone in the lab was receiving reassignments. Maybe some *were* being terminated. But then why was she spared? Or maybe *she* was the only one being reassigned. Maybe everyone else was returning to the Hamilton County lab *except* for her. Had they found something during their investigation already? Maybe they were protecting her from something…or someone. Or maybe they were singling her out for some reason. Her imagination was getting the best of her. She was starting to freak herself out.

None of this was making sense. She flipped back to the second page. The bottom right corner had a box with information on who to contact with questions. It was blank. No phone number, name, email…nothing.

So, who the hell was she supposed to contact with questions? She filtered through the remaining pages of the document again. It only contained the employment application with instructions to have all pages completed prior to arriving for work. Nothing with contact information.

What about the person to contact if the envelope had been tampered with? Gina thought. She returned to the front of the document and found Chief of Police Bruce Stanford's name, but no phone number or email address.

How can they leave that information out? Gina thought. *Obviously, the moron who put this document together should be terminated.* She was mentally lashing out. Wanting to blame someone for missing information. Gina placed the documents back in the envelope.

She really wanted to blame someone for turning her life upside down. And one name quickly came to mind. Nick Casey. She grabbed her purse and exited her car. She walked back to the entrance door. The officer with the iPad was there to greet her once again.

"Excuse me. But can I go back in and speak with Police Chief Stanford? I have some questions."

"One moment," he said as he checked his iPad again.

"It's Gina Teducci. You just let me in a little while ago."

"I'm sorry, but you've been removed from the list of approved personnel."

"Are you kidding me?" Gina scoffed.

"I'm sorry, Miss Teducci, but I can't allow you to enter the building."

"This is crazy. I was just in there with him. I walked out to my car but didn't leave the lot." She held up the envelope. "I just have a few questions and his name is…" Gina stopped herself. She realized she was about to give out confidential information. *Shit.*

The officer was waiting for her to finish.

"His name is the only one I can remember," Gina covered with a lame excuse.

"I'm sorry. Like I said, I can't allow you to enter."

Great. Now what? Gina thought. "Thank you," she said and walked back to her car. She wouldn't make a scene. She wouldn't jeopardize the fact she had been spared from losing her job. *But to what degree?* she wondered.

What would Atlanta have in store for her? And why Atlanta? She was being sent to a city that she had no ties to. It was like someone hit the reset button on her career...on her life, without her consent. She liked the life she had in Jersey. She wanted to keep that life, not start a new one.

She would miss her co-workers: Roger and Claire and the other techs she worked with. Starting a new job all over again, learning their procedures, working alongside new people wasn't sounding appealing at all. She had barely gotten her feet wet at the Hamilton County lab and now she was having to do it all over again. Her life was being tossed into turmoil and she couldn't share one detail about it.

What a giant shitstorm Nick had created for all of them. Not to mention everyone else involved with the trial. Gina supposed she should feel lucky. She thought about all the people who were suddenly having their lives upended. She supposed Nick's had been as well. He was in prison now. Everything had changed and not for the good.

Gina got back to her car and climbed in, setting her purse and the envelope on the passenger seat. Her bamboo plant was lying upside down on the floor. Dirt and water scattered across the floor mat. It must have gotten tossed when she threw everything on the seat earlier. She left it there. She didn't care now. She pulled her door shut. She started the car and drove off. Atlanta was waiting for her.

CHAPTER 13

Gina's flight touched down at Hartsfield-Jackson Atlanta International Airport. She plucked her phone from her purse. It was nine thirty p.m. It took her another hour to exit the plane, pick up her luggage in baggage claim, and rent a car. She was given a Ford Explorer. A roomy SUV. Much larger than her Honda. This would take some getting used to, but she liked it.

It had more technology than her four-year-old Honda, but most of it was easy to figure out. And what she didn't figure out didn't matter. She didn't plan on needing the SUV for long.

Traffic was marginal on the drive to the hotel. She'd taken the time at home to research her hotel, the route to the hotel from Atlanta's airport and her surrounding area where she'd be staying, prior to heading to the airport. It made navigating through an unknown city much easier. She arrived at the hotel fifteen minutes later. She checked in and went to her room. Room three forty-five.

Gina entered, flicked on the lights, and wheeled her luggage inside. She locked the door and looked around at the space she would call home for the time being. It was modern and smelled like new carpeting. A spacious kitchenette suite with a separate king bedroom. She looked out the window. There wasn't much to see this time of night except the other hotels nearby.

She unpacked, hanging some clothes in the bedroom closet, and folding some into the dresser drawers. She unpacked toiletries and took a hot shower. She had eaten at home before flying out. Her last meal at home until who knew when.

She had emptied out her apartment refrigerator, took out the trash, and watered her plants before leaving. She hoped they would survive until she got back. She even vacuumed and dusted, leaving her place clean and organized for her return. Hopefully, that wouldn't be long. Megan had a key to her place so, she could always ask her to stop by and check on things if this reassignment took longer than…Gina didn't want to finish that sentence.

She let the hot water stream down her back. She was already missing her apartment. Her creature comforts. Her daily routine. She hadn't even been gone twenty-four hours yet.

She climbed into bed, still wide awake. The shower did nothing to rid her of her anxiety. It was too quiet. Like solitary confinement. She flicked on the wall-mounted television and lowered the volume to create white noise. She lay awake, staring at the ceiling, watching the glow from the television flicker.

She had called her mother and Megan earlier in the day to let them know she'd be gone for a few days, possibly a week. She told them that she had a New Jersey-related case to work on in Los Angeles with Roger and Claire. She had lied to them and it felt rotten. She promised to call and check in as her work allowed.

She had no idea what to expect tomorrow. No idea how long she would be in Atlanta. Her reassignment was *"open,"* which was noncommittal.

Plucked from her career and her life and stowed away in this hotel by authorities she most likely had never even met, and she couldn't reach out to anyone. Like she'd been imprisoned for some wrongdoing.

It made her think of Nick. She wondered how he was handling prison. Now that she was eight hundred miles away from New Jersey, she wasn't sure when she would be able to go see him. And even though he had told her not to visit him in prison, she had every intention of doing so. She still wanted answers to her questions. Only now she wasn't sure when that could happen. She rolled over and eventually fell asleep.

When her phone alarm went off the next morning, Gina woke with a start. She'd tossed and turned most of the night and felt like she'd only had five minutes of sleep. She fumbled for her cellphone. The jazzy little jingle kept getting louder by the second. Her fingers found the button and turned it off. Peeking one eye open told her it was five thirty. She threw the covers off, letting cool air invade her warm cocoon. If she allowed herself two extra minutes under those covers, she would fall right back to sleep. She pulled herself out of bed and was showered, dressed, and ready to leave in an hour.

She made a quick stop at the hotel breakfast bar to grab some fruit, a pastry, and coffee to go, then she left the hotel. Inside her SUV, she punched the crime lab's address into the GPS. She was on the road sitting in traffic on the highway twenty minutes later.

My first day at a new job, she thought. The completed application sat on the passenger seat. She had left the remaining documents from the confidential package in the safe in her room along with her Walther PK380 handgun. She wanted to get her clearance before bringing it to the lab.

Gina arrived at the Atlanta lab way earlier than expected. It had taken her only forty minutes with traffic. She would sleep a little longer tomorrow. She checked in and was introduced to Sophia Ramos who was a mid-forties petite Puerto Rican with flawless skin and dark features. She was polite but firm. Gina imagined she ran a tight ship around the lab.

Sophia would be her new supervisor. Her new Roger. She introduced Gina to several other lab technicians. Gina was sure she wouldn't remember anyone's name by the end of the day.

Most of her morning was spent filling out paperwork with the human resources department, taking a drug/alcohol test, having her fingerprints taken for the background search, and having a cubicle assigned to her.

Her cubicle was smaller than the one she had at the Hamilton lab. And it would remain pretty much the way it was. A laptop, phone, calculator, and a wall calendar. Any personal items she used to decorate her space at the Hamilton lab remained at home. She wouldn't make it too comfortable, because she didn't plan on staying too long. Case files would eventually fill the drawers and floor space. She made out her list of required office supplies as Sophia had asked.

Listening to the bustle of the crime lab beyond the cubicles made her homesick for the Hamilton lab. She kept waiting for Roger or Claire to walk by, or anyone that she recognized from her previous job. But of course, that wouldn't happen. At least it was comforting to hear the familiar sounds again.

Her meeting with Chief Stanford yesterday had been upsetting. The lab sitting quiet and dark had been depressing. She was glad that was behind her now. *One day at a time,* she kept telling herself. Pretty soon she would be hitting her stride again here in Atlanta. Things would get better. And by then she would hopefully be returning to New Jersey.

"Are you still working on that list?" Sophia asked.

"I am," Gina said, handing her the short list.

Sophia reviewed it. "That's it?"

"I don't require much."

"Suit yourself," she replied. "Come on. I'll give you a tour of the lab and then get you to work."

Walking through the corridors, Sophia pointed out, speaking in a brisk manner, "The drug chemistry lab where we analyze submissions for presence or absence of controlled substances." She turned to her left. "Across the hall here is the biological sciences section. We'll come back to that since it's where you'll be working."

Gina was well-acquainted with all criminal lab sectors, but it couldn't hurt to get the full tour and learn her way around Atlanta's. She glanced at the biological lab where she would be stationed. It was a modern facility with state-of-the art equipment, much like the Hamilton lab. Aside from a different interior design palette, it was pretty much the same.

She followed Sophia down the corridor of glass partitions. "Criminalistics is in here," Sophia said as they entered the workspace. "We have this separated out into five subsections." She pointed them out. "Hair and fiber analysis there, paint and polymer analysis here, glass and fire debris analysis right there, shoe print and tire track comparisons over there, and here is food and product tampering."

Gina nodded, familiar with the set up.

"This way," Sophia continued.

Gina followed her to a closed- off room.

"Firearms identification section here for examining any physical evidence related to the illegal use of guns and weapons." She held the door open for Gina to enter. "And of course, for testing all types of guns and ammunition as well as fired ammunition components recovered from shooting scenes."

Gina stood in the middle of the room that resembled a small shooting range. The walls were reinforced and insulated to muffle the explosion of gun fire when testing firearms. The workstation included their testing equipment and computers to report their findings in the national database.

"I think this is a better set up than Hamilton's," Gina said.

"Come on." Sophia exited the room and continued down the corridor. She cut across the lab to another corridor. "In here is the questioned documents section, to examine any kind of writing or print, and the materials containing that writing or print." She moved to the next room. "And here we have the trace evidence section, which I'm sure you're familiar with."

"I am," Gina replied. She'd spent plenty of time at the Hamilton lab performing trace analysis tests on materials like paint, glass, hairs, fibers, gunshot residue…physical comparisons of a material, fire debris for accelerants, and impressions for foot and tire tracks. She found it fascinating and enjoyed the science of it.

Sophia stopped outside the room. "We'll stay out here since we're not covered up."

Gina watched three forensic scientists dressed in full protective gear working with microscopes and instruments, testing evidence samples.

Sophia pinched her arm. "Moving on."

They continued down the corridor, stopping at a large classroom. "We use this room for the crime scene section. The team meets in here to discuss cases, evidence, and testimony. We also use this for proficiency training of all our personnel."

Gina poked her head into the room. A group of scientists and lab techs sat around the conference table discussing their case. An overhead projector displayed photos of a bloody crime scene. *A violent shootout,* Gina surmised.

"And way down here," Sophia waved a hand over her head, pointing down the hallway as they walked to a solid metal door. "Is the collision reconstruction garage." She pushed through the metal door. Gina followed close behind.

Much like the Hamilton lab, the garage resembled an auto lube and tune facility. Three car lifts, an underground pit for draining car fluids, and two walls of equipment. Some for mechanical purposes and some for computer analysis and reporting. A mid-nineties Caprice was on one of the lifts. The garage smelled of gas fumes, chemicals, and decay.

"The Caprice was involved in a suicide," Sophia said. "It's obvious what happens in here."

"Reconstructing collisions and recovering evidence from car-related crimes," Gina answered.

"Yep. Let's get you set up in the lab," Sophia said, as she reentered the lab. They made their way back around to the biological lab and entered the glass-walled room.

"We utilize polymerase chain reaction technique for all DNA testing." She looked to Gina. "Hamilton uses the same, doesn't it?"

"We do." Another piece of equipment Gina was familiar with. This was her comfort zone. The PCR Thermo Cycler processed samples of blood, semen, or saliva. Evidence coming from homicides, sexual assaults, home invasions, assaults, burglaries…hit and run fatalities… even from human remains that the medical examiner was working on.

"Looking familiar?" Sophia asked as she walked Gina to the U-shaped workstation.

Gina nodded yes, feeling her anxiety subsiding by the minute.

Sophia continued. "The PCR Workstation here minimizes cross-contamination of evidence." Her hands motioned non-stop, indicating as she spoke. "Two microscopes here." She said, pointing them out as they walked to the opposite side of the workstation. "And over here…"

"This for CODIS." Gina pointed out the computer equipment.

"Yes," Sophia answered. "If your DNA doesn't link you to a suspect in the FBI's National DNA Index System, then you enter their profile in the combined DNA Index System database here."

"Right," Gina said. She was beginning to feel like herself again.

"The laptop at your cubicle is only used for clocking in and out and research," Sophia said. "This computer here," she referenced the one set up next to the CODIS computer. "Is for you to input all case evidence and reports. This one is linked to all the lab sectors. All case information goes in here."

"Same as Hamilton," Gina replied.

Sophia pointed towards the far side of the lab. "A printer, scanner, and copier machine are over there for everyone to use. And coolers and cabinets for storing samples." She turned back to Gina. "Any questions so far?"

"No. It's everything I'm familiar with."

"Good," she replied. "Let's grab your lab gear and get you to work."

Sophia got her set up with a lab coat, gloves, and protective eye wear from the supply room. They returned to the biological lab.

"Samples are dropped in here unless it's handed to you by one of the scientists." Sophia referred to a large metal basket on one of the lab tables. "Some cases require a rush. If there's any you don't get to by the end of the day, place them in the proper storage."

She plucked one of the sealed evidence envelopes and handed it to Gina.

"I'll oversee your first few days."

Gina took the evidence envelope and went to work, cutting blood samples from two different articles of clothing and from three pieces of a car's interior parts. The case involved a carjacking fiasco.

She also tested semen samples from bed sheets of a rape case and cotton swabs of saliva pertaining to the same investigation. Before she knew it, the day was over. She had run tests on eight separate samples and entered her findings in the case files on the computer.

Sophia had micro-managed the entire time. It would take some getting used to, having someone standing over her shoulder watching her every move. Gina felt like she'd taken a giant step backwards in her career.

At the Hamilton lab, she had been on her own for over two years. She missed having a supervisor who was confident in her work. But it would come again. She just needed to be patient.

"Tomorrow won't be so crazy," Sophia said. "You can join us for lunch. Get to know the team."

"I'd like that," Gina replied. "Thank you."

"Ok. Quittin' time, kiddo. See you tomorrow," Sophia said. "Oh, and Gina?"

Gina looked over to her as she was shedding her lab gear.

"If anyone asks you about what happened at Hamilton…"

"I don't know anything."

"Right. And I want to know who's asking."

Gina accepted her request, then left the lab to collect her things in her cubicle. She clocked out on her laptop and left for the day, walking out to her SUV. She'd survived day one. It could only get better from here. Sophia had seemed impatient at times, but Gina assumed that came from the responsibility of overseeing the crime lab. She was quite the opposite of Roger and that would take some getting used to. In the end, Gina was thankful to still be working in a crime lab. It certainly beat the alternative.

CHAPTER 14

Gina stopped at a grocery store on the way back to the hotel. She picked up items to cook dinner in her room for the next few nights. Dining out alone didn't appeal to her, especially in a strange new city. She also grabbed some wine, bottled water, snacks, yogurt, and fruit.

On her way back to her car, Gina scanned the parking lot. She couldn't shake a feeling that someone was following her. Being unfamiliar with her surroundings and knowing no one, was unsettling. She was letting her imagination get the best of her.

She got back to the hotel, put the groceries away, then changed into workout clothes. She hit the hotel gym for some weights and cardio exercises for an hour. Sticking to her workout routine brought a sense of normalcy. She returned to her room and showered, then made a bowl of pasta with fresh tomatoes and basil and opened a bottle of wine.

She'd missed the evening news, but not catching any highlights of Friday's mistrial didn't bother her. She could search online for information, but she just wanted to put that aside for the time being. Gina selected a movie to watch instead. *Gone in Sixty Seconds.* She'd seen it before, but that didn't matter. It was action and entertainment.

Gina sat alone at the small dining table, eating her dinner, and drinking her wine. She couldn't wait to go back to work in the morning. This hotel living was going to try her patience. She felt like a lab rat undergoing isolation analysis.

She finished dinner and took her plate to the sink. There was a knock on her door. She looked out the peephole. She didn't recognize the man.

He was tall. At least six foot one or two. Dark hair and skin. Maybe Hispanic, maybe African American. It was hard to tell. The hallway lighting cast down behind him, making him out to be a shadowed silhouette. He held up a badge for her to see through the peep hole and knocked again.

Gina couldn't make out the badge information. "Who is it?" she asked.

"Detective Reuben Alvarez. Atlantic City P.D."

Atlantic City, not Atlanta, Gina thought. *Something to do with one of her cases back in New Jersey, possibly? But why was he here?* "What is this regarding?"

"Can you open the door so I can explain?"

No. I don't know you and I wasn't expecting you. Gina was on guard now. It was possible he was here on the lab's behalf, but there should have been a call from the front desk letting her know someone was here to see her. How would he have known her room number? *Shit!* A trace of panic rippled through her. Was there no end to the stress she'd been enduring?

"Give me a minute."

Gina bolted to the bedroom and to the safe. She quickly entered her five-digit code and wrenched open the door. She snatched up her gun, checked her magazine, reloaded the gun, then made her way back to the door, loading a bullet into the chamber.

She unlocked the deadbolt and then the latch. She kept the gun concealed behind her as she opened the door to detective Alvarez. Gina was right. At least six foot two with the build of a pro linebacker. He was wearing a straw hat with a floral print shirt and khakis, looking more like a tourist than a detective. *Possibly private investigator or undercover,* Gina thought. *But why was he here to see her?*

"Gina Teducci?" he asked, tucking his credentials into his pants pocket.

"What is this about?"

"Is that you?"

"Yes."

"Can you come with me for a moment?"

"To where? Why?"

"Just down the hall. Room three twenty-seven. I need to discuss a case with you."

Gina hesitated. "Which case?"

"One you haven't been made aware of yet."

OK, this is getting weird now, she thought. "How did you know I was here?"

When he didn't answer, she started to close the door. "I'm sorry, but…"

His hand extended to keep her from closing him out. "It'll only take a minute."

Yeah, a minute to clobber me over the head and attack me, you sick pervert. She wasn't believing the detective bit. "At least tell me what it's about." *And then I'll decide if I trust you.*

"I can't. I have to show you."

"Evidence?" Gina asked. Her train of thought switching gears. "Did something happen in room three twenty-seven?"

"It's happening as we speak."

"What?"

He wasn't making sense. Apprehension was getting a grip on her. *How can a crime case only require a minute of her time?* She decided she wasn't trusting detective Alvarez and liking him even less. She wanted to call someone to verify who he was, but who? She had no contacts in Atlanta. At least none that she could trust to be looking out for her well-being. And no one in New Jersey was supposed to know of her assignment. She thought about calling the front desk.

"Please. Just follow me to the room. Like I said, it'll only take a minute. I'm pretty certain what you find there will answer your questions."

Not if you kill me. "Can I see your badge again?" she asked.

Reuben removed the leather wallet containing his badge and credentials. He opened and he held it up for her to review. *Atlantic City Police – Special Investigations number four five four five.* It looked authentic, but these days counterfeit credentials were hard to detect. Especially in a situation like this. She memorized his badge number.

"Special Investigations for what?" Gina looked up to him.

"Narcotics."

"A drug-related crime?"

He gave her a blank stare, seemingly becoming impatient.

"Give me a minute to change clothes," Gina said.

He agreed. Gina closed the door, locked it, and went to the living room. She set her gun on the coffee table and grabbed a small notepad and pen and jotted down the detective's name and badge number. She left it on the table, then went to the bedroom.

She changed out her yoga pants for jeans and pulled on a sweater and Sketchers. She returned to the living room and grabbed her gun, tucking it into her waistband. She put her cellphone in her pocket along with her room key and left the room.

She stayed two steps behind detective Alvarez, walking down the hallway to room three twenty-seven. Instinctively, she scanned the pale taupe walls, dizzying multi-colored carpet, and ceiling for clues to whatever crime she was about to investigate. Everything looked pristine. Like the hotel had just opened its doors the week before.

They arrived at room three twenty-seven. Reuben removed the room key, swiped it in the cardlock, and opened the door. He walked in first, then held the door for her. A tingle chased down Gina's spine, not knowing what to expect. But that happened anytime she arrived at a crime scene. Or it could have been the fact that she still didn't trust Alvarez.

She crossed the threshold and entered the room. A whiff of grilled onions carried through the room. The victim had been eating or had just finished eating a burger or sandwich or something with sautéed onions. It overpowered the new carpet smell that lingered in the hallway.

Reuben closed the door and walked past her into the room. Gina followed, her eyes scanning every inch of the room as she went. High-end computer equipment and files covered the dining room table. Visually examining surfaces for evidence, for clues, for...

"Nick?" She stopped abruptly. Her adrenaline amped up, seeing him standing there. He was clothed in jeans and a flannel shirt and not orange prison scrubs. His detective's badge was clipped to his belt. His police issued firearm was holstered in a shoulder harness.

"I assure you, Gina, this is legal," he said, reacting to her reaction.

Gina walked farther into the room, closer to him. "What is this, Nick? What are you doing here? How are you out of prison?"

Her eyes probed his face, neck, and hands for bruising or signs of having fought his way to escape, but there were none. In fact, he appeared to be fine. As if the whole prison ordeal never happened.

He looked over to Reuben. "You've met Reuben Alvarez."

Gina looked over to Reuben. "I…yes. Well, sort of," she whipped her head back around to Nick. "What the hell is going on here, Nick?"

"Give us a minute?" he asked Reuben.

"No problem," Reuben replied. "Gina."

He tipped his hat, then exited to the adjoining room through an interior door. There was commotion going on next door, but Gina wasn't interested in that right now. It also hit her that Nick hadn't referred to him as *detective*.

"Come and sit, Gina," Nick said, making his way to the fine tweed fabric sofa. The same gray one that furnished her room. He sat down and faced her.

"I'm having trouble with the fact you're sitting here in front of me, in this room. It's…"

"I know. I can explain," he said.

"Oh, so now you can explain? At the courthouse…"

"I couldn't say anything."

Gina didn't respond.

"You should probably take a seat," he suggested.

His tone sounded grave. A sinking sensation hit the pit of her stomach and her mouth was cotton dry suddenly. Her body seemed resistant to movement as she made her way to the sofa. She reached behind under her sweater and slid her gun from her waistband, setting it on the coffee table, and sat down.

Nick eyed her gun then raised his eyes to her. "Keep that with you at all times."

"I usually do. What's going on here? Is Alvarez really a detective?" she pointed towards the other room.

"I'll explain him and the others later."

Gina glanced over her shoulder towards the adjoining room. *There were others. And he didn't clarify Alvarez as being a detective, which told her...*

"For starters, I'm not on the run," he said. "You can relax. My being here is legal."

Gina turned back to him. "I..." She exhaled. She wasn't sure what to believe.

"Gina." He leaned forward with his elbows resting on his knees. "I would never put you in harm's way. I want you to know that."

His words carried a deep note of sincerity. Her posture relaxed some. She would give him the benefit of the doubt. Her adrenaline spike somewhat returned to normal. She would hear him out. Listen to whatever it was he came here to tell her.

"Ok," was all that she said. He seemed relieved to hear this.

"What I have to tell you, Gina," He paused, staring at her, unblinking. "It's, it's pretty hard to say."

Jesus, what?! Gina thought. "Explain to me how you got out of prison."

"I'll get to that. I just want to..."

"What?" Gina blurted out. "Just tell me, Nick. Say what you have to say." His beating around the bush was aggravating to no end.

"It's not by accident that you're here," he said. "In Atlanta."

"What does that...I was reassigned here. By the state."

"At my request," he said.

Gina's heart sank. An alarm went off inside her. "What do you mean?"

"I'm still working my investigation. Not the D.A.'s investigation. My private unofficial investigation."

Gina struggled to make sense of what he was telling her. *How did that involve her?*

"I'm still undercover," he said. "Everything to do with this. Everything to do with you. It's why you were instructed not to talk to anyone. You didn't talk to anyone, did you? Before coming here?"

"I...no. Well...yes. I did," Gina said. *Shit!* She couldn't think straight.

Nick straightened his posture, obviously not pleased with this bit of news. "Who'd you talk to?"

Gina suddenly felt small. "My mom, and Megan. She's a close friend of mine."

Nick chewed on this for a moment.

"But I didn't say anything," Gina responded quickly. "At least nothing about this. About coming here to Atlanta. I just said I had a case to work in Los Angeles. That I was going with Roger and Claire."

Nick winced at this.

"Really? Was that wrong?" she blurted out. "The instructions gave no indication as to what I was supposed to say, or not say." Gina was upset and pissed off. *How was she supposed to know?*

"OK, calm down." He held up his hands. "I'll handle that. Don't worry about it."

Gina scoffed. "It seems that all I've done lately is worry."

Nick leaned forward again. "Gina, I need to tell you about the investigation."

She searched his eyes. They were that cool steely blue again, like they had been at the courthouse. He seemed bothered by what he was about to tell her.

"This is about the mistrial," she said. "Joe D'Amato. This parallel investigation you said you're conducting."

"That's part of it," he said.

"You're here to tell me that you're working for Joe. To justify what you did in court to help him walk from the charges, and that you somehow want me to accept that."

"No."

"Then I don't understand. The lab had three key pieces of evidence linking Joe to multiple crimes," she said, holding up three fingers on her right hand. "One of them being a murder. The DNA doesn't lie, Nick. I tested some of that DNA. I know for a fact…"

"This has to do with Joe, yes," he said, interrupting her. "But it involves your family, too."

Gina flinched. It was a bold accusation. "How so?"

Nick paused, as if to choose his words carefully. "This has to do with your sister Sirrina. Some of it, anyways." He thought for a moment, then said, "A lot of it, actually."

"Sirrina?" Gina asked. This threw her for a loop. "That was so long ago." She barely whispered the words.

"I know," Nick said. "But something came up that…well…it was cause for me to re-investigate what happened to her. Guiseppe as well."

"Guiseppe?" Gina asked. "Joe's nephew?" She felt the air escape her lungs. "He's the one who…" Her throat tightened. Tears formed in her eyes. "I can't believe you're sitting here telling me this, Nick. It hurts, you know that, right?"

"Gina," Nick said. "I need you to stay focused here. Listen to what I'm about to tell you."

Gina wasn't so sure she wanted to hear what he had to say. Her insides churned. She wiped her eyes with shaking hands. But after a moment she reconsidered. As much as she was hesitant to know what he was going to tell her, she wanted to know. She inhaled a deep breath and prepared to listen to him.

"I need you on board with this, Gina, because I'm going to need your help, ok?"

"Ok." Her voice was strained. Her nose was running. She reached for a Kleenex on the side table and wiped her nose. She seemed to do that a lot. Like worrying.

"There were questions surrounding the yacht explosion at Lincoln Marina," Nick continued. "The explosion that killed Sirrina, Guiseppe and his two friends. Questions that I was hired, privately, to investigate."

Gina considered this. "Joe?" she said. "But it was an accident. That's what the investigation found. I've read the reports myself."

Nick was quiet.

"You found otherwise?" Gina asked.

"Maybe."

"Maybe?" Gina nearly shouted.

"I'm still investigating."

Gina let his words sink in, then she backed down. "What do you know then? What can you tell me?"

"You're undercover now, too, Gina," he said. "No one can know what we're doing here. And no one can know what I'm about to tell you. Is that clear?"

His intensity scared her. "Understood," she said.

"A string of events led to Sirrina's abduction from the Wildwoods," Nick said. "The yacht explosion at Lincoln Marina was a cover-up. Guiseppe and his friends were murdered. It wasn't an accident."

Gina felt like she'd just been pushed off a cliff. Her heart skipped erratically in her chest. "Sirrina, too," she whispered.

Nick was quiet.

"Nick?" she asked. "Sirrina too, right?" Nick's expression caused her anxiety to spike.

"Gina, there's a chance Sirrina wasn't on board the yacht."

She gasped. "What?"

Nick pressed his hands together, interlocking his fingers. His knuckles turned white from the pressure. They were strong hands. And she focused on them to deflect from what he was telling her.

"Gina?"

"Where would she...what happened to her then?" Gina heard herself ask.

"It's why we're here, Gina," Nick said.

Gina was reeling from his words. An ache balled up in her throat. He was being vague. Or she was having trouble understanding what he was telling her. Either way, it was driving her mad.

"Why are we here, Nick? What happened to Sirrina?" she demanded, lifting her eyes to meet his.

"The people who took her that night." Nick paused, grappling with how best to tell her.

"Just say it, Nick," Gina nearly growled.

"They're part of a trafficking ring," Nick said.

"I don't understand." It was a knee-jerk response. She *did* understand what trafficking meant, but...

"They sold her," Nick said.

Gina was certain she was dreaming. Any moment now, her alarm would sound, waking her up. That jazzy little jingle that annoyed her. Now she wanted to hear it more than anything. Maybe the high-pitched ringing coming from somewhere was it and it just sounded different now. She couldn't place it. Numbness enveloped her and the room spun. It was a strange sensation for a dream.

"Gina." Nick reached out and took hold of her hands. "Take a deep breath. Come on." He squeezed her hands.

His touch startled her. She was unaware that she'd stopped breathing. His voice sounded hollow. Distant. She sucked in a deep breath.

"Another one." He squeezed her hands again.

Gina did. Followed by a few more ragged breaths. The room slowly stopped spinning. She eventually regained control. And when she did, she began crying. It wasn't a dream. It was a nightmare. He pulled her close and held her. Gina wasn't sure what was worse, Sirrina's abduction and murder sixteen years ago, or this news. Nick held her tight, letting her cry until the tears finally subsided. She backed away, wiping her eyes. She reached for more Kleenex and blew her nose. Nick's words echoed in her head.

"What...what does this mean, Nick? Is she..." Gina couldn't bring herself to utter the words. The shock of it all still had a grip on her.

"Gina, we can't get our hopes up here," he said. "It's been sixteen years."

Gina couldn't help but think her sister may still be alive, but she was afraid to say it. Afraid she might jinx any chances of finding her.

"Gina?" Nick squeezed her hands again.

Gina raised her eyes to him.

"We're here on the slightest possibility that Sirrina may still be alive," he said. "And I stress slightest. Ok?"

"Why here? Why Atlanta?" Gina asked. Her voice was raspy from crying.

"It's where the evidence is leading me. An informant gave up the name of the man she was sold to," Nick said. "Atlanta's his playground."

Gina wished he had chosen a better word than playground. But she looked to him now in a much different light. He wasn't the bad guy at all. Quite the opposite, in fact. He was here solving her sister's murder. A murder that had supposedly been solved sixteen years ago. A murder she had wanted Joe D'Amato to pay for, because his nephew Guiseppe had caused Sirrina's death.

"What about Joe's trial?" Gina asked. "Was it true what you said? The evidence and testimony had been falsified?"

"It was," he replied. "People are going to pay for that. But that's another matter altogether. That'll wait until I'm finished solving this piece of the investigation. Or at least until I'm satisfied that I've exhausted all efforts in doing so."

Gina's heart lifted a little. She appreciated hearing those words. "You said Sirrina wasn't on board the yacht when it exploded. Is there any chance Guiseppe and his friends weren't either?" she asked with hope.

Nick released her hands. She hadn't realized he was still holding them.

"No," he said positively. "Their bodies were recovered and identified just as the investigation reported."

She had only been twelve when it happened. Some of what she learned about that night was from her family and news reports. But it wasn't until she was in college working as an intern in the crime lab that she was able to learn more details from reading archived reports.

She didn't remember reading about any doubts as to Sirrina having been on board. They had recovered children's clothing from the water. It had been assumed it was Sirrina's clothing. But what trace evidence had they found? Gina couldn't remember the reports mentioning that.

She recalled how the crime scene had been critically compromised by the port police and the public. Much of the evidence was either destroyed in the explosion, damaged in the water, floated away in the Hudson's current, or eaten by marine life.

And Gina never thought to question that after being trained as a forensic scientist. Guilt consumed her now. Apparently, no one had thought of this during the investigation, either. It was a sickening realization. And now Nick's investigation was uncovering an entirely different result. She wondered what this would bring.

"Who do you think was behind the set up?" Gina asked.

Nick was quiet.

"Do you know?" she probed.

"Let's just say that I'm not ready to say yet."

"What kind of answer is that?" Gina snapped at him. She studied him for a moment. His expression told her that he knew, or at least knew something. "It's someone I know," she said. It was a statement, not a question.

"I'm trying to keep you safe, Gina," he said. "Don't go asking too many questions."

"How can you expect me not to?" she shot back at him. "It's what I do for a living."

"I'm only going to give you information that I think you need to know, as you need to know it."

"That's…" she stopped herself. She reconsidered the remark she was about to fling at him. She had to imagine he was taking a huge risk including an amateur as part of his investigative team. Which made her wonder. "Why am I here?"

"I was getting to that," he said. "For two reasons. You're going to be analyzing DNA samples as we get them."

"From?"

He didn't answer.

"At the lab?" Gina asked. "They know why I'm here?"

"No. Like I said, no one knows the truth. Don't talk to anyone about this, especially at the lab. As far as they're concerned, you're here on a temporary transfer because the Hamilton lab is closed for an investigation that you're not a part of. Your limited experience only allows you to test DNA samples and find matches."

"But that's not true," she cut him off.

His patience was unwinding. "I know. This is your cover here. You only have experience to work in the DNA lab. We don't want you out in the field on crime scenes collecting evidence on cases that we're not here to work. We need you testing DNA. It's the only way for us to get a positive I.D. And you're the only one who can access NDIS and CODIS. The lab is only aware there's an ongoing investigation into trying to bust up a trafficking ring. Around here, that's everyday business. They don't know about me and they can't. All they know is that when you find a match, you'll report it to Reuben Alvarez. His role in this is lead detective on the case that the samples will reference. He's part of my crew that's here working with me on this."

"There's a crew?" Gina asked.

Nick smiled at her. It was touching. It was the first time either of them had a light moment between them.

"There is," he said. "I can't do this alone. And I'm the only one of the crew that can log into the system. If I do, I'll be flagged and identified here in Atlanta, and we don't want that."

"I'll be flagged and identified, too," Gina said.

"Right. But you have a reason for being here and searching the database."

Gina thought for a moment. "You said you and I are the only ones who can access the database," Gina said. "What about *detective* Alvarez?" Gina was sure to put emphasis on the word detective.

"My guys work in the private sector. That's all I'm going to say."

Gina understood. "What will you be doing?" she asked.

His expression quickly turned grim. "Nothing you want to know about."

Gina instinctively looked to his gun and badge. "Will you be safe?"

"I hope so."

Gina raised her eyes to him, not liking the sound of doubt in his words. "Tell me you're going to be safe," she insisted.

"I can't, Gina, and I won't," he replied. "You know that there are no guarantees in this line of work."

There was a long silence before she spoke again. It was a truth she found hard to accept.

"What's the second thing I'll be doing?" she asked.

"We'll need to take photos of your face to have on our phones for identifying..."

He didn't finish his sentence. Gina withdrew, feeling violated by the thought. She wasn't sure how to respond.

"I know this sounds bad, Gina, but it's our best chance at finding Sirrina. As kids, the two of you could have been twins. Even though you're four years apart, the resemblance was obvious. We're hoping that resemblance still exists, at least to some degree."

Gina understood now. "I'll do whatever you need, Nick."

"I was hoping you'd say that," he replied. "We need to do this tonight."

CHAPTER 15

Gina followed Nick into the adjoining room. Room three twenty-five. This was where the onion aroma was coming from. Pizza boxes lay open on the kitchen counter of a double room just like the one she had come from with Nick. The décor and layout were the same as hers, except hers had a king bed.

Reuben Alvarez sat at the dining room table with another man. Two laptop computers occupied their attention. A folding table held a printer and electrical equipment Gina didn't recognize. One other man sat on the couch, preparing field case test kits. The coffee table was cluttered with camera equipment, binoculars, and files. Command central for their investigation.

"Guys, I want you to meet Gina Teducci," Nick said to the three men. "You already know Reuben."

Reuben stood up from the dining room table and walked to her, extending his hand. "Pleasure again."

Gina laughed. "Was it the first time?" She didn't think so. He scared the crap out of her.

"Absolutely," he replied, then returned to his seat.

Nick introduced Chico Ruiz next. He was lean and heavily tattooed. He stood and shook Gina's hand. "Nice to meet you, Gina." His artwork was fascinating. She would ask him about it at some point.

"And over here we have Maurice Williams." Nick referred to the hulking African American man occupying the couch. Case boxes of buccal test swabs, hand sanitizer, latex gloves, tweezers, plastic tubes, and a variety of evidence envelopes lay strewn on the floor space around his feet and on part of the coffee table.

He stood and side-stepped the clutter on the floor, extending his hand. "Call me Ice."

"Ice. Got it," Gina replied. His powerful build, like Reuben's, had Gina feeling a little better knowing these guys would be backing Nick. Not that it appeared Nick couldn't take care of himself.

"Have a seat at the table there with Chico," Nick said, referring to the dining room table.

Reuben pulled a chair out for her. "Thank you," she said as she took a seat.

Nick and Reuben took up the other two chairs, joining them. Chico's fingers were flying over the laptop keys. She glanced to Nick who was watching her, almost gaging her reactions to the situation. She had plenty of questions she still wanted to ask him, but it would wait until later.

Chico turned the laptop towards her. "I'll need your access, Gina," he said.

The FBI national database home page was on the screen, prompting for an identification. Gina looked to Chico. "You have FBI clearance?"

"Not in this case," Chico replied.

"How did you do that? Hack into the FBI's database?"

All three of them looked to Nick. "It's what he does, Gina." Nick replied. "Computer hacking and cyber terrorism."

Gina brought her attention back to Chico. "And using my login information doesn't trace this back to you," Gina stated, understanding.

"Right. None of the agencies can know it's me logging in," Chico said. "Most of my assignments…"

"She doesn't need to know about." Nick cut him off.

Gina weighed his response and decided not to test his patience. She turned back to Chico.

"Agencies? Plural?" Gina asked Chico. "Meaning?"

"Meaning FBI, Homeland Security, DEA, and ATF," Nick replied.

"Should I just speak to you?" she directed her question at Nick.

He didn't respond, but his expression came across loud and clear.

"Just so you know, this is way above my pay grade." Gina positioned the laptop so she could type. "I'm not sure you'll be able to access the information you're looking for through my credentials." She began typing her login information.

"I took care of that," Chico said.

Gina stopped typing and looked over to him. "What does that mean?"

"It means you have top level security clearances," Nick replied, as if she had just asked for the time of day.

Gina suddenly felt at odds. A strange mix of emotions were brewing. Her suspicions were raised. It was like walking barefoot through a swamp at midnight, not sure of where her next step would land her.

"Is this...am I...?" She wasn't sure she wanted to ask.

"You're not doing anything illegal." Nick finished her thought for her.

"How is it...? Never mind." She wanted to know how he managed getting her clearance, but thought about his earlier comment. She wouldn't ask too many questions. Instead, she finished logging in on Chico's laptop then spun it back to him.

Chico positioned the laptop, and his fingers began to fly over the keys once more.

"Can I get you something to drink, Gina?" Reuben asked.

"A beer would be good," she replied.

"Make it five," Nick said. "We're going to be here a while."

"Coming up," Reuben said.

Reuben went to the kitchen, then returned handing out beers to the group.

"While I'm up, Gina, can you come over here and stand against this white door? I'll need pictures of you on our phones." He waved his cellphone to her.

Gina took a drink of her beer, then went to have her head shots taken by Reuben. He took several pictures with each of their cellphones. It felt uncomfortable, knowing these men would be circulating images of her face to a public she didn't know. A trafficking public. It made her uneasy, but knew it was necessary. This was for her sister, and she would do anything to help Nick's investigation to find her.

After her photo shoot, she took her beer and went to kneel on the floor next to Ice.

"Mind if I help?" she asked.

"Not at all. You know this better than I do."

Gina went to work packing the three case kits for evidence collection. "Why only three cases?"

"That's all we need," Ice replied.

That meant one of them wouldn't be in the field collecting samples. Gina looked back to Nick. He had moved his chair to sit next to Chico. His back was to her. The printer on the side table began spitting out paper.

She took another thirty minutes to help Ice finish up the field kits. She returned to the dining room table, plucking the papers from the printer on her way. She studied the face of a man on the printout. She shuffled through the remaining pages. Horacio Lorenzo Torres...

Nick snatched the papers from her grasp. She flinched and looked up to him.

"It's probably best of you don't read too much of this information," he said.

It stung a little, him not wanting her to know some things. But she would trust his authority in not wanting her to have too much information. They both returned to the dining room table and took their seats.

"I would think that my top-level clearance would allow me to review all documents and evidence." She gave him a slight smile.

"That top-level clearance gives *us* access," Nick said, referring to his crew. "We all have our part in this. I need you focused on the DNA testing."

He gave her a look as if to say, "Got it?" Gina assumed he didn't want her knowing too much of what they might find relating to Sirrina's circumstances. Especially since he wasn't sure himself of what they might uncover. He was protecting her, and she would accept that.

But he had to know that her career placed her amid heinous and horrific crimes on a regular basis. This wasn't new to her. What was new, was the fact this time it involved a personal connection for her. For him as well.

It would take extra effort to not get emotionally absorbed in this investigation. That started with her not reviewing the paperwork Nick had taken from her moments ago. Horacio Lorenzo Torres. She would remember that name.

Nick stood up. "I've gotta make some phone calls in the next room," he said to her. "You good to hang out here for a while longer?"

"Sure. Whatever you need," Gina replied. Although she wasn't sure what else she could do to help. She wondered if he just felt better having her in the room with them instead of down the hall by herself.

Nick walked to the room next door. Reuben collected the remaining printed papers and returned to his seat. He was thoroughly engrossed in his work. Gina moved to sit next to Chico.

"Whatever appears on this screen," he looked to her. "You didn't see."

Gina received his message loud and clear. He went back to typing. Pages of information were scrolling past pertaining to Horacio Lorenzo Torres. Gina was able to scan some of the information as it flew past on the screen. Birth certificate: born in Juarez, Mexico November eighteenth nineteen sixty-nine. *That would make him fifty.* Gina thought. *That made him thirty-four when he acquired Sirrina.* Gina took a swig of her beer to wash down the terrible thought.

Social security information, bank records, mortgages; all flew past on the screen. Vacation villas and European sports cars flashed past intermittently with crime scene photos in between the pages of text and reports. His criminal record was a lengthy one. Auto chop shops, trafficking guns, drugs, and stolen goods. Now he was trafficking humans.

Nylon jog suits were apparently his choice of attire, as if he knew his squatty paunchy frame had nothing appealing to offer. The darkness of his thinning hair matched the circles under his eyes. Two poorly capped teeth the color of dirty gauze drew your eye to his crooked smile under a thick moustache. The folds of his neck swallowed up his chin and jawbone.

Gina was having a hard time imagining this scum bag had something to do with her sister's abduction. It pained her to think Sirrina had been alive all these years trapped with the likes of this pig.

Chico took a cord and plugged his cellphone into the laptop. He scrolled on his phone for the pictures Reuben had taken of her and a moment later her image was on his screen. He clicked through the photos; front, side, hair tied up, hair hung down long, smiling, serious, and he loaded them all onto the laptop.

"You photograph well," he told her.

Gina responded with a slight smile and took another drink of her beer. She watched Chico's fingers flow in rapid succession over the laptop keys. His eyes were trained on the screen, watching the results of his entries display columns of numbers and letters. Then a green graph appeared, and a series of colored digital lines began connecting to matching colored dots. The graph moved in different directions, then started to take on a 3-D image. His fingers never stopped moving over the keys.

It was fascinating to watch him at work. No manual, no instructions, no diagrams, just the information contained in his memory. Gina went to school with students like him in college. It was like their brain was hardwired directly to the computer and their fingers were an extension of that connection. Each time he would enter some information, a new and more complete image of a human head appeared on the screen.

"So how does this work exactly?" Gina asked.

"Basically, I'm creating a new template," Chico said without skipping a beat on his entry input. "Since Sirrina was only eight years old when she was abducted, chances are there's no biometric measurements of her within the national database. I'm creating a current template to download into the database using a composite of your facial measurements, and cross referencing that with a graphic composite I'll create for Sirrina." He paused to allow the computer to work. "Facial, iris, and fingerprints can be measured from a high-resolution image with an algorithm that will compare the physical details. This way when we enter the suspect's," he turned to look at her, "or in this case the victim's image, hopefully we'll land on a match."

"In essence, you're entering Sirrina in the database as a twenty-four-year-old. A version of what she might look like today."

"Pretty much, yeah," he said. "This template along with the fingerprints and DNA should give us our match for identifying."

"How will you be able to match that?" Gina asked.

"Sirrina's prints are already in the database. Her DNA, too."

His comment surprised her, but then she remembered. "Her school records."

"That's it," Chico said.

Gina recalled having to submit her fingerprints and saliva swab the first day of kindergarten. Pertinent information if a child ever got hurt or went missing. Parents had to sign permission forms to allow the school to collect the samples. It seemed like a fun game for the kids at the time. Little did she know that would come around to possibly save her sister's life.

Gina realized that her own prints had been taken three more times since then. For her college application, before she started work at the Hamilton lab, and then just today for her start at the Atlanta lab. She never thought about Sirrina's prints already being in the system, though. She had completely forgotten about kindergarten.

"Do you do this a lot?" Gina asked. "Hack into the database to create templates?"

"It's part of what I do," he replied. "Professionally. Cyber terrorism and computer hacking investigations."

"For the government?"

"For whoever," he replied.

Gina wasn't sure she wanted to know who whoever was. *Don't ask too many questions. Isn't that what Nick told her?* she changed the subject.

"I learned some of the differences in forensic science and biometric technology in college," Gina said. "I'm kind of familiar with what you're doing."

"Forensic science is utilized after the occurrence of a crime or event," he said. "Biometric technology is typically used before an event occurs. Like what we're doing here tonight. I'm creating a biological or physical composite for future recognition purposes." He continued talking to her while his fingers worked their magic. "In a forensic investigation, no one knows what evidence, if any, will be discovered or collected until the investigators arrive at the scene and collect it." He turned to her. "That's your job." He smiled at her, then continued his work and his explanation.

"In biometrics, a person's traits or features are known in advance." He stopped typing and looked at her again. "Basically, we'll be using your facial image to identify the girls we'll be investigating. It's not a guarantee, but it's giving us a strong lead."

Gina liked him. He had a calming effect on her. And if it weren't for the fact that they were looking for her sister, she might actually be enjoying this process of working with him.

"How do you know where to look for Sirrina?" Gina asked.

He nodded towards Reuben and the paperwork he was filtering through. "It's all there."

Chico went back to work and didn't give her any more information. She knew that what they were about to embark on wasn't going to be good.

The tattooed artwork had her attention now. Full sleeves covered both of his forearms. His right arm had two fish, a red and black one, intertwined in colorful flowers and abstract designs. His left arm had an animated black dragon spitting fire. Its nostrils flared with wide angry eyes.

"What are the images of?" Gina asked pointing to his tattoos.

Chico looked down and extended both arms, examining the artwork. "The two Koi." He ran his hand over his right arm. "Is meant to bring success and bravery to the one who wears it." He looked up at her. "The red Koi signifies love." He smiled.

"Is that for your wife?" Gina asked.

"I'm not married," he said. "It's for my little girl, my parents, my brother and sister." He touched his left arm. "The dragon symbolizes wisdom, power, and great strength."

Gina caught that he didn't mention his little girl's mother. She wondered what had happened there as she took another drink of her beer.

Chico tapped his hand over his heart. "The triangle of my Jiu Jitsu training is here." His shirt had that covered up. He relaxed his hands in his lap. "And the tiger is meant to bring strength, courage, and good luck."

Gina searched his artwork, not finding one. "Where's the tiger?"

"On my back," he said with a smile. "I'll save that for when we get to know one another a little better." He winked at her.

Gina smiled back at him. She appreciated the banter.

"Are you working in here or hitting on her?" Nick asked as he re-entered from the adjoining room. The door between the two had been propped open for easy access.

Gina and Chico looked to him. "Just clearing some heavy karma is all," Chico said.

"Unh, hunh," Nick replied, walking over to stand behind him and view the laptop screen. A digital image of Gina's likeness was coming to life.

Gina smiled up at Nick then looked back to the screen. "He's very talented."

"Thank you," Chico replied. "But your work at the lab is what's going to matter in this case the most." He typed in more alpha and numerical sequences. "The DNA match will be our confirmation. It's what we're hoping for here."

There was an awkward silence.

Nick squeezed Chico's shoulders. "Maybe you should work more and talk less."

"That science has always fascinated me," Chico said, ignoring Nick. "She knows." He referred to Gina. "We all have these inherited organisms from our parents that identify us. Am I right?" he asked her.

"Yes," Gina responded, smiling at his enthusiasm.

"Humans have twenty-three chromosomes, each carrying numerous genes," he confirmed with Gina. "Correct me if I'm wrong, each gene occupies a fixed specific position known as locus, or loci for plural?"

"That's right," she replied, impressed.

Chico continued. "And an allele is a variation of that trait in the locus." His hands were flying over the keys again as he spoke. "By analyzing these small variations and scanning for a match, you can identify individuals."

"You've done some studies on forensic sciences," Gina said.

Chico stopped working to look at them both. "I studied some of it in college, but I learned more about it when I was researching my family history."

Gina looked to Nick. "Basically, DNA contains the recipe for the proteins responsible for the process of our development."

"You're speaking a foreign language to me," Nick replied. "I'll take your word on what you two science geeks just said."

"I'll second that," Reuben chimed in.

"It's interesting stuff, man," Chico said.

Nick squeezed Chico's shoulders. "Get back to work, Einstein."

"Yeah, yeah, yeah," Chico said, returning to his computer work.

Nick kept his focus on the laptop screen. His expression seemed serious, almost edgy. It was obvious he had a lot on his plate right now with this investigation. He moved to stand over Reuben's shoulder.

"Any luck with our guy?"

"Plenty." Reuben handed Nick a stack of papers.

Nick sorted through the pages. "When do we start?"

"Tonight," he replied. "I was just about to set up the solicitations." Reuben stood and stretched to reach for the second laptop on the table. Gina moved to push it to him. "Thanks." He returned to his seat and got to work with solicitations.

"Where's he working from?" Gina asked Nick.

Nick shot her a look. Reuben and Chico kept their heads down, minding their work.

"Right," Gina said, half to herself. "Don't ask questions."

She stood up and downed the rest of her beer. She moved to the kitchen and threw the bottle in the trash and returned to the living room.

"If you're done with me here, I'm going to turn in for the night," she said to no one in particular.

There was a collective nod from the group.

"I want all of you to know that I truly appreciate what you're doing here for my sister," Gina said. "Thank you."

Chico gave her a quick glance and a wink, not skipping a beat on his work. Reuben and Ice acknowledged her appreciation. Nick set the paperwork down with Reuben and came over to her.

"Need an escort back to your room?" he asked.

She considered his offer for a moment. There were things she wanted to discuss with him, needed to discuss with him. It had been on her mind all night. But right now, amid their work here, it just didn't seem right to unload on him.

"No. I'm good," she replied. "You have plenty going on here. I just need to grab my things from the other room."

She moved past Nick into room three twenty-five to collect her purse and gun. She would talk to him tomorrow. Nick followed behind her. When she turned to leave, he was standing inches from her.

"Something's up," he said.

"It can wait."

"What is it?"

"I just need to clear the air about some things is all, but now's not the time."

"What things?"

He wasn't going to let this go. "I owe you an apology, Nick."

He tucked his hands into the front pockets of his jeans. "That's not what I expected to hear. And that doesn't seem like something that should wait." He displayed an irresistible grin. "An apology for what?"

"Some really awful misconceptions about you, your actions. And about Joe as well."

His grin faded, but he remained quiet.

"I'm sorry. I just...I was way out of line for thinking what I was thinking about you."

"Like what?" he asked.

"Nick, this probably isn't the best time or place to…"

"I wanna know. Like what?"

He didn't seem angry or upset as much as he seemed concerned for her well-being.

"That you sided with Joe. That you accepted some sort of deal with him to have his case tossed. I had been trying to reason with the fact you threw your career away by perjuring yourself on his case." She looked down to her gun in her grip. She set it back down on the coffee table. "I was pissed that you wouldn't talk to me at the courthouse." She raised her eyes to him. "You were going to prison. That scared me. I was worried about what would happen to you being incarcerated with felons you helped imprison. And I was pissed and worried that I was losing my job. Not to mention the stress of having to undergo an F.B.I. interrogation. And I was upset at the chaos you caused at our lab. Your actions upended all our lives. I began to doubt you. I blamed all of it on you. Blamed you for looking out for yourself and Joe."

There was a long silence between them. Nick gave her words serious consideration.

"I'm sorry, Gina," he said. "But now that you know…"

"Yes. Now I know why," she said. "I just needed you to know what I had been thinking and that I was sorry for thinking it."

"Apology accepted. But seriously, Gina, after what I've put you through these last few days, I'm surprised you even wanted to speak to me again." His smile was infectious.

"Well, you've redeemed yourself in a most unexpected and remarkable way, Mr. Casey."

"Were you really worried for me?"

His smile melted her insides. "Somewhere in all that mess, yes. I was worried," she said. "It also dawned on me how little about you I really know."

He gave her a quizzical look.

"I mean personally," she said. "Your career's an open book. Plenty of media, case reviews, and talk around the lab about that. But we grew up together and then we grew apart. I realized during this ordeal that we lost contact with each other shortly after Sirrina…" She almost said died, but now she wanted to think positive. "Before what happened at the Wildwoods. I thought I knew you, but realized it was based on what I had read and heard about you."

She paused for a moment, wondering if he had anything to say. When he didn't, she continued. "Anyway, it upset me that I was having doubts about you and your actions."

Nick reached out and took hold of both of her hands.

"Do you trust me, Gina?" he asked.

"Yes," she replied. "But if you'd asked me that a few days ago, I would have hesitated."

"And I wouldn't have blamed you," he said. "You've dealt with a lot of shit these past few days. I would have felt the same. Anyone would."

She squeezed his hands, liking the feel of holding him.

"The rest we can work on," he said. "Nothing would make me happier, Gina, than you wanting to get to know me. I'm looking forward to sharing some personal time with you."

Gina felt a stirring deep inside. She wanted to reach out to him. He moved in close and pressed his lips to her forehead. He cast his eyes down to her.

"But this isn't the time or the place I want to do that," he said.

Gina deflated a little, but she understood. She chided herself for thinking those thoughts. Sirrina was all that mattered right now. She looked down to their hands clasped together, then she lifted her gaze to him.

"Thank you again, Nick. The words sound empty and hollow, but I want you to know how much I appreciate what you've done. What you and the guys are doing."

"I know," he replied. "Get some sleep. I'll talk to you tomorrow."

He released his hold on her. She collected her gun and they both walked to the door. He opened the door for her, and she brushed past him.

"Goodnight, Gina."

"Goodnight, Nick."

She made her way back to her room. She heard his door close. Gina was sure sleep would come easy for her tonight. Knowing Nick was just down the hall gave her security and the hope of finding Sirrina.

She wanted to call her parents, her friends, someone, anyone, and share the news, but she couldn't. It felt deceitful not confiding in any of them. But she wouldn't risk any possibility of harming Nick's case. She slid her room key in the lock, entered her room, and went to bed.

CHAPTER 16

Gina looked at her cellphone on the nightstand once more. It was one o'clock in the morning. Twenty minutes later than the last time she looked at it. Sleep wouldn't come tonight. Having Nick and his crew down the hall from her room hadn't helped, either. If anything, it made her want to stay up and theorize on how to find her sister.

All she could think about was Sirrina. Where she might be now. What her life had been like. How scared she must have been that night at the Wildwoods when she was taken. Was there any chance they would find her? And what would that be like, to have her sister suddenly back in her life after sixteen years? Sixteen years of knowing she was dead.

Gina's thoughts fired in rapid sequence. She played so many scenarios over and over again. And what about her parents? How would they handle the news? It would be an ultimate shock, no doubt. Having gone through the grief of losing a child, only to have her come back into their lives again was unthinkable.

But then Gina thought about the alternative. What if they didn't find her? What if she was left with the fact that Sirrina may be alive but nowhere to be found? Knowing this would torment her for the rest of her life. And would she…should she, ever tell her parents about what she and Nick and his crew were trying to accomplish? That they'd had a possible lead into Sirrina being alive, but they'd failed to find her? How would her parents ever be able to handle that? Would it be better to just not say anything?

The continuous thoughts tortured her. She became restless, tossing and turning in bed, trying to block out the questions. She finally gave up and got up at one fifteen. She wrapped herself in a blanket and moved to the living room, turning on the lamp next to the couch. She sat down with her cellphone and Google searched information on human trafficking. Probably not the best decision, but the subject matter had a grip on her now. She couldn't let it go.

In her line of work at the crime lab, she had been involved in criminal and missing persons cases of trafficking. It was a slave trade. It was difficult to process cases of people exploiting humans for commercial gain. She'd reviewed enough police reports of prior investigations to know the realities of what happened in those cases. Children, teenagers, and young adults were sold into prostitution and introduced to drugs, and most were physically and mentally abused.

Some were runaways who wound up living on the streets. Some had been in abusive relationships and some were abducted from a normal life. Most were sold on the premise of making money to make a better life for themselves. But in the end, they were just sold. Like a commodity.

Gina had learned to process evidence in cases that involved trafficking, or any explicit activity, from a scientific standpoint. To always remain detached and never allow fear, judgment, or her opinion to enter the equation. It was good advice that worked for the cases that she processed. It was her chosen profession, and one she couldn't allow emotions to interfere with. Instead, she concentrated on performing a series of tasks to arrive at conclusions to include in her report.

But this was different, now, being as Sirrina was involved. It *was* personal. She was researching information from a completely different perspective. In reading the stories and articles, Gina was imagining Sirrina as the victim. The horrific details and events she possibly had been exposed to. Gina's raw emotions surfaced now that she accepted the possibility that Sirrina had been forced into that life. Into that nightmare.

Tears spilled down her cheeks as she continued to read. She wondered what Nick had been thinking by including her in his investigation. Certainly, he would have considered the impact this would have on her. Having to acknowledge the fact that Sirrina might be a victim of this horrific life.

Or maybe it was his detective mind following the best lead no matter the consequences. Either way, she wanted to imagine he had a difficult time making the decision to include her and then having to tell her. There would have been no easy way to approach this matter. He deserved so much credit for having followed through with that.

And his concern for her well-being earlier seemed genuine. In the end, she concluded he was working the strongest angle of his case, hoping to bring positive results. And that meant recruiting her to help with his case.

Continuing to read the subject matter became too upsetting. Instead, she looked for news regarding Nick and the mistrial. She searched for news relating to recent court cases at the William J. Brennan courthouse. Not including Nick as her primary search seemed smart. Of course, there was plenty of news fodder on the D'Amato mistrial posted.

She opened the most current article from The Star-Ledger and scanned the contents.

"Allegations amid the controversial mistrial of crime boss Joe D'Amato continue to circulate. The F.B.I. and the Hoboken police department remain tight-lipped as to any evidence that corroborates the testimony of detective Nick Casey that evidence and testimony introduced into the case were falsified. And while Detective Casey perjured himself during the trial and was arrested, it is unknown as to where he will be serving his sentence. Sources say that due to the nature of his arrest and the fact he's incarcerated criminals within the prison system, it is imperative for his safety that his incarceration remain unknown to law enforcement and the public. There are on-going investigations into the Hoboken police department, the New Jersey district attorney's office, and the Hamilton crime lab regarding corruption suspicions."

Gina continued reading. The article mentioned her director, Detective Jerry Pulia, as a strong lead in the case, but no accomplices. It stated other suspects were being questioned, but no names were mentioned from the department. District Attorney Benjamin Forrester was mentioned as a cooperating witness, and it said there were possible suspects within the D.A.'s office, but again, no names were mentioned.

When the story mentioned the crime lab, Gina tensed, afraid to read about any of her co-workers having participated in the corruption or possibly linking her somehow with the corruption. But there was little written about the lab. It only mentioned they were still conducting their investigations, without reporting names.

Gina wasn't sure where that landed her. Was she in the clear, as Nick said? Or would they be calling her back for more questioning? It didn't surprise her how little had been uncovered or reported to date. The F.B.I. was giving very minimal information to the media. And they would continue to do so.

The fact the police department, the D.A.'s office and the crime lab were under investigation would have tales of past cases spinning. It could possibly call into question every case that had been tried by any one of these institutions. It had the potential to create a firestorm of lawsuits. Not to mention every case would have to be reinvestigated and re-tried in a court of law.

She scanned the remaining article. It went on to detail the history of corruption that plagued the police department and the state of New Jersey. The last portion of the article recapped the D'Amato crime family, reiterating crimes from the last thirty years. It also mentioned her family as part of those criminal tales.

Gina didn't care to read about historic news. She checked out a few more online reports on the mistrial. Most of them were running the same platform. She would continue to read the news in the coming days. It would be her only source of information for the time being.

Calling her supervisor Roger for any updates, or even talking to her family and friends so soon, was out of the question. She wasn't accustomed to lying, and she didn't trust herself to not say something about being in Atlanta and then having to explain why. She was tired now. She switched off her phone and went to bed.

When Gina arrived at work that morning, she was dragging. She had a second cup of coffee, but the caffeine was slow to kick in. She prepared the Lysis Mix and the Purification Mix for the samples she would be testing.

The three other techs on her team were busy at work with their own cases. They were cordial but detached. The awkwardness of having a recruit, Gina supposed. She figured in time they would come around. It didn't bother her. She had her own case to think about. One she wouldn't be sharing with any of them, anyway.

She walked over to the cooler and storage cabinets and removed twelve evidence envelopes then returned to her station. Sophia met her at her workstation.

"Good morning," she said. "Can you come with me for a minute?" She spun on her heel, not giving Gina a chance to respond. Gina got the impression she wasn't happy about something.

Gina followed Sophia to her office.

"Take a seat please," she said, closing the door behind Gina.

Gina scanned the many plaques and awards nailed to one wall. Zen artwork framed in black metal covered another wall. A six-foot tall human anatomy poster was tacked to a wardrobe closet: a full skeletal and vascular rendition. Books, manuals, human skulls, and other scientific gadgets filled a floor-to-ceiling bookcase.

Sophia scooted in her chair behind her desk and rested her elbows and forearms on the desk as she peered at Gina. "You worked late last night."

"I'm sorry?" Gina replied. *Was she asking or telling?*

Sophia pursed her lips and turned to her laptop, plugging in some information. "You were busy accessing the FBI's national database last night, were you not?"

Gina's pulse quickened. *Was she in trouble for that? How did she...*

"For approximately six hours," she continued, looking back to Gina. "My, my."

"I was..."

"I wasn't aware you had that level of clearance, Miss Teducci."

I do now, Gina thought. Sophia sounded bitter, almost pissed off. What could she say? She obviously had the proof right there in front of her.

"Is there a problem?" Gina asked nervously.

Sophia only responded with a blank stare. Obviously, she had a problem with this.

"I'm sorry," was all Gina could think of to say, afraid she might step deeper into the shit Chico had just placed her in.

"Don't apologize, Gina," Sophia replied. "If anything, I should be apologizing to you."

"Come again?"

Sophia sat on the edge of her chair. "Imagine my surprise, learning that you clearly out- rank me here at the lab. I should be taking direction from *you*. I only wished you would have said something to me yesterday instead of letting me tote you around the lab like you were a first-year intern."

Sophia's tone had turned bitter. Gina was dumbfounded.

"No. Not at all, Sophia," Gina offered. "I needed to familiarize myself with your lab."

Sophia grimaced at her weak response. "Your reassignment package stated clearly that you were only to be working in the biological lab," Sophia continued. "Testing DNA samples. I misunderstood that to mean that your experience was extremely limited. Obviously, a mistake on my part."

Gina remained quiet, not wanting to say the wrong thing.

"Apparently, you're to utilize the lab at your discretion. The case that you're working on is coded at a highly classified sensitive material level. My staff and I are to steer clear of any work you're processing. So, I won't offer to help in any way since that's out of the question."

Gina detected a hostile note in her tone. She obviously wasn't happy with what was taking place in her lab.

"I'm sorry, Sophia. I'm not sure what to say."

"Stop apologizing, Gina. This is your job," Sophia snipped. "Of course, we still have other cases to work here as well. But no one will interfere with what you're here to accomplish. And I certainly won't be standing over your shoulder micromanaging your work."

That explains the distant attitudes from the other scientists in the lab, Gina thought. *What the hell had Chico done while logged in under her identification last night?* she wondered. Whatever it was, it worked. She had breathing room to work now.

She had been worried about having to answer questions from Sophia about her case. Having to keep information from her to protect Nick and his crew and their case. Why hadn't Nick told her Chico was going to do this? She would have been better prepared to handle Sophia's assault this morning.

Sophia's comment had Gina wondering if she might have been reprimanded in some way for overseeing her work yesterday. She almost seemed threatened by Gina's presence. Gina hoped not. This was becoming uncomfortable. She had hoped to make a smooth transition here, but that didn't seem likely now.

"Well," Sophia stood up. "Back to work then."

Gina stood. "Yes." She started to walk out, then turned back to Sophia. "Are we still on for lunch today?" Gina gauged Sophia's reaction.

It was slight, but Gina caught it. A faint pinch in Sophia's expression and a delay in her response.

"Sure. I'll let you know when."

Gina wouldn't count on it. She left Sophia's office and made her way back to the biological lab. Six evidence envelopes were in the metal basket on the tabletop. She picked them up and noticed all six of them had detective Reuben Alvarez's name as the requester. She returned to her workstation, adding the six new samples with the twelve she had left there when Sophia arrived.

She went to work, cutting the tip of the cotton off the swab letting it fall into a test tube. She did the same with the remaining seventeen swabs. Then she added the Lysis Mix to each test tube. She was in her zone now. She blocked out everything going on around her. She only focused on her work as she carried out the next twenty-plus steps in processing the samples, getting them ready for the DNA test.

When the DNA testing was complete, she moved to the computer to run the results through the database. As the person matches came up on her screen, she made reports of each one, then filed the information in separate electronic files. She would email the results to the corresponding names of the requesters, as noted on the evidence envelopes.

When she got to the samples from Reuben Alverez, her adrenalin spiked. Each time a person match appeared on her screen; Gina flinched. There had been a match to all six of his samples. All of them had similar traits and features as Gina, but none of them were Sirrina. And each one gave Gina pause. *Who were these girls? How had they ended up here, being processed as a missing person and trafficked victim? Was anyone looking for them?*

"...lunch with us?" Sophia was asking.

Gina snapped from her thoughts. "I'm sorry?"

"Lunch," Sophia said. "I was asking if you wanted to join me and the others. Are you ok?"

Gina noticed that her attitude seemed more relaxed now.

"I, yes. I'm fine," Gina replied. "I'll need to take a raincheck for tomorrow, if that's ok. I have a lot to work on here."

"Can I bring you something back?"

Her offer was genuine. "That would be great," Gina replied.

"I don't know where we're going yet, so,"

"Anything is fine. I'm not picky."

Sophia accepted and left her.

Gina went back to her work, finishing up a report on another victim. *Maybe they wouldn't find a match for Sirrina. Maybe she somehow managed to escape the situation that put her there in the first place,* Gina thought. *Maybe she started a new life far away from this vile existence. But then why didn't she come home? Why wouldn't she come back to her family? Could she have been too damaged, or broken, or scared to come back home? Maybe she felt guilt or shame or even anger. Anger towards her sister for allowing this to happen to her.*

When Gina left the lab, it was nearly six o'clock. Exhaustion from lack of sleep made her neck and shoulders ache. She drove back to the hotel with the sandwich Sophia had bought for her. She had not stopped to eat and now her stomach was growling.

As she entered her room, her cellphone text ringer went off. She turned on the lights and set her things down on the dining room table. She took her phone from her purse and read the text. It was from Nick.

"Have you had dinner yet?"

She typed back, "No."

"Dinner at my place when you're ready. Room three twenty-seven."

Gina smiled. "Ok," she texted back.

She moved to the bedroom, stripped off her clothes and took a shower. She was dressed and ready to leave thirty minutes later. The shower had revived her. Or maybe it was the prospect of joining Nick for dinner that had livened her up. She stuck her phone back in her purse and locked her gun in the safe, then left her room.

CHAPTER 17

Gina knocked on the door of room three twenty-seven. Nick answered a moment later.

"Hi there." She smiled with a flutter of excitement.

"Hey," he smiled, holding the door open for her.

Gina entered and did a quick once over. It appeared that only Nick was in the room. And something smelled delicious. Her stomach growled, reminding her again that she hadn't eaten lunch. The door adjoining the two rooms was closed.

"Where is everyone?" she asked.

"Working. Beer?" he asked, heading for the kitchen.

"Sure." Gina walked to the living room and sat on the couch. Nick had to-go boxes of eggplant parmesan, garlic bread, and salad. Takeout from somewhere. It looked and smelled delicious. Nick returned with the beers and sat next to her on the couch.

He popped the tops off and handed one to her, grinning, seeming relaxed now. He held his bottle up to her and they clinked bottles before taking that first ice cold sip.

"Where's this from? It looks and smells amazing, and I'm starving," she said, setting her beer down and grabbing a fork and knife.

"Uncle Vito's," he said. "It's only a few blocks from here. Reuben's good at finding these gem hole-in-the wall joints with food that rocks."

They dug into their dinners.

"Thank you for this. Your timing was impeccable."

"That's because your GPS let me know when you got here."

Gina's chewing slowed. "You're tracking my GPS?"

"You better believe I am." He chewed his food and took a drink of beer. Off her look, he asked, "What?"

"Nothing." She looked back to her food. "I guess I didn't realize I was being followed."

"There's one of us watching you at all times, Gina."

"Am I in danger here?"

"No. Just a personal request of mine." He took another bite of eggplant.

She wasn't sure how to take that. "Something interesting happened at the lab today."

"What's that?" he asked, drinking his beer.

"Apparently my security clearance with the lab outranks everyone I'm working with there, including my supervisor, Sophia."

He took another bite of eggplant and chewed for a minute. "That's right."

"That would have been good information to know before going in this morning. I would have been better prepared for Sophia's inquiry."

"You knew we were increasing your security clearance."

"Yeah, but not to the level…" She didn't finish her comment because it didn't seem to be of much importance now. It's what her role in his investigation entailed.

"You did ok, right?" His response was too casual.

"The point is, I'm not sure I'm comfortable with that level of clearance. I'm not qualified for…"

"You're processing DNA samples. You're qualified."

"When will you tell me more about the case?"

"Eat your dinner. It's getting cold."

"Don't do that." She poked his forearm with her fork. "I'm being serious."

"I am too, Gina," he said, wiping his hands and mouth with a napkin. "I told you from the beginning, I'm only going to give you information as I think you need to know. The less you know about this right now, the better."

"But why?" she pleaded. "This case has everything to do with me. It's my *sister* we're here trying to find. Why can't I know more details? And if I'm not in any danger, as you said, then what's the harm?"

"Because I haven't figured all of it out yet," he replied. "I'm not going to say anything that will lead to speculation. That doesn't do you or any of us any good."

Gina couldn't fault him for thinking that. If that was true, then he was right.

"Ok. But when you know, will you tell me?" she asked.

Nick laughed. "Geez, you're as bad as a kid on Christmas morning."

Gina took a sip of her beer, waiting for an answer.

"I'll tell you. Ok?"

"Thank you." She ate more of her eggplant. "This really is delicious," she said with her mouth full of food. "It's making me homesick for my mom's eggplant parm."

They quietly enjoyed dinner for a few moments.

"How about we change the subject from work?" he asked.

"Nice way to skirt the issue, Casey, but ok." She smiled at him before drinking her beer. "What can we talk about that's not classified or restricted?" She was teasing him now.

"You're relentless," he said. "How about resolving how little you know about me personally? What can I tell you?"

She took another bite of her dinner and chewed as she considered her answer. "Everything."

"Can you narrow it down a bit?"

"How is it you're working for Joe?"

"Gina..."

"I wasn't referring to the case," Gina responded, then thought about her question. "But I guess it leads back to the case, doesn't it? What I meant was how did you come to know Joe? Him being a criminal and you being a detective?"

Nick took another bite of his dinner, giving her question some serious thought.

"If I'm out of line just tell me," Gina continued. "I only know of your remarkable record as a detective. All I'm saying is that it clashes with the likes of Joe D'Amato."

He set his fork down and wiped his mouth with a napkin. "You know, you and me, we're not so different," he said, chewing his food.

"No?"

"I guess I just assumed you knew more about me," he said, finishing his bite. He looked straight at her. "Joe's family to me, Gina."

She stopped her chewing. He had her full attention.

"Obviously not a blood relative, but yeah." He took a drink of beer. "I was eleven when my parents died in a car accident. I had to go stay with my aunt Mary and her five cats."

Gina swallowed her food, smiling at the memory. "That's when you moved to our neighborhood from Brooklyn."

"It's probably why I can't stand cats today," he remarked. "My aunt worked at one of Joe's car dealerships."

"I don't think I ever remember you mentioning that growing up."

"You probably never asked."

Gina shrugged her shoulders. "Probably because it didn't matter. We were kids," Gina replied. "My dad and uncle built those dealerships for Joe."

"Teduccis and D'Amatos did a lot of business together back then." He raised his eyes to her. "They still do."

"I know," Gina said. "My grandfather and Joe's father did a lot for one another growing up. And it was Joe who helped get my father established here in the states when my parents moved here from Italy." Gina reflected on that memory. "I can tell my fathers had mixed emotions about Joe's trial." She poked her fork at her eggplant. "And I channeled my anger at Joe during his trial, because it was his nephew that caused what happened to Sirrina."

"I know, and I understand that. You didn't have all of the information."

"I still don't," Gina said, looking back to him. "And neither do you."

"No. I don't. But what I do know is that Joe took care of us. My aunt Mary and me. I owe him everything. He's been like a father to me."

Gina didn't expect to hear this.

"My aunt had her hands full with me," he continued. "I was a punk kid growing up. Every day she'd tell me that trouble was gonna beat me home." He laughed at the memory. "She was right. I wanted to blame someone for the cards I'd been dealt. Joe straightened me out."

He looked down at his beer. Some serious considerations seemed to be brewing in his mind. Life lessons from a crime boss, she imagined.

"What did he do?" Gina asked.

"He took me hunting," Nick said, talking to his beer. "Just him and me." He raised his eyes to her again. "We came across a deer in the woods, and he told me to shoot it."

Gina began to lose her appetite.

"I positioned myself for the kill." Nick was animated, acting out the moment for her. "Lined up the deer in my scope, and before I pulled the trigger, he asked me why I was about to shoot the animal." Nick smiled at the recollection. "Balancing his rifle in my hands, it felt like it weighed as much as I did. I wanted him to know I had everything under control. But deep down, I was scared shitless, about to kill this innocent animal, and then he asked that question. I turned to him, thinking he'd lost his mind or something. And then he asked me again, 'why are you shooting the deer?' I knew I didn't have the answer. I lowered the rifle to my side. He squeezed my shoulder and said 'that's exactly right. If you don't have a damn good fucking reason for killing, then you don't.'" Nick took a drink of beer. "He was right." He pondered the thought. "If I had killed the deer because he told me to, then I wasn't a man of principle."

"What happened after that?"

"I worked for him for quite a few years, but I won't go into details on that." He ate some more eggplant.

Gina wouldn't ask for details. She was aware of the rackets Joe operated, so she had a clear idea what Nick had been involved in.

"The Cadillac project steered me away from the criminal path."

"What was that?"

"We were at Joe's horse farm north of the city. We entered one of the barns where he had a nineteen forty-nine Cadillac stowed away. Just sitting in a corner rusting away. He put me to work restoring it from top to bottom, inside and out. We brought it back to a garage that a friend of his owned. Calvin Daniels. If I wasn't in school, I was at the garage working with Calvin. I learned a lot from the old guy, too." Nick paused to reflect for a moment. "Joe seemed inclined to keep me on the right side of the law. Keep me from walking a criminal line. I guess he saw potential in me that I didn't see. I was too young and stubborn." Nick owned up to that comment. "Joe paid for my education, college, the academy." Nick laughed. "I think he half expected I would come work for him as his private security detail. He wasn't too thrilled with my career choice."

"I'm sure he is now," Gina replied. Nick's reaction made her realize that her words stung. She obviously wasn't completely past blaming Joe for Sirrina yet. "I'm sorry. I didn't mean for that to sound the way it did."

He didn't respond.

"I'm sure Joe's pleased at what you've become," Gina said. "Your career and reputation speak volumes. He's gotta be a proud pop."

They both smiled at the thought.

Gina changed the subject. "Have you ever been shot?"

"I have," he replied, crunching into a bite of garlic bread. When he finished chewing, he said, "Once, here." He pointed to just under his right clavicle bone. "Hurt like a son of a bitch."

"You weren't wearing a vest." It was a statement, not a question.

"I can't always wear one undercover."

Gina wasn't happy with that bit of reality. "It's ironic, isn't it?" Gina said. "That we both picked careers in law enforcement."

"Another beer?" he asked, standing up.

"Sure."

He retrieved two more beers, then popped the tops off.

"What happened to you after Sirrina," Gina hesitated, not wanting to say it. "You know."

Nick was about to take another drink but stopped. Her question appeared to strike a nerve with him.

"It brought back some heavy feelings from losing my parents a few years earlier," he said. "It was hard watching you and your family go through that. Losing Sirrina. I felt responsible for her disappearing that night."

"You did?" His comment surprised her.

"Well, yeah. To some degree," he said. "We had hung out together all day, you and me. I should have come with you and Sirrina and Jimmy instead of going to the pizza joint with the others. Maybe, who knows. Maybe none of it would have happened."

"Nick." Gina never realized he had been holding guilt inside like she had been. "I…wow." His words caught her off-guard. "You can't do that, you know. You can't let the guilt…"

"I know," he said, cutting her off. "I focused that energy elsewhere. A different direction."

"By becoming a detective?"

"It's helped." He studied his beer. "But when that happened to Sirrina, I felt, I don't know." He looked over to her. "Like I let you and your family down. Especially your old man. Joe always had good things to say about Carmine. It just…"

He didn't finish his thought.

"Do you still feel that?" Gina asked.

"No. I was fifteen at the time. I had a lot to learn." He drank his beer then set the bottle down on the table. "I'll admit though, it's what kept me from pursuing you."

"You thought of pursuing me?" Gina smiled with intrigue. "I always figured you thought I was too young for you. That you wanted to date older, experienced high school girls instead."

"I did, and I did," Nick replied, laughing.

Gina punched him playfully.

Nick became sincere. "But I still thought about you."

Gina felt a pang of loss. "You know you broke this girl's heart," she said.

"I know."

Gina watched him reflect on his thoughts. She waited for more from him.

"After what happened to Sirrina, what we had been through with that ordeal, we all needed time to heal and recover from it." He looked over to her.

A quiet sadness reflected in his eyes and tugged at her heart.

"There was so much anger and blame between both our families," he continued. "And as time passed, it just seemed to be something grim that would wedge itself between us. Nothing good would come of it. I thought you would be better off with someone else. Someone who hadn't experienced the tragedy firsthand with you. Someone good who wasn't heading down a criminal path the way I was. You deserved so much better, Gina."

"And now?" Gina asked, surprised by his profoundness.

"Now, well, I won't say I was wrong. I stand by my reasons. But some things are different now."

"Only some things?"

He poked his dinner with his fork, considering his response. He looked over to her. "Sixteen years ago, what happened to Sirrina sent us our separate ways. And now sixteen years later, what happened to Sirrina has brought us back together."

"Irony? Fate?"

Nick shrugged his shoulders. "I don't believe in that. Call it whatever you want. I just know I'm not going to make the same mistake I did in assuming you'd be better off without me."

His blue eyes bore right through her. She noticed the fine lines at the corners of his eyes deepened as he smiled. His two-day old beard gave him a rugged appearance that very much appealed to her. She reached over and gripped his forearm. This time no one would call out "no contact allowed" through a speaker behind two-way glass.

Gina breathed a sigh of relief. "For a first…whatever this is, you sure give a girl a lot to think about."

"You wanted to get to know me."

"I did, and I *did*," she joked, paraphrasing him.

"We save this." He motioned with his hand, referring to the two of them. "We know exactly what this is. But we save this until we wrap up the investigation, ok? I've put too much into this investigation to lose my head in the middle of it. And I know that if we took this a step further, I would lose my mind over you, Gina." His eyes searched hers. "This investigation is too important to too many people that mean everything to me. Especially you." His conviction was clear.

She squeezed her hand on his arm. It was not what she wanted to hear, but she agreed with him. "This is cruel and unusual punishment, Nick Casey."

He frowned at her comment. "Come here." He wrapped his arm around her and pulled her close to him. He kissed the top of her head, holding her tight. "I'm hoping this will be over soon."

"Me, too."

They spent another hour catching up on each other's lives and careers over the remainder of their beers. Nick's cellphone rang. He walked away from her to take the call. A moment later he went to the door adjoining the two rooms, walked through it, and closed it behind him.

Gina guessed it was for the best now that they hadn't gotten romantically involved tonight. It still bothered her that she couldn't be a part of everything going on with her sister's case.

She cleaned up the remnants from their dinner and threw it in the kitchen trash. She took a wet towel and cleaned up the table. She sat back on the couch, waiting for Nick.

Gina replayed their earlier conversations in her mind. She was glad they'd been able to spend some quiet time together getting to know one another. It seemed strange to think that being she's known him most of her life, but after tonight, she realized she hadn't really known him at all. And now knowing what she'd learned about him, she found herself wanting to know more. He was so easy to be around. There was a comfort, a warmth, a security just being near him.

Gina had dated a few times over the years, but she never recalled feeling the same way about any of them. Like there was no connection. It's probably why those dates never amounted to anything. She wondered now what would become of her and Nick.

Nick entered the room just then. "I've gotta work, Gina."

That was her cue to leave. She collected her purse and walked over to him. "I guess I'll see you tomorrow then," she said.

"I meant what I said earlier."

"I know."

Gina wanted his investigation to be over with. She wanted to find Sirrina in the worst way, because she also wanted Nick. She placed a hand on his cheek. His beard felt wonderfully masculine to the touch. She leaned up to him and placed a kiss on his other cheek. Kissing his lips would have been a mistake. "Stay safe." Her voice was a strained whisper.

"I'll try."

It took all of her will to turn away from him and walk out the door.

CHAPTER 18

Nick returned to room three twenty-five to follow up on the information Reuben and Chico had obtained. Flicking on the television, he scrolled through the guide, looking for a movie. Any movie. It didn't matter because he wouldn't be watching. He just needed some background noise to cancel out the quiet of the room. Too much of his work required him to sit in solitude while working surveillance.

That time was best utilized thinking through his plan and the people who would be impacted by his investigation. This investigation would impact plenty of people. He had run his plan through his mind top to bottom, inside and out too many times to count.

Even the detour to Atlanta now, trying to locate Sirrina, had been well thought out, not only by himself, but with the help of Reuben, Leo, Ice, and Chico. Tonight, he would just run through the file once more. It was all he could do, since he couldn't very well go out in public. He wouldn't run the risk of someone identifying him.

The media had been running too many stories about the mistrial, plastering his face on the screen for all to see. He would have to hunker down in this hotel room for one more night.

There were limited choices on TV. He made his selection, then moved to the kitchen to grab a bottled water. He thought about Gina again. He was glad they had been able to spend some quiet time together. He would be leaving in the morning and wasn't sure when he would be returning. His crew would keep him informed of her well-being. Not telling her tonight felt deceitful, but he wasn't ready to answer the flood of questions she would have assaulted him with.

It was also why he didn't delve too far into his past with Joe D'Amato. Not long after Sirrina's abduction and death, Joe had requested for Nick to keep his distance from the Teducci family. Namely, Gina. It had been a true test of his will. Nick had spoken frequently about her to Joe. It was how Nick learned of the Teducci and D'Amato alliances. Gentlemen's agreements dating back five generations. Generations that were rich in mafia history.

Those agreements were based on respect and loyalty. And had it not been for Joe and Carmine upholding that respect and loyalty, the two families would still be going at each other today. It had been Carmine's generosity to see past holding the D'Amato family responsible for Sirrina's death, acknowledging that Guiseppe had acted on his own and not at the request of Joe or anyone affiliated with the D'Amato family. It was how both families were able to continue their respective operations in corruption, keeping a stronghold on the city and state governments for their personal gain.

Nick had a tough time turning a blind eye towards it. He was sworn to uphold the law while backing a man who manipulated the law to serve his needs. Nick joined the police academy with his eyes wide open, knowing someday he would find himself deciding whether to continue in law enforcement while turning his back on Joe, or siding with corruption and turning his back on law enforcement.

He never imagined the two would become one. In the end, he chose which criminal to back and that was Joe. He also never imagined investigating Guiseppe's murder would lead him to Atlanta to seek out Sirrina.

Nick wasn't sure how much Gina knew, but he was guessing not much. Carmine would have done his best to protect her. To protect all his kids. Gina had three older brothers with wives and children of their own. There would be a place and time to reveal the truths. He only hoped his investigation would bring the closure they deserved.

Confiding in Gina tonight had given him some insight to his career choice, his past, and what he wanted going forward. Unsure of what his investigation would uncover, he was sure of one thing: he wanted Gina in his future.

It had taken sheer will to not pull her to him and kiss her full on the mouth when she kissed his cheek goodnight. But he knew he wouldn't have been able to stop himself with just a kiss. He would have wanted more…much more. And he saw it in her eyes, sensed it in her reaction when he cut the night short, that she wanted the same. But he couldn't compromise his investigation by starting something with her without knowing how things would end with this case.

He pulled up a chair at the dining room table. File folders were spread out, some of them open with photos of young women. The evidence of shattered lives. Some battered and bruised, some strung out on drugs, and some anorexic and malnourished.

There were daunting images of anemic complexions and protruding skeletal features. Some covering the signs of exhaustion with heavy make-up, others with colored hair; black, blonde, orange, red, blue, purple, teal, green; a kaleidoscope to counteract the misery. Outfitted in flimsy garments, standing on street corners, leaning into cars, and walking into The Georgia Star Inn. Reuben's surveillance captured it all.

Unfortunately, none of the girls resembled Sirrina, or what they concocted Sirrina to look like now. If they didn't find her working out of Horacio's locations, then hopefully one of the girls would recognize the photo of Gina. Or maybe it would spark the slightest clue of where to look for her, a lead, anything to go on.

Two other locations, The Riverside Inn and The Orchards motel, rounded out Horacio's prostitution enterprise. These were the three locations Nick's crew would be targeting. All three were owned by Horacio under the limited liability corporation of El Rey LLC. Translation; The King LLC. *A spineless degenerate is more like it,* Nick thought. *The King. Really? He lacked imagination, too.*

Having three locations to cover unexpectedly changed his plan, not to mention added more time. He had unfinished business waiting for him back in New Jersey. Business that pertained to Guiseppe's murder. But taking care of this piece of his investigation is what mattered most right now.

Nick logged into his laptop and accessed Reuben's notes. According to his intel, The Georgia Star was the busiest of the three. It was a two-level slump stone structure built in a "L" shape. Asphalt shingles, black wrought iron railings, with twenty-six peach colored room doors. Each with black iron numbers signifying the room. The ten rooms at the short end of the "L" were where Horacio's girls worked. The remaining sixteen rooms were rented out to friends, business associates, or to unsuspecting guests.

His other two locations ran comparable operations. The Riverside Inn was similar in construction to the Georgia Star, but with twenty-two turquoise doors. The Orchards motel was a low one-level yellow vinyl sided "U" shaped structure with twenty red doors.

Each property location had electronic files attached. Mortgage records dating back to the initial construction, previous ownerships, current loans, property tax records, insurance policies, financial statements, most likely doctored or falsified. Statements that made Horacio appear as a law-abiding citizen. But that wasn't Nick's concern. His investigation pertained to Sirrina. The trafficking violation would end Horacio's career. At least while he was incarcerated. Nick filtered through the remaining records, then moved to the schedule.

Tonight, Reuben was manning the Georgia Star, Ice had the Riverside Inn, and Chico was on The Orchards. Operation One Hundred for Twenty-Four was under way. Chico had hacked into Horacio's computer, gaining access to his secure website.

Over the course of this investigation, he would be setting up solicitations for prostitutes every night. Posing as any one of a hundred characters. It didn't matter because they never asked. And only one specific request: the girls needed to be early-to mid-twenties. More specifics might raise suspicion.

Not wanting to use the motels for their operation, they would have taxis pick up the girls from the motels and drive them to another location, like a shopping center parking lot. Somewhere busy where the girls would feel safe, and no one would pay attention to a girl climbing out of a cab and into an SUV.

Nick rifled through the paperwork and found a stack of generic pre-printed release forms. Each victim would need to give their consent to have their DNA tested by signing one of these documents. They would include the consent form with the sample inside each evidence envelope. These would then be couriered to the Atlanta crime lab and delivered to Gina for DNA testing.

Each victim would be given one hundred dollars in exchange for their saliva sample. They would be given an extra fifty bucks to give to Horacio upon their return. His cut. Nick was banking on the fact that a hundred bucks would appeal to these girls enough to not give them up to Horacio. All they had to do was sign a form and say ahhh.

And they would only be collecting samples from twenty-four-year-old girls. Once they were out of the cab and inside the SUV, the first order of business was to verify their age. If they weren't twenty-four, they wouldn't be swabbed.

All would be asked to identify the photos of Gina, and Sirrina's digital image. And all would be offered help through a local shelter or rescue organization. If they accepted, the cab ride would re-route the girls to one of those locations instead of returning them to Horacio. If they refused the help, they would be paid and sent on their way. Unfortunately, Nick knew that most of the girls would choose the latter and continue working.

His plan seemed like such an elaborate process, having to involve so many players to locate Sirrina. It would have seemed easier to just pick up Horacio and question him on Sirrina's whereabouts. Beat the answers out of him if need be. But what if he lied? Or what if he no longer had contact with her? What if she had escaped, run away, overdosed, or died? They would never know the truth because Horacio would never give it to them.

He wondered how much luck, if any, they were going to have in finding Sirrina. It was a shot in the dark at best. Sixteen years was a long time. Sirrina had only been eight years old when she was sold into this hell. It was too much to hope she had escaped and too despicable to think she'd survived.

Scenarios played out night after night for Nick. He didn't expect a brighter side to any of this. No matter what they found, the results would be devastating. Sixteen years subjected to this life… He thumbed through the photos again. She would be so damaged. Mentally and physically. He wondered how he would ever prepare Gina and her family for that reality.

But he was getting ahead of himself. They needed to find Sirrina first. It would start with Horacio. Nick plucked his file from the stack and flipped through it. He would like nothing more than to come face to face with him: middle-aged Mexican scum pushing flesh for cash. A real piece of shit. Nick fantasied about the ass-kicking he would deliver to this wretched degenerate. Nothing would give him more pleasure than to remove him from existence. Joe had told him a long time ago; you better have a damn good fucking reason for killing. This qualified.

Nick continued to peruse his file. Horacio grew up in Juarez, Mexico, running auto chop shops. He immigrated to the U.S. in the early nineties and continued operating chop shops and dealing drugs. That led to trafficking: guns, drugs, and humans. Arrested twice but never convicted. Nick would see to it that the conviction stuck this time. That was, of course, if he survived an encounter with Nick.

Nick's cellphone rang. The display read Leo. Nick pressed "accept."

"Yeah."

"We might have a situation up here," Leo said.

"What's that?"

"Your boy's got D.A. Forrester rounding up a court order for him to come and pay you a visit in prison."

"Which prison? My incarceration location hasn't been disclosed to anyone," Nick replied.

"Your boy Jimmy's throwing around plenty of cash to get some answers to that question. And three of the players have dropped out of sight."

"Who?" Nick asked.

"Rotello, Nunzio, and Chu."

"Sounds like Jimmy might be cleaning house."

"I can try and dig a little deeper, see if I can find out more on them."

"No, stay with Jimmy," Nick said. "I was heading back to Jersey in the morning, but I guess I'm heading there now."

CHAPTER 19

Early morning mist swirled in the shafts of dawning daylight piercing the tall trees of a quiet New Jersey neighborhood. One elderly resident appeared in his bathrobe with his white terrier companion to retrieve the newspaper from his driveway. He waited patiently for the dog to tiptoe through the dewy lawn and complete his business, then both retreated inside his house. That had been the only stirring of this Norman Rockwell neighborhood so far, other than the tree squirrels and blue jays going about their business foraging and nesting.

Nick glanced at the dashboard clock. Five twenty-eight. He sat in the back seat of Leo's silver crew cab pickup. The tinted windows kept him obscured from sight. Leo sat in the driver's seat. If anyone called it in as a suspicious vehicle, it would be traced back to a shell corporation owned by Joe. And any inquiries pertaining to Joe D'Amato had been flagged and were being sent directly to Sergeant Jim Slater and Chief Bruce Stanford.

The house they were watching this Thursday morning was three doors down. Across the street from the resident who had just come out to pluck his morning newspaper from the driveway with his terrier. The patience of surveillance was wearing thin for both Nick and Leo.

Nick was running on fumes physically and mentally. He'd left Atlanta just after eleven p.m. the night before and landed an hour and forty minutes later at Newark Liberty International airport. Leo was parked on the tarmac in the silver pickup as Joe's Hawker Beechcraft Premiere private jet taxied to a stop.

Nick departed the aircraft, having gotten maybe thirty minutes of shuteye. The pilot was the only other passenger, and he remained on board. Nick and Leo left the airport and hit an all-night diner to re-fuel on pancakes, ham, and eggs while discussing a strategy for approximately an hour. Then for the next three and a half hours, they sat parked in this spot up the street from Detective Jerry Pulia's home. Each of them caught maybe a thirty-minute nap.

Detective Jerry Pulia walked out the front door of his four-bedroom Tudor-style home at precisely five thirty. Dressed in a maroon track suit and white running shoes, he performed warm-up stretches on the front porch. After a deep cleansing breath, he trotted down the front steps on to the stone walkway that led through the manicured yard.

Once he reached the sidewalk of East Alder Lane, he began his morning jog. Still on paid administrative leave pending the investigations, he continued this part of his daily routine, according to Leo. They allowed Jerry to get into his run before Leo moved to start the truck.

"Wait," Nick said from the backseat.

Leo looked in the rearview mirror. A car was pulling out of a driveway coming their way. Leo let the car pass. One more car started in the house next to Pulia's. Leo waited for the car to back out and proceed down East Alder Lane. The neighborhood was coming to life. The working crowd was getting an early jump on their commute. Nick was anxious to get this done before anyone spotted them.

When all was quiet, Leo started the truck and followed Jerry, far enough behind to not be suspicious. When East Alder Lane rounded a bend to the right, it left the residential neighborhood behind and became a narrow two-lane country road. Most residents leaving the neighborhood would veer to the left at this point, heading towards the main highway.

Leo sped up to pass Jerry, then came to an abrupt stop just ahead of him. Jerry stopped hard in his tracks. Nick flung the rear passenger door open and stepped out. Jerry was about to turn and run in the opposite direction when Nick called out to him.

"Get in, Jerry. We need to talk."

Jerry halted his retreat and did a double-take. He hadn't recognized Nick in his street clothes and baseball cap. But his voice was unmistakable.

"Nick?" he called out between heavy breaths. He bent forward, pressing his palms to his knees, winded from the half mile jog.

"Hurry up before someone comes by," Nick called back to him and then climbed back inside the back seat of the truck, leaving the door open.

Nick twisted sideways in his seat to look at Jerry out the rear tinted window. He was being careless now. Out for a run on a deserted stretch of highway without a gun for protection or a cellphone to call for help. Nick could tell this because the bulk of any firearm would have been visible under the thin nylon jog suit. Not to mention his stride would have been hindered by it. And if he had a cellphone on him, he would've detected that through the nylon fabric, too.

Nick kept his eyes trained on Jerry as he looked around, considering his options. When nothing seemed plausible, he walked to the pickup and climbed into the back seat next to Nick. He closed the door. Leo put the truck in drive and continued down East Alder Lane. It remained a deserted strip of country road.

Jerry wiped beads of sweat from his face with his sleeve, breathing unusually hard from his short jog. His cheeks blushed red from the cold air mixed with his blood circulating under pressure. He apparently hadn't been at this jogging routine for very long.

"How the fuck is it that you're sitting here and not in a prison cell?" Jerry huffed between breaths.

Nick didn't respond.

"Jesus," he muttered half to himself. "Who else knows?"

"No one. And it's going to stay that way," Nick replied.

Jerry smiled. Devious thoughts were obviously running through his mind that Nick wasn't liking.

"I think you know not to cross me, Jerry."

"You fucked us all, Nick. You know that?"

"No. You fucked yourselves. You sided with a man who has no future."

Jerry thought about this. "Jimmy Teducci?"

Nick remained quiet.

"What does that mean, he has no future?" Jerry asked, sounding stressed. "What do you know about him?"

Nick didn't answer, allowing Jerry to stew with his thoughts. Jerry peered out his side window as the truck bounced along a dirt road now, no longer on East Alder Lane. His gaze came back to Nick with an odd expression. It wasn't surprise or worry or anger. It was more…

"I prided myself on being a good detective, you know?" Jerry said, then cast his eyes down to his hands clasped on his lap. "To serve and protect," he scoffed. His body jiggled as the truck continued off-road. "I served and protected the wrong people. I let down…"

His thought trailed off and he glanced back to the grassy meadow they were driving through. A moment later it became a thick forest. Leo pulled the truck into a densely wooded area and parked. He climbed out, leaving Nick and Jerry to talk and to keep an eye out for hikers.

"Cut the mea culpa crap, Jerry," Nick said. "You're not sorry one bit."

Jerry snapped his head back to Nick with anger.

"It was your choice and your choice alone to take those deals and accept the payouts," Nick continued. "No one forced you. But I'm not here to judge."

Jerry seemed unsettled.

"I just need some answers," Nick said.

"Yeah? Me, too," Jerry shot back. "How the fuck did you pull this off, Casey? Getting out of prison. D'Amato's gotta be spending half his fortune to fund his defense in all this."

"Never mind about me," Nick replied.

"You're no better than me, serving and protecting a criminal like him," Jerry chided.

"I never implied I was."

"What, better than me?"

Nick didn't answer him.

Jerry shifted his gaze back out to the surrounding forest. "I guess if I had been half the detective you were, I would have seen this coming." He brought his gaze back to Nick, looking defeated. "What do you want to know?" Jerry asked, the wind leaving his sails. He was ready to talk.

"What happened to the Janet Sardello car bombing case files?" Nick asked.

"That wasn't your case. Why do you care?"

"Just answer the question," Nick shot back.

Jerry chewed his lower lip, contemplating his answer. "From what I know, the FBI fucked that up during their raid of the crime lab. It's been missing ever since."

"Lying to me now isn't going to buy you more time, or save your ass, Jerry," Nick replied. "There's video footage of you removing the files from Gina's office. Where did you take them?"

Nick was lying at this point, but he hoped Jerry would believe him enough to give up the information. He needed to link the Sardello car bombing with Jimmy, and those files were the only way to do it. If he had the files in his possession, he could use them to coerce a confession out of Jimmy for Guiseppe's murder. He could offer Jimmy…

"What video footage?" Jerry cut into his thought.

"The crime lab security cameras."

Jerry thought long and hard about this. "There's no…" He stopped, confused. He was having difficulty recalling. "Are you sure?" he asked.

"I am," Nick answered with certainty. His ex-partner was doubting what he should know wasn't the truth. There was no video recording. There were no security cameras within the lab. Something he should have been privy to, but seemingly never paid attention to. His detective mind taking a backseat to his criminal behavior.

"Shit," Jerry exclaimed. "So, the FBI's going to…"

"It's only a matter of time, Jerry. Where are the files?"

Jerry exhaled, leaning his head back against the headrest. "I'm fucked."

"Where are the files?"

Jerry was studying the headliner. "I gave them to Jimmy."

That was a punch to Nick's gut. "You what?"

Jerry flopped his head, looking over to him. "Jimmy paid me four-grand to take them from the lab and deliver them to him."

"Four-grand."

"Yeah. I was supposed to go through the file and make sure nothing was traced back to him. File a report from the crime lab that the evidence was inconclusive."

"But you didn't do that?"

"No. I never had a chance. He just wanted the files returned to him as soon as possible. But he still paid me the full amount."

"But the files remained unchanged?"

"Yeah." Jerry sounded irritated. "That's what I said."

That was good news for Nick. That meant the Sardello bombing could still be linked to Jimmy. And he could also have conclusive evidence matching the Lincoln Marina bombing. When Nick had reviewed the Sardello file before it was sent to the lab, he had found similarities in the explosive devices used in both bombings.

This, coupled with the fact that Jimmy had bribed Jerry to tamper with the evidence and then demanded to have the files, was now stolen evidence. It would be enough to convict Jimmy of both bombings. He would be sent to prison for life without the possibility of parole.

"Where did you deliver the files?" Nick asked.

"To his office. I met Jimmy there last Sunday."

"When no one else was around."

"That's right."

"And lying to the FBI about them losing the files during the investigation, who's idea was that?"

Jerry considered his answer for a long moment. "It was mine." Jerry looked out to the forest once again. "In exchange, Jimmy's going to talk to district attorney Forrester about pushing the blame for the D'Amato mistrial on the others to keep me in the clear. That was our deal."

"Keeping you in the clear from fabricating three key pieces of evidence?"

"Yeah," Jerry scoffed.

"That's a pretty tall order."

Jerry remained quiet.

"You believe him?"

Jerry didn't answer. The red in his cheeks had faded. His complexion was pale now, almost sickly. His wide blue eyes stood out in contrast.

"What others?" Nick would leave nothing to chance. He wanted to be sure all the players would be involved.

Jerry looked back to Nick. He almost appeared relieved to be confessing his sins. "Sergeant Rotello, Officer Nunzio, prosecutor Chris Schuler from the D.A.'s office and Claire Chu from the crime lab."

Nick was satisfied. "I have one more thing for you, Jerry."

"What's that?"

Nick leaned forward to the front passenger seat and plucked a cellphone off the seat and sat back down. He waved the phone to Jerry. "This entire conversation has been recorded."

Jerry leaned his head back, mentally kicking himself. He punched his fist into the headliner.

"You go to anyone, and I mean anyone, about what we talked about here this morning, I turn this over."

Jerry looked to Nick, deflated. "What does it matter? I'm fucked either way."

"At least give me the chance to finish my investigation. Try to be a good detective once again. Do the right thing here and keep this under wraps."

Jerry closed his eyes, pressing his fingers to them and rubbing intently as if he were trying to wake up from a bad dream. He stopped and looked to Nick.

"Now what?"

"Now, you get out of the truck," Nick replied.

Jerry flinched, looking scared. "Why?"

"Because you're out for your morning run, Jerry. Now run home."

Jerry exhaled relief. Nick supposed he had thought the worst was about to happen to him. Jerry opened his door, climbed out, and closed the door. A moment later Leo climbed into the driver's seat, started the truck, and drove away, leaving Jerry standing in the woods.

~~~~~

As the silver pickup drove out of the woods and turned right onto East Alder Lane, Jimmy sat parked in his black Lexus, obscured from view. He had been on his way over to Jerry's house to pressure him into participating in his meeting with the D.A. at the Hudson County courthouse.

Jimmy was hoping that D.A. Forrester coupled with Detective Jerry Pulia would result in Judge Bailey giving up Nick Casey's place of incarceration. It was a likely possibility that the judge hadn't been informed yet that Pulia was a suspect in the FBI's investigations. And if so, he would grant them the information to discuss trial details and clarifications.

But as Jimmy drove down Jerry's street, he passed Jerry jogging in the opposite direction. Jimmy hadn't realized it at first and didn't come to the realization until he was halfway down Jerry's block. By the time Jimmy turned his car around and rounded the bend on East Alder Lane, Jerry was climbing into the backseat of a silver pickup. Jimmy followed from a safe distance. When the truck turned off the road, Jimmy parked and watched, hidden and waiting.

From his distance, he could only make out the driver: an African American man, maybe mid-thirties. It appeared no one else was in the truck with him. He waited for the truck to drive out of sight before starting his car.

Jimmy turned onto the dirt road and followed it into the wooded forest. It was possible Jerry had remained in the silver pickup and Jimmy hadn't been able to make him out through the tinted windows. But that thought quickly subsided. Up ahead, he spotted Jerry sitting on a large boulder with his head hung down.

Jimmy drove up to Jerry, stopping a good ten feet away. Jerry looked up. It took Jerry a moment to realize it was Jimmy behind the wheel. No longer concerned with having Jerry join him and Benjamin at the courthouse, Jimmy was now concerned with who Jerry had been meeting with in the silver pickup.

Jimmy put his car in park. He pulled his handgun from under the front driver's seat. He opened the center console and removed a pair of latex gloves and a silencer for his gun. He tucked both the gloves and silencer in his coat pocket. He tucked the firearm into his waistband, concealing it with his coat. He turned off the ignition and climbed out.

"Jimmy?" Jerry said. "What are you doing here?"

Jimmy closed his door and came around to the front of the car.

"Let's take a walk, Jerry."

Jimmy stood impatiently, watching Jerry calculate how Jimmy knew he was here in the woods. His detective mind spun theories. Jerry stood slowly and walked towards Jimmy. Jimmy pressed a hand on Jerry's back, turning him back towards the woods. Dry branches and leaves crunched underfoot as they walked deeper into the forest off the trail.

"I just came from a hike Jimmy, I don't need..."

"Shut the fuck up and walk."

Jerry stopped abruptly. "Fuck you, Jimmy. What is this? What are you doing here?"

"Who was in the truck, Jerry?"

"What truck?"

Jimmy diligently pulled on the latex gloves, then removed the gun from his waistband and waved it in front of Jerry. Jerry put his hands up in defense.

"Jesus, ok, ok." His wide blue eyes were panic stricken. He lowered his hands to his side. He looked around as if hoping for someone to come along and intercept them. But the only witnesses were the birds chirping merrily in the trees above.

"Move," Jimmy said, waving the gun towards the woods.

Jerry began walking. Jimmy followed a few steps behind, attaching the silencer to the end of his gun.

"Talk to me, Jerry."

Jerry stopped again, turning to face Jimmy. "No one you need to be concerned about."

Jimmy stopped a few feet away from him. "I'll be the judge of that. Who was it?"

Jerry eyed the gun again noticing its added hardware. His posture sagged. Jimmy could see there wasn't any fight left in him.

"Like I said. No one." It was a meager response.

"Come on, Jerry, humor me. Throw a name out. Lie to me for chrissake. Don't just stand there and play me for an idiot."

"I'm done, Jimmy," Jerry countered.

"What the fuck is that supposed to mean?"

"It means I'm done. I'm done with all of this. I don't want to be this corrupt person anymore. I've had it; with you, with the department, but mostly with myself."

"What is this, a coming to Jesus moment for you, Jerry? It doesn't work that way."

Jimmy pointed his gun at Jerry. He wasn't about to take any chances with Jerry talking to anyone and implicating him.

"No, no, no, Jimmy wait," Jerry pleaded.

He looked pathetic now. Jimmy had had enough.

"Jerry, Jerry, Jerry. You can't detour from the path you've been on, to a path of righteousness. You're too far gone for that."

"Jimmy, please,"

Jimmy fired a shot into Jerry's chest, sending him tumbling to the ground. The silencer muted the blast, but Jimmy instinctively surveyed his surroundings, making sure no one was in the vicinity. Shooting someone in broad daylight was a foolish thing to do. Jimmy knew better.

Jerry lay face down in the dirt, writhing and wheezing in pain. Jimmy walked up and stood over him. He fired two more shots into Jerry, killing him.

CHAPTER 20

The Terrace Room at New York's Plaza Hotel on Fifth Avenue at Central Park South was buzzing with three hundred guests for the black-tie event. Awards in journalism, publishing, and advertising had been announced and distributed earlier in the day by national and international media judges at the Lincoln Center Theater.

Jimmy had missed that part of the event, having been sidetracked with other pressing business. Chloe had been disappointed. It turned out that she had much to celebrate tonight. She had been an award recipient. Apparently, to be nominated for an award was an achievement not easily attained. And to win one was next to impossible without remarkable grit and creativity. Chloe had won two awards.

Jimmy vaguely recalled Chloe describing her accomplishments in between them both showering and changing clothes for tonight's party. One award was for an article written about homelessness. It had been a case study or something to that effect. Jimmy couldn't remember the details. The other one was a CLIO award for innovative media.

Obviously, it was a big deal. Jimmy probably should have been excited for his bride-to- be, but he wasn't in the mood for celebrating tonight. Killing Jerry Pulia earlier in the day was sapping his festive spirit. He was still trying to figure out who Jerry had been talking with in the silver pickup and what the content of that conversation might have been.

Jimmy watched his future in-laws, Daniel and Charlene Morgan, circle the room. They were the hosts of this social event. A private party for three hundred of their most respected colleagues. An event to celebrate the cache of awards received by Morgan Publishing.

Morgan Publishing had been founded by Daniel's grandfather over seventy years ago. It was originally a small book publishing house that began in a one-level warehouse in Brooklyn. Daniel's father grew the company by adding media and advertising components to their label. And he moved their offices to Madison Avenue in Manhattan.

Daniel and Charlene improved on those successes by adding online content in publishing, advertising, and social media. They had become a major contender in the publishing and advertising realm.

Wait staff scurried between the tables, ushering trays of champagne and hors d' oeuvres that appeared too artistic to eat. Fine linens draped the dining tables, topped with crystal, fine China, silverware, and flowers.

Jimmy sat at a table of twelve with Chloe by his side. The din of conversation was rising with the alcohol consumption, drowning out the string quartet playing on one of the terraces. Journalistic socialites reveled in their achievements and rubbed elbows with power players that could be their next big story. Chloe excused herself to go mingle.

An empty chair sat on either side of Jimmy now. Chloe's friend Megan sat one chair away from him, engrossed in conversation with the others at their table. They made a few attempts to include Jimmy in their discussions, but he had no interest in any of the people at their table. Well, except maybe for Megan. Jimmy had entertained a few indecent thoughts about her already tonight.

She was thin, almost fragile, Jimmy noticed. Her long blond mane hung straight down her back, nearly to her waist. The strapless dress she wore highlighted sun-kissed skin Jimmy wouldn't mind running his tongue over. He was drawn in by her sensual lips, glossed in soft pink, as she spoke with the others. Her light green eyes sparkled when she laughed. Jimmy licked his lips. He imagined what she'd taste like. He allowed his thoughts to wander, because he was in a place he didn't want to be tonight.

He couldn't remember the names of the other guests. He didn't care. Two of them were writers and two of them were from the editing department of Morgan Publishing. The other four were their spouses or significant others. It wasn't like him to not remember a name. He felt out of his element, and that surprised him. There were plenty of politicians present tonight. Plenty of legislators ripe for lobbying, but he just wasn't in the mood.

He turned his attention to the menu card at his place setting. Following hors d' oeuvres would be a six-course meal prepared by six different chefs. Each one was preparing his or her own masterful creation with a wine pairing. Jimmy could feel a headache coming on. He was getting a glimpse of what next month held for him. When he and Chloe tied the knot, he would be inducted into publishing royalty. Chloe's parents would host a grand spectacle to celebrate the wedding of their only child.

The Morgans knew how to entertain. Their soirees were renowned. Jimmy had no doubt their wedding would be a highly publicized event that he would rather do without. He could already imagine the outcome. It was going to draw the Teducci family into the headlines once again. Corruption hype would overshadow their wedding nuptials.

But that wasn't what bothered Jimmy. He wasn't concerned about the impact it would have on the Morgan family. He cared for Chloe, but he didn't love her. His marriage to her was simply a means to an end. She put her career ahead of him, and that was fine with him. He had plans of his own.

What bothered him was that the D'Amato mistrial would still be fresh news. Jimmy would have to relive his failure to put Joe behind bars all over again. His stomach felt sour now. He took another drink of champagne, wanting something stronger.

Jimmy's gaze wandered the room, landing on Chloe. She had the ears of four other individuals, captivating them with journalistic flair. Jimmy marveled at her poise and charm. She would do well to uphold the sterling reputation of the Morgan Publishing empire.

Empire. Jimmy scoffed to himself. It was a noun used in an online blurb that he'd read recently. Jimmy recalled a statement claiming that their reputation had been built on facts, not fabrication. Jimmy thought that part might change once they were married. Having access to unlimited media products would serve Jimmy well in his lobbying career.

He knew Chloe's aspirations for him were to run for a political office. She had mentioned it on more than one occasion since their engagement. And each time she mentioned it, Jimmy gave the thought serious consideration as far as she was concerned. But he had no intentions of running for or holding any type of political office. Lobbying suited him fine.

Jimmy wondered how Chloe had ever been able to convince her parents that marrying him was a good idea. He smiled to himself, taking a sip from her glass of champagne. He imagined she'd sold them on the premise of grooming him for a promising political career.

He took another drink, but the champagne wasn't dulling his boredom. Having to sit in a room full of reporters and marketers enduring Chloe's spotlight was making him edgy. He thought about Jeanette. He would prefer to be lying in bed with her right now, getting his dick sucked and his brains fucked out by her instead of sitting here feeling like a chump in a chimp suit. Chloe had a way of doing that to him. Making him feel diminished.

Chloe returned to their table, vaporizing his thoughts. She continued chatting non-stop. She was in her element. Megan sat next to her, sharing details about his and Chloe's upcoming wedding. Endless babble droning on and on about dresses and shoes and food and gift registry; blah blah blah. His head began to throb listening to them.

"Have you heard from Gina?" Chloe asked Megan. "I tried calling her again today. I was hoping she was going to make it tonight." Chloe turned, giving Jimmy's arm a playful punch. "I can't believe your cousin isn't here. She's going to be my maid of honor. How could she miss this?"

Jimmy shrugged. He was more in tune to Megan's expression of obvious annoyance.

"No," Megan replied.

"Is she back from L.A. yet?" Chloe asked, turning back to Megan. "She was only supposed to be gone for a week, right? Or was it two? I can't remember. I've been so busy."

Their conversation had Jimmy's interest now, but he remained quiet.

"I told you that in confidence, Chloe." Megan's green eyes flashed on Jimmy then back to Chloe.

"What's the big deal?" Chloe looked to Jimmy then back to Megan. "Why is she in L.A.?" Jimmy asked.

Megan deflated and took a sip of her champagne. She was obviously upset that Chloe had mentioned Gina's trip to L.A. *Why?* Jimmy wondered.

Chloe broke the awkward silence, speaking to Jimmy. "She had a case to work on out there. She went with a couple of techs from the lab." Chloe spun back to Megan. "Why was it a big deal not to say anything?"

Megan shrugged her boney shoulders. "I don't know. Gina just asked me not to tell anyone where she was going."

Chloe laughed. "That's silly. It's her job." Chloe waved a dismissive hand. Jimmy had his eyes trained on Megan. Her cheeks were flushed now. Her eyes downcast to her glass of champagne. *What was she not saying?* Jimmy wondered. He would remember to circle back around to her later in the night and find out.

Chloe's parents stopped by their table. The media moguls, as Jimmy had come to refer to them. Chloe was a spitting image of her mother: sharp angular facial features that topped a dynamite body. Full, rounded breasts and soft pouty lips. Charlene could have been Chloe's older sister.

And she had a head for business, just like Chloe did. Jimmy was staring at his future in this accomplished couple and it looked good to him. Chloe's father came from a legal background, which he had pursued along with journalism. He worked behind the scenes with a team of attorneys, handling all legal and financial matters. Jimmy thought there could be some conflicts with him later down the line, but Jimmy would worry about that then.

Jimmy had done his homework on them prior to asking Chloe to marry him. He was impressed by their achievements, if not a little envious. The Morgans were the real deal. A power-couple. Their combined talents and ambition had carried their success.

Jimmy had talent and ambition, too, but in a different arena. He could be charming and persuasive when bending the ear of a certain politician, aiming for a piece of legislation to rule in his favor. He could also be ruthless and fierce when things didn't go his way. Like Joe's mistrial.

He doubted very much that the Morgans had the sort of talent and ambition required to right a wrong of that nature.

Jimmy missed what everyone at their table was laughing at, but he didn't care. His thoughts shifted. Because of the mistrial, because of Nick Casey, he had been forced to make new arrangements. Nick had sabotaged his original plan and the outcome of his goal. There was nothing Jimmy could do to fix that now.

Instead, he focused on limiting the risk of any of the players turning on him. He would engage some general housekeeping measures to make sure no one spoke to law enforcement. By this time tomorrow, all threats would be eliminated. Well, all except for one. Nick Casey.

Jimmy had hired professionals to hit their marks all on the same night. Tonight. This would ensure none of the players involved would panic and talk, or run, like Claire Chu from the lab had done. Jimmy had found out through his sources that she boarded a plane bound for Hong Kong earlier today, but she would meet her demise once she landed. And the rest of them would meet theirs tonight. Just like Jerry had this morning.

If Claire had left immediately following the mistrial, Jimmy might not have figured out her plan. She might have gotten away. Now, he only had to focus on Nick Casey. He already knew how to take care of him, he just needed to find out where he had been incarcerated.

Hugs and congratulations with the Morgans continued from the guests at their table. Jimmy tuned back into the conversation. The Morgans were gushing heartfelt sentiments of how pleased they were to have Jimmy joining their family. Whatever. It benefitted him to use their publishing firm to solicit bribes for advertising. He would play the doting fiancé. He wrapped an arm around Chloe and kissed her cheek for good measure.

Her parents left their table shortly afterwards, to circle the room. Three hundred guests to schmooze and flatter and receive compliments from. Plenty of ass-kissing going on in the room. People wanted to bask in the glow of the Morgans' talent and success.

And if Jimmy had been able to shake his foul mood, he would have been circling the room himself, glad-handing and soliciting for his own benefit. But what was to take place later tonight, mixed with the image of Jerry Pulia's body writhing in pain face down in the dirt, kept penetrating his thoughts.

Jimmy instinctively flexed his right hand. Phantom vibrations from the gun firing in his grip kept recurring. It had been a while since he'd shot someone. He preferred explosive devices. A method that killed without physical involvement or mental aftermath from having witnessed the kill.

The image of Jerry rolling over to face him repeatedly pierced his thoughts. His wide blue eyes looking up to him with panic. Sobbing from the pain. Dirt and leaves and debris from the forest floor plastered to his sweating face. His body quivered when Jimmy pumped two more bullets into him.

Jimmy rubbed his eyes. It wasn't like him to let images like that command his thoughts. Maybe this time it was the fact that there were so many about to meet the same fate as Jerry. Maybe it was proving to be too much to ignore now.

Jimmy gulped down the last of Chloe's champagne. He needed to focus his attention elsewhere before his thoughts spiraled out of control. Most of the guests were seated for the six-course menu that hadn't even begun. It was going to be a long night. Jimmy excused himself and went to the bar.

"Jamison, neat," he told the bartender.

When his drink arrived, he downed it and asked for a double. When the second one arrived, he took his drink and sat at the end of the bar. Alone. He searched the headlines on his cellphone.

There were plenty of stories posted regarding detective Pulia's murder. Jimmy rubbed his eyes again. It wasn't going away. That little nagging itch causing him to question his actions. Wondering if he had covered his tracks. He had acted in haste this morning. He replayed each detail once again as he sipped his whiskey.

After murdering Jerry, he drove over twenty miles before pulling up to a convenience store fuel pump. Pump number four. He walked inside, purchased a burner cellphone and a water, paid with cash, and left the store. He took care to wear a baseball cap and sunglasses and kept his head down to avoid revealing too much to the security cameras inside the store.

On the way back to his car, he ripped open the packaging and removed the phone. He tossed the packaging into a trash can on the fuel pump island. He started towards his car and then remembered the latex gloves he wore to shoot Jerry with. He reached into his pocket and removed them. He returned to the trash can and discarded the gloves. He kept his back to the store so the exterior cameras wouldn't have a clear image of what he had been tossing in the trash.

He climbed back inside his car, closed the door, and drove away. Twenty minutes later he pulled into a drive-through car wash to clean off any dust and debris from the dirt road. Like Jerry's face when it slammed into the ground after collapsing from the first bullet.

Jimmy dialed the number to the Hoboken police department customer service while his car crept along in the car wash. He purposely did not dial nine-one-one. Long fiber strips slapped and squirmed their way across the hood of his car, slathering soap suds up and over the windshield.

When a woman's voice answered, Jimmy reported having spotted a possible gunshot victim while hiking in the woods near a residential neighborhood off East Alder Lane. He also reported having seen a silver pickup truck leaving the area with a mid-thirties African American man behind the wheel.

Next came the large blue spinning brushes attacking the front, sides, and rear of his car. None of this had been part of his original plan. If only Jerry had stayed home this morning instead of taking a ride in a silver pickup, Jimmy wouldn't have had to kill him yet. He hadn't planned on killing Jerry until after he found out where Nick had been imprisoned. Improvising, he made the anonymous call to direct the police away from him.

When the woman asked for him to hold so she could transfer his call to an officer or detective, Jimmy hung up. He had given her enough information. Powerful streams of water sprayed down, followed by high-powered blowers. Jimmy watched the bubbles and beads of water jiggle and scatter across the hood and windshield, eventually evaporating. Just like Jerry's bulk had jiggled when the bullets ripped through his body.

Jimmy wished that image would evaporate from his mind. He recalled his car rolling out into the sunshine, sparkling clean. He drove over to a trash can, opened his door, tossed the burner cellphone in, then left the carwash.

The rest of his day had been a lost cause. He had driven down to Hudson county to meet district attorney Benjamin Forrester. The court order Jimmy paid Benjamin to round up turned out to be a waste of time. Judge Bailey had remained tight-lipped as to where Nick was being incarcerated. They were concerned for his safety, is what the judge had told Benjamin.

The only positive that came out of the trip down there was that Benjamin had been authorized to review the video footage of Nick Casey leaving the courthouse jail. He was one of seven inmates loaded into the prison transport van and driven away. But to where, was not disclosed.

Jimmy had hoped to sit in with Benjamin during both accounts, but he hadn't been given authorization. And that didn't surprise him. He wasn't anyone directly involved with the case. Instead, he sat in the waiting room until Benjamin returned.

Of all the players in his plan, Nick posed the biggest threat now. Something Jimmy hadn't been prepared for. Taking Nick out was his number one priority. Jimmy had people standing by, waiting for his instructions. It would be a matter of making a phone call. And it could have been taken care of by now if only he knew where they had carted Nick off to.

As much as he wanted to do the killing himself, he wouldn't be able to with Nick in prison. But his hired professionals would be able to. This job was going to cost him a small fortune. But knowing Nick would be gone from this life forever would be worth every penny.

And he would pay it, too. Jimmy knew better than to try to negotiate payment on a contract for hire. Whatever they demanded; he would give it to them. He had learned a long time ago the repercussions of not paying the agreed upon amount. He had also learned not to use the same people more than once.

One-time hired professionals don't know you. They didn't want to know you. They just wanted their instructions and their payment for doing their job. Period. And they'd do a good job because they wanted to get paid without hassle.

Jimmy had hired separate individuals to take care of the remaining players. He had wanted Jerry Pulia handled by someone else, too. But this morning, well, shit just happened. So much for that plan.

In any event, having witnessed Jerry climbing into the silver pickup truck and taking a drive to the woods, Jimmy knew he couldn't trust any of his players anymore. Jerry was talking to someone. Most likely the Feds. Most likely cutting himself a deal. There was no telling how much information he'd spilled to them.

Since the mistrial, Jimmy had been through Joe's case in painstaking detail. There was nothing directly connecting Jimmy to any of it. It would all be hearsay. They couldn't prove the bribes, the pay outs, the corruption leading to the mistrial, none of it. He was in the clear. So why did he want to kill anyone that could point a finger at him?

Because like his father once told him in a drunken stupor, your secret is safe so long as those you told it to are dead. He was right. It was probably the only time Jimmy could recall giving his old man credit for something. And Jimmy wasn't going to leave anything or anyone to chance.

Jimmy downed the rest of his whiskey. Tomorrow would be one week since the mistrial where Nick's testimony had upended months of planning and preparations to put away Joe D'Amato for a good long time. Long enough for Jimmy to make his move, taking over contracts in New York.

The ten thousand dollars Jimmy had paid Nick up front to carry out his part of the plan was gone. But that didn't matter to Jimmy. What mattered was that Nick went back on his word, back on their deal. He single-handedly blew apart a great plan. A full-proof plan. A plan that would only work once. Jimmy would never have another opportunity like this to put Joe D'Amato behind bars. And *that's* what mattered to him.

Nick should have been dead five days ago. The secrecy of his location was wearing thin on Jimmy. He needed to find the right person to give up the information. There was always someone willing to talk for the right price. And if not, blackmail was a useful alternative that...

"Honey?" Chloe was standing by his side at the bar. "Are you ok?"

Jimmy bounced from his spiraling thoughts and looked over to her. She looked exquisite. The long black sequined dress hugged her curves. Thread thin shoulder straps, a plunging neckline, and low-cut backline exposed plenty of creamy white flawless skin.

Jimmy thought of whisking her off to a side room somewhere and plunging himself into her. She would most likely object to the idea. Jeanette, on the other hand, would have obliged his desire.

"Can I get you another one?" the bartender asked.

"Yeah. I'll take it to go." The whiskey was improving his mood.

The bartender poured him another double shot of Jamison, then left to tend to other patrons. Jimmy took his drink and slid off his barstool. "I'm fine," he answered Chloe.

He took her arm and walked with her back to the party. *Who at this party tonight would have that information?* Jimmy wondered.

CHAPTER 21

This same night, Nick entered the Plaza Hotel just before eight thirty, taking precautions to shield his identity with a Harley Davidson cap, tinted riding glasses, and a heavy leather jacket. He used a service entrance, following hotel staff through a single door as they entered.

Leo remained in the silver pickup parked in a loading zone near the Pulitzer Fountain. Hopefully being parked in this area wouldn't pose any problems. If it did, Nick had left him his badge to use, alleging official police business.

Nick rode a service elevator up to the sixteenth floor. He was on his way to meet with Joe D'Amato to give him the latest details. He would also be receiving Joe's instructions for his next move. Nick had no doubt Joe would be asking him to take care of Jimmy, possibly as soon as tonight.

It would be the first time Joe would make that request of Nick. To kill someone. To some extent that bothered Nick. He was concerned that it would change things between him and Joe.

The elevator doors glided open and he stepped off into the carpeted hallway. He followed the numbered arrows to room sixteen ten. He knocked twice. A moment later a man in a tailored suit opened the door. It was Eddie, one of Joe's security detail. Nick knew him well. He had selected and trained Eddie and one other, Sean. And he had used both men earlier today. Sean was currently sitting with Jeanette at a safe house in New Jersey.

"Hey, Nick," Eddie said, swinging the door fully open. "Come in. Joe's in the living room to the right."

"Thanks," Nick said, shaking Eddie's hand before walking past him into the suite.

Nick removed his cap and glasses as he walked to the large living room, furnished in Edwardian luxury. Not Nick's taste, but what did he care?

Joe reclined on the gold fabric sofa, reading a newspaper. Outfitted in slacks, a dress shirt, and loafers, he appeared relaxed and rested. The aromas from what must have been Joe's dinner still lingered in the air. Joe set the paper down and stood to shake Nick's hand and embrace him.

Joe had reserved this room knowing the Morgan Publishing party was taking place downstairs. And knowing Jimmy would be attending. Even though Judge Bailey's orders had been for Joe to not leave the state of New Jersey, Nick knew Joe's connections could work their way around that order.

Nick set his cap and glasses on the coffee table and draped his leather jacket on the back of a side chair. He glanced out the tall windows before taking a seat. Central Park was just across the street, but too dark to appreciate this time of night.

"Drink?" Joe asked.

"No. I'm good. Thank you," Nick replied, scanning the room.

A dining room, small kitchenette and wet bar rounded out the two-room suite. A propane fireplace flickered in the wall next to Nick. The setting seemed more appropriate for the two to engage in a chess game rather than discussing Jimmy's fate.

Eddie took a seat at the dining table with a section of the newspaper. Joe poured himself a mug of tea at the bar, then returned to the sofa. He tossed aside the newspaper he had been reading and sat perched on the edge of the sofa.

"How are you, Nick?" he asked.

"I'm good."

"You look like shit," Joe replied. "When was the last time you got any sleep?"

Nick shrugged his shoulders. "Don't worry about me."

"I do. You risk a great deal in this condition. To yourself and to others." He sipped the steaming mug of tea.

"I'll sleep plenty when this is over."

Joe eyed him over his mug, not satisfied with his response. When Nick didn't say anything else, Joe set his mug down on the coffee table and eased his weight back to sit fully on the sofa.

"I'd like to hear your thoughts on the matter downstairs," he said. "We both know these things can't be rushed. But the sooner the better for all concerned."

"Let me take you through the events of today, before you make any decisions," Nick replied.

Joe did not react, but Nick could tell his calculating brain was churning full speed ahead like always. He was patient and careful in his actions. And he never reacted.

If you didn't know Joe, you would think he hadn't heard a word you said or had possibly misunderstood you. Or was maybe even flat out ignoring you. But Nick knew him. Too well. Joe was an exceptional listener. A practice he principled himself on. And a lesson he had taught Nick as a kid: you have two ears and one mouth. Use them accordingly.

His nature was eloquent and courteous, and he was as good as his word. Always making sure everyone got a fair shake, on both sides of any deal he made. Unfortunately, every now and then there was some dumb fuck who thought he deserved better.

If you crossed him, you crossed a line there was no turning back from. Calculating and ruthless would best describe Joe's demeanor at that point. Nick had witnessed this side of Joe plenty of times growing up. And for no good reason. There was no need to cross Joe. He took care of his family, whether it was under his roof or under his organization.

Of course, his organization was built on corruption. And of course, that corruption conflicted with Nick's career path. But, neither of them split hairs over the fact. There was corruption on both sides of the law. It was Nick who had had to come to terms with that fact. And he had. When he decided to back Joe and not his department.

"Fine. Let's have it," Joe responded, bringing Nick back to their meeting.

"Jimmy should be in a holding cell," Nick said. "But things didn't play out the way I planned."

"Sometimes plans have a mind of their own."

"Leo and I couldn't have been more than five miles away from Jerry when Jimmy found him," Nick said, feeling the weight of guilt. "It had to be Jimmy that killed Jerry. And I'll be able to prove that once we process the gun we found at his office."

Joe gave a slight nod, leaned forward to pick up his mug, then he leaned back again.

Nick continued, "After Jerry told me that Jimmy had paid him to deliver the Janet Sardello car bombing case files to him, I wanted to search Jimmy's office and apartment for them. We were headed to Jimmy's office after leaving Jerry. Leo obtained information through the district attorney's office that a warrant had been granted to D.A. Benjamin Forrester to access evidence from your trial at the Hudson county courthouse. The warrant was limited and specific, only allowing the D.A. to view recorded evidence of my transfer."

"And what did that entail?" Joe asked.

"A video recording of me stepping off the elevator in the G1 garage of the courthouse and climbing into the prison transport van."

"That's it?"

"That's it."

"So, they're not aware that your van was stopped by Sergeant Jim Slater just outside the courthouse and that he pulled you off of that van and re-routed you back to the courthouse?" Joe clarified.

"No. And we used the personnel garage G2 on the third lower level, where cameras are minimal. No one thought to ask about viewing that video footage."

"And no one has thought to talk to the transport van driver?"

"Not yet." Nick said. "If they do, his information will have them answering to Sergeant Slater."

"Good," Joe replied.

"We knew Jimmy would be meeting the D.A. at the Hudson county courthouse to take part in the warrant search, so we thought we knew where he was going to be. It would give us time to meet Jerry and search his office and apartment. Shortly after our meeting with Jerry in the woods, Leo consulted the tracking device he'd been using to follow Jimmy. That's when we realized Jimmy wasn't on his way south to Hudson county, but was leaving Jerry's location." Nick paused for a moment, thinking about Jerry. "Not realizing Jerry had been shot, we started our tail on Jimmy. We followed him for three stops: a convenience store, a carwash, and his office. After that, he headed south to Hudson county. Leo and I hung back at his office. That's when I called for Eddie and Sean to come help us." Nick tipped his head to Eddie, who was still reading his newspaper. "We were going to search Jimmy's office. If we didn't find anything, we were going to hit his apartment afterward."

Joe sipped his tea, listening to every detail.

"Jimmy's assistant Jeanette was the only employee there," Nick continued. "I used my badge and a simulated warrant to get her to open Jimmy's safe. After that, Leo had Sean take her to a safe house. He's keeping her there until I have Jimmy in custody, or..." Nick didn't finish his sentence because that depended on what Joe would ask him to do tonight.

Joe nodded.

"I searched the safe." Nick continued. "Found a nine-millimeter handgun with a silencer still attached, five- grand in cash, some contract documents, and the Sardello case files."

Joe showed no emotion. "Stupid prick," he muttered. "There's a reason that kid never amounted to anything, and never will."

"Why he didn't destroy em', I don't know. But it's to our benefit," Nick replied. "We bagged, tagged, and boxed it all up." Nick paused, looking down to his interlocked fingers. He tapped his thumbs together, recalling what he had witnessed while searching Jimmy's office.

After Leo and Eddie had left Jimmy's office with the last of the boxes, Nick had walked over to the wall of windows behind Jimmy's desk. He gazed out to the Hudson and New York, absorbed with the view: watercraft and ferries gliding over where the Lincoln tunnel lay submerged under water.

His gaze had slowly made its way north, landing on Lincoln Marina. He'd flinched when the marina came into view. A surreal moment. It was where his investigation had begun. The explosion that had killed

Guiseppe and his two college friends. Where Sirrina had supposedly perished as well.

Nick thought there were only two reasons that Jimmy would want that view from his office: a sight that had been the scene of such a horrific event. Guilt or gratification. Nick was betting on the first one.

"Are you ok?" Joe asked.

Nick brought his attention back to Joe. "Yeah."

"You don't look it," Joe said. "If it's too close…" He paused a moment, rethinking what he wanted to say. "Don't make me regret accepting your desire to carry this thing out personally."

"I won't," Nick said. He hadn't realized he was giving Joe doubts.

"Is that it?"

"No," Nick replied with renewed energy. "After his meeting in Hudson county, he made his way back to Jersey. We started tailing him again and followed him to Liberty State Park. He met with three separate individuals over the course of an hour." Nick paused.

"For?"

"Contracts. For the lives of Sergeant Rotello, Officer Nunzio, and prosecutor Chris Schuler. All three of them tonight."

"Jesus." Joe sat forward, placing his mug back on the table. "In one night."

"It's how I would do it," Nick replied.

"There's no doubt he has one earmarked for you, then."

"I know I would," Nick answered.

Joe appeared bothered by this comment, but didn't say anything, so Nick continued. "As the individuals left the park, I called in their plate numbers to Sergeant Jim Slater. He gave me their addresses. I had three of your people round them up." Nick referenced Joe. "They have them holed up in a hotel in Jersey."

"And the contracts?" Joe asked.

"We bought them out, offering double the price Jimmy was going to pay."

Joe nodded, satisfied with that result.

Nick recalled getting to the hotel after the contract killers had been rounded up. When he entered the room, he hadn't expected to see the three men lined up on the couch. Hands zip-tied and black cloth shrouding their heads.

Joe's men had taken precautions to protect Nick and Leo's identity. He learned the three hitmen knew nothing of each other. And that they had each been assigned to kill one individual in exchange for ten thousand dollars. It didn't matter how, it just had to be done by tonight.

"We have one in the wind," Nick continued. "Claire Chu."

"From the crime lab?" Joe asked.

"Right. None of them knew the name. So, either Jimmy's not bothering with her, which would surprise me, or he's got something set up for her when she lands in Hong Kong tonight. I won't be able to help her, if so."

"Her choice to flee," Joe said.

"Do you blame her?"

"It's not for me to worry about," Joe commented. "Or you."

Nick thought about the call he'd received from Joe earlier in the day. Joe had been contacted by Sergeant Slater regarding an anonymous tip on the shooting in the woods, reassuring Joe the tip would be filed as inconclusive.

It had been a close call with Jimmy showing up. More troubling was how close he and Leo had been to Jerry. They could have possibly saved him. He also realized that Jimmy may have spotted them with Jerry in the woods.

"Any possibility Jimmy saw us today with Jerry?" Nick asked. "Would he know I'm not in prison?"

Joe nodded. "No. Like I told you earlier, when Sergeant Slater called me about the anonymous tip, they hadn't made an ID on Leo and they stated that he was the only person in the truck. You weren't spotted. I got an update from the sergeant less than an hour ago. Still nothing. Your cover's still intact."

"You think it was Jimmy who called it in?"

Joe shrugged. "Whether it was or not, no one is looking for you. That's all that matters."

Nick accepted this, but deep down, he was bothered by it.

"Where are you with Atlanta?" Joe asked.

"Nothing yet," Nick replied, knowing that wasn't the answer Joe wanted to hear.

Joe didn't respond.

"We'll take Jimmy tonight," Nick said.

"No. Hold off on that course of action." Joe held up his hand in gesture.

Nick was surprised by his request. "I thought you wanted Jimmy taken care of as soon as possible," he said. "Once he finds out that his hired contractors didn't do their jobs, he's going to figure out someone's working against him. He could be a flight risk."

"He's not going anywhere," Joe said with confidence.

"Do you know something that I don't?"

"He's predictable," Joe said. "When he finds out his contractors didn't perform, he'll want answers. He'll hire someone to find the contractors he paid, and that's going to take time. Time he's not aware that he doesn't have. And he won't pay out another thirty-grand to anyone else until he has his answers, because he likes his money too much. By then, well…"

Joe didn't need to finish that sentence.

Maybe Joe was right. But Nick had also known Jimmy to panic when faced with a threatening circumstance. "We'll need to protect those contractors."

"I'll take care of that," Joe said. "You take care of Atlanta."

"And Jimmy?"

Joe pondered this for a long moment. "I'll let you know when I'm ready for Jimmy." He circled his index finger around the rim of his mug. "He won't be killed." Joe raised his eyes to Nick. "I'd like you to solve your case in Atlanta first. But either way, Jimmy will go to prison. I can guarantee you it won't be a pleasant stay for him. I'll get more satisfaction from that."

Nick felt a strange mix of relief and remorse wash over him. He nodded, agreeing with Joe. His cellphone rang. Leo read on the display. He took the call.

"Yeah?"

"We might have a situation here tonight."

"What's that?"

"Gina decided to attend the Morgans dinner party tonight," Leo said. "She entered the hotel twenty minutes ago. I needed to confirm it was her before calling you."

Nick refrained from reacting in front of Joe. "Alright, thanks," Nick replied, rubbing a hand over his tired eyes. "I'll be down in a minute. Stay put in the truck."

Nick disconnected the call and pushed his phone back into his pocket.

"Problem?" Joe asked.

"Nothing I can't handle."

"Gina's here."

Nick looked over to him.

"I could hear Leo's side of the conversation," Joe said.

"Not for long." Nick stood and pulled on his jacket.

Joe stood up and they shook hands. "I'll wait to hear from you," Joe said.

Nick collected the rest of his things, placing the Harley Davidson cap back on his head and slipping on his tinted shades. Eddie stood and began to walk towards them.

"I can let myself out," Nick said to him.

Nick left Joe's room to go find Gina.

CHAPTER 22

Gina sat with Megan at their table for twelve, sipping champagne and chatting amicably with the eight other guests. The two seats to Gina's left were vacant when she'd arrived twenty minutes earlier. Megan told her Chloe had gone off to collect Jimmy from somewhere.

A small army of servers began ushering in the first course of the meal. Some balanced silver serving trays loaded with small plates dotted with artsy morsels. Others glided around the room clutching a wine bottle in each hand, pouring the wine selected to pair with the first course.

Gina was entertained by it all. "I feel like royalty tonight," she said to Megan. "I'm glad I came."

Megan sipped her wine. "Oh, me, too. And yes, everyone should get to experience a night like tonight at least once in their life, don't you think?"

"I do," Gina replied.

They clinked their wine glasses and sipped. Gina was glad she'd made the last-minute decision to fly up from Atlanta. Even though it would be a quick turn-around, she would get to enjoy a special night with her two best friends. She couldn't wait to see Chloe's reaction.

Jimmy and Chloe made their way back to the table.

"Gina." Jimmy spoke louder than necessary.

"Oh my gosh!" Chloe shrieked. "You're here!"

Gina looked up to them. She had to admit, her cousin was handsome. Even more so decked out in a tux. His cheeks were flush, and his smile beamed at her. And Chloe of course looked fashionable and radiant in her little black sequined get-up. Gina set her wine glass down and stood to greet them.

"Jesus. Get a look at you," Jimmy said, pulling her to him in an uncomfortably tight embrace.

"Hey, cuz," Gina said, still pressed up against him.

He pulled back, holding both of her arms out. "Damn, aren't you a hot number tonight."

Gina caught a heavy whiff of alcohol on his breath. Obviously celebrating Chloe's big night.

"Jimmy!" Chloe chided him, pushing her way between them. She gave Gina a tight embrace rocking her back and forth. "Yeee, I'm so glad you made it. What a surprise." Chloe was ecstatic. She pulled away. "You do look stunning tonight," she said with an infectious smile.

Even in heels, Chloe was still two inches taller than her. "So do you," Gina said.

Gina smoothed a hand over her full-length Armani slip of a dress: a halter-neck couture sheath of jade knit that fit her curves perfectly. Her hair was tied up with a fancy clip revealing the open back of the dress. She felt wonderfully sexy in the long gown and heels.

"All three of us look stunning tonight," Gina remarked, holding an arm out to both Chloe and Megan. "And congratulations on your awards, Chloe."

The three of them embraced each other.

"Thank you," Chloe said.

"Lord, take me now, with them." Jimmy reveled, pressing his hands over his heart.

Gina thought Jimmy seemed overly animated. She wondered if there was something other than the alcohol energizing him tonight. Her criminological mind was always at work.

Chloe playfully smacked Jimmy's arm. "I think someone's had a few too many."

"Not even," Jimmy scoffed.

"How about a picture?" offered one of the guests at their table.

"Oh, great idea," Gina replied. "Use mine." She readied her cellphone and handed it over to the guest.

The four of them lined up with arms around one another. Gina felt Jimmy pull and squeeze her waist a little too tight. She smiled for the picture, then broke away, taking her phone from the guest.

"Thank you."

Gina returned to her seat, setting her phone on the table, and then scooting in her chair. Jimmy snatched up her phone.

"Hey," Gina said, trying to snatch it back from him, but he was too quick. She had case sensitive information on it, so it bothered her that it was in his possession. Not to mention that Nick's number and text messages were under her most recent activity.

He scrolled for the picture. "Relax. I'm just sending this to me and Chloe." He sent the picture then returned her phone to the table next to her plate.

Fortunately, he had placed it face down on the table, because when it rang a moment later, Nick Casey was on the display. Her heart skipped a beat. That had been a close call. She reprimanded herself, needing to be more careful.

"I have to take this." She excused herself.

Gina made her way to a quiet corner of the room, answering the call as she walked. "Hello?"

"It's Nick."

"Hey. How are you?" She tried to sound casual. She covered the receiver, not wanting him to hear the festivities going on in the background. She was sure he wouldn't be happy with her decision to leave Atlanta for the night.

"Not enjoying the night as much as you are."

Was he being sarcastic? She couldn't tell. And she couldn't tell him where she was. But she didn't want to lie to him, either.

"I was just…"

"Never mind," he cut her off. "Tell your guests you need to take a call at the front desk. Don't say anything more. Meet me at the bar next to the Fifth Avenue entrance."

"You're *here*?" Gina was stunned. At the *hotel*?"

"I am," he replied. "Make it quick. I'm risking someone seeing me here."

"Right."

Shit. Gina's hands were shaking as she disconnected the call. Had he followed her? Why else would he be in New York? She was compromising his cover by not adhering to his plan. Why had she decided to come tonight? *Shit. Shit. Shit!* She was kicking herself. Chloe and Megan would have understood if she couldn't have made it. She could have said work was keeping her in L.A. longer than planned, which wouldn't have been a far stretch from the truth.

She had just thought it would be a nice surprise to show up on Chloe's important night. And it had been a nice surprise. Chloe had been so excited and giddy just moments earlier. But she doubted Nick would care. He would only care about the fact she had made him follow her here tonight. Caused him to risk his position and his investigation. The worst part was that she knew better.

Gina made her way back to the table. She set her phone down.

"Apparently, I have a call waiting for me at the front desk." Gina said as she bent down to retrieve her clutch purse off the floor.

Jimmy snatched up her phone and began scrolling through it. Before Gina realized what he was doing, it was too late. The look on his face said it all. He'd found Nick's name on her caller ID. Gina felt panic rising inside her. Jimmy was speechless. His dark, calculating eyes held her surprised expression, not saying a word. Then his lip curled into a grin.

"Come on, honey," he wrapped an arm around Chloe, pretending he hadn't seen Nick's name. "Get in the pic with me." He took a selfie of himself and Chloe. He reviewed the picture with Chloe, then looked to Gina. "I need to hit the head. I'll go with you." He stood up.

Gina straightened, clutching her purse. "I think I can manage on my own," she said. "It's probably just work or something." She waved a dismissive hand.

"Nonsense." Jimmy spoke with a proper English lilt. "Allow me the pleasure to escort my darling cousin to the front desk on my way." He held out an arm for her to take, looking spiteful.

"Oh, that's sweet," Megan said.

"Knock it off, Jimmy." Gina forced a smile, ignoring Megan. "Can I have my phone please?"

Jimmy was drunk. And Gina could see that he wasn't about to let this opportunity to pull her aside escape him. If she flat out refused his escort, he would make a scene.

"I'll hang on to it until we get to the front desk," Jimmy responded.

"Why?" Gina wasn't appreciating the game he was playing. "Just give it to me." If he didn't hand it over, she would let him have his way. She wouldn't make a scene in front of everyone at their table and embarrass Chloe.

"Hurry back so your food doesn't get cold," Chloe chimed in.

Thanks a lot, Chloe, Gina thought. Jimmy was staring her down, insisting she take his arm. She wouldn't go to the bar Nick mentioned. Once Jimmy went to the men's room, she could go find Nick and get him out of the hotel before Jimmy saw him.

Gina gave in. Her heart was pounding as she took Jimmy's arm. It had seemed a harmless idea when she decided to fly up to New York for this one-night event.

Turns out it was a terrible idea. A bad decision. A mistake to not support Nick in Atlanta. He would be pissed. And she wouldn't blame him. He was risking everything to find her sister. She knew better than to compromise an investigation. She would never forgive herself if something happened to him. If she had just stayed put in Atlanta, none of this would be happening right now and Nick's cover would still be intact. When she and Jimmy reached the reception desk, Gina turned to him.

"Can I have my phone now?"

"No."

"Jimmy, just give it back to me. I'll see you back at the table." Gina tried her best to ward him off.

He grabbed a hold of her wrist and pulled her close to him. "I'm not going anywhere, Gina." His tone was resentful. "I'm curious who your mystery caller is. Let's go find out, shall we?" He pulled on her arm as he stepped closer to the reception desk.

Gina resisted. "Let go of me, Jimmy. How absurd."

He spun around to face her. "I think there's something you need to share with me."

"Let go of me, Jimmy." Gina pulled against his grip.

He smiled. "You wanna make a scene?" He squeezed harder on her wrist. "I'll be happy to." His eyes darted around the reception hall. He pushed his weight against her, driving her back towards the entrance of the bar where Nick had told her to meet him.

Gina stopped their momentum by digging her heels into the carpet runner. "Have you gone completely crazy, Jimmy? What's the matter with you?" She growled at him, pursing her lips, trying to keep her voice in check. "Let go of me." Gina resisted panicking but could feel her heart beating faster in her chest. He was looking at her like a crazed lunatic.

Jimmy released his grip on her wrist. "Is he calling you from prison?"

Gina didn't want to lie to him, but she needed to protect Nick. "Yes."

"Where is he?"

"I can't say, Jimmy." She rubbed the sore spot on her wrist from Jimmy's grip. "Why do you care anyways?"

"Never mind. I just need to talk to him."

His adrenaline seemed amped up. His chest heaved deep breaths that reeked of alcohol.

"About what?"

Jimmy didn't answer. His eyes were dark and full of rage and fixed on her.

"You're scaring me, Jimmy. What's…"

He gripped her wrist again, moving close to her. "You should be scared." His teeth were clenched, and his face was inches from hers.

"Let her go, Jimmy." Nick's voice rang out behind her.

Gina spun her head to see Nick standing close behind her. She was practically sandwiched between him and Jimmy. Plenty of heat and tension rose from them both. Jimmy released Gina's wrist.

"No fuckin' way." Jimmy exhaled. His face paled. But not for long. That look of rage quickly reappeared.

A long, heavy silence hung between the three of them. Gina sidestepped, opening the space between them. Watching Nick and Jimmy, she remembered the two of them having a similar exchange when Nick recanted his testimony.

"How the fuck did you pull this off? Hunh?" Jimmy nearly shouted at Nick.

"Keep your voice down," Nick shot back, noticing guests and staff were paying attention to them now.

"Fuck you, Nick," Jimmy replied. "You don't tell me…"

"Jimmy." Gina cut in, taking a hold of his arm bringing his attention to her. The alcohol was running rampant in his system. "Jimmy, Nick is…"

"Gina!" Nick called out, startling her.

Gina whipped her head around to Nick. A sense of urgency was being directed at her from him. "What? I was just going to tell him…"

"Nothing." Nick cut her off again.

His expression came across loud and clear. Shut the fuck up. So, she did. She looked back to Jimmy who was intently watching their exchange. Gina let go of Jimmy's arm and took a step closer to Nick.

"Excuse me, sir." A uniformed hotel employee walked up to Jimmy. "I'm afraid we're going to have to ask you to leave."

"Fuck you," Jimmy shot back at the meager hotel employee. Jimmy turned back to Gina and Nick.

"Jimmy," Gina countered in a calming tone. "You've had a few drinks tonight. It might be best…"

Jimmy bent forward into her face. "Fuck you, cousin. You don't tell me…"

Nick pressed a hand on Jimmy's shoulder, pushing him backwards. Jimmy's arms flew up, pitching against Nick's grip just as two security guards came from behind Jimmy, each taking an arm. They wrestled with him as he shouted out obscenities, then they ushered him to an exit through the bar and out a side door. A small crowd of onlookers stopped to watch the scene unfold.

Nick pulled Gina into a quiet corner, away from the gawking crowd. He looked down to her. "You alright?"

She rubbed her wrist, looking down at the red abrasion Jimmy's grip had left on her. Nick took her hand in his, smoothing his fingers across the mark. Gina raised her eyes to him.

"I'm sorry, Nick."

She dropped her gaze back to his hand, holding hers. It was difficult to look him in the eyes. What a mess she had caused for him.

"I just…"

She just didn't think it through. She should have stayed put in Atlanta. Period. She knew that now. But the words couldn't get past the ache in her throat.

Nick folded her into his arms, holding her tight. Relief enveloped her. She wrapped her arms around his waist, absorbing the comfort of his embrace. He could have said a lot of things just then, making her feel worse. But he didn't. He just continued to hold her. The hotel manager approached them.

"I'm so sorry, ma'am. Are you alright?" he asked apologetically.

Gina looked over to him. "I am. Thank you."

"My staff just informed me of what happened. Do you wish to press charges or file a complaint?"

"No. I'm fine. Really."

That was the last thing she wanted to do. Although she assumed Nick probably wanted to. Jimmy had just had too much to drink. He obviously couldn't handle his liquor. She would make a mental note to talk to Chloe about it.

"Very well. If you're joining us as guests, the hotel would like to comp your room."

He was a tall thin silver-haired gentleman wanting to right a wrong. He stood looking to them both.

"We're not," Nick replied. "We were just here for a night cap in the bar."

"Ah. Well then. Allow us to pick up the tab," he insisted.

"Already taken care of," Nick replied.

The manager frowned, reaching a hand inside his coat. He removed a card from his vest pocket.

"This card is for complimentary drinks the next time you visit with us." He was doing his best to remedy the situation.

Nick took the card from the manager. "Thank you."

"Good evening. If there's anything else I can do, please let me know," the manager said. He spun on his heel and walked away from them.

Gina realized she was still holding on to Nick. She dropped her arms to her side, clutching her purse in one hand.

"I believe you have a plane to catch," Nick said.

His comment caught her off-guard. She detected a hint of hostility in his tone. He was still stinging from her screw up. For a fleeting moment, she had imagined taking the hotel manager up on his offer to stay in a room for the night, with Nick. But that quickly passed.

Nick's mind was on the investigation. As it should have been. Gina silently criticized herself for fantasizing about Nick. She nodded. She headed toward the exit.

"Hey," Nick called out to her.

Gina stopped, but took a moment before turning back to face him. He took two steps to meet up with her.

"Next time, give me a heads up when you decide to deviate from the plan."

"I got it. Loud and clear. It was a stupid move on my part." Gina countered bitterly.

Still trying to get her emotions under control, she turned to walk again, but he caught her arm and spun her back to face him.

"I'm not mad, Gina."

"No? Well, I'm mad at myself." She bit off the words, wishing she had stayed in Atlanta.

"Don't be. It doesn't suit you."

"How would you know what suits me, Nick?"

His eyes slid down over her. "That dress definitely does."

His unexpected compliment shut her up. He had this wonderful way of drawing her in. His expression was charming and mischievous. But the mixed signals she'd been receiving since they started working together confused her. Annoyed her, really. He said he wasn't mad, but how could he not be? He was patiently waiting for her response.

"Thank you," was all she could come up with.

"No. Thank you." He pulled her to him and brought his lips down to hers in a kiss.

Gina's breath caught as his mouth crushed hers. Pleasure pulsed through her as his tongue found hers. It was a sensual and passionate moment. She lifted her arms, wrapping them around his neck. She smelled leather from his jacket mixed with soap or cologne or whatever it was. It was manly and intoxicating. His hands were around her waist, pulling her tighter against him. The mixed signals now became clear. It was a wonderfully delicious kiss. A kiss she had imagined on several occasions recently. The upsetting reunion fell away. It was the two of them in this moment and nothing else. She didn't want it to end, but he pulled away. He pressed his lips to her forehead, then looked down to her.

"When this is over," Gina said, raising her eyes to his. "Remind me to wear this dress again."

Nick exhaled with a smile. "Deal."

They left the hotel holding hands. Once outside, she tucked in close to Nick to shield herself from the cold. He stopped to remove his leather jacket and wrap her in it. It was bulky and heavy and warm, and it smelled like him.

"Can I keep it?"

"How about I get you one that fits you instead."

"Then it wouldn't be yours."

"Come on."

He grabbed her hand and led her to a silver pickup parked in a loading zone. A tall, athletic man stepped from the driver's seat.

"Gina, this is Leo Bradford. Also, part of the crew. Leo, Gina Teducci."

Gina shook his hand. "Nice to meet you."

"Likewise. But…"

"I'll explain later," Nick replied curtly. Gina detected that note of hostility again.

Nick's cellphone rang. He removed it from the pocket of his jeans. "It's Reuben," he said to the two of them. "Yeah," Nick answered.

He walked away from them, trying to get a better signal. His silhouette was a black shadow against the Pulitzer Fountain cascading water over its tiers, highlighted by landscape flood lights. Gina could still feel his kiss. Her lips tingled and tasted like him. She could smell him on the leather jacket that warmed her bare skin beneath. And she could feel his hands caressing her body, holding her tight. She jolted from her thoughts when he spun around to face her and Leo. His expression conveyed shock.

Gina felt a stab of panic. She looked to Leo. "What is it?"

"I don't know."

Nick took long strides back towards them.

"What is it? What happened?" Gina asked when he reached them.

"We might have caught a break in Atlanta."

Gina's heart leapt into her throat. She half-choked and swallowed. "Sirrina?"

"Yeah," Nick said. But Gina sensed it wasn't all good news.

"To the airport?" Leo asked.

"I'll need you to continue your detail here," Nick said to Leo. "We'll catch a cab to Newark."

"Got it. No problem," Leo replied.

"Let's go." Nick turned to Gina then started towards Fifth Avenue.

Gina said goodbye to Leo and fell into step with Nick. He hailed a cab and they climbed in.

"Newark Airport," Nick told the driver. He removed his wallet and counted out some bills. He fanned out hundred-dollar bills to the driver. "There's an extra three hundred for you if you get us there in half the time without getting pulled over."

Gina was pushed back in her seat as the driver sped up, dodging and weaving through traffic and pedestrians. Nick sat back in his seat.

"What did Reuben say?" Gina asked.

"Not much. Just that the informant might be a flight risk and to get there a.s.a.p."

Gina's thoughts were going a mile a minute. What if this was it? What if this was the break they had been hoping for? What if they found Sirrina?

"Put your seatbelt on," Nick said to her.

"Hunh? Oh." Gina hadn't realized that she hadn't fastened herself in. She reached for the seatbelt and stretched it over the bulk of leather, locking it in place. Nick called someone to arrange an immediate flight to Atlanta. *Who did he know with the airlines that could pull that off for them?* she wondered.

Everything was a blur. But then she remembered the party. Chloe and Megan, and Jimmy. What was she going to say? Certainly, Chloe and Megan were missing her by now. She reached for her cellphone inside her purse. She dug through the contents, but it wasn't there. Where did she...?

Gina sucked in her breath. "Shit!"

"Hold on please," Nick said into his phone, looking at her with concern. "What?"

"My cellphone."

"What about it?"

He wasn't going to like it, but she couldn't lie to him about it. "Jimmy has it."

He stared at her unblinking as their cab sped through town.

"Yes. We'll be there in less than thirty minutes," he said into his phone. He paused for the person to speak, keeping his eyes glued on her. "Two passengers and one pilot. All adults."

One pilot? Gina thought. But she wouldn't interrupt Nick with her concerns. She turned her attention out her side window, unable to look him in the eye. Another screw-up on her part. New York was passing by in a blur. She recalled the moment when Jimmy snatched up her phone off the table to take a selfie of him and Chloe.

"Hartsfield-Jackson Atlanta International." Nick said into his phone, then waited again.

Nick placed a hand on her knee, bringing her attention back to him.

"Was it locked?" he asked her

"What?"

"Your cellphone. Was it locked?"

Gina thought for a moment. "No."

"Thank you." Nick hung up and immediately began dialing another number. His eyes darted out his side window, out the front windshield and then back to her.

"Chico," he said into his phone. "I need a favor. Put a block on Gina's cellphone immediately." He paused for a moment. "Security breach."

Gina listened to him rattle off her phone number to Chico. She remembered Jimmy refusing to return her phone to her in the lobby of the hotel. And then Nick was there, and he and Jimmy were having words, and then they escorted Jimmy out of the hotel. With her phone in his coat pocket. And then it was just her and Nick. She felt completely incompetent.

"I'll call you when we land," Nick said to Chico. He hung up.

"Chico's taking care of it," Nick said. "He'll have a new phone for you when we get to Atlanta.

Gina acknowledged him, keeping her focus out her side window.

"It happens, Gina."

"What's that?" she brought her attention back to him.

"Losing a cellphone," Nick said. "Usually, they get stolen. It happens in our line of work."

But she hadn't lost it. And it hadn't been stolen. She had been irresponsible with it. Gina wasn't sure if he was just telling her this to make her feel better. She shook her head without responding. She half expected him to ask how the hell Jimmy wound up with her cellphone in his possession. But he must have come to the same conclusion she had. There wasn't anything more to say about it. Chico would handle locking her phone so no information could be accessed, and no calls could be made or received.

Forty-five minutes later they were on board Joe's private jet, taxiing down the runway headed for Atlanta.

~~~~~

Jimmy had watched Gina and Nick exit the hotel and make their way to the silver pickup parked in the loading zone. The same silver truck that picked up Jerry and took him to the woods. And the same tall African American man was driving.

Jimmy's thoughts were muddled by the whiskey, challenging his efforts to put the pieces together. He paced in Central Park, across the street from the Plaza Hotel, scrolling through Gina's cellphone. What was Nick was up to? And how the hell had he been able to skirt going to prison? He could only think of one answer: Joe D'Amato.

Unless Nick had connections of his own, which could be possible. But that didn't seem likely. The more logical conclusion was that Joe had organized Nick's release. *But why?* Jimmy continued to pace.

Was Nick working something out for Joe? If so, what was it? Or maybe Nick owed Joe for something. He'd already proven to be a corrupt detective, working with Jerry Pulia. Jimmy rubbed his head with his free hand, trying to figure out Nick's angle. He stopped pacing to scroll on Gina's cellphone again. He came across information in Atlanta, Georgia. Traffic whizzed by on Central Park South. He drew his gaze to the hotel across the street. Nothing was making sense.

Searching Gina's phone further, he found information regarding the Atlanta, Georgia crime lab, an Atlanta hotel, airline information for flights to and from Atlanta, and the airport car rental agency. Gina hadn't been working in Los Angeles. She'd been in Atlanta, Georgia. *Why?* Jimmy wondered. And why had she lied to Megan about where she was?

Jimmy found Nick Casey in Gina's contacts. He dialed the number, not knowing what he would say as it rang. An automated voicemail answered. Jimmy hung up and dialed again. Again, the voicemail. He dialed the number three more times. His mind was spinning, trying to put the pieces together.

He copied the Atlanta information and Nick's phone number to his cellphone. Then he dialed Chloe's number. Her voicemail answered. He left her a brief message that he wasn't feeling well and was taking a cab ride home. He apologized, told her he loved her, and hung up.

Jimmy hailed a cab. Now that he knew Nick wasn't incarcerated, he wanted answers. *Why was Nick at the hotel tonight?* Gina seemed surprised to see him there, too. But the two of them also seemed to have something going on. *Was Gina helping Nick?*

Jimmy scrolled through Gina's cellphone while cruising in the backseat of the cab. He didn't find anything more than what he already had. His gaze turned out the passenger side window. His grand plan had fallen apart thanks to Nick, forcing him to take extreme measures to protect himself. Those measures would be carried out tonight. There was only one thing left to do. Kill Nick. And he would use Gina to accomplish this.

CHAPTER 23

On board the private jet, Gina sat belted in on the two-person sofa facing the narrow aisle. Nick sat across from her in one of two captain's chairs separated by a small table. It was her first time on a private jet, and she found it to be small but well-appointed. It could carry five passengers plus one pilot. But tonight, it was only Nick, herself, and the pilot.

Nick had been on his phone texting and making calls since their takeoff. Gina sipped a diet soda, trying to settle her stomach. The culmination of what had gone down tonight, and now the possibility of having a lead into finding Sirrina, was taking its toll.

It probably didn't help that she hadn't eaten anything since breakfast this morning, which had consisted of a stale croissant and orange juice from the airport before flying to New York. When she had arrived in New York she'd gone shopping for a dress and shoes for the evenings event. Gina didn't stop to have lunch because she'd been planning on enjoying a Michelin Star dinner at the Plaza Hotel, but that didn't happen. And it wasn't hunger she was feeling now anyways, it was exhaustion.

Nick hung up, unfastened his seatbelt, and moved to sit next to her on the sofa. He rested his right knee on the sofa, sitting sideways to face her. His right arm stretched out across the top of the sofa nearly touching her.

"We need to talk."

"Conversations that begin that way are rarely good," Gina replied.

When he didn't respond, Gina prepared for troubling news. "What is it?" she asked.

"Earlier tonight you were upset for having made the decision to fly to New York."

"I still am."

"You wouldn't have made that decision if you'd had all of the facts."

"What do you mean?"

"When we first talked about this case, I told you I would only give you information regarding the investigation that I felt was necessary. Tell you what you needed to know on a limited basis. To protect you."

Gina placed her soda can in the arm rest cup holder, not liking the vibe she was picking up from Nick.

"What fact would have kept me from going to New York to be with Chloe and Megan?"

"Your cousin Jimmy."

Gina half laughed. "I'll admit. He's a force to be reckoned with. And he obviously can't handle his liquor. He proved that tonight. But he's..."

"My investigation." Nick cut her off.

Gina flinched, not sure if it was flight turbulence or Nick's comment that caused her queasiness. "What does that mean? I don't understand." A stab of panic pinched her insides.

"Jimmy's my unofficial investigation. He's the one..."

"Responsible for Sirrina?" Gina heard herself saying the words but couldn't wrap her head around the logic. The moment felt thick and in slow motion. A flood of questions and recollections hit simultaneously, crowding her mind. She wanted answers. She wanted explanations. She wanted Nick to be wrong. How could Jimmy be responsible? And if he was...*why*? Tears welled up in Gina's eyes. Her emotions suddenly got the best of her. She looked to Nick.

"Are you sure?" It was barely a whisper. The culmination of emotions caused her body to tremble. She recounted the night at the Wildwoods. She recalled Jimmy's stint in the mental hospital from trying to commit suicide. Family gatherings without Sirrina. Joe's trial. The aftermath of Joe's trial. And still none of it was adding up to Jimmy having been the culprit.

"It's not making sense, Nick. Are you sure about this?" she implored. "I don't mean to question your capabilities and judgment, but I'm having a hard time making the connection."

"I'm sure," he said. "I'm sorry, Gina. I'm sorry I didn't tell you sooner, and I'm sorry it's Jimmy."

Nick spent the remainder of the flight to Atlanta bringing her up to speed on his investigation and preparing her for their meeting with the trafficking victim.

~~~~~

It was nearly midnight as Gina and Nick rode the hotel elevator up to the third floor. When the door opened, they stepped out.

"Give me ten minutes to change clothes," Gina said to Nick. She started towards her room.

"You've got five and come to room three twenty-five."

Gina rushed to her room and changed into jeans and a sweater, tossing the beautiful jade green gown in a heap on the bed next to Nick's leather jacket. Her mind hadn't stopped spinning since stepping foot onto Joe's private jet. She'd been surprised to learn that Nick had the jet at his disposal. She'd been surprised by a lot of information tonight.

Nick had overwhelmed her with details of his *unofficial* investigation. Not initiated by the department, and not initiated by the D.A.'s office. Initiated by Joe D'Amato. And Joe hadn't spared any expenses or resources to help him work his investigation into finding Guiseppe's killer. An investigation that included finding her sister.

Gina found herself feeling grateful for all that Joe was doing to help Nick. An unexpected emotion, since she originally had wanted to see Joe behind bars for Sirrina's death.

She was running on fumes now, but this meeting with one of the trafficking victims was giving her a jolt of energy. Someone who could possibly lead them to find Sirrina. Somehow, Reuben had convinced her to stay the night at their hotel. She was cooperating and willing to talk with them about Sirrina.

Gina pulled on boots and practically ran down the hall to room three twenty-five. She knocked, invigorated from her sprint. Nick joined her in the hallway and closed the door behind him. He pointed to room three twenty-six directly across the hall.

"In here," he said.

Gina was on pins and needles, wondering what this person might know about her sister. And afraid she might not like what she heard.

"Remember what we discussed on the flight." Nick looked down to her. "Whatever you hear in here tonight, keep your reactions buried deep. We don't want to upset her, and she doesn't need to know this investigation is personal, ok?" He seemed more concerned for Gina than for his investigation. He knocked on the door and looked down to her.

Gina nodded in agreement. She wouldn't make any promises to him because she couldn't guarantee she wouldn't react to some horrific detail the victim might share. Working a crime scene, she was practiced at detaching herself emotionally from the victim. But this was her own flesh and blood they would be discussing.

Reuben opened the door. "Hey. Come in."

Nick stepped aside to let Gina enter ahead of him. The room was the same king bedroom kitchenette layout as her room. Chico and Ice were apparently not joining them, and Nick had told her on the plane that Leo had stayed behind to continue keeping tabs on Jimmy.

Nick came up behind her. They stood in the dining area. Reuben made his way to the living room.

Gina focused on the young woman perched on the edge of the sofa. Mid-twenties, skinny, almost scrawny, and pale, with short spikey copper red hair. She wore a bathrobe and was barefoot. The lamp light on the side table highlighted her pitted complexion. She wore no makeup and appeared weary but twitchy. She lit a cigarette and eyed the newcomers with suspicion.

Gina recognized the signs of drug abuse from many cases she'd worked on. Being involved in trafficking, the victim's circumstances likely involved drug abuse, prostitution, and possibly homelessness. Reuben had said she was twenty-five, but she could have easily been mistaken for much older.

"Gina, Nick, this is Amber," Reuben said, as he lowered himself into a side chair across the coffee table from Amber. The three of them acknowledged one another. Gina glanced down to the table that was littered with files, printed digital images, and a tape recorder.

Nick placed his hand on Gina's lower back, coaxing her forward. "Take a seat on the couch with her," he whispered in her ear.

Gina agreed without saying anything. Her throat felt swollen and she didn't trust her voice to speak. The possibility that her sister may still be alive was becoming very real. This girl, Amber, could be the link to finding Sirrina. It was as if she were facing her sister right here, right now, at this moment, and it scared her. She made her way to the couch and sat on the edge, on edge, the same as Amber was. Gina couldn't take her eyes off Amber, absorbed in the possibilities.

Nick pulled a chair from the dining room over to the coffee table and sat next to Reuben.

"Is she alright?" Amber asked, referring to Gina. "She's kind of freaking me out."

Her southern drawl snapped Gina from her trance.

Gina's eyes darted to Nick. His expression reminded her, *keep your emotions buried.* "I'm...yes." She turned back to Amber. "Sorry."

Amber studied her and Nick for a moment, toking her cigarette. Gina knew this to be a non-smoking floor. In fact, the entire hotel was non-smoking. She assumed Reuben had given her the cigarettes to keep her...well...to keep her. At least long enough until Nick and Gina arrived. Gina considered lighting one up for herself, even though she wasn't a smoker. It might have helped curb her nervousness. She drew in a deep breath instead.

"These are the two we've been waitin' for?" Amber asked Reuben.

"They are," Reuben replied. "Gina and Nick," he pointed to them, respectively.

"Yeah. You said that already," Amber shot back. "You've also recorded everything I said earlier. I don't see the reason why I should have to repeat it all again." She consulted her drugstore wristwatch. "I really need to get back to work. Horacio's gonna have a shitfit if I'm gone again tonight."

"This won't take long," Reuben soothed.

"Yeah. You told me that, too. You know I work for a real shitbag. I don't want to have to pay for this, if you know what I mean."

"I do," Reuben replied. "And we discussed that earlier."

Gina watched the two of them exchange a long look and Amber appeared to back down. Gina wondered what the two of them had talked about.

"What's your story?" she asked Nick.

"We're looking for someone."

"Yeah. I got that already from the big guy here." Amber pointed to Reuben. "Said it's a private contract." She flicked her ash in a drink glass half filled with melting ice cubes. "You're not cops or detectives or any kind of law enforcement, right?" Her beady eyes darted to Nick and Gina.

"No," Nick responded.

"What about you?" She pointed to Gina.

"No," Gina replied.

Amber toked her cigarette. "What do you do?" Amber asked Gina.

Reuben cut in. "Amber, if you don't mind, we'd like to…"

"No, that's fine," Gina cut him off, looking to him then back to Amber. "The least we can do is give her peace of mind for what she's doing for us." Gina smiled warmly at Amber. "I'm a student. College. Fourth year."

"Yeah? What college?" Amber's hand shook as she toked her cigarette.

"Georgia State."

"What's your major?" Amber squinted her eyes as if she were interrogating a suspect.

"Biology."

Amber was stumped. "What does that teach you to be?"

"A lot of things," Gina replied. "For me, it's criminology."

"The study of crime?" Amber asked.

"Right."

"Like a CSI?"

"Hopefully, Someday."

"Ain't that law enforcement?" Her eyes darted to all three of them. "I watch TV. I know."

"Not exactly," Gina replied. "At least not yet. I'm still just a student."

"Just a student." Amber smiled, revealing bad dental hygiene. "You're a smart one, though," she concluded, toking her cigarette once more before dropping it in the glass. "You're the one in the photos on the cell phone he showed me, aren't you?" she looked to Gina and Reuben both.

"I am," Gina replied.

"Are you the private contractor?"

"Amber, can you let us ask the questions?" Reuben interjected.

"Can I have another hit before we start?" Amber countered.

"After you've answered our questions," Reuben replied.

Gina glanced down to Amber's bare feet. She detected the needle marks and bruising on the tops of both her feet. Amber caught Gina looking. She recessed herself back on the sofa, folding her legs and feet under her. She tucked a pillow under her right arm, ready to talk.

The top of her bathrobe spread open. If she hadn't been borderline anorexic there would have been ample cleavage displayed. Instead, a boney breastplate was all that she exposed. Gina thought she had probably been pretty at one time. And could be again, if she were able to get herself clean.

Reuben leaned forward and switched on the recorder. "This is Reuben Alvarez, continuing with Amber and now also with Gina and Nick." He thumbed through a substantial stack of digital images on the coffee table. Gina noticed they were printed images of the woman Chico had designed. What Sirrina possibly looked like at various stages of her life.

He turned the stack to face Amber and fanned them out in front of her on the table. The images revealed different characteristics. Hair color ranging from blonde, brunette, black and red. Different skin tones. Different weight and bone structure. It was amazing to see the depth of Chico's work.

"This again?" Amber squawked. "I've done this three times for you already."

"Four," Reuben replied. "And now once more please."

Amber leaned forward, scanning the pages. After a moment, she plucked the image with tangled light brown, almost blond hair. Sunken brown eyes and hollowed cheeks. It was an image that was portraying life-long drug and possibly physical abuse.

"Like I told you." She held the page up to Reuben. "I know her as Sasha."

Reuben accepted her choice. "Right."

Gina's mind raced to conclusions from the image she'd picked. Even though these were digital likenesses of Sirrina, Gina knew what the real-life image would reveal. The thought of it hit the pit of her stomach. She swallowed against the bile that threatened to come up, forcing herself not to react in front of Amber.

"Can I see, please?" Nick asked, holding out his hand. Amber handed the image to Nick.

Gina watched him study the face in front of him without reaction. He handed it over to Reuben.

"What can you tell me about her?" Nick asked.

Amber helped herself to another cigarette. She lit it and sat back on the sofa, continuing to sit on her legs. Her robe top remained propped open. "Probably not as much as you hoped to hear." She blew out a stream of smoke.

Gina noticed her whole body was trembling now. If she didn't have another hit of heroin or meth or whatever her drug of choice was soon, she would be useless to them. And if she did have another hit of heroine, or meth or whatever, she would be useless to them. She was at that in between stage, but not for much longer.

"She works for Horacio?" Nick asked.

"That's what the big guy here asked, too." Amber referred to Reuben again. "At first I wasn't sure. She looked familiar, but I couldn't place where I had seen her. And then it clicked." Amber snapped her fingers. "She had worked for Horacio for a long time, but then she was gone."

"How long ago?" Nick asked.

"Mmm...four, maybe five years." She toked her cigarette again.

"And you don't know where she might be now?"

"I wasn't done," Amber shot back.

Nick held up his hands apologetically.

"I do know where she's at."

Amber leaned forward. She took a drink from a soda can that was on the coffee table. She seemed to hesitate, stalling at the most crucial part of her narrative. Gina wanted to throttle her to force the information from her.

Amber leaned back on the sofa and looked down, noticing her bathrobe had pooched open. She made a minor adjustment to close it up, sort of.

"I thought maybe she got lucky and found a decent John and was working on getting herself cleaned up. You know?" Her eyes fell to the images on the table. "That's a false hope some girls have. Figuring out a way to escape Horacio. Some fantasize of a different life far removed from where they're at." Amber toyed with the tie on her robe. "I guess it keeps them going." She flicked her ashes in the glass. The ice cubes had melted all the way down now. "That and the drugs." She gave a half laugh. "I don't have those delusions."

"So, did she find a decent John or not?" Nick asked.

"No. Quite the opposite."

"If she isn't working for Horacio and she didn't find a decent John…"

"She's Diego's property," Amber said, cutting Nick off.

Gina pressed her hands together, fighting off her reaction. Amber's words echoed in her ears. *Diego's property*. They were still uncertain if this was Sirrina that Amber was talking about. *But what if it was?*

"Who's Diego?" Gina and Nick asked simultaneously.

Amber unfolded her legs and began to stand up. Gina reached over, placing a hand on her arm.

"Please, Amber," Gina spoke calmly. "This is very important."

"And my life isn't?" she shot back to her.

Gina quickly retracted her arm. "Of course, it is." Gina replied. "I just meant…"

"We want to help her," Nick cut in. "The same way Reuben offered to help you."

"Ha!" She laughed. "That's sweet. And I'm sure it would make ya'll feel better, too. But there's no helping us. Heck, a lot of us are here by choice 'cause it's the only choice. Take me for example, I'm the biproduct of a stripper and a small-time drug dealer. This life's in my

DNA." She turned to Gina. "You'll learn that in CSI college," she jested. "And it's in the DNA of most of us out there."

Gina wouldn't dare correct her analogy. Instead, she found herself hoping Amber would be able to make a better life for herself than this one.

"You don't have to let your environment control your life, Amber."

"No?" Amber replied. "I'm a number, Gina. You hearin' me?" Her eyes darted to all three of them, turning defensive. "Horacio doesn't call us by our names, he calls us by our room numbers. The room numbers we service for him. I'm twenty-one. How's that for environment?" She lashed out, toking her cigarette, and blowing the smoke in Gina's direction. "I can guarantee you, Miss CSI, there's no greener grass over the fence for me. No college education in my future. No, no house in the suburbs with a white picket fence and a puppy dog in the yard." Amber's trembling worsened. "I make my living sucking dicks, cradling balls, and swallowing cum shots from strange men every night. Lying face up, face down, or bent over whatever piece of furniture can handle the pounding these Johns give me while fucking any orifice they choose." She suddenly turned amused with her captive audience. "Heck, some even bring props or toys to enhance their experience."

She leaned forward to flick her ashes in the glass, then drew her hand down the cleavage of her robe, toying with Nick and Reuben. "Whatever gets them off."

She licked her lips, holding both of their gazes for a moment. When neither reacted, she leaned back on the sofa once more. "That's the life. That's my life."

She toked on her cigarette, blowing out another stream of smoke. "I've danced and stripped; I've been filmed and photographed." She laced her fingers with the tie of her robe, feigning a pouty little starlet. "But Hollywood hasn't come calling yet."

She paused for a response. When she didn't get one, she continued. "What do you suppose they'd do about this if they had?"

She extended both arms straight out in front of her, quaking uncontrollably. She pulled up the sleeves of her robe, revealing track marks and bruising. Ashes from her cigarette broke off, landing on the photos. She retracted her arms, placing them in her lap and looking straight at Gina. "This is not the makings of a happily ever after."

Gina was sorry she had pushed too far with Amber. Her lack of self-esteem mixed with fear and maybe shame had Gina reconsidering saying anything further. She didn't want to upset Amber more than she already had.

Reuben moved to collect the photos, shaking off the ashes.

"Sorry about that," Amber said.

"No problem," Reuben replied.

"The offer that the big guy here made me." Amber pointed to Reuben. "Was more than generous. A lot of girls in my position would jump at the chance to take it. But I'm not like a lot of girls. I'm Horacio's girl. If I ever acted on that and took the offer, I would end up like your girl." She pointed to Nick, then dropped her cigarette into the glass of melted ice.

"Meaning?" Nick asked.

"I'd become Diego's property. A mule."

"Drugs?" Reuben asked.

"Yep." Amber pointed to him, gesturing a make-believe pistol in her grip. "He uses his girls as either a distraction for smuggling or as the transporter. It's dangerous and he's a mean son of a bitch if anything happens to his precious drugs."

Gina, Nick, and Reuben quietly absorbed Amber's story.

"At least Horacio gives us girls some freedoms," Amber continued. "We come and go as we want so long as we return each night to work. He gives us a decent place to live. Maids clean the sheets regularly. He pays us to get a hot meal and supplies us with drugs. Most importantly, he doesn't beat us."

"A few minutes ago, Horacio was a real shitbag. Now he's a prince?" Reuben asked.

Amber scoffed. "No. He's far from a prince. But he's a hell of a lot better than Diego. Diego keeps his girls locked up." Amber bent towards Reuben to make her point clear. "You only wind up being Diego's property from trying to escape Horacio's operation."

"Speaking from experience?" Reuben asked.

Amber didn't answer.

"Amber?" Reuben asked. "Did you…"

"Once." Amber cut him off.

"A minute ago, you spoke as if you never…"

"It's not something I want to talk about, ok?" Amber became defensive.

Another quiet moment passed between the four of them.

"How did you leave Diego to go back to Horacio?" Nick asked, skipping ahead.

Amber sat quiet.

"Amber. Answer the question," Reuben said.

"I had to do a favor for Diego first," Amber replied bitterly.

"A favor?" Reuben asked. "What kind of favor?"

Amber deflated. "I had to kill a man. One of Diego's men." She brought her eyes back up to them. "Diego said he was DEA."

A heavy silence ensued.

"What did you do, Amber?" Nick asked.

"I shot him in the back of his head while he was screwing one of the girls."

Gina gasped, unable to control herself. All eyes turned to her.

"And was he DEA?" Nick asked Amber to keep her on track.

Amber shrugged her shoulders. "I don't know. I think Diego just wanted to see if I could do it."

"And that earned you a pass to return to Horacio?" Reuben asked.

Amber nodded yes. "It's far from a great life, but I know I'm a hell of a lot better off than being under Diego's roof. He likes to beat and torture. He gets a real satisfaction from it. I was told it has something to do with when he was a kid. I never asked for more details."

Gina felt nauseous. Knowing that Sirrina had possibly tried to escape made her stomach boil. She felt like shouting and crying all at once. Nick stood up and walked to the kitchen and returned a moment later. He handed Gina a bottled water from the refrigerator and returned to his seat.

Gina couldn't speak to thank him. She just twisted off the cap and gulped down half the bottle to relieve the knot that was lodged in her throat.

"Did I upset you, Gina?" Amber taunted.

"No," Gina replied, replacing the cap on the water bottle, fighting to keep her wits about her.

"Ya'll wanted to know." Amber shrugged it off as if she'd been talking about the weather.

"Let me get this straight. Diego works for Horacio?" Reuben asked.

"No. The other way around," Amber answered. "Horacio works for Diego."

"Where do we find Diego?" Nick asked.

"Unh, Unh." Amber took up her position on the sofa again, tucking her legs under herself and hugging the pillow tight to her body. She was rocking and trembling. She was scared and in bad need of a fix.

"Amber, please," Gina pleaded. "This is so important for us to find her. Please help us."

Amber gave Gina a long hard stare.

"Can I see the photo I picked out?" she asked Reuben.

Reuben handed her the image she had selected from the pile. Amber studied the image in depth, then looked up to Gina.

"Is she your sister?" Amber asked.

"It doesn't matter, Amber," Gina replied.

"It does to me," Amber said.

"Why?" Gina asked

"If she were my sister? I'm not so sure I'd want to find her," Amber said. "Especially knowing she's been in Diego's possession. The man's a ruthless animal."

Gina wished she'd stop saying things like that. Her stomach churned. She drank more water to avoid throwing up. Gina wasn't sure if Amber was just being spiteful and wanting to hurt someone. She was showing signs of withdrawal and could've been lashing out because of it.

"It's exactly the reason we want to find her," Nick said.

"I've said all I'm going to say." Amber turned to Reuben. She unfolded her legs, leaned forward, and switched off the tape recorder. "I'd like my payment, if you know what I mean."

"I do," Reuben replied. "Not until you tell us where to find Diego."

"I can't say." She looked to all three of them. "He'll kill me."

"You can stay here until we've located the girl," Reuben said. "You'll be safe here."

"It's Sasha," Amber said. "I told you, her name is Sasha. And I won't be safe here. If I don't go back tonight, then I'll have Horacio wantin' to kill me. Or worse, he'll send me back to Diego. I can still make up a lame excuse for being gone last night and part of tonight. But if I'm gone any longer, forget it. I might as well be answering to Diego."

"Give us an address, Amber," Nick said.

"No fucking way," Amber shouted.

Reuben shot up out of his chair and grabbed a hold of her frail arm, yanking her off the couch.

"Ow, shit! What are you…" Amber fought against his grip. Her bathrobe flailed, scattering the digital images, sending them floating to the floor.

Reuben pulled her close to his body and practically carried her out of the room and into the bedroom, slamming the door closed.

"What's he doing?" Gina demanded from Nick.

"His job," Nick replied.

Gina could hear Reuben and Amber's voices from the next room but couldn't make out what either of them were saying. She looked to Nick, but he wasn't going to say any more. He scooped up the photos. One of them was the image that Amber had selected. Nick studied it once more before setting it on the coffee table. He placed the remaining pages back in the folder.

Gina wanted to leave. She didn't want to be here in this room any longer. She kept imagining it had been Sirrina sitting there with her on the sofa. Listening to her sister tell her of the life she had no choice in. Amber's words cut her to her core. But she couldn't leave. She wouldn't leave before finding out where Diego was. Because that's where Sirrina was. She hoped Reuben could convince Amber to give up Diego's information.

Gina strained to listen to their conversation, but it was quiet now. Gina looked over to Nick as he took a seat next to her on the sofa. He was about to say something when the bedroom door opened.

Reuben walked up to Nick. He handed him a slip of paper with something written on it. From what Gina cold see it was an address, but she couldn't make out what it said. A rush of relief and hope washed over her.

Nick studied it for a moment. "You think it's good?" he asked Reuben.

"I do," Reuben replied. "She picked that same image from the stack five times." Reuben pointed to the digital image of the blonde girl with sunken eyes and hollowed cheeks. A haunting image Gina wouldn't soon forget.

Nick folded both the address and the image and tucked the papers into his jeans pocket as he stood.

"Thanks, man," Nick said, holding his hand out to Reuben.

Reuben shook his hand, then they both looked to Gina.

"Let's go," Nick said to her.

Gina felt like she was floating through a bad dream. Reuben had been successful in getting Diego's location out of Amber. *What had he said to her to change her mind?* Gina wondered as she stood up.

"Please thank her for me," Gina said to Reuben.

"Will do."

Gina moved towards the door. As she passed by the bedroom, she peered inside. Amber lay sprawled out on the bed in a drug induced high.

CHAPTER 24

Monday morning. Nick sat behind the wheel of Reuben's rented SUV, watching the address Amber had given them for Diego. Reuben sat in the passenger seat, smoking a cigarette, and Ice was in the back seat. Reuben extinguished the cigarette in the ashtray.

For two days they'd been on surveillance. Nick wondered if Amber was even still alive. He hoped so. He would never forgive himself for having used Amber in this capacity if Diego harmed or killed her.

Nick had thought of raiding Diego's house and hoping to find Sirrina. If she wasn't there, they could at least save the girls who were there. Maybe they could knock Diego around, threaten his life to give up intel on Sirrina's whereabouts and hope they would get an answer.

But the fact that Amber recognized Sirrina's photo seemed to be the best angle at this point. And that meant using Amber.

They had kept her in the hotel for one more night. Nick and Reuben had convinced her to help them. In return, they offered protection, getting her into a recovery program and a better future. Or at least a future far removed from Diego and Horacio.

Amber declined their offer. She asked for cash and a guarantee they would get her out of Diego's house alive. Nick and Reuben agreed, even though both knew there were no guarantees in any of this. It was a shitty situation, but one Nick hoped would bring positive results. The only way they could help Amber after this was if she wanted it. His focus remained on Sirrina. She was what mattered most right now.

The plan had been for her to call Horacio and tell him that she'd tried leaving, but it didn't work out. She played the part of damsel in distress perfectly. And just like Amber had said, Horacio came to pick her up. And he didn't return to The Georgia Star Inn. He didn't return to the Riverside Inn or The Orchards Motel, either.

Instead, he brought Amber to this ten-acre parcel in a heavily wooded subdivision.

The main house and two out-buildings sat behind vine covered walls and fencing. Lush landscaping and manicured gardens mimicked the surrounding neighborhood. A tranquil setting with a monster in its midst.

Chico had been emailing information on the location to Nick. The main house was fifty-four hundred square feet. Six bedrooms, seven baths with a basement. One of the two out-buildings was categorized as a workshop/garage. The other was noted as storage.

Nick wondered what exactly "storage" meant. All three buildings had plumbing, heating, and air conditioning. Diego could have girls stashed in any one of them or all of them. Had Nick and his crew enlisted the help of Atlanta law enforcement, they would have been able to secure a warrant and raid the property. But since Nick was conducting this as unofficial business for Joe, they wouldn't be involving Atlanta law enforcement or the FBI...yet.

Nick was studying a diagram Chico had made. It gave the layout of the property with distance markers between the buildings, and perimeter fencing with gate locations and security cameras. It also noted Diego's protection detail. Six armed men on duty twenty-four-seven.

Diego's wife and four sons remained in Brazil as far as Chico's information provided. This would make raiding the property less challenging.

Nick engrossed himself in figuring out the perfect time to strike, what entry points to take, how to eliminate the protection detail, securing Diego until he had Sirrina safely removed from the property. And possibly eliminating Diego as well.

But acting on that plan required proof that Sirrina was there. Nick hoped to have confirmation of that before making a move. And that confirmation would come from Gina. Amber's role in this was to obtain an item containing Sirrina's DNA for Gina to test. That confirmation would solidify Jimmy's responsibility for Sirrina's abduction. It was imperative information.

Amber had a list of potential objects to smuggle out. Anything that would have Sirrina's hair, saliva, fingerprints, or blood on it would do. It had been a huge risk, relying on a drug addict to pull this off, but she was their only chance. If she couldn't pull this off, Nick would have to involve Atlanta in the raid, and would lose control of his investigation.

He couldn't afford for that to happen. It would raise too many questions. Questions that would compromise protected resources. Key personnel in various sectors of government. Resources that Joe D'Amato paid a great deal of money to use at his discretion.

As much as it went against Nick's principles as a law enforcement agent, he would safeguard those resources. He owed it to Joe. Nick held very few people in such high regard. Joe topped the list of those he valued and cared for most in his life. Gina was becoming a close contender.

He switched his thoughts back to Amber. He hoped that the methadone injections Reuben had been giving her would work. She seemed responsive to the opioid that reduced the heroin craving and withdrawal symptoms. *But for how long?* Nick wondered.

She just needed to keep her wits about her long enough to pull this off. But Nick had no idea how or when she would do it. It could be another week for all he knew. Experience told him work like this couldn't be rushed. But the unknowns troubled him. It was the only part of his plan that he couldn't direct her on. Amber was on her own for this part of the operation. He didn't like not being in control. And now here it was day two, and still no sign of her.

He had tried to supply her with a cellphone, but Amber refused. She told them Diego would confiscate it as soon as she arrived at his house. Nick felt uneasy that she had no way to contact him or Reuben. Part of the shitty situation.

A neighbor drove by, taking notice of their SUV, but kept moving. They wouldn't be able to stay parked on the street for much longer without raising suspicion. It would only take one concerned neighbor.

Nick thought about Jimmy, now. He was a nagging detail that was starting to fester in the corner of Nick's mind. Leo hadn't been able to get a tail on him. Jimmy could pose serious problems now that he knew Nick hadn't been incarcerated.

Leo had followed Jimmy's Lexus from the Morgan Publishing party back to Chloe's apartment in New York knowing Chloe was driving and that Jimmy wasn't with her. Leo had lost track of Jimmy during the conversation outside the Plaza Hotel with Nick and Gina. Leo assumed Jimmy had gotten a ride back to Chloe's apartment by taxi or Uber, but that hadn't been the case. Leo had also reported to Nick that Jimmy hadn't been spotted at his New Jersey apartment or his office, either.

Nick's attention was drawn to the Dolly Parton wig-wearing neighbor walking her three Pomeranian pups harnessed with rhinestone leashes. She was hard to miss. They had seen her yesterday morning at approximately the same time. Her plump figure hobbled down the street decked out in neon orange track gear and white sneakers. She was one property away from Diego's. She could be that concerned neighbor.

"Is that what southerners refer to as gumption?" Reuben asked.

"It's something," Nick replied.

Nick was about to start the SUV to take a lap around the block when his text ringer sounded off. He plucked his cellphone off the center console and read the message aloud. "Soda can baggie trash at curb."

"From Amber?" Reuben asked.

"Maybe. I don't recognize the number."

Nick glanced back to the Dolly Parton neighbor approaching the driveway. At the same time, a muscled man wearing a black short-sleeved shirt, black jeans and black sneakers wheeled a large trash can down Diego's driveway.

Ice leaned up from the backseat, resting his elbows on the front driver and passenger seats. "One of Diego's protection detail?"

"That would be my guess," Reuben replied.

The electric iron gate swung open. The neighbor stopped at the bottom of the driveway, letting her dogs do their business on the parkway lawn. Muscle man continued rolling the trash can down the long driveway to the curb. He waved to the neighbor lady. She waved back. He made his way back up the driveway, closing the gate behind him. In the distance, Nick heard the trash collection truck roaming the neighborhood.

"Shit," Nick said. "We need that trash."

"She's too close," Reuben said pointing to the neighbor. "And nosy enough to cause problems."

Ice began clearing the rear cargo area of their SUV and stuffing the contents in the backseat with him. "As soon as she leaves, pull up to the curb," Ice said. "I'll jump out. You pop the hatch. I'll pull the trash bags from the can and throw them in back. We'll be gone in two minutes." He slipped on a pair of latex gloves.

"The security camera on the front gate's going to record us," Nick said.

The trash truck rounded the corner at the far end of the street, picking up trash on Diego's side of the street.

"We don't have a choice," Ice said, pulling his hoodie over his head and slipping on dark shades.

"We'll be gone before they realize what we're doing," Reuben said. "If they're even monitoring the cameras."

The neighbor lady was in the process of picking up after her pooches. She shuffled to Diego's trash can, dumping the plastic bags of dog waste in the can. She closed the lid and began limping back in the direction she had come from. The trash truck was closing in, two houses away.

Nick rolled up the tinted windows. "Make it quick, Ice."

Nick started the SUV and made a beeline across the street, stopping in front of Diego's house. He popped the hatch. Ice jumped out of the backseat and hustled to the can.

Nick watched in his side mirror as Ice flipped open the lid, searched the contents, removed an item, and closed the lid.

"Right on," Nick said, keeping his eyes on Ice.

Ice slammed the SUV's hatch closed then jumped in his seat behind Nick. "Go, go, go!" He called out, pulling his door closed.

Nick pulled away from the curb just as the trash truck was pulling away from the next-door neighbor's house about to stop at Diego's. The noise of the trash truck drowned out their actions. Nick glanced to the neighbor lady as they drove past. She was too preoccupied with her dogs to notice them.

"Does this fit the text message?" Ice asked, leaning forward holding up a Ziplock bag containing a crushed soda can.

"It does," Nick replied. He pressed down on the accelerator, driving out of the neighborhood.

"It wasn't in the bagged trash," Ice said. "Amber tucked it in the corner on top of everything else in the can. She made it pretty obvious for us."

"Amber came through," Reuben said.

"She did," Nick said, a jolt of optimism hitting him.

"Of course, the neighbor's bag of dog shit had to land on it." Ice removed his gloves, tucking them into the duffel bag on the seat next to him.

Nick and Reuben chuckled.

"Hey, it's a small price to pay," Nick said.

"Yeah, yeah," Ice replied.

Forty minutes later, they pulled into the crime lab parking lot. Nick called Gina and had her come out to meet them. She took the Ziplock bag from Ice through the rear window. Nick watched her face pale as she studied the contents.

"If we're lucky, that will have Sirrina's DNA on it," Nick said.

Gina snapped her eyes up to him.

"You'll find Amber's DNA on it, too," he added.

Gina nodded. "Ok." But she remained rooted in place.

"Gina?" Nick said.

"I...yes...I'm going." She was obviously shaken.

"You alright?" he asked.

"Yeah," was all she said. She turned and sprinted across the parking lot and into the crime lab.

~~~~~

Nick wasn't the only one working surveillance that morning. Five spaces away and one aisle over, Jimmy sat parked in a rented car, watching Gina. From his vantage point, he couldn't make out who was in the SUV. He watched Gina run back inside the crime lab. A moment later, the SUV started up and left the parking lot.

Jimmy remained parked. His focus was on Gina. She was his target. She would lead him to Nick. Jimmy wondered if Nick had been in the

SUV. And if so, what had he given her? He considered following the SUV but changed his mind. He would wait for Gina.

He was parked next to the Ford Explorer SUV Gina had been driving. Jimmy had run scenarios every which way, trying to figure out what the two of them were working on. If she were in fact working at the crime lab, it could very well just be a position transfer since the New Jersey crime lab was still under investigation.

But if not, then what had she been up to? And with Nick? Their involvement indicated some sort of collaborative work. But here in Atlanta? Nick wouldn't have jurisdiction. Maybe it was a case that the two had worked on previously. Or maybe them working together was all coincidence.

Jimmy was tired. Running on little sleep. And this over-analyzing was driving him half crazy. He needed answers. He'd been following Gina for two days now.

He'd been lying to Chloe, making up excuses for his whereabouts since Friday night. Claiming a work emergency needed his attention in New Jersey and he would be staying at his apartment there. Chloe wouldn't check his story because she was too wrapped up in her own work.

He'd checked into a hotel across the street from Gina's hotel. He was being careful not to be seen by her before he was ready. He'd tried to pick up Gina twice now, and twice he had failed. The first attempt he had flat out chickened out. He wasn't sure why, but he hadn't felt ready to take her at that moment. Something felt off. And he'd learned to trust his instincts.

The second time, he was within reach of her in her hotel parking lot when two men approached her and started up a conversation. Jimmy didn't recognize them. They only spoke for a few minutes, then all three of them walked into her hotel together. It appeared that Gina knew the two men. It was possible she had met them in the hotel at some point. Jimmy had gone back to his hotel to re-think his plan. And now here it was, day three, and he still hadn't taken action.

He decided that picking her up in the crime lab parking lot might be easier. Less people around than at her hotel. He slipped his hand into his coat pocket, feeling the outline of the handgun. It was a Glock nine-millimeter he'd purchased upon arriving in Atlanta. She wouldn't scream and she wouldn't run. He knew Gina. If anything, she'd take a swing at him.

He glanced at his Rolex. Ten fifty-five. Hopefully, she would go to lunch. Alone. His plan was to take her then. If she didn't leave for lunch, he'd be stuck here for another seven hours, again. She had worked both Saturday and Sunday, not leaving the crime lab until six. He wasn't cut out for surveillance work.

CHAPTER 25

Gina's gloved hands shook as she removed the soda can from the Ziplock bag. She carefully examined the crushed object with an LED-lit magnifying glass attached to her workstation. The hair samples jumped out at her immediately. Two, maybe three strands wound tightly around the lift tab of the can. Her heart pounded with the discovery.

She took a pair of tweezers and carefully unwound the hairs to free them from the can. Amber had done her job well. She examined them under the magnifying glass. Half of the strand was dark brown. The same color as Gina's hair. The other half was the lighter blonde shade that coincided with the digital image Amber had chosen. The result from previous hair coloring.

She placed them into a paper envelope and set them aside. She went back to the can. She carefully worked to straighten out the tin. She inserted a cuticle stick inside the wrinkled evidence and gently pushed the stick along the insides of the tin, working out the creases and dents until she had a fairly smooth-surfaced can.

She swabbed the can three times for saliva samples, placing each swab in individual envelopes and setting those aside with the hair sample. Then she dusted the can for fingerprints. She was able to lift two full and three partial prints.

Her heart was racing, and her mouth felt parched. Shaking hands made the task of processing the evidence nearly impossible. She broke out in perspiration, even though the air temp in the lab was set at sixty-three degrees. Most days she had to wear layers to keep warm.

Gina took her samples over to the respective workstations and processed each sample accordingly. Lab techs came and went, but for the most part the lab was unusually quiet for a Monday.

She was glued to the computer monitor as it ran through the database, searching for matches. It seemed like an eternity. Gina glanced at the clock on the wall. It was nearly one in the afternoon already. She'd skipped lunch. She wasn't hungry. She waited patiently, wondering, *what if?*

Another two hours passed before Amber's face popped up from a fingerprint match. Gina felt her heart skip before realizing it was Amber. Her legal name was Lindsay Amber White. Gina had been right. She was pretty. The photo of her obviously had been taken prior to her drug addiction.

The CODIS computer continued to scan for matches on the remaining samples. Gina logged into a separate computer to make a report on Lindsay Amber White. She pulled up a police record on her. Two arrests for drug possession and one for prostitution.

She printed out the reports and placed them in a file she made for Amber. She also printed out information from the Department of Motor Vehicles and credit reporting agencies. Amber had no credit to speak of, and the motor vehicle department gave three separate addresses for residency, all within the Atlanta area. Gina placed all this information in Amber's file.

She took a quick bathroom break. On her way back to the lab she stopped in the lunchroom to buy a bag of chips, some peanut M&M's, and a water from the vending machines, then hurried back to the CODIS computer to continue watching it scan for results.

Four more hours passed before it happened. A second match had been found. And there she was. Sirrina Marie Teducci. A weightless sensation struck Gina, like she was falling from a high place. Her breath caught in her throat.

"Oh my god," she whispered out loud to no one.

It was Sirrina's kindergarten photo. The one that had been taken during the fingerprinting exercise at their school. Gina couldn't take her eyes off Sirrina's face staring back at her from the monitor.

Moments later, the hair and saliva samples came back with positive matches. Both presented Sirrina's kindergarten photo as well. It also pulled up the digital image Chico had created within the database. A current image of what she might look like today.

It had worked. They had found her. More precisely, Nick had found her. None of this would be happening right now if it weren't for him. It all seemed impossible, yet there she was. Sirrina was alive. *Her sister was alive!*

Gina couldn't help but feel as if she and her family had abandoned Sirrina all those years ago. She'd been alive all along.

Gina choked up and began crying, unable to look away from Sirrina's image. All the hope mixed with the fear of not finding her had built up to this moment. The emotional rollercoaster she'd been on for the past two weeks overwhelmed her now.

Questions fired off in her head. She was unsure of what was to come. She had processed the samples from the soda can and confirmed that it was in fact Sirrina. But Gina had no idea where Nick, or Amber, for that matter, had retained the soda can from. Where had they found her? Was she safe? Was she with Diego? If so, how had they gotten to her?

Nick hadn't given her any details when he delivered the soda can. And now that she thought about it, she hadn't asked him. She'd been so astounded with the fact they had given her an item that possibly contained Sirrina's DNA on it that she forgot to ask.

Gina wanted to laugh and cry and yell and scream and jump for joy all at once. But the shock of it all kept her rooted on the stool. Besides that, she didn't want to draw attention to herself in the lab.

She thought about her parents. She wanted to call and tell them, tell her brothers and her family and her friends, but she knew it was too soon. She needed to talk to Nick first. Her sobbing continued. It was so damn unbelievable. The image of Sirrina blurred and distorted through her tears.

Gina wiped at her tears and looked at the clock. Seven-fifteen. Sophia had left hours ago, and so had most of the techs on her rotation. She was glad no one from the night rotation had interfered with her work. She didn't know any of them and wouldn't have wanted to explain what she'd been working on; let alone why she was crying.

Elated, Gina wanted to call Nick and share her findings with him as soon as possible. She had sent him two text messages earlier, letting him know she was still waiting for results. She didn't have privacy to speak freely in the lab, so she would wait until she was in her SUV before calling him.

Instead, she sent him one more text message: "It's a match. It's Sirrina. I'm leaving the lab in about thirty minutes. I'll call you on my way back to the hotel. Gina."

Gina brought the results screen back up on the monitor. She printed out the screen shots of both Lindsay Amber White and Sirrina Marie Teducci. She logged out of the database and carefully sealed up the samples and placed them in their proper storage containers.

She printed out the reports of her findings and made copies. She placed the originals in an envelope, sealed it, and would take those with her to lock in her desk drawer in her cubicle. The copies she folded up and placed in her purse to take with her. She wanted to show the results to Nick and Reuben and Ice and Chico. Results they had made possible. Results they would confirm were real. Results that left Gina no doubt her sister was alive.

She clocked out for the day at seven thirty-five.

When she exited the lab, the glare of LED lights shone against the twilight sky. The day had been a blur. She ran across the parking lot to her SUV. She was shaking with anticipation, wanting to call Nick. The text she'd sent him earlier couldn't convey her excitement and appreciation. She fumbled in her purse for the key fob. Her eagerness was causing clumsy hand coordination that was working against her. She pressed the button on the key fob, unlocking the doors.

CHAPTER 26

After leaving the soda can with Gina, Nick returned to the hotel with Reuben and Ice. Chico had been busy laying out their arsenal for the raid. The four of them packed four large canvas duffel bags full of firearms and ammunition, smoke grenades, nylon cuff restraints, night vision binoculars, communication devices, flashlights, and miscellaneous tools and equipment.

When the packing was finished, the remainder of their day was spent converging around the dining room table, examining, and re-examining Diego's property diagram that Chico had researched. Nick had received two separate text messages from Gina that no results had been found yet, keeping him informed on her work at the lab.

By late afternoon, a team of six special forces soldiers arrived at their hotel room. They had been recruited and organized by Reuben to aid in their mission tonight. All were ex-military combat soldiers who worked private security assignments.

Nick went over the plan for their operation and the property diagram he now had tattooed in his memory. If all went as planned, they would have no problem accessing the property.

The unknown was once they were within the confines of the property. The only intel they had was that there were six protection detail on sight and Diego. Surprises weren't uncommon during operations like this. Their resources were limited since this undertaking was unofficial. That resulted in limited information. And they had no idea how many victims besides Sirrina and Amber they would find once they had the property in their control.

They needed forty minutes to get to Diego's house from the hotel. It would be dark upon their arrival. They ordered pizzas, checked, and re-checked their gear, and swapped stories of combat and prior cases as they waited for nightfall before taking action. It helped to get their minds focused on the mission.

Nick checked his cellphone. Seven o'clock. That was his planned departure time, but he still had no confirmation from Gina. He had decided that, whether or not he got that confirmation, he would move on Diego tonight.

"Let's move out," he said to the group.

"We haven't heard from Gina yet," Reuben said.

"I know," Nick replied.

Reuben, Ice, and Chico quietly accepted Nick's request.

The ten-man team slipped on bullet-proof vests then filed out of the hotel rooms, hefting the duffel bags. As Nick brought up the rear, he considered the impressive sight his crew made. If any hotel guest appeared in the hallway just then, they would fear some sort of hostile takedown was about to happen. And it was, just not at this location.

The men used the stairwell and exited out a side door to avoid the lobby. Fortunately, they made it out without drawing attention to themselves. They piled into a black panel van that Reuben's men had arrived in and headed to Diego's house.

Ten minutes into the drive, Nick's text ringer went off. He removed his cellphone from his pocket and read the text from Gina. Delight and relief surged.

"We got a match," he called out to everyone. He couldn't help but smile. It was the news he'd been waiting for. Sirrina was alive. And they were going to get her. The powerful realization struck his core.

"That was Gina?" Reuben asked.

"It was." Nick said. "She's leaving the lab in a while. Said she'd call later." He was all smiles as he tucked his phone back in the pocket of his jeans, over-energized now.

"Whooo!" Ice clapped his hands once, hyped and anxious. "Let's get this done, boys," he called out.

"Nothing like a rescue operation to get the heart rate amped," one of the soldiers called out.

The mood in the van shifted into high gear. Adrenalin pumped up. And the remaining drive to Diego's house did nothing to stifle that energy. Even though traffic delayed them an extra twenty minutes.

Nick had the driver park a block away. He wanted to survey the area before making their move. Overhead streetlights and residential landscape lighting were sparse, giving them plenty of shadows to work in, but he wanted to wait for the sky to turn dark. Twenty minutes later, that detail was satisfied.

"Let's do this," Nick called out.

Chico slid the four bags down the center of the van floor. The crew got busy arming themselves with weapons, ammunition, and communication devices.

Nick fastened the last of his ammunition magazines to his belt, his adrenalin amped up and ready to put his plan into action. He consulted his cellphone. Eight-thirty. Time to strike. And still no word from Gina. He'd expected a call from her sometime during the drive. She should have been back at the hotel by now. But it was possible she'd gotten distracted or delayed at the lab.

He couldn't be sidetracked by that now. He silenced his phone. His team of nine sat ready and waiting for a command from him. He would catch up with her after their mission was complete. And by then, he hoped to have positive news to share with her.

"Let's move," he said.

One of the soldiers fired up the van and circled the block with the lights turned off, parking a short distance from Diego's property. The driver did a once-over, scanning the neighborhood from his vantage point.

"All clear," the driver said.

Nick slid the rear side door open. They exited the van, quickly making their way to Diego's property. Within minutes they had scaled the vine-covered fencing and scattered to their respective positions.

With the element of surprise, one by one Diego's protection detail was taken down quietly without a struggle. Nick came up from behind to the last of the protection detail sitting at the kitchen island. He placed the guy in a chokehold until he blacked out, leaving him slumped over his plate of food. Nick fastened nylon zip ties around his wrists and ankles.

He plucked the man's cellphone from the counter. He removed his own phone from his pocket, scrolling to the text message Amber had sent. He typed in a reply and hit send. The man's cellphone text ringer sounded, and Nick's message appeared. It was by sheer luck that Amber had been able to send him the message while this guy was taking out the trash.

"That's six," Nick said to his crew through a wireless communication device attached to the collar of his shirt. He'd been the only one to access the main house so far.

"Move in. Soft. First floor only." He gave his crew the order. He wanted the element of surprise saved for Diego. He tucked both cellphones in his pockets.

The remaining nine men of his crew entered the main house from various entry points in quiet precision. Nick pointed upstairs. Handgun drawn, he moved first. Reuben and Chico fell in line behind him. Ice and the other six scattered throughout the house.

Within minutes, Nick found Diego in the master bedroom, dimly lit by one bedside table lamp. A wall-mounted television was tuned to a Spanish broadcast. Diego sat on the edge of the bed, removing a needle he'd just plunged into a young girl's arm.

From across the room, Nick couldn't tell whether it was Sirrina or not. She looked to be about Sirrina's age and had the same color hair. She was naked and half-covered with the bed sheet. Nick raised his handgun, pointing it at Diego.

"Get away from her, Diego," Nick called out.

Diego whipped his head around at the sound of his voice.

"What the…" Diego lunged for the nightstand table. Nick fired off one shot, purposely missing Diego, but causing him to recoil.

"All good." Chico responded through his mic clipped to his shirt collar to the remaining crew downstairs.

"Are you out of your fucking mind?" Diego shouted. "Do you know who I am?"

He stood facing Nick in a gold bathrobe that hung open. His paunchy midsection drooped over his white boxer shorts. Thick curly black hair, damp from sweat or from showering, framed his dark beady eyes and groomed beard.

"Yes, I do," Nick replied, calmly keeping his gun trained on the fifty-three-year-old swine as he stepped further into the room. Reuben and Chico came up behind him, guns drawn.

"Got him," Reuben said.

"On your knees, hands behind your head," Nick said to Diego.

"Fuck you, man. How'd you get past my security?"

Nick took three long strides to close the gap between them. Nick stood a good seven inches taller than Diego.

"Alright. Alright." Diego wobbled as he carefully lowered himself to kneeling on the carpet. He threaded his fingers behind his head. Nick indicated to Reuben as he holstered his gun. Reuben restrained Diego's hands behind his back with nylon zip ties. Nick turned to the girl on the bed.

Chico kept his gun drawn on Diego. "Target secure. Repeat. Target is secure." He spoke through his mic again.

"Jesus." Nick wavered as his adrenalin pulsed. "It's her," he nearly whispered to himself. It was Sirrina. He'd found her. He could feel it deep inside him as he covered her naked, frail, and scarred body. Even in the dim light he could tell it was her.

He pulled his gloves off and lowered himself to the edge of the bed. Slowly raising a hand, he gently pushed the hair away from her eyes. She lay unconscious. He removed a small flashlight clipped to his belt. His other hand gently lifted one of Sirrina's eyelids. He shone the light in her eye. Her pupil was dilated. He checked the other one...same.

"Get your hands off my Sasha," Diego yelled at Nick. "You don't touch her. She's my best..."

Reuben knelt behind Diego, clutching him in a headlock. "Not another word out of you or I'll twist your fuckin head off."

Nick ignored Diego, keeping his focus on Sirrina. Her skin was white and veiny with bones protruding. A combination of anorexia and drug abuse. Her lips were nearly blue and matched the bruising on her arms from needle use. He identified scarring from small cuts with a sharp object of some sort mixed with burns from cigarettes.

Nick pressed his index and middle finger to her neck, feeling for a pulse. It was there, barely. He secured his flashlight to his belt, lost in the moment as he watched over her. His thoughts mulled over how Gina and her family were going to handle this tragic blessing of having Sirrina back in their lives.

He pulled his gloves back on, then plucked the syringe from the bed and moved it to the nightstand. From somewhere in the house one of the crew called out.

"Down here!"

Nick looked to Diego. "You better pray I don't find any more like her." Nick stood and slammed his fist into Diego's cheek, sending him face down to the floor. Nick looked to Chico.

"Stay here with him." He turned to Reuben. "Let's go." Nick hurried from the room with Reuben on his heels.

"Where?" Nick called out.

"Basement," Ice called up to him.

Nick flew down the stairs and to the basement. Two of Reuben's soldiers stood at the entrance.

"Back there." One of the soldiers pointed towards the far end of the room.

The basement stairwell landed in a large windowless carpeted room that was sparsely furnished. The smell of decay mixed with perspiration, sex, blood, urine, and god knows what else, emanated.

Bedroom furniture occupied one corner, with cameras and lighting surrounding it. Presently, it was all sitting dark. Nick noticed blood stains on the bedding. That explained the bodily fluids he smelled. Reuben and Ice surveyed the area further while Nick moved towards the far end of the room that led to a long hallway. The odors worsened. For all Nick knew, there was a dead body or two down here.

Several doors lined both sides of the hallway. Nick approached the first door to his right that was open. He removed the flashlight from his belt again, shining it into the room. It had the makings of a small jail cell. Windowless, a twin bed pushed in one corner with worn tattered bedding, a small dresser, no mirror, a desk and chair with books, a notepad and pencil. Nick entered the room while Reuben and Ice moved on. He thumbed through the notepad. The pages were blank.

"Nick," Reuben called out.

Nick moved back out to the hallway. He heard voices that sounded like crying. A beating taking place. Definite crying mixed with grunting and growling sounds.

"In here," Reuben said.

Across the hall was a TV room. Nick found Reuben and Ice standing with two more soldiers. One held a television remote control.

"Diego likes recording himself with the girls," Reuben said.

"A real sicko," Ice added.

Nick looked to the TV and saw a poor-quality video of Diego beating and assaulting one of the girls. The excitement of finding Sirrina diminished as disgust and rage quickly reached a boiling point inside Nick.

"Turn it off," Nick said to the soldier.

Nick's eyes probed the room. A sofa and two chairs, books on shelves, coloring books, crayons, puzzles, board games on a card table: the entertainment area. And the wall-mounted television that was now dark and quiet.

"Collect any recordings you can find and put them in the van." The two soldiers acknowledged Nick's request.

Nick continued down the hall. Next to the entertainment room was a large bathroom. The shower and toilet were stained and moldy with damp towels hanging on the curtain rod. Filthy laundry filled a hamper, and toiletries scattered the countertop. Musty odors stemmed from this room.

Nick moved to the next bedroom across the hall. It was the same as the first bedroom except a body lay covered in the bed. Nick flicked on the small table lamp.

"In here," he called out.

Reuben and Ice entered the room as Nick knelt next to the bed and pulled the blankets back to reveal a young girl, maybe eleven or twelve. Her bony frame was dressed in a tank top and underwear. She reacted wearily to them being in her room. She was half comatose on whatever drug Diego had pumped into her. She had the same scarring and bruising on her delicate, battered body as Sirrina had.

"Jesus. What is this place?" Ice asked.

"Hell," Nick replied, but kept his focus on the young girl. "We're gonna need paramedics." He looked up to Reuben. "Check the other rooms."

Reuben called in for emergency personnel as he and Ice left the room. Nick listened to her shallow breathing. He checked her pupils. Dilated. Just like Sirrina's. The girl flinched at his actions. She placed her cold delicate hands on his forearm to stop him. It cut Nick to the core, seeing this young girl in this circumstance.

He carefully tucked her arms back under the covers, listening to the guys going room to room down the hallway. He could hear their voices but couldn't make out what they were saying until Reuben called out.

"Nick? Get down here."

Nick jumped to his feet and bolted from the room. He rushed down the hall to where Ice was standing. Nick took two steps into the room and froze. There were two beds in this room. The stench of death permeated the space.

"Holy shit," Nick said.

"She didn't make it." Reuben pointed to one of the beds. "O.D. would be my guess."

Nick could make out the outline of a body covered in a sheet about the same size as the girl he'd just left in the other room.

Reuben stood at the foot of the bed where Amber lay sprawled out in her bra and underwear, bruised and bleeding. There were blood stains on the sheets and splattered up the wall next to the bed.

Nick moved in closer to examine her. Her face was beaten beyond recognition. The swelling, coloring and caked blood indicated she'd been this way for a while. Her copper red hair was her only identifier.

"Is she breathing?" Nick asked. He checked her pulse by pressing fingers to her neck. Immense guilt consumed him.

"Barely," Reuben replied.

Nick felt a faint erratic pulse. He covered her with the sheet and blanket from her bed.

He turned to the other bed and lifted the sheet just enough to view the dead young girl. Blonde. Frail. Scarred. Her skin bluish gray. The stench was overwhelming. She'd been dead for at least two days.

"Son of a bitch."

Nick replaced the sheet over her. He looked back to Amber, then to Reuben.

"This is on me," he said, pointing to Amber.

"No, it's not man," Reuben shot back.

"Yeah. It is," Nick countered as he strode past him back out into the hallway.

"Nick," Reuben yelled after him.

Nick strode straight down the hallway to the open room. He rushed past the men standing by and took the stairs two at time into the house.

"Nick?" He heard Reuben calling after him

When Nick reached the staircase on the main level, he took those steps two at a time as well. He rushed towards the master bedroom. Reuben continued calling out after him.

Nick pushed through the master bedroom door, taking long strides over to Diego. He pulled him up to his feet, then slammed his fist into Diego's face, knocking him backwards into the bed. Diego groaned and caught his balance against the bed and stood. His hands were restrained behind his back.

"Son of a bitch!" Diego shouted. His teeth were stained with blood.

Chico stepped out of Nick's way.

"You like to beat 'em?" Nick examined Diego's restrained hands. His knuckles were cut and bruised from beating Amber. "Let's see how you like it, motherfucker." Nick went at Diego again, slamming his fist into his face. Diego grunted as he fell backwards on top of Sirrina. Nick pulled him up and off the bed, punching him once more. Chico didn't try to stop him. Diego's body fell against the bed once more, sliding down the side of it, folding to the ground. Nick delivered one more blow to Diego's head just as Reuben entered the room.

Reuben didn't try stopping Nick, either. Diego was nearly unconscious when Nick finally stopped. He'd let his rage get the best of him. It was something he'd always held in check, but not this time. He straightened and backed away, huffing, and flexing his gloved hand, feeling the swelling of his knuckles. He looked down to see his gloved hand wet with Diego's blood.

The three of them studied Diego's body slumped on the floor, half propped up against the bed. He was bleeding and moaning and wheezing in pain. Nick looked over to Chico and Reuben. Ice entered. The four of them shared a moment of silence. Sirrina lay motionless in the bed.

"Can any of you think of a reason this piece of shit should continue breathing?" Nick asked, looking to each one of them.

All three shook their heads no.

Nick pulled out his gun. He looked to the nightstand table. He holstered his gun and pulled open the drawer where he found a small metal container. He popped it open to find Diego's heroin stash. Reuben helped Nick through the process of making multiple doses of the drug, loading the syringe Nick had placed on the nightstand earlier.

When it was full, Nick stood over Diego with the syringe in his gloved hand. He knelt in front of Diego. Diego's head bobbled. He tried to focus on Nick through the blood of his beaten and swollen eyes. Blood and drool strung from his mouth, connecting with the hair on his chest. Beads of sweat trickled down his temples, mixing with the blood oozing from the cuts around his eyes. He began to pant.

"You won't," Diego huffed some more. "You won't get away with this."

"Wrong." Nick held up the syringe. "It's you who won't get away with this, anymore."

Diego squirmed, trying to free himself. "No, no, no!"

Nick dug his knee into Diego's thigh and pressed his left hand against Diego's battered face, pinning his head back against the bed. In one motion he stabbed the needle into Diego's neck and released the drug into him. Within seconds, Diego's body went limp.

Nick wiped the blood from his gloved hands on Diego's robe, then removed a pocketknife from his belt. He pushed Diego's weight aside and reached behind him to cut the nylon restraint. He handed it over to Chico.

Nick stood up, replacing the knife in his belt, leaving the syringe stuck in Diego. The four of them watched Diego's body convulse. Spittle foamed around his mouth. After a moment, his body lay still. Nick checked for a pulse. Nothing. He straightened and moved to sit on the edge of the bed next to Sirrina. He heard sirens arriving.

Within minutes, paramedics, police, and detectives swarmed the property. Two Atlanta detectives entered Diego's room with guns drawn. Nick remained seated on the bed with his hands up displaying his badge. Reuben, Ice, and Chico stood surrounding Diego with their hands up. The two detectives looked to Sirrina, then to Diego. Nick observed the detectives. Seasoned. Plenty of experience between the two.

"What happened here?" one detective asked, referring to Diego.

"Looks like he had an accident with a needle," Nick replied.

Nick waited for more from the detectives, but nothing else was said. Paramedics entered the room. The Atlanta detectives holstered their guns and directed them to Sirrina. Nick stood and moved aside so they could help her. Nick felt the stares from both detectives. He pocketed his badge and turned to them.

The same detective that spoke to him before commented, "I think you have some explaining to do."

Nick knew they had recognized him, either from the news or police briefings. Nick would have to explain his being here to these two and hope they would support his efforts. Nick nodded, accepting the request. As the paramedics carted Sirrina out of the room, Nick, his crew, and the two detectives followed.

Downstairs in the foyer, they watched several more paramedics cart away Amber and the other sedated young girl in the basement. The dead girl was carted out by the coroner and eventually so was Diego. Diego's protection detail was arrested.

Nick and his crew were questioned by the Atlanta detectives. Nick was able to explain their undercover position without giving up too many details. He still needed to protect his private investigation that wasn't yet complete.

He told the Atlanta detectives they had been acting on an anonymous tip. As far as Atlanta was concerned, they had been following a lead to track down Diego and Horacio as part of a trafficking ring. They gave up Horacio's three hotel locations, so that would keep them busy for a while.

In the end, Atlanta ended up seizing hundreds of thousands of dollars' worth of drugs, cash, and weapons. The two other buildings on

Diego's property had been equipped for his drug processing and packaging operation: a substantial score for Atlanta's police department.

Nick and the guys headed back to the van after being questioned and released. In depth questioning and statements would be given later at the Atlanta police station. There would be jurisdiction issues brought up by Atlanta, but Nick had chief of police Bruce Stanford back in New Jersey to clear that up for them.

Nick wanted to get to the hospital as soon as possible, and he wanted to get there with Gina. He'd had his cellphone muted during the raid. There were five missed calls from Gina. He climbed into the passenger seat of the van while playing his voice messages.

The first one: "Hi, it's Gina. Call me as soon as you get this."

Reuben climbed into the driver's seat while the rest of the crew piled into the back of the van.

The next three calls were hang-ups. The last one was Gina asking him to call a.s.a.p.

Nick dialed her number as the van drove away from Diego's neighborhood.

"Hello?" Gina answered.

"Hey. It's me. I'm sorry I didn't call sooner, but I've got great news, Gina. We found her. We found Sirrina. She's going to be ok. She's on her way to the hospital right now. I'm coming to get you and we'll head there together." Nick felt a rush of excitement and relief at being able to share the news with her.

There was a long pause before she answered. "That's nice. I'm happy for you. But do you think you can stop by the hotel before you go? I'd like to talk to you about something."

Nick was floored by her response, but only for a moment. Something was up. He detected it in her tone and more importantly in the words she spoke. "What's going on, Gina?"

Reuben looked over at him.

"I'm not staying in room three twenty-five anymore," Gina said. "The couple next door in three twenty-seven were up all night. Couldn't get any sleep. I'm now staying in room three forty-five."

Nick paused on that message for a good long moment, knowing Gina had always been checked into room three forty-five. He and the guys had been occupying three twenty-five and three twenty-seven.

"Got it," Nick replied. "I'm on my way."

"How long?" she asked.

"Less than thirty."

"An hour?" she asked. "Try and make it sooner if you can."

"I will. Can you talk?"

Gina hung up on him. Nick's adrenalin was nearly off the charts now. She had made it clear in her responses that she was in trouble. She needed him now, but he was a good thirty-five minutes away.

Nick disconnected from the call looking to Reuben. "We've got a problem?"

"With Gina?" Reuben asked.

"Yeah. We need to get to the hotel. And I mean *now!*" Nick slammed his fist down on the center console repeatedly indicating his urgency. Reuben gunned the accelerator.

CHAPTER 27

Gina disconnected from her call with Nick. Jimmy backhanded her across her face, sending her stumbling backwards in the living room. She caught her balance, nearly falling over the coffee table. She sat down on the edge of it. She tasted blood in her mouth and her lip stung. It felt numb as it began to swell.

"Jesus, Jimmy. What the…"

"You think that's funny? Pulling that little stunt?" Jimmy yelled. "You think I'm stupid?"

He came at her again, pulling her by her hair, forcing her to stand. His free hand gripped her face and squeezed hard.

"Ow, Jimmy! What are you doing?" Gina cried out. She clawed at him, scratching his face.

He pushed her hard, sending her backwards, tripping over the coffee table. This time she landed with half her backside on the table, then tumbled between the table and sofa. She scrambled to get to her feet, but Jimmy was standing over her. He swung his hand and slapped her hard, sending her backwards on the floor. Gina thought she might black out from the hit. The stinging pain hit her with full force.

Jimmy bent down and gripped her by her shirt, yanking her to her feet. The momentum made her head spin and she fell into him. He pulled her over to the dining room. Gina struggled to free herself and fight against him, but it was no use. He overpowered her. With one hand firmly gripped on her arm, he used his other hand to pull a chair from the table, spinning it around. He pushed her down into the chair.

He gripped her face once more, tugging her head to face him. "Don't you move."

"Jimmy, I didn't…"

Jimmy pulled his arm back and made a fist. Gina threw her hands up in front of her face. But he didn't strike her.

"Shut the fuck up and sit there."

Gina's heart was racing. She was in pain and felt swelling where blood was rushing to her injuries. Bruising would be forming from the trauma he'd inflicted on her. She'd made the mistake of giving Nick a heads up, but she had to think it would be worth it. He would be the only person that could get to her in time and save her from Jimmy's wrath.

When she had left the lab tonight, Jimmy had been waiting. As soon as she climbed into her SUV, Jimmy flung open the passenger side door, climbed into the SUV, and pressed his gun against her ribs. The whole episode took her by surprise.

He told her his plan and threatened her life if she didn't cooperate. Knowing he was Nick's investigation, she did as he asked. She knew him to be dangerous now. His plan was to ambush Nick here at the hotel. In this very room. Gina needed to buy some time.

"Jimmy, calm down for a minute," she pleaded. "Nick's not going to be here for almost an hour. Talk to me. What happened? Why are you doing this? Why are you going after Nick?"

Jimmy ignored her, rifling through a large duffel bag he had sitting on the dining room table. Gina placed a hand on his arm.

"Jimmy, please talk to me."

She had been trying to reason with him for the last hour while they waited for Nick to return her call. Jimmy caught her hand and twisted it backwards, nearly breaking it. Gina fell to her knees from the chair, trying to ease against his grip.

"Ow, shit! Jimmy!" Gina cried out. She balled a fist with her free hand and punched him in the groin, causing his knees to buckle. He fell in front of her. When she tried to stand and make a run for it, he grabbed her legs. Her body slammed down on the carpeted floor. They struggled and fought on the floor, but he easily overtook her, pinning her to the ground.

"Shut the fuck up before someone hears you." He let go of his hold on her. "Get back in the chair."

"Can I use the bathroom first?" she asked.

"No, dammit. Sit."

Gina did. She rubbed her wrist and arm from Jimmy's attack. "Can you at least bring me a wet towel for my face?" she asked. She was trying to think of anything to stall to give Nick time to get to her.

Jimmy continued to search through the duffel bag. He removed a roll of duct tape and began peeling it. The first piece went across her mouth. Gina sat in stunned silence. Jimmy was taking this too far. He cinched her hands behind the back of the chair. She tried to fight against him, but his grip was too strong. He knelt on the floor in front of her and taped each of her ankles to the legs of the chair.

She thought about kicking him in the groin and trying to escape, but that didn't seem feasible with a chair anchored to her back. She was still dazed from the blows he'd given her. The room hadn't stopped spinning yet. She felt sick to her stomach.

Gina watched him work the tape. She imagined he was putting the pieces together now. Realizing that Nick had been investigating him. He seemed panicked and not in control of his situation. Gina didn't know the extent of Nick's investigation, other than it involved Sirrina's disappearance.

Gina wanted so badly to talk to Jimmy. To plead with him. But her mouth was duct taped shut. She moaned and mumbled, hoping he would remove it. Instead, he stood towering over her. He balled his hand into a fist and held it inches from her face.

"I told you, shut the fuck up."

He moved behind her and tipped the chair back on its rear legs. Gina felt her stomach flip. Jimmy spun the chair and dragged it into the living room, placing it in front of one of the side chairs. Gina faced the door to the room. Jimmy sat behind her in the side chair. She couldn't figure out what he was doing. She felt like he was....*Jesus*...he was going to use her as a human shield for when Nick entered the room.

She moaned through the tape again and tried to pivot to face him but couldn't. He just sat there in silence. It made Gina's blood run cold. What was he thinking? What was he anticipating doing to her? To Nick?

It continued for nearly ten minutes. Gina thought she would go mad. It was unnerving as hell.

He abruptly stood up, startling her. He moved to the dining room table while reading something on his cellphone. Apparently, that's what he'd been doing. He rifled through the large duffel bag again. He removed a strip of something and carried it over to her.

Gina moaned through the tape once again. Tears sprang to her eyes as soon as she identified what he was holding: a strip of explosives banded together in a belt.

"There, there." He said, patting her knee. "We'll get you wired up, so when Nick gets here, he'll be focused on rescuing you from this little contraption. He'll never see me coming from the bedroom." He bent down close to her face. "And you won't be able to warn him." Jimmy straightened, holding up the belt of explosives. He carefully laid them across her knees. "Don't move."

Gina could hardly breathe. Jimmy had lost his mind. She was sure of that now. She watched him return to the dining room table and dig through the duffel bag once again. His gun sat just to the left of the bag on the table.

Suddenly, an explosive sound and shattering glass filled the room. Gina tried to duck and ended up tumbling over in the chair. She about blacked out, thinking the explosives would blow her to pieces. From the floor she watched Jimmy move towards her, but his attention was focused on the hotel room window. Gina felt the cool night air rush into the room. She arched backwards, noticing the window had a gaping hole in it.

The door to their room exploded open. Nick was the first one to enter. He had his gun drawn and pointed at Jimmy.

"Don't move, Jimmy," Nick called out to him.

But Jimmy spun from the window, attempting to head for his gun. Nick quickly intercepted him. Nick pushed his weight forward, tackling Jimmy to the floor.

"No!" Jimmy yelled out. "I'm going to kill you, dammit!"

They wrestled on the ground just inches from Gina's head. Grunting and fists punching into flesh. She tried her best to shield her face from getting kicked or punched. Seconds later, Reuben, Ice, and Chico entered the room, taking control of Jimmy and his gun. They rolled Jimmy face down and secured him with nylon restraints.

Jimmy began sobbing. "No! Goddamn you, Nick! This ain't over yet." He continued blubbering and cursing at Nick.

Nick ignored him as he crawled to Gina on his hands and knees. When his eyes caught sight of the explosives, he froze. Their eyes met, sharing a staggering moment. Gina felt panic and dread course through her.

"Guys?" Nick called out. "This isn't over yet. We're gonna need the bomb unit up here."

"What?" Reuben said. He and Ice and Chico all stopped their movements to look to Gina.

Nick looked over to Reuben. "Get him out of here," he said, referring to Jimmy. "Call for the bomb unit and have the hotel evacuated."

"You to," Reuben replied. "Get your ass up."

"I'm staying," Nick countered.

Reuben walked over to Nick, standing over him.

"Stop moving," Nick called out, holding up his hands.

"Get your ass up and out of here, Nick. That's an order," Reuben commanded.

Gina felt sick. If she threw up, she would gag and choke with the tape over her mouth. She fought to swallow against the churning in the pit of her stomach.

"I appreciate it, man, I do. But I'm not leaving her." Nick was adamant.

Chico and Ice hauled Jimmy out of the room. Reuben and Nick shared a long, heated stare before Reuben finally relented. He looked to Gina.

"Hang in there, Gina. We'll have you out of here in no time."

Gina closed her eyes, knowing he was attempting to comfort her. When she opened them again, Reuben was gone, and Nick was kneeling beside her. He worked at the tape on her mouth, peeling it back slowly. Gina moaned and then yanked her head against his grip, pulling against the tape.

"Do it quick and get it over with," she mumbled between swollen cut lips.

"Jesus." Nick traced his fingers over her face, taking in her cuts and bruises.

"I'm fine," Gina said.

"I'm not," Nick replied. He pulled a pocketknife from his belt and extended the blade. He examined the explosive device half-concealed under Gina. "Is it attached to you?"

"Not yet. He was working on that when you blew a hole through the window."

Nick looked over to the window. "Nice shot, hunh?" Nick said. "One of Reuben's guys in the hotel across the way." He brought his focus back to her.

"Was it wired up?"

"No. He didn't get that far."

Gina caught that Nick breathed a sigh of relief. His moves were slow and precise as he cut the tape from her hands and feet, freeing her from the chair.

"Part of your weight is laying on the device," Nick concluded. "We wait for the bomb unit to clear you. Try not to move."

Twenty minutes later, the bomb unit arrived, suited up in detonation gear. They immediately plucked Nick from the room. Next, they secured Gina and got her separated from the device. The second bomb tech escorted her from the room and down the hallway to where Nick was waiting. She never felt him catch her as she blacked out.

CHAPTER 28

Gina sat beside Sirrina's hospital bed, watching and listening to the monitors blip and beep as they registered her sister's condition. It was just before midnight. An IV drip was giving Sirrina vital fluids as she lay unconscious. Gina still couldn't believe this was her sister. It all seemed like some sick, twisted dream. How could this have happened to her? How could their lives have been lived in such opposition?

She looked across the room at Nick, stretched out in a chair too small to fit his tall, muscular frame. His head was leaned back against the wall, his eyes closed. He looked so peaceful. She owed everything to him.

Gina looked back to Sirrina. She traced a finger over her forearm. Over the scars. Scars that would run deep. Scars that would impact her sister mentally even more than physically. Gina wondered how Sirrina would come out of this. Many of Gina's cases dealt with this exact circumstance, so she knew the probability of permanent mental health issues. Sirrina would be undergoing treatment for years to come.

Gina heard the door open and turned to see the nurse standing there.

"Your parents are here," she said.

"Thank you," Gina replied.

The nurse left. Nick sat up.

"It's probably a good idea for me to wait here," he said.

Gina agreed. She walked down the corridor to the nurse's station. Her parents turned to face her. Gina had told them she'd been in a minor accident and that she was in the hospital. She could tell they'd been stressing the entire trip here.

They embraced her and her father cupped her face.

"Jesus! What happened? You ok?"

Her parents looked at her with deep concern.

"I'm fine. Let's go in here for a minute so we can talk."

Gina pointed them to a small, enclosed waiting room. The moment was weighing heavily on her. The three of them entered and sat in a quiet corner.

"I have some very good news to share with you that's going to come as quite a shock," Gina said.

"Well, for starters," Carmine said. "What are you doing in Atlanta? Your mother and I have been worried sick the entire trip down here. You're supposed to be in L.A. Imagine how we felt when we got the call you had been in an accident three thousand miles from where we thought you were."

"Dad," Gina sighed. "I'll explain all that. Just…"

"Was the accident your fault?" he asked. "Was anyone else hurt?"

"No. There wasn't an accident, Dad."

Her parents looked at her, confused.

"What happened, Gina?" Jackie asked. "Your face…look at you." Her mother's hand caressed Gina's cheek.

Gina took hold of her mother's hand lowering it away from her face. She drew in a deep breath. "I'm in Atlanta helping Detective Nick Casey on an undercover case. Everything I tell you right now needs to remain between us, because it's still an ongoing investigation."

Jackie slid her hand from Gina's grip. Gina watched her parents process her words.

"Investigation for what?" Carmine asked a little too aggressively.

"Sirrina," Gina answered.

Her parents flinched simultaneously, but her answer left them speechless. Gina recalled how she'd felt when Nick revealed the same information to her.

"This is going to be really difficult for you both to understand," Gina almost whispered.

"What?" Carmine asked.

"Tell us what it is, Gina," Jackie expressed with concern.

"We found Sirrina," Gina said.

Her parents' expressions registered surprise, and their faces paled in unison.

"What do you mean, you found her?" Carmine bit off the words bitterly. "She's…we…"

Anger and confusion kept him from finishing his sentence. Gina's heart was racing just as she imagined her parents' thoughts were. She watched the two of them try to get a grip on what she was telling them. Since there hadn't been a funeral for Sirrina they were trying to piece together the past with this moment right now. It pained Gina to put her parents through this, but the outcome would be worth it.

"We found her, Dad. She's alive."

"*Gina!*" Jackie cried out. She choked up and couldn't finish whatever else she was going to say.

Gina couldn't hold back tears any longer. "We found her," she sobbed.

Carmine embraced Gina and Jackie together. "Christ, I'm trying to wrap my head around this, Gina. How can this be?" he asked, pulling back. "It's been sixteen years. Where's she been? What happened to her? How did you…?" He choked up. "Jesus. I can't believe what you're telling us, Gina."

"I can't either," Gina said in between sobs. "I've witnessed it all and I still can't believe it."

Gina gave them as much detail as she thought they could handle but didn't explain Jimmy. She would save that for later. She needed to reveal the truth in small doses. Just as it had been revealed to her. It was the best way for her parents to absorb the shocking news. After a lengthy explanation about Nick's involvement, and her involvement with his case, they went to Sirrina's room.

When they entered, her mother broke down. She rushed to Sirrina's bedside.

"My baby," she cried. She placed a shaking hand over her mouth, and the other on Sirrina's forehead.

Nick brought a chair over and steered Jackie into it. Carmine stood rooted in place, staring in disbelief at his youngest daughter, hooked up to machines. It rendered him speechless.

Jackie continued sobbing, stroking Sirrina's head and running fingers through her tangled hair, dismayed at Sirrina's condition.

"I can't believe…Why did this happen?" Jackie looked to Gina and Nick. "What happened to her?" She could barely speak between sobs.

The scene crushed Gina. "Not now, Mom," Gina replied. "Just be here with her."

Carmine sat in a chair and took a hold of Sirrina's hand. He was still in shock at seeing her lying there.

"Nick and I are going to the cafeteria to get some coffee. We'll let you have some quiet time with her."

"Don't go," Jackie called out, looking up to Gina. Panic shone in her expression. "Stay here."

Carmine reached across the bed and took Jackie's hand. "It's fine. Let them go."

"What if she doesn't come back?" Jackie was nearing hysterics between sobs. She dropped her head on the bed and cried uncontrollably. Carmine squeezed Jackie's shoulder and stroked her arm to comfort her. He looked to Gina and Nick.

"Go," he said. "She'll be alright."

Gina's heart sank. It was the first indication that her Mom wasn't going to be ok from this ordeal. Just as she'd suspected. Who would be? Her family was going to need serious healing. But, in the end, they would have Sirrina back in their lives again.

"Sirrina?" Jackie wiped her tears and leaned over Sirrina. "She just squeezed my hand." Jackie glanced to all of them appearing desperate, then she looked back to Sirrina.

"Mom?" Sirrina whispered.

"Yes!" Jackie cried.

Gina and Nick closed in at Sirrina's bedside. Sirrina's eyes blinked open and tried to focus.

"Mom?" Sirrina said again, her voice was barely audible.

"Yes, honey. I'm right here." Jackie was crying, stroking Sirrina's head.

Carmine took hold of Sirrina's other hand. Sirrina twitched and closed her eyes. Gina stood over her father squeezing a hand on his shoulder as tears ran down her cheeks.

"Daddy, I'm sorry," Sirrina whispered again. Tears rolled from her closed eyes and then she was asleep.

Carmine cried for his daughter. "I'm here, sweetheart. You're going to be fine. Everything is going to be fine." He caressed her hand.

"This is a good sign," Gina said. "She knows you're here. She's recognized your voices."

"Gina?" Sirrina came to again.

Gina moved next to her father and took Sirrina's hand. "I'm here, sis. It's Gina. I'm right here."

Sirrina opened her eyes again. "*Gi....na.*" She gave Gina's hand a slight squeeze. "You came...you...found...me." Sirrina exhaled and closed her eyes.

Gina choked up and couldn't respond. Her sister looked so fragile it broke her heart. Her parents were just as heartbroken.

"She needs her rest," the nurse announced.

Gina and Nick looked to the nurse, not realizing she'd entered the room. Gina moved out of her way.

"I'm giving her a sedative, so she'll be asleep for some time now," the nurse said, as she infused Sirrina's IV drip with a syringe of medication and then noted this and Sirrina's vital signs on her laptop.

"Can we stay?" Carmine asked.

"Sure, preferably two at a time," the nurse replied, then she left.

Gina wiped her eyes. It had been an emotional moment having Sirrina regain consciousness, even for just a few minutes. It made Gina hopeful in her recovery. She had recognized them. Sirrina had heard their voices and recognized them. Gina hugged her parents.

"She's going to be ok," Gina said. "Nick and I will be in the cafeteria. We'll check back in a while."

This time Jackie didn't cry out. She was too absorbed with Sirrina.

As Gina and Nick turned to leave, Carmine caught Nick by the arm. "You and me are gonna have a talk later." He gestured to Nick with anger in his eyes.

Nick quietly agreed. He and Gina slipped out of the room and made their way to the cafeteria. They found a quiet table in a corner to catch their breath. They sipped hot coffee and chowed down a hot meal together. It was the first sense of normal either of them had felt in a while. The food left much to be desired, but that didn't matter. What mattered was that they were together. Safe. And so was Sirrina.

Within the hour, Gina's brothers, sisters-in-law, nieces, and nephews all arrived at the hospital. The lounge/waiting area was overrun with the Teducci clan. They took turns going to see Sirrina in her room in between rounds of assaulting Gina and Nick with questions. They answered and explained as best they could without giving too much detail. It was like being mobbed by a media circus. Gina was surprised that the hospital staff didn't ask them all to leave from the disruption they were causing.

When the chaos finally calmed down, Nick pulled Gina aside.

"As much as I don't want to ask you this," he paused.

"What?" Gina felt that familiar sinking feeling, seeing his expression.

"I still have unfinished business with Jimmy," he replied. "And I need you and Carmine to come with me."

"My dad? Why?"

"I can't say right now."

"Nick, please don't do that. Just tell me."

"I can't. And I won't. Not here." He looked over to her family, huddled together. "Just tell them we have some final reporting to file." His eyes came back to hers. "As far as getting Carmine to leave with us, tell him we need one parent present to close out some final paperwork. He doesn't know anything about Jimmy yet, and I don't want him to."

Gina could tell there was a lot behind what he was asking of her. She wouldn't question him further.

CHAPTER 29

Thirty minutes later Gina, Nick, and her father were seated around a table in a small interview room at the Atlanta police station. A uniformed officer had brought them coffee and asked them to wait for further instructions. As soon as the officer left, closing the door behind him, Carmine turned to her and Nick.

"OK, what the hell is going on here?" Carmine snapped.

That was probably the tenth time he'd asked them that question since leaving the hospital. Gina placed her hand on his arm.

"Dad, please. Don't get upset. This is…"

"I am upset, dammit. How could I not be? I should be at the hospital with your mother. Why haven't you answered my questions? Why am I here?"

"I assure you, Mr. Teducci, you'll want to be here for this," Nick answered.

Carmine turned his anger towards Nick and was about to respond when the door opened. New Jersey Chief of Police Bruce Stanford entered, followed by Joe D'Amato. Nick stood up as they entered. Joe closed the door behind him. Gina watched her father's gaping expression. Gina squeezed his arm. Her father was a powerful man, and rarely lost his cool. But Gina had to think he was about to lose his cool over this.

"Carmine Teducci, this is New Jersey chief of police, Bruce Stanford." Nick made the introduction.

Bruce approached the table and he and Carmine shook hands. "I'd say it's a pleasure, but I'm in the dark here, chief."

"We'll have that cleared up in a bit." Bruce stepped back and turned to Joe. "And I believe you already know this gentleman."

"Yeah," Carmine replied bitterly. "This just keeps getting better."

Gina watched her father absently rub his chest. She wondered if the culmination of events might be causing him more stress than she realized. Joe moved around the table, extending his arms to Carmine.

"I assure you Carm," Joe said, pulling Carmine into an embrace. "Very soon, this will all make perfect sense."

"Lots of assurances going around from two people that should be in prison right now," Carmine said, looking at Joe and Nick.

"Please, if you will all take a seat," Bruce asked.

Gina watched her father survey the men around the table. He rubbed his chest once more as he lowered himself into his chair. She had to imagine his head was spinning as he tried to put the pieces together. She felt awful withholding information from him and her mother, but it was for the best.

"I'm here in the capacity of liaison between Mr. D'Amato and the Atlanta police department," Bruce said. "Though this has been an unofficial investigation, the Atlanta folks have extended every courtesy to me and to Detective Casey to wrap up his investigation. For starters, giving us use of this room. We'll be moving down the hall shortly. But before we do, I'll let Detective Casey fill you in on some details."

Carmine listened intently to Bruce, while Joe watched Carmine. At least Gina had some insight as to why they were here. Her father was completely in the dark and about to hear some shocking news. She was grateful that her mother wasn't present. Nick stood at the head of the table.

"As you're aware, Mr. Teducci, I perjured myself at Mr. D'Amato's trial. I testified that I was running a parallel investigation that proved evidence and testimony had been falsified. I have verbal and written proof that Detective Jerry Pulia, Sergeant Rotello, Officer Nunzio, prosecutor Chris Schuler from the D.A.'s office, Claire Chu from the crime lab, and myself, had all been paid by one person to plant evidence and falsify testimony in order to convict Mr. D'Amato and send him to prison."

"Who?" Carmine asked.

"Your nephew. Jimmy Teducci."

Carmine's jaw dropped open. He looked to Joe, and then to Gina, then back to Nick. "No. That can't be. That's not…" He couldn't finish his sentence.

Gina watched her father's face pale and that worried her. She knew the extent he had gone to, helping Jimmy over the years. It pained her to have to put him through this. But as he was listening, Gina was also now learning the details.

"We'll be pressing charges against him for these crimes as well as the murder of Detective Jerry Pulia," Nick added.

"Oh my god." The words fell from Gina's lips. She was just as stunned as her father hearing this.

"Why this special meeting? Am I involved somehow?" Carmine asked. "I mean, with my businesses…with work? Is there something I need to know? Should I have my attorney here?"

"No. This is all on Jimmy," Nick reassured him. "I can prove Jimmy was acting alone."

"When will you arrest him?" Carmine asked. "You know where to find him, I assume."

Gina was surprised her father was thinking so far ahead, as if the shock had already dissipated. Or maybe it was the shock that was talking.

"We already have him," Nick replied. "He's here." Nick gestured to the police station.

"I don't understand. Why Atlanta?" Carmine looked to the faces around him. "What's this got to do with what happened in Jersey?"

Nick took a long breath. He seemed to want to choose his words carefully. He had to be exhausted from all he'd been doing. Gina reached over and placed her hand on her father's arm, keeping her focus on Nick.

"There's more, but I need to prepare you for this next part," Nick said.

"Out with it already," Carmine barked at Nick.

Gina squeezed his arm, but he seemed oblivious to her presence. His eyes were glazed over with fury.

"When Joe found out what I had learned in my investigation, that Jimmy had planned to have him sent to prison, it confirmed a suspicion of his that he'd had for a long time. A suspicion I'd held for a long time, too." Nick said. "About sixteen years long."

Nick paused here to allow Carmine to absorb what he was saying. It didn't take long. Gina watched the shock register on her father's face as he looked to Joe. "Sirrina?" he nearly choked on her name.

"And Guiseppe," Joe added.

The color drained from Carmine's face. He sat rooted in place, as if no words could form. Gina imagined he was feeling the same horrifying shock she had when Nick gave her the same news. And he wasn't even hearing the worst of it yet. Her father turned to her.

"You knew this?" he barked at her.

"Dad, I…"

"What? *What?!* How could you keep this from me? From your mother?"

"Carmine," Joe called out. "This isn't on her. It's not on any of us."

Carmine looked as if he were about to explode.

"We're only just now wrapping up the case, Mr. Teducci," Nick explained.

Carmine shot a hard look to Nick.

"How was Jimmy involved with Sirrina? What happened? Explain that to me." He slammed a closed fist on the table. His anger turned his face bright red.

"That's why we're here," Nick said. "I wanted you and Joe and Gina present for my interview with him. I want you to hear what he has to say. And I'll let you know if the evidence says otherwise."

Carmine chewed on this bit of information. He looked to Gina. Then he looked to Joe. And then he looked back to Nick.

"You think that's a good idea, detective?" Carmine asked. "Because I'm gonna want to kill the son of a bitch."

"Dad!" Gina grasped his arm.

"No. He's right, Gina," Nick said. "It's not anything that the two of us haven't already thought." Nick referred to Joe and himself.

Gina instinctively looked to Bruce. The chief of police. It couldn't be prudent for them to be saying what they were saying in front of him. But their words seemed to be landing on deaf ears.

"When do we do this?" Carmine asked.

"Right now," Nick said.

Ten minutes later, Gina, her father, Joe, and Bruce sat in a small observation room that held four plastic chairs and nothing else. A large one-way glass window viewed into an interview room. Jimmy sat handcuffed to a stainless-steel table that was bolted to the floor. There was one other plastic chair on the opposite side of the table in the carpeted room, and two cameras were mounted near the ceiling in opposing corners.

Nick entered the room holding several thick file folders and a small device. He placed the contents on the table, then pulled a key from his pocket. He unlocked and removed the cuffs from Jimmy's wrists, placed the cuffs on the table, then he sat down across from Jimmy.

Jimmy sat back in his chair, rubbing his wrists. He looked to the glass window.

"Who's watching?" Jimmy asked.

His voice came through a wall-mounted speaker in the observation room.

"No one. It's just you and me, Jimmy."

"Right." Jimmy obviously didn't believe him.

Nick opened one of the files and removed evidence photos one at a time. He placed them in front of Jimmy to review.

"What's this?" Jimmy asked.

"Look at 'em. You tell me."

Jimmy studied the photos. Gina caught the ever so slight recognition on his face. Nick continued laying down photos. Gina couldn't make out what they were, but Jimmy knew. He picked up a few of them to examine them closer.

"How the fuck did you get this?" Jimmy blurted out, holding a few of the prints.

"Care to explain?"

"No. I want my lawyer."

"I'll get your lawyer. But tonight, it's just you and me here in Atlanta. They don't have jurisdiction over this case. We'll be taking you back to Jersey in the morning. That's when we'll talk with your lawyer." Nick hesitated for a moment. "I just wanted to satisfy my own curiosity."

Jimmy sat quietly listening.

"See, I have the gloves and the gun you used to kill Detective Pulia. Gunshot residue on the gloves will verify the gun, so will the bullets from Detective Pulia's body. I have the burner cell phone you used to call the police after you shot him. I have recorded evidence from the men you set up to take out Sergeant Rotello, Officer Nunzio, and prosecutor Chris Schuler." Nick held up the small device he'd brought in. "All are willing to testify that you hired and paid them to kill those three individuals. You'll be going away for a good long time, Jimmy."

Nick allowed his words to resonate with Jimmy. Jimmy's complexion paled.

"But I haven't given any of this up, yet," Nick continued. "And I can make it all go away."

Jimmy raised his eyes to Nick. "Like I'm going to trust you, you fuckin' traitor. I paid you ten-grand up front. Half your bribe. And for what? You screwed me, Casey."

"That was the deal I worked out with Joe. And that deal has been satisfied. Now I want to deal with you, Jimmy."

"How fuckin' stupid do you think I am?"

"Not stupid. Desperate."

"Fuck you."

"You sure?"

Jimmy chewed on Nick's words for a moment. "How do you make this disappear? What do you want?"

"I just want clarification on something. It's..." Nick cast his gaze away from Jimmy, thinking of what words to use. "It's one of those things that's hard to explain." He brought his attention back to Jimmy. "When your gut instinct tugs at the corner of your mind, a nagging question that just won't go away until you have clarity. You know what I mean?"

"Maybe. What's the question?" Jimmy asked.

Gina knew right then that Nick had him. She felt a rush of mixed emotions as she watched Nick work him.

"Sixteen years ago. The night at the Wildwoods. Sirrina. What happened?"

Jimmy flinched, "What? That was," he scoffed. "Why are you asking about *that*?"

"Like I said, it's one of those things that's hard to explain. It's kind of like a splinter under my skin that surfaces now and then. I can't rid myself of it."

"I don't know what to tell you."

"Tell me what happened," Nick said. "What *really* happened."

"You know. You were there, asshole."

"But I don't know. That's what bothers me. Even today."

"Fuck you for bringing this up, Nick. She was kidnapped and killed. She's dead, Nick. My cousin Sirrina is dead."

Nick leaned forward on his elbows. "What if I told you she wasn't? What if I told you she was alive...here...in Atlanta.?" Nick tapped a finger on the table.

Jimmy bolted out of his chair taking a swing at Nick, clocking him square in the jaw. Nick's head flung back from the sucker punch and he nearly tipped backwards in his chair.

Gina gasped as her hands flew to her mouth.

Nick quickly recovered. He came around the table to face Jimmy.

"Try that again, asshole." Nick baited him.

Jimmy swung again, but this time Nick caught his fist mid-swing. Nick returned fire, punching Jimmy in his face. The two of them went at each other in a full-blown brawl. Gina expected someone to enter the room and break it up, but no one did. Within seconds, Nick had Jimmy pinned to the floor face-down.

"Are we gonna talk or are we gonna fight?" Nick pressed on Jimmy's back.

Jimmy panted and squirmed for a moment, then relented. His face was beet red from Nick's pressure. Nick stood and hoisted Jimmy to his feet, pushing him to the chair and forcing him down in his seat.

"Do that again and there won't be any deal."

Nick righted his chair that had tipped over during the brawl. He wiped blood from his lip with the back of his hand, then wiped his hand on his jeans. He lowered himself into the chair. Jimmy touched fingers to the cuts and abrasions on his face. Nick clearly had won that round.

"Were you serious about that? Sirrina's alive?" Jimmy asked.

"Yeah."

"How? How is she? Where is she? What....? Jesus Christ." Jimmy pressed his hands to his face, rubbing at the disbelief and smearing blood. He looked at his hands and wiped them on his shirt and pants.

"That's what I want to hear from you. How?" Nick asked.

Jimmy leaned back in his chair, looking up to the ceiling for a long moment, gathering his thoughts. He brought his attention back to Nick.

"That was a long time ago. I was just a kid. A stupid punk kid."

"You were eighteen."

Jimmy sneered at the comment. "If I tell you this, I've got your word all of that evidence goes away?"

"It does."

Jimmy squirmed in his seat, thinking how best to approach his explanation. Gina watched her father squirm in his chair as well. Anger and fury were undoubtedly coursing through him.

"OK, look," Jimmy said. "I got jammed up. This guy I met in college, an older guy. Glen Langley was his name. He got me and some others involved in some investments. He seemed like a good guy. He was going to teach me the ropes to start running and managing my own investment strategies, which were bogus. A Ponzi. He was supposed to be teaching me how to run the scams and he ended up screwing me in the process. He took me and some other guys for a lot of money. I had borrowed money to invest with him, and when Glen skipped town, I didn't have a way to pay back the debt."

"Who'd you borrow money from?" Nick asked. "To invest."

"This dude Glen had introduced me to. Manny Contreras," Jimmy scoffed.

"Stupid fuck," Carmine said. Gina placed a hand on his knee. His focus was set hard on Jimmy. Gina hoped this wouldn't send him over the edge.

"They were working together?" Nick asked. "This Glen and Manny?"

"No. I don't think so," Jimmy replied.

"The guy who wants you to invest with him sets you up with a guy to borrow money from for you to invest, and you don't think the two of them were working together?"

Jimmy pondered this for a good long moment.

"Stupid fuck," Joe commented this time.

"I don't know. Maybe," Jimmy offered.

"So, what happened?" Nick asked.

"I owed Manny a hundred grand by that time. The interest had been adding up quick. Faster than I realized." Jimmy shrugged. "Anyways, Manny kept calling, hounding me for the payback. Turns out he'd been following me, too. That's why Sirrina was taken. He mistook her as being my little sister. He held her for ransom until I paid him the money."

"So why didn't you tell anyone? Go to the police. Call your old man or Uncle Carm. They could have paid the ransom."

"My old man and me weren't talking at that time. He wouldn't have helped me anyways. Lousy prick. And I wouldn't tell my Uncle Carm. It would have pissed him off to no end. And given him one more reason to look down on me. Twist the screws of control a little tighter." Jimmy motioned as if working a screwdriver in his hand. "So, I lied. I lied to the police in my statement about what happened to her. My old man laid into me when we got home that night. Beat the shit out of me. That was expected. That's when I faked taking my own life."

"You faked your suicide attempt?"

Gina gasped.

"Yeah. And it landed me in a cushy rehab resort hospital. Uncle Carm set it up for me. I had thirty days to recover. That gave me thirty days to fix my problem."

"The Pines," Nick confirmed.

"Yeah. It gave me time to plan. I channeled my best Glen Langley strategy, scamming three women who were in the recovery program. I raised half the ransom and set a meeting with Manny. I snuck out of the hospital, brought Manny the money, but he didn't have Sirrina. He said…" Jimmy paused for a good long time here. "He said he'd already unloaded her." Jimmy reflected on the moment. "Said he had sold her to some guy in Atlanta."

Carmine bolted up from his chair. "Jesus Christ. I'm going to kill that son of a bitch."

Gina grabbed his arm. "Dad."

Carmine looked down at her, fuming.

"Dad let Nick finish the interview. Sit down. We need to hear this."

Carmine looked back to Nick and Jimmy. He eased himself back into his chair. Gina gripped his hand.

"Shocked the shit out of me," Jimmy continued. "I'd never heard of someone doing that before. Selling humans." Jimmy shook his head, reliving the ordeal.

"It's called trafficking, Jimmy."

"I know that now," Jimmy replied bitterly. "I just meant, at the time, I didn't…" He waved a hand to dismiss the rest of what he was going to say.

"Continue," Nick said.

Jimmy frowned. "Manny and his guys beat the crap out of me. Said if I went to the cops, they would kill me. Said Sirrina was most likely dead already. They took the fifty grand I brought with me and left. I made it back to The Pines that night and locked myself in my room. The next day I picked a fight with a newcomer, you know, so I had an excuse for the beating Manny had given me." Jimmy seemed to drift in thought. "How the fuck did you find her?"

"Finish your story, then I'll tell you."

"That's it. You wanted to know what happened to Sirrina. I just told you."

"Did you think to ask Manny who he sold her to? Did you think to try and find her? To get help?"

"Hey, fuck you, Nick. You weren't there. You didn't have to face…" Jimmy tossed his head back, taking some heavy breaths. "I believed them when they told me she was probably already dead. I mean, how could she…" He looked back to Nick. "It scared the shit out of me, ok? Is that what you want to hear?"

"I want to hear the truth about what happened."

"I'm telling you, asshole."

"How did you come to blame Guiseppe D'Amato for her abduction?"

Jimmy hesitated on this one. "What the fuck is this?" Jimmy looked to the glass window then back to Nick. "Really?"

"I told you. Clarification. Just the two of us talking about the past," Nick responded casually. "You could be sitting alone in a jail cell if you prefer." Nick gauged Jimmy. "It's a slow night at the station. I've got time to kill until we head back to Jersey in the morning. And I know you've got time to kill."

"Just the two of us talking, hunh?"

"That's it." Nick was cool and confident. "You've told me this much already. You might as well get the rest of it off your chest. I'd have to imagine this has been a pretty heavy weight to carry around with you all these years." Nick scrutinized Jimmy. "Am I right?"

Jimmy traced his fingers over the handcuffs on the table, pondering his situation for a long moment, then said, "I had to clear my name from any further investigation into her abduction. I set up Guiseppe to take the fall."

"Motherfucker," Joe growled.

"How?" Nick asked.

"Arrrggghhh," Jimmy scratched his head hard with both hands. "I can't believe this."

"Just tell me." Nick said. "I'm probably the only person you can share this with that would understand what you did and why." Nick was baiting him again.

"Glen had set up an alias for me." Jimmy's focus returned to Nick. "Driver's license, passport, bank account, the whole nine yards. I was Jimmy Salazar in Glen's investment world. When he bailed, I went looking for him. I tossed his office and found his client book. I took that with me and blew up his office in case he had any other evidence lying around."

Jimmy paused.

"Go on," Nick prompted.

"I found Guiseppe's name in the client book. I remembered him from college. We had a couple of classes together. The guy was a real simpleton. It was a no-brainer. I convinced him and two of his college buddies that I had taken over Glen's operation at the college. I arranged a meeting on my supposed yacht: 'Killing Time,' docked in Lincoln Marina."

"Whose yacht was it?"

"Hell, if I know." Jimmy shrugged. "I scoped out the marina and found one that looked buttoned up for the season. I climbed aboard, broke in, and made it look as though it was in use. I rigged the engine compartment with explosives to detonate with a burner cell phone and, well, you know what happened there."

"How did you explain Sirrina having been on board? The kid's clothing that was found."

"When I went to purchase the makings for my explosives, I picked up some kid's clothes, too. I just scattered them below deck in the living quarters of the yacht."

"Mother of Christ," Carmine exhaled.

"Shortly after the explosion," Jimmy continued, "I told my Uncle Carmine and Joe D'Amato that Guiseppe had been making threats against the Teducci family. That he was going to start putting pressure on the Teduccis to push them out. That he was planning on taking control of some of the Teducci's lucrative contracts and that he would use any means possible to do it. And that it was obvious the yacht in the marina had been rigged by Guiseppe to take me out, but that Guiseppe's plan had backfired on him and ended up killing, well, you know," Jimmy paused, "Obviously, Joe and Uncle Carm figured that one out amongst themselves, because they never went to the police about it, which is how I assumed they would handle it." Jimmy grinned, proud of his accomplishments.

"All this time you've let Joe and Carmine believe Guiseppe was to blame," Nick said, digesting Jimmy's words.

"What? So, now you run to Carm and Joe and tell them the truth? Be the good detective and earn some points with the families?" Jimmy asked bitterly.

"No. At some point your conscience will get the best of you and you'll tell them."

"It hasn't yet," Jimmy replied.

"You're a piece of work, Jimmy Teducci," Nick said.

"Whatever," Jimmy replied sorely. He looked down to his hands clasped in his lap. "And now it's on your conscience, too." He lifted his eyes to Nick. "This was good. You and me. Just two friends talking it out."

Nick let the comment pass. "How'd you get Pulia and the others to go along with your plan?" Nick asked.

"How do you think?"

"I'm curious what that cost."

"Enough."

"Lobbying pays better than I thought these days," Nick quipped.

Jimmy displayed indifference. "I lobby for legislation, that legislation earns contracts for construction, Uncle Carm's company is awarded the contract, and Uncle Carm pays a kickback for said contract." He was proud, almost gloating. "The thing is, Uncle Carm never questioned why the kickback amounts had increased over the last year. The extra money he was paying went to fund my plan."

"You motherfucker!" Carmine bolted up out of his chair again.

"Let me get this straight." Nick leaned his elbows on the table. "You got Carmine Teducci to pay for taking down Joe D'Amato without his knowing?"

"In a roundabout way, yeah." Jimmy was definitely gloating. "Worked like a charm."

"Until it didn't."

"No thanks to you, asshole."

The two of them were silent for a long moment.

Carmine and Joe shot a look to one another. Gina couldn't believe the magnitude of Jimmy's confession. And he had just implicated her father. She looked over to chief Bruce Stanford. His gaze was set hard on Nick's interview of Jimmy. Gina wondered where this would land her father.

"What happened to Claire Chu from the crime lab?" Nick asked.

"Claire, Claire, Claire." Jimmy half smiled. "She met her demise in Hong Kong. The only part of my plan that you didn't fuck up."

Jimmy's cavalier response sent shock waves through Gina. She watched Nick digest his response as well.

"So, tell me how you found Sirrina?" Jimmy asked.

"One more thing," Nick said. "The Janet Sardello car bombing."

Jimmy hesitated. There was that glimmer of recognition in his reaction again. Ever so slight, but Gina caught it.

"What about it?" Jimmy asked.

"Was that your handiwork? I know she caused a lot of grief for a lot of people," Nick baited him again.

"And what if it was?"

"Just another one of those nagging spurs in the corner of my mind. It felt like your signature on the bombing."

"Like you said. She was a problem for a lot of people I worked with. I remedied the problem."

Nick pulled the Sardello case file from the bottom of the stack of files he'd brought in. He watched the recognition register on Jimmy's face.

"How did you get that?"

"Jeanette, your office squeeze, was kind enough to open your safe for me."

Gina soured, thinking of Chloe.

"Shit," Jimmy said half to himself. "It doesn't prove I did anything."

"It proves a lot, Jimmy. You paid Detective Pulia to pull this from the crime lab and deliver it to you before the FBI raided the lab."

Gina felt her blood run cold. That case file had just been assigned to her before Roger pulled it.

"You can't prove that." Jimmy countered. "And now Pulia's dead."

Nick sat quiet for a moment. "Just out of curiosity, I have confessions from three contract killers for Rotello, Nunzio, and Schuler." Nick picked up the recorder for reference. "But there wasn't one for me. What did you have planned for me?"

Jimmy sneered. "I was gonna have you taken out in prison."

Nick absorbed his truth. "Yeah. It's how I would have done it," Nick replied. "That explains why you went to the Hudson county courthouse with D.A. Forrester. You were trying to find out where I had been transferred to."

"Bingo," Jimmy replied.

"And you're right. Pulia's dead," Nick responded. "But you killed him after we got a recorded statement from him."

Jimmy folded his arms and leaned back in his chair. Realization registered in his expression. "That was you. The silver pickup in the woods near Pulia's house last week." It was a statement, not a question.

"Bingo," Nick replied. He sat back in his chair, studying Jimmy.

"You think you're so fuckin smart, Casey." Jimmy retorted. "When I get to Jersey my lawyer's gonna bury all of this." He referenced the files on the table. "You won't be convicting me of any of it."

"Maybe not," Nick replied. "But then again, maybe I will."

"You can't use any of this, what we discussed here tonight." Jimmy waved a hand indicating the files and recorder on the table. "You can't use that against me since you didn't read me my rights yet. You said yourself before we started, that this was just the two of us talking." Jimmy pointed to the one-way glass window where Gina, Carmine, Joe, and Bruce continued watching. "No witnesses, no observers, implying off the record." Jimmy pointed to the cameras in the two corners of the room. "It's even on the recording. Those cameras are my evidence that you coerced me into giving you my statement. That you violated my rights."

Nick smiled. "I'll let you in on a little secret, Jimmy."

"What's that?"

"The cameras haven't been recording us."

Jimmy looked up to them again, now with more scrutiny.

"The red light would be on if they were recording," Nick said. "See? No red light."

Jimmy turned back to Nick, recalibrating his thoughts. "Then it's like I said, off the record. You still don't have anything to pin on me except your word against mine."

"And how do you think that's gonna play out for you, Jimmy?"

Jimmy's face reddened with anger. "My attorney's gonna chew you up and spit you out, Casey. You've already earned a reputation for perjuring yourself in court. And when he's done, I'm gonna take you out, for good."

"Jimmy, there's not an attorney within a thousand miles of Jersey that's going to want to touch your case. "Nick sat forward. "And I can assure you, if you do find an attorney stupid enough to try your case, you can be certain he or she will be deterred before the first motion can be filed. Am I making myself clear?" Nick paused for a moment. "At best, a first-year public defender is all you can hope for. It'll be the D.A. doing the chewing and spitting out."

Jimmy sprang up from his chair and leapt across the table, scattering the files. He went at Nick, bowling him over in his chair. They both landed on the floor and broke into an all-out brawl once more. Fists landed solid punches into each other's faces, chest, ribs, anywhere they could make contact.

Gina stood and went to the glass window. Her heart pounded with mixed emotions. Her father and Joe joined her.

Nick over-powered Jimmy by flipping and sending him flying upside down over Nick's head, slamming into the wall. Nick got to his feet and went after Jimmy before he could stand up. Nick connected with a solid punch to the side of Jimmy's head, rendering him half unconscious.

Nick rolled him over face down. He grabbed the handcuffs from the table and secured them on Jimmy's wrists. He stood up and yanked Jimmy to his feet. Jimmy appeared dazed from the hit. Nick pushed Jimmy down in his chair again and wiped blood from his own mouth with his forearm. Jimmy was oozing plenty of blood himself.

Nick moved to pick up the files and paperwork that had gone flying while keeping an eye on Jimmy. He placed the files on the table. He righted his chair and placed it square in front of Jimmy. Nick sat down inches from Jimmy, waiting for him to recover from the blows Nick had delivered. Nick snapped his fingers in Jimmy's face, bringing him into focus.

"Just so we're clear here, Jimmy," Nick said. "You're going away to prison for a good long time and there's not a damn thing you can do about it."

"Fuck you, Nick."

"No. Fuck you, Jimmy. I finally have the answer to what I've felt in here all along." Nick pressed a fist over his heart. "I'm only sorry it's taken me sixteen years to prove it. You gave yourself away that night at the Wildwoods when Sirrina was taken. You were the only one of us kids who knew her that wasn't scared or crying. I watched you, pacing, confused, angry, detached...guilty." Nick jammed his finger into Jimmy's shoulder.

Jimmy's bloody, beaten face contorted as he tried to focus on Nick. He began to sob.

"You can't cry for her now, Jimmy." Nick said.

Nick stood up and looked down at Jimmy. He read him his Miranda Rights. He looped his hand under Jimmy's arm and hoisted him up. Jimmy's head bowed as he sobbed. Nick walked him out of the room.

Gina squeezed her father's hand. They wrapped one another in a tight embrace. Gina reflected on the events. Nick had known, deep down, like a sixth sense, that Jimmy had had some involvement in Sirrina's abduction that night at the Wildwoods.

Her mother had felt something, too, all these years. Gina had a glimpse of it when Jimmy had dinner at their house, but she hadn't questioned it. Her mother had described him as an opportunist without a conscience. Gina had no idea that her mother had suspected Jimmy. Deep down. Like Nick. Why hadn't Gina or her father sensed it?

Her family had done so much for Jimmy over the years. Gina had loved and trusted him like one of her brothers. Had looked up to him. He was the one she clung to that night at the Wildwoods, so afraid until Nick and the other's arrived. She felt such betrayal now hearing his words. His confession.

"I'll give you folks some time," Bruce said as he exited the small room.

Gina pulled back. "Dad, what happens now? With what Jimmy said, about you?"

"Let me assure you that none of this will blow back on either of us," Joe said, referring to Carmine and himself.

If Gina had learned one thing from this unofficial investigation, it was that Joe had some important and powerful connections. She trusted his assurance.

Joe extended his arms to them, and all three wrapped each other in a long embrace.

CHAPTER 30

It was nearly one-fifteen in the morning when Gina entered the Homewood Suites hotel where Jimmy had held her. Police caution tape was being removed by two uniformed officers. That meant detectives had wrapped up their investigation. The hotel manager approached her.

"I'm sorry ma'am, but the hotel is closed." He furrowed his brow at her bruised face. "We had a..." He looked to the cordoned off areas not sure how to respond.

"Yes, I was here when the disturbance occurred."

"It was more than a disturbance." The manager scoffed looking at her more closely and recognizing her. "So, that was you. I wasn't sure, but the..." He gestured to his own face referring to her cuts and bruises. "Are you alright?"

"Yes, I just need to collect my things from my room. Is that possible?"

"Of course. I'll have to escort you, though."

"Fine."

"Room three forty-five, correct?" he asked.

"Yes," *a room number I'll never forget.*

Gina followed the manager to the elevator, skirting their way through the investigation scene, and up to the room.

After leaving the Atlanta police station, Gina had dropped her father off at the hospital. Joe took a taxi to the airport to head back to New Jersey. And Nick stayed at the police station to finish processing Jimmy.

It was hard to believe they were all still functioning at this hour. But given the magnitude of the truths that were revealed through Nick's investigation, it was no wonder.

Gina entered room three forty-five with the manager. She recalled the terror Jimmy had inflicted on her. A large sheet of plywood covered the broken window. Broken glass and debris littered the room, including the toppled chair Gina had been duct taped to.

"This must have been quite an ordeal for you," the manager said.

Gina snapped from her thoughts. "I'll just be a minute."

"Please, take your time. I think the police are done working in here."

"They are," Gina called out from the bedroom. *Otherwise, they wouldn't be allowing us to walk through the crime scene, you moron.*

Gina was sure he didn't deserve her annoyance. She was beat. She packed her things including Nick's leather jacket and the jade green dress she'd worn for the Morgan Publishing party.

Gina reflected on that night at the Plaza Hotel. Her and Nick shared their first kiss. She hadn't known the truth about Jimmy yet. And they hadn't known that Sirrina was still alive.

It was all so damn unbelievable what Nick's investigation had revealed. The hotel manager was right. This had been quite an ordeal. And not just for her. So much had happened to so many people. She thought of Chloe. Her friend was going to be devasted by this ordeal as well.

Gina collected the rest of her things and rejoined the manager in the living room.

"I was working with three other men that were staying down the hall in rooms three twenty-five and three twenty-seven. Can I collect their belongings as well?"

"Mmm, I believe those men checked out a while ago. But they did leave a bag downstairs for one fellow, Nick Casey."

"Right. I can take that one with me."

The manager frowned. "I don't think I can do that."

"I assure you Mr....." Gina looked at his name tag, "Giles..."

"Patrick."

"Patrick," Gina said. "I'm authorized to take Mr. Casey's belongings. He'll be occupied at the police station for quite some time yet. In fact, I'm heading back to the police station from here and can deliver his belongings to him. Please. It's been an extremely long day, as you can imagine."

At this point, Gina didn't care that she had lied to him. She wasn't heading back to the police station. She was exhausted. She was headed to another hotel closer to the hospital and had no idea when she would be seeing Nick again. She would send him a message that she had his things.

Patrick nodded. Whether he agreed with Gina or just felt sorry for her at this point, he relented. "Follow me."

When they returned to the lobby, Patrick hefted a large duffel bag out from his office and brought it around to Gina's side of the reception counter.

"I'll carry this one for you to your car."

"Thank you, Patrick."

It was just after two a.m. when Gina checked into the Marriot Hotel across the street from the hospital. She was looking forward to going home and sleeping in her own bed again very soon. She was glad Nick had suggested moving to another hotel.

Patrick had offered to put them up in another room when he helped Gina to her car, but Gina was sure she wouldn't have been able to stay at that hotel. Not after what had gone down there. Plus, the convenience of being across the street from the hospital made sense.

As much as she wanted to be at Sirrina's bedside, she needed sleep. She got to her room, took a hot shower, slipped into a cotton tank top and underwear, brushed her teeth, then went to bed.

She had left a key for Nick at the front desk, not knowing when he would be returning, if at all. She had sent him a text letting him know this, and that she had his belongings from the previous hotel. She had just dozed off when she heard the room door unlock and open.

Gina sat up in bed and turned on the end table lamp as Nick entered the room. They shared a long quiet moment. So much had gone down in the past week and a half that the quiet seemed overwhelming now. Gina got out of bed and went to him. They kissed and wrapped their arms tightly around one another. The sheer exhaustion from all the happenings finally slipped away.

Nick felt warm and secure and smelled like soap. At some point he'd been able to clean up from the brawl with Jimmy. His hands slid down her backside, gripping her ass. Gina's pulse quickened. Nick pulled her up and she wrapped her legs around his waist, still locked in a kiss. He carried her to the bed and laid her down. He stripped off his clothes and she did the same while admiring his lean muscled physique, now marred with cuts and bruising from Jimmy. She held her arms out to him and he lay on top of her.

His mouth met hers in a charged kiss while his hands explored her body. Nothing would stop them now. This was their moment. Exhilaration coursed through her and she felt him grow hard against her bare thigh. Their breathing was labored as they yearned for one another. His hand slid up her side, finding her bare breast. She took pleasure in the feeling of his warm body resting against hers. He cupped and squeezed her breast while trailing kisses down the side of her neck.

Gina pressed her hips against him. She didn't want to wait any longer. She'd wanted this moment to happen for so long…wanted him. His hand slid from her breast and down her side, then caressed the inside of her thigh. She shivered against the chills that shot through her. His hand slowly traced the way between her legs. Her breath caught as his fingers slid inside her. Hot, delicious sensations hit her core. Gina sighed. She could barely contain herself. A low groan escaped his lips between kisses against her neck, then his lips were on hers once more.

He shifted his hips and was inside her. Gina gasped with pleasure. Her breathing escalated with his. She brushed her hands over his back, sliding down to caress his ass, exploring the physique she'd fantasized about on too many occasions. She moved her hips with his, then locked her legs around his waist. Their lovemaking was filled with heat and passion and longing for one another. Slow, rhythmic moves soon led to a quicker pace until they both climaxed.

Nick laid soft kisses down her neck as her fingers traced down his spine, feeling the damp of sweat on his back. He pulled his head back, looking down to her seeming mesmerized by the moment. Gina touched her fingers to his bruised face and cut lip. He took her hand and kissed her fingers, then brought his lips to hers once more for a soft, loving kiss. He lifted his head to look at her again.

"I think you were supposed to be wearing that sexy green little number you had on at the Plaza."

Gina laughed. "I don't think we needed it." She lifted her head off the pillow to kiss him again.

"I had planned on taking a shower before taking you," Nick said. "But dammit." He looked down and cupped her breast once more. He licked and kissed her nipple. He lifted his eyes to her. "You got the best of me, Gina."

"How about I join you in the shower now?"

After another lingering kiss, Nick rolled off her and pulled her from the bed. They took a hot shower, making love once more in the shower, and then fell back into bed. They slept soundly for the first time in over two weeks.

In the morning, they made love again, ordered room service, showered, and went to the hospital to be with Sirrina and Gina's family for the rest of the day. Unfortunately, Sirrina remained unconscious for the duration of her hospitalization in Atlanta. Gina had hoped she would hear the wonderful sound of her sister's voice again, but the heavy sedation was aiding with her detoxification.

Two days later, they transported Sirrina to a hospital in New Jersey. She still had not regained consciousness. The doctors had told Gina and her family that would change in the coming days.

Jimmy had been transported back to New Jersey the day before. He sat in a jail cell at the Hudson County Correctional Center awaiting his arraignment. Bail had not been proffered. His arraignment was scheduled for Monday morning at eight a.m. Gina had mixed emotions about attending. She knew Nick would be there, and of course her father and Joe, and most likely Jimmy's parents.

It was Sunday morning when Gina woke to these thoughts. She turned to look at Nick. He lay on his side facing her. She watched his body rise and lower with each breath. The cuts and bruising from the Jimmy fight still colored his face. Her abrasions from Jimmy's assault were still healing as well. They made quite the couple. His eyes lifted open: those bright clear blue eyes she'd come to know and love. They squinted slightly as he smiled.

"You're watching me sleep?" he mumbled half in the pillow, drowsy from sleep.

"Only for a second," she said. "You looked peaceful."

"Go back to sleep, babe," he murmured, wrapping his arms around her.

His body felt warm against hers. She was content. Happy to be home in her bed with him beside her. She closed her eyes and fell back to sleep.

CHAPTER 31

Gina attended the arraignment with Nick on Monday morning, along with her father, Joe, and her Uncle Anthony. Her Uncle Frank, Jimmy's father, attended as well, but he didn't sit with them. Chloe sat next to Gina, holding her hand, and Megan sat next to Chloe. When news about Jimmy broke, the media hadn't been kind to the Morgans. Gina had spent a good deal of time consoling Chloe between time spent at the hospital. It hadn't been easy for any of them.

The arraignment went pretty much the way Nick said it would. Jimmy was to be remanded until trial, so no bail was set. Federal prosecutors would be seeking indictments from the grand jury for two counts of first-degree murder, two counts of second-degree murder, one count of voluntary manslaughter, aggravated assault, bribery, child abuse, kidnapping, conspiracy, extortion, money laundering and tax evasion.

Gina knew the process would be lengthy. With so many charges being brought against Jimmy, the prosecutors had their work cut out for them. They would need to demonstrate to the grand jury that there was enough evidence to indict Jimmy on any one or all the charges.

Once the grand jury decided which charges to bring forth for trial, the prosecutors would move forward with their case. Jimmy would be going away for a long time if convicted. And Gina had no doubt he would be. His court-appointed attorney wouldn't be doing him any favors.

Gina had been given a two-week personal leave of absence from work to take care of family matters. The crime lab was still under investigation, as was the D.A.'s office and the Hoboken police department.

Good to his word, Chief of Police Bruce Stanford had cleared Nick of the perjury charge as well as any wrongdoing regarding his unofficial investigation. The remaining parties involved in Jimmy's conspiracy would be arraigned later in the week. Multiple charges were being filed against Sergeant Rotello, Officer Nunzio, and prosecutor Chris Schuler for falsifying evidence and testimony in Joe's case.

Judge William Bailey was undergoing a federal inquisition regarding his possible involvement in the corruption, but Nick had told Gina that the judge hadn't been involved in his investigation and would most likely be cleared.

Gina had been shocked and saddened to learn that District Attorney Benjamin Forrester would be charged for accepting bribes to fund his campaign. Jimmy ratted him out to the federal prosecutor, most likely in desperation to benefit himself in his own trial.

Gina had liked and respected Benjamin. The news had been such a disappointment. She had no doubt that more fallout from Jimmy's arrest would surface in the coming weeks and months. There had been too many people involved for it not to.

Trying not to get too caught up in the media fodder, Gina was spending most of her time at the hospital with Sirrina. She went in the mornings and afternoons to read to her. Sirrina would remain unconscious through the heroin detox process, but Gina thought it would help to read to her. Plus, it gave her something to do.

Her mother spent practically every waking hour at Sirrina's bedside, and it was beginning to take its toll on her. Gina wouldn't say anything to her about it until next week. She would give her mother this week to reunite herself with the daughter she thought she'd lost sixteen years ago.

Gina's aunts and cousins brought a never-ending supply of food to the hospital. They offered platters of lasagna, manicotti and baked ziti, meatballs, and eggplant to the hospital staff. Along with sweet treats of cannoli, cookies, and cream-filled sfogliatelle. It was what her family did. They cooked. In times of crisis or joy, sorrow or sickness, stress or pleasure…there was always food.

It was how Gina's family coped with things. Her mother said it was the process of preparing the food that brought the healing or gratification more so than the eating. But the eating was a close second.

On Friday morning, Gina sat next to Sirrina's bed reading excerpts from a travel magazine. Her aunts had taken Jackie to the cafeteria for some tea and homemade sweet bread. Gina didn't hear the door open, and a moment later Nick's arms wrapped around her from behind, startling her. He bent down, pulling himself close to her, nuzzling her neck.

"Can I steal you away this afternoon?" he whispered in her ear.

She set the magazine down on the bed and placed her hands on his arms around her neck.

"What did you have in mind, detective?" She smiled.

He kissed her neck once more, then moved to sit across from her in another chair next to the bed.

"A little something that I thought you might enjoy."

"You're not going to tell me?"

"Nope." He took Sirrina's hand.

Her hand looked so delicate and pale against his. Gina watched him share the moment with Sirrina. Some emotional thoughts or maybe prayers seemed to be at the forefront of his mind.

Gina knew that he and Reuben had tried to help Amber get into a rehab facility. But in the end, she'd only asked for money and a plane ticket to Ohio. She was going to go live with a friend. Gina knew it wasn't what Nick had hoped for her, but he and Reuben both gave her their numbers and told her to call them if she ever needed help. It was the best they could do. Amber didn't want rehab.

"What are you thinking right now?" Gina asked.

Nick kept his focus on Sirrina, "Whether she'd mind if I stole you away for the afternoon."

Gina smiled.

"She's strong, like you," he said, looking over to Gina. "Your mother, too."

"I'm not so sure about that."

"She just needs time. We all do."

Gina agreed.

"So?" he asked.

"What?"

"This afternoon?"

"You didn't say what it was."

Nick stood and came back to her side of the bed. "Be ready by one. I'll pick you up at your place." He bent down and tipped her chin up, giving her a quick kiss. Then he left the room.

At 1:05 Gina sat waiting in her living room, scrolling through emails. She heard the rumble of a motorcycle idling outside. She walked out onto her balcony and peered down to the street from her third-floor apartment.

She watched a guy dressed in a leather jacket, boots, jeans, a helmet, and sunglasses back a sleek black and chrome motorcycle against the curb outside her building. He killed the motor, climbed off, and removed his helmet. It was Nick. Gina had to admit, the biker image roused something deep inside. It was very appealing.

"What are you doing?" Gina yelled down to him.

He looked up to her. "You ready?"

Gina felt a rush of excitement at the prospect of riding on his bike. "Two minutes. I need to change my shoes."

Gina quickly changed out of her sandals into low-heeled boots, put on a heavier sweater, grabbed her purse, and practically ran out of her apartment.

She met Nick on the curbside. She took in the bike: a sleek black and silver Harley Davidson. The afternoon sun reflected off the chrome. And there was plenty of it.

"It's beautiful," Gina said. "I didn't know you rode."

"There's a lot you don't know about me." He smiled and opened the fiberglass side bag. "It's part of my mystique."

Gina laughed.

He removed a bundle of leather and shook it out, handing it to her.

"Try it on," he said. "This one should fit you better."

Gina took the jacket and pulled it on. He remembered the night at the Plaza Hotel.

"It fits perfect," she said. "But it's still not yours."

He handed her a helmet and sunglasses. She put on the gear as he swung a leg over the bike, righted it, and fired it up. Loud and powerful. The sound vibrated through her. Gina was thrilled. She couldn't imagine a better way to spend the afternoon together. She climbed on the back and wrapped her arms around his waist, tucking her hands inside his jacket pockets.

"Where to, mystery man?" she asked.

She caught his smile in the side mirror.

"Hold on."

He gave the throttle a rap and tore off down her street. They made their way out of her neighborhood, and then along the Hudson River on Palisades Parkway north, and then headed up to Bear Mountain State Park. The sun felt warm, and the air was cool. She rested her chin on his shoulder as he shifted through the gears. The brisk air stung her cheeks the faster they rode. He was right. This was just what she needed.

Sirrina had a long road ahead of her, and Gina would be there every step of the way. So would her family. Gina was grateful for the turn of events that brought her sister back into their lives. And now she was falling in love with the man who had made that happen. The man she'd had a crush on sixteen years ago. She couldn't ask for more.

Photo by Chelsea Schmitz

ABOUT THE AUTHOR

Cathy Wilson grew up in southern California, called Phoenix, Arizona home for twenty-five years and now resides in California's wine country. When she's not working on her next novel, she's gardening, hiking, and enjoying RV travel with family and friends. Please visit her at www.cat@writetoentertain.com.

www.ingramcontent.com/pod-product-compliance
Lightning Source LLC
Chambersburg PA
CBHW022139170626
46807CB00005B/1994